IF
6
WERE
9

IF 6 WERE 9

JAKE LAMAR

 Crown Publishers • New York

Published by Crown Publishers, New York, New York.
Member of the Crown Publishing Group.

Random House, Inc. New York, Toronto, London, Sydney, Auckland
www.randomhouse.com

CROWN is a trademark and the Crown colophon is a registered trademark of
Random House, Inc.

"Fire and Rain," words and music by James Taylor © 1969, 1970
(Renewed 1997, 1998) EMI BLACKWOOD MUSIC INC. and
COUNTRY ROAD MUSIC INC. All Rights Controlled and Administered
by EMI BLACKWOOD MUSIC INC. All Rights Reserved.
International Copyright Secured. Used by Permission.

Printed in the United States of America

Design by Leonard W. Henderson

Library of Congress Cataloging-in-Publication Data
Lamar, Jake.
If 6 were 9 / by Jake Lamar.—1st ed.
1. Afro-American college teachers—Fiction.   2. Radicals—Fiction.
I. Title: If six were nine.   II. Title.

PS3562.A4216 I38 2001
813'.54—dc21
00–031416

ISBN 0-609-60537-2
10 9 8 7 6 5 4 3 2 1
First Edition

For Dorli

CHAPTER 1

"FUCK THIS SHIT! FUCK THIS fucking fucked-up bullshit!"

It was not Reginald T. Brogus's most eloquent moment, but the two profane sentences he muttered, hissed, and, at times, almost sobbed as he paced up and down the floor of my dimly lit and cluttered kitchen might have served as something of a motto or a mantra for the man in all his incarnations over the past twenty-five years. Whether in the guise of a beret-flaunting, pistol-wielding revolutionary or a pipe-sucking, red-suspendered neoconservative, Reginald T. Brogus, in his bombastic way, was always saying the same thing.

"Fuck this shit! Fuck this fucking fucked-up *bullshit!*"

But Brogus had none of his usual bravado in my kitchen that night. Or rather, morning. The red digits on the bedside clock radio had glowed 2:27 as I groped for the bleating telephone. Brogus was calling me on his mobile. He said he was standing out on Maplewood Road, right in front of my house.

"You gotta let me in, Clay. Please!"

I grumbled about the hour, asked what Reggie's problem was. He wouldn't tell me. He just kept begging me to let him in. I told him to go around to the back door. Penelope snored lightly as I fumbled in the dark for my bathrobe. It would take much more than a telephone call and me bumping loudly into furniture to wake my wife when she's in one of her comatose sleep zones. I closed the bedroom door behind me and crept gingerly down the stairs. Pen could not be roused but I didn't want to risk waking the twins.

Still groggy as I walked into the darkened kitchen, I dragged my slippered feet across the linoleum floor. Clicking on a small lamp that rested beside the four-inch black-and-white TV on the kitchen table, I saw the broad silhouette of a man at the back door, the door whose top portion was a clear pane of fortified glass decorated with frilly yellow curtains, the door that led out to our backyard. Despite my hectoring lectures on household safety, Penelope and the girls were constantly forgetting to lock the back door. Turning the doorknob, I discovered that the rear entrance to our home had, once again, been left unlocked while we slept in our beds.

Reggie Brogus stood on my back step, wearing only a blue warm-up suit with white trim and dirty white Nikes on his feet. I found his attire odd for two reasons. One, this was the morning of February 17, 1992, and we were living in Arden, Ohio, a flat, windswept, virtually treeless frozen tundra of a college town where spring tended not to arrive until sometime around Memorial Day. And two, Brogus was, at this point in his life, a blubbery three hundred pounder who looked as if his main form of physical activity was chewing.

"Yo, Clay, man, you gotta help me."

Brogus's eyes looked even more bugged out than usual behind the Coke-bottle-thick lenses of his black-framed glasses. I hustled him into the kitchen, warning him to keep his voice down. Somehow, I wasn't alarmed by Brogus's showing up like this. Maybe I was still too sleepy to be scared. And everybody knew Reginald T. Brogus had a penchant for the melodramatic. I flicked on the overhead fluorescent light. I had just enough time to take in the mountain of smeared dishes and glasses towering in the sink when Brogus cut the overhead off.

"That's too much light, man! You crazy?"

I sat down at the kitchen table, in the 40-watt glow of the little lamp. "Chill out, Brogue," I grumbled.

That's when Brogus began his pacing and feverish cursing. "Fuck this fucking *fucked-up* bullshit!"

I yawned silently, my left index finger rubbing at an obstinate bit of mucus encrusting my left upper eyelashes. "You're gonna have to be more specific, man," I croaked. Though Brogus was clearly a desperate man, I still wasn't taking him all that seriously. Like a lot of other black folks, I hadn't taken Brogus seriously since the 1970s.

"Why don't they just shoot me? Huh? They wanna destroy me so bad? Why don't they just drive a stake through my fucking heart!" Brogus was beating on his fleshy chest now as he stalked about the linoleum. His voice catching, he sounded like he was on the verge of tears. "Wouldn't it just be easier to kill me? Do they have to *torture* me?"

They? At first, I assumed Brogus was talking about our colleagues on the faculty at Arden University. Then I remembered how legion were the enemies of Reggie Brogus. "They" could have been resuscitated radicals from the Black Panther Party or backwoods white supremacists or vindictive agents of the FBI or the CIA or the IRS or wine-sipping, cheese-nibbling, left-wing media types or any member of the female gender. Brogus was, even by the standards of the day, a bit paranoid. As I began to worry about this unexpected visit, I tried to keep that fact in mind. I still did not know the big fact, would not know it until I saw it with my own eyes—the fact that the nude, strangled body of a white girl, a student of our university, was sprawled on the couch of Reginald T. Brogus's office in the Afrikamerica Studies department.

*   *   *

Remember, I am speaking here of 1992—of *early* 1992. The realm of credibility had not yet expanded to its current galactic proportions. Though the Gulf War a year earlier had begun to make the incredible credible, on the night that Brogus showed up panicked on my doorstep, O.J. Simpson was still best known as an ex-jock TV talking head, Mrs. Simpson still had *her* head fully attached to her body, Slick Willie Clinton looked like just the latest in a string of Democratic losers, and everybody assumed that the verdict in the trial of the white cops who were videotaped beating the shit out of poor black Rodney King in L.A. would, of course, be guilty. In February 1992, a naked corpse—let alone a naked white female corpse—in a professor's—let alone a black male professor's—office still had the ability, if not to shock, then, at least, to surprise.

But, trying to calm Brogus down as he paced and cursed in my kitchen, I still didn't know about the body. Such a thing was beyond my imagining. I still lived my life within the old parameters of the credible.

"You gotta come with me," Brogus said, breathing hard and heavy. "We gotta go to my office. You gotta see this shit. You will be my witness."

"Witness to what? And keep your voice down."

Brogus finally stopped pacing, stood still, and raised his hands to his face. He pressed both palms flat against his vast and squarish expanse of forehead and stared at the floor. He seemed to be trying to regulate his breathing, to steady his nerves. He lumbered toward the table and sat across from me. His flabby butt spilled over the sides of the spindly wooden chair. He propped his elbows on the table and entwined his chubby fingers. He did not look directly at me. His froggy eyes seemed focused on a spot just behind me, on something only he could see in the darkened corner of the kitchen. "You will be my witness," he said in a low growl.

"Witness to what, Reggie?"

Brogus shook his head slowly from side to side, continued to stare past me, into the shadows. "To the shit . . . to this fucking shit they put in my office."

"Your office. At school?"

Brogus nodded slowly, froggy eyes staring eerily behind his thick glass lenses. "Don't you see?" he growled. "It's not enough to kill me. They want to ruin me."

Considering myself very clever, I immediately leapt to the wrong conclusion. Drugs. Somebody must have planted some coke in Brogus's office. Whether presenting himself as a radical or a right-winger, Brogus had always been vehemently antidrug. In both of his books—*LIVE BLACK OR DIE!: A Militant Manifesto*, published in 1968, and *An American Salvation: How I Overcame the Sixties and Learned to Love the U.S.A.*, published in 1984—he had railed about how dangerous drugs were to the black community. It followed, then, that if one of Brogus's innumerable enemies had wanted to shame and discredit him, a fiendish way to do so would be to plant drugs in his office, thus making him not only a criminal, but also a fraud.

"I think I understand," I said to Brogus. "But, hey, man, why come to me? Don't you think you ought to call the police?"

"THE *PO*—LICE!" Brogus fairly shouted.

"Shhhhhhh!"

"What the fuck you think the *po*—lice gonna do wid my black behind?" Brogus was looking right at me now, speaking quickly, in an angry rasp. "It might be the fucking *po*—lice did this shit in the first place!"

"Okay, okay," I said, raising a hand to calm him. "Bad suggestion."

"Them motherfuckers never could keep my ass in jail. They came up with all kinds of trumped-up charges back in the seventies—and I *always* beat the rap!"

How strange it was to hear the Republican Reginald, at the denouement of the Reagan-Bush era, damning the cops the way Revolutionary Reggie used to back in the day. Only a few months earlier, Brogus had publicly defended the excessive use of force employed by the cops who had battered Rodney King. Clearly, the brother was having some kind of a breakdown. "Look, Reg, what do you wanna—"

"Whatthefuckisthat?" Reggie hissed, the five words running together, sounding like one. He spun halfway around in his chair, stared at the back door.

It took a moment, but I soon heard what had startled Reggie, the faint crackling sound, the scratch of nails on wood. Brogus abruptly spun back around, causing the chair beneath him to creak, and glared suspiciously at me, as if I were somehow responsible for the mysterious and insistent scratching noise. Perhaps, in a way, I was.

"Relax," I said, rising from the table and walking over to the closed door of the kitchen pantry, the little walk-in closet filled with dry goods and sundry household provisions. I opened the pantry door and looked down at the two silver eyes glowing in the shadows.

"*Yow!*" Dexter said in his squeaky little voice. Our sleek, midnight black cat liked curling up on one of the lower shelves of the pantry and sometimes we forgetful humans in the house inadvertently trapped him in his cozy lair. Dexter raced out of the kitchen, his claws clicking on the linoleum.

I returned to the table. "What were we saying?"

The Dexter incident seemed to have gotten Brogus even more worked up. "You gotta come with me," he said, huge eyes staring, imploringly, straight into mine. "You gotta write about this shit. You gotta expose what's goin' on in the press. You will exonerate me!"

"Whoa, whoa, whoa, Reggie! I'm not a reporter anymore. I'm nothing. I'm just a fucking journalism professor."

"You gotta come with me. Right now!"

"Reggie, look at me, I'm wearing a bathrobe."

"Then get dressed, motherfucker! You gotta see this shit!"

"Aw, come on, Reg . . ."

"Clay!" Brogus leaned forward and took hold of both my wrists in his enormous hands. "You owe me, man. You *owe* me!"

It was true. I did. But what's more, I have to admit, my interest was piqued.

"To believe this shit," Brogus rasped, "you gotta see it."

*　　*　　*

Some, I am sure, call it my exile.

Clay Robinette? In Ohio?!?! Ohmigod!

Being the laughingstock of your profession—at least in New York—is not as painful as you might think. What one mainly feels is an itchy-scabby sort of annoyance. Why the fuck should I be the one to get caught doing what everybody else does and gets away with? I could hear my former colleagues chortling over their expense account salads, mock-lamenting my fate. A nervous indulgence on their part. Any one of them had to know she/he could be next.

You remember Janet Cooke, don't you? Sister on the *Washington Post*, won the Pulitzer back in '81 or '82 for a story about little Jimmy-Johnny-Jackie, a six- or seven-year-old black junkie living or dying in the ghetto. Anyway, turned out the whole story was fake, completely made up by Janet, who subsequently was stripped of her prize, her job, her reputation, and her future. Most people figured she got what she deserved. Anyway—I was no Janet Cooke. I got caught making up a few quotes. From a few anonymous, and sometimes imaginary, sources. I did this a handful of times in a handful of articles. Believe me: I am not the only journalist who has done this. I always played by the rules of the game as

I found them to be. But I got exposed, trashed, ostracized, blackballed, and, finally, more or less, run out of town.

A credit to the race: that was the compliment back in olden times. Well, Janet Cooke was considered a debit to the race. Though my case was never exposed to as much publicity as hers was (What prize, after all, did I ever win?), I, too, was regarded by some as a disgrace to black people. I never felt that way about myself. Hey, I was a mediocre journalist. I never aspired to anything but mediocrity. You know how black folks always say a black person has to be twice as good as a white person to get half as far? Well, that may or may not be true. All I want to do is uphold my right to mediocrity. To be a very good journalist is very hard. To be a mediocre one is easy. All I ever wanted was to be a mediocre journalist. I reject absolutely the notion that I must be twice as mediocre as my mediocre white colleagues in order to be considered half as mediocre. Why, simply because I am black, must I be held to some rigid standard of excellence? My God, look at all the mediocre white people—let alone white journalists—out there! I am neither proud nor ashamed of my mediocrity. But my *right* to mediocrity, my freedom to be as mediocre as any mediocre white person, must be seen as one of the ultimate goals of racial progress, don't you think?

By February 1992, I was no longer mediocre—I was a failure. That is to say, I considered myself a failure. But I was, it must be said, an amiable failure. A few months shy of my thirty-fourth birthday, I figured I had had my shot at a decent career in journalism and blown it. Another chance would most likely not come along. Don't get me wrong: I did not think that my life was over. I loved my wife and our daughters; they, more than anything I did for a living, gave meaning to my life. But, in terms of career, I considered myself a washout. There are worse things one could be.

I guess you could say Jerry Shamberg rescued me—though I hate to think of it in those terms. Back in the fall of 1986, I had written a profile of the new dean of Arden University for *A Bite of the Apple*, a now-defunct glossy weekly for upscale New Yorkers. The obscure, boringly respectable Arden U. had just received a gift of $100 million, left to the institution in the will of a reclusive steel industry heiress who had been an undistinguished member of the Class of '07, never married, and had no close relatives to leave all her dough to when she expired. A few shrewd members of Arden's board persuaded the traditionalists among them to use the huge endowment to transform Arden into a "hot" or "cutting edge" university. They wanted to spend that money creating a "buzz" about the school. Their goal was to transform dull, mediocre Arden into a popular magnet for wealthy, sophisticated students, the sort of students who were drawn to places like Brown University in Rhode Island or Oberlin College, which had always overshadowed Arden as Ohio's school of choice for the smart progeny of the sort of upscale New Yorkers who read magazines like *A Bite of the Apple.*

"We as educators are producers. The students are consumers," Dean Jerry Shamberg said to me during my interview with him. "It is our job to create a good product that our consumers, or their parents, will be happy to pay for. I'm not just running a university here. I'm running a business!"

A wily Brooklynite, Jerry Shamberg had a doctorate in psychology and a master's in business administration from Harvard. Arden University had paid an obscene amount of money to lure Dean Jerry away from the College of the Dunes on Long Island, which, during his ten years of stewardship, had metamorphosed from a joke college for potato-headed hicks into an expensive playground college for the children of rich Manhattanites who summered in the Hamptons. Though it was rumored that some students at the College of the Dunes actually majored in volleyball, the school's reputation soared. Shamberg seduced high-profile academics with immense—for academics, that is—salaries. He hyped the school incessantly to his pals in the New York cognoscenti. Applications for admission multiplied exponentially. Donations poured in. Some parents were said to have engaged in bidding wars to get their kids into the joint. The trustees of Arden University hoped that Dean Jerry Shamberg could work the same magic in the flat, frigid wasteland of Ohio.

I had always thought Shamberg came across as an asshole in the article I wrote about him. But the piece in the October 1, 1986, issue of *A*

Bite of the Apple turned out to be a publicity bonanza for Arden U. Two and a half years later, I bumped into Shamberg on Madison Avenue. He had read of my exposure as a fabricator of quotes and sources. "At least you quoted *me* accurately!" he said with a big, honking laugh.

The itchy-scabby annoyance of my disgrace was particularly acute that afternoon. I told Shamberg I had been unable to obtain even the lowliest of freelance magazine assignments in the past six months. My agent was advising me to get a day job. On the spot, Shamberg offered me a teaching gig at Arden University. I told him I'd never even taken a journalism course let alone taught one before. He said it didn't matter. I told him I was damaged goods, totally discredited as a journalist.

"Hey, you're controversial!" Dean Jerry boomed. "Controversy's good! It sells!"

*   *   *

And so, in the fall of 1989, I became a professor of journalism and creative nonfiction—whatever the fuck that is. (Actually, I suppose "creative nonfiction" might be a polite term for what got me excoriated and blacklisted in the media world.) As college professors go, I was paid handsomely. Despite the relentless dreariness of Arden, Ohio, it seemed a pretty good place to raise a family. Penelope had never been very keen on New York and never liked the journalists' milieu. She and the twins took to Ohio right away. And, to tell the truth, I didn't have that much trouble adapting either. As far as I was concerned, I'd tumbled off the stepladder of mediocrity. At the age of thirty-one, I settled into the comfortable rut of failure.

There was another reason—besides my decimated professional status—why I was happy to get out of NYC. Racially, things were getting a little too intense for my pacifistic temperament. In April 1989, a young white woman—an investment banker—was jumped while jogging in Central Park, brutally raped, beaten, and left for dead by a gang of black teenagers. In August, a black teenager was gunned down by a mob of white thugs in Bensonhurst, Brooklyn. The two attacks brought all of the city's barely sublimated race hostility roaring to the surface. I had a feeling things were only going to get worse. I didn't want Amber and Ashley—yes, my daughters are named Amber and Ashley—spending their formative years in that sort of charged atmosphere.

Which is not to say that Arden, Ohio, was any bastion of peace, love, and understanding. *Issues* were always in the air: multicultural studies, affirmative action, freedom of speech versus sensitivity to minorities. Forgive me if I could never get particularly worked up about these very important issues. But I soon became aware that most white and all "minority" members of the faculty were constantly judged by students and by each other on where they stood on these and all those other very important issues. You would be judged not only by the opinions you expressed but by the way in which you expressed them, how you dressed, where you lived, who you hung out with, and who you fucked. Of course, this sort of thing goes on everywhere. But on a college campus—with its prickly commingling of willful diversity and willful self-segregation—what you said you believed and how you acted on those beliefs took on a concentrated significance.

For not the first time in my life, I felt lucky to have a black wife.

*   *   *

February 17, 1992—2:45 a.m. I parked my Volvo in a lot behind the Mathematics building. I lived about a mile from the spot. Brogus had wanted to walk it, thinking we would call less attention to ourselves. I told him there was no way I was walking a mile, through the snow, in the middle of a night when the local temperature was 15 degrees Fahrenheit (wind chill factor: –2). Besides, I said, who would see us? Nobody was up and about in Arden, Ohio, at this hour on a Sunday night. During the short drive, Brogus kept muttering curses to himself and saying how I would be his witness. I stepped out of the car, into the iron cold. I pulled the bushily lined hood of my parka over my head. Brogus stood on the other side of the car, in his warm-up suit and sneakers. He wasn't even wearing a T-shirt: black and white curlicues of hair sprouted from the zippered V midway down his fleshy chest. Had Brogus *run* to my house?

"Aren't you cold?" I asked.

"Fuck it," Brogus said. He looked around the huge empty parking lot as if he thought someone might be hiding somewhere. Wispy clouds of his breath floated in the icy night air.

The brief rush of enthusiasm I had felt about this little excursion as I had dressed quickly in the dark—clumsily throwing a heavy cable-knit sweater and black jeans over the thermal undearwear I slept in; pulling on thick woolen socks and Timberland boots as Penelope snored lightly in the bed—had all but vanished. What had I been so excited about as I hurried back downstairs to meet Brogus, who was, by then, pacing furiously around the foyer, murmuring obscenities? A story! My old reporter's instincts had come bristlingly back to life. I smelled a story! Remember: at this point, I still think Reggie is talking about drugs, that somebody must have stashed a fucking kilo in his office, hoping to frame him for possession or maybe even *dealing!* It instantly occurred to me that this would make a sensational piece for *Esquire* or *GQ* or *Vanity Fair.* The daily media—newspapers, radio, TV—were bound to be full of this story, at least for a day or so. But I would be privy to the inside stuff on the Reggie Brogus Affair. If there was indeed a story there and if I could write the shit out of that story, I knew I could get it in one of the sleek monthlies. Then, I'd be right back in the game! Clay Robinette: The Comeback Kid.

Brogus was silent as we trudged the short distance from the parking lot to the Mathematics building, head down, hands thrust in warm-up suit jacket pockets, elbows flaring, feet coming down hard, trying not to slip and fall—across the frozen walkway. The flat, wide open sprawl of Arden University lay before us, its drab and blocky red brick structures looking, as usual to my eye, like someone's naive idea of what a university should look like. There was a certain forced and self-conscious state-liness to the architecture. As if some earnest Ohioan had re-created his fantasy of New England—or even Olde England. But there was no ivy crawling up the walls of Arden University's Halls and Houses. There were hardly even any trees dotting the quadrangle. As Brogus and I trudged along an asphalt walkway, a thin layer of ice covered every-thing. There wasn't all that much snow on the ground; shiny patches of white here and there. But ice coated all. Frosted, spiky blades of green and yellow grass glittered in the moonlight.

Afrikamerica Studies was not yet a full-fledged department with undergraduate majors, Ph.D. candidates, or a building of its own. The '91–'92 scholastic calendar marked the second of Afrikamerica Studies' two years as a "pilot program." A few courses were offered under the auspices of Afrikamerica Studies. But there was, as of yet, no official status, no official funding for, and no official chairperson of the department. In September 1992, it would become a real major and might even get its own building for faculty offices. But in February '92, Afrikamerica Studies still occupied one suite of offices on one floor of the old Mathematics Department building.

We stood at a side entrance to the Math building, Brogus fumbling with his keys. He seemed to have calmed down a bit in the short trudge from the parking lot. As we entered a darkened vestibule of the building, he spoke almost matter-of-factly. "Turn on the flashlight."

Back in my garage, I'd picked up one of those silvery baton flashlights to take with us, but clicking it on discovered the batteries were dead. In its place, I had brought along a clunky, unwieldy beacon that you had to carry by its sturdy handle, the sort of light more suitable for nighttime roadwork crews than for two professors creeping around a Math building at three in the morning. Brogus and I both gasped at the little atomic blast of light that occurred when I switched on the beacon. We were standing in a wide stairwell with metal steps and bannisters. The stairs looked hard and somehow sinister in the harsh blue-white light.

"Damn, Clay!" Brogus hissed, blinking wildly in the metallic glare.

"I told you, it's the only working flashlight I had."

Brogus grumbled something unintelligible and started climbing the stairs. I followed close behind, hauling the heavy beacon and thinking what a ridiculous waste of time this was. Hell, there probably weren't even any drugs in Reggie's office at all. Whatever the fuck was in his office, I had the feeling there was no story in it for me. Brogus led me through a pair of swinging doors on the second floor landing and we started down a long, gleaming corridor. The Math building had been constructed in 1955 and its hallways were designed and decorated in a way that probably seemed all modern and space-agey futuristic then, but now just looked comically dated.

"Turn that thing off," Brogus snarled at me over his shoulder. I switched off the light. We stopped at the door of the Afrikamerica Studies Department. I could hear Brogus's keys jangling as my eyes slowly adjusted to the darkness. I saw the silhouette of the door swing open. I could not make out much in the shadows, but I knew the room we had just entered. It was the reception area. I knew there were prints of works by Romare Bearden and imitation African masks hanging on the walls of this small enclave where the department's part-time secretary had her desk. I heard Brogus close the door behind me. For the first time since Brogus had called me, I felt scared.

I nearly jumped when Brogus brushed up against me. Both his beefy hands were touching me now. He was feeling for the big, clunky flashlight. He grasped it by the handle and gently took it away from me. I felt another of his hands on my back. "I'll lead you to my office," he rasped in the dark. With Brogus's hand pushing gently on the back of my parka, I moved forward. With my right hand, I felt my way along a wall of the short hallway that I knew led to Brogus's office. Reggie stopped abruptly and tugged on my parka. I stood still. I could hear Brogus's keys jangling. It sounded as if his hands were trembling. "Fuck this shit." Brogus's voice sounded like it was about to break again. I heard his key turn in the lock, heard the soft whine of his door swinging open. "Fuck this fucking fucked-up bullshit," Brogus said in a voice now choked with tears.

I had never been a crime reporter. Never covered the police beat; never visited a morgue, notebook and pencil in hand. I had, until that moment, never even seen a dead body before. From almost complete darkness I now found myself in a world of blazing blue-white light. I saw her there, naked, her skin looking eggshell-white in the weird light. She was facedown on the couch. The couch was muddy brown, fake leather. I saw the deep groove of her spine, the pale mounds of her ass. Her legs were spread slightly, but I could not see her vagina. Yellow socks covered her feet. They were short socks, barely concealing her ankles. Her right arm hung over the edge of the couch, her hand splayed awkwardly on the floor. Her left arm was twisted around her head at an unnatural-looking angle. Her head, too, was contorted in what I immediately realized could only be a gruesome attitude of death. Had her neck been broken? I could not see her face or her neck or her shoulders. They were obscured by a turbulent mass of crimson hair. And still all that registered with me was that this woman was so clearly not asleep, not alive. Though I had never seen it before, this was recognizably, unmistakably, death. I was so mesmerized by the peculiar contortion of death that the body was utterly unfamiliar. I don't know that I said anything.

"Look what they did to me," I heard Brogus sob. "I didn't do anything, man. I didn't do shit!"

Dreamily, almost involuntarily, my body moved toward the couch. I could feel my knees bending. I reached down. My hands were covered in what my wife called my "astronaut gloves"; absurdly thick thermal wear, the black gloves looked almost as if they were inflated. It did occur to me, as I reached for a fiery swath of her hair, that, this way, I would not leave any fingerprints anywhere. I squatted beside the couch as my gloved hand brushed aside a curtain of hair. Incredibly, perhaps, the first thing I recognized was Brogus's suspenders. They were decorated in a screaming, red-white-and-blue stars-and-stripes design that made Brogus look like a black, overfed Uncle Sam whenever he proudly wore them. The suspenders were twisted knottily around the woman's neck. I brushed back another stream of hair and only then did I see. The face was puffy and bore a bruised-bluish tint. Her eyes and her mouth were open. The hideous torsion of death had made her lovely body unrecognizable to me. But now I looked into her face, her expression frozen, eyes wide open, mouth a perfect O. It was Pirate Jenny, also known as Jennifer Esther Wolfshiem; also unknown, I hoped, as . . . What is the correct term these days? What was it back then? The contemporary euphemism escapes me. And so I fall back on the quaint, the archaic, the genteel. She was my mistress.

CHAPTER 2

I WON'T LIE TO YOU. My first instinct was to run. I was in a squatting position when I recognized Jenny, her head tilted unnaturally on the couch, her eyes and mouth hideously, intimately wide open, her face only inches from mine. I simultaneously recoiled and sprang upright. *Lemme get the fuck outta here.* I stared down at Jenny, at the body that was so suddenly familiar. I don't know how long I stood there, in the blazing blue-white light, in Brogus's windowless, bare-walled office, staring at this body I had once caressed, ravished, been inside, this body that even now gave me an erotic rush at the same moment that I was thunder-struck by its lifelessness, sickened by the violence that had been done to it. *Lemme get the fuck outta here.* I do not think I said the words out loud. But there was nothing else going on in my mind. Not a single legal or moral consideration. The pain of losing Jenny, the horror of her being murdered, had not yet kicked in—not really. Though I could hear Brogus breathing heavily behind me, I was not, at this moment, thinking of him either. My system of rational thought had crashed. I had reverted to pure instinct. *Just lemme get the fuck outta here.*

I was movin'. Not quite running, but damn near. I must have made it from Brogus's tiny office, down the short hallway of the Afrikamerica Studies Department, to the door of the reception area in about four strides. "Clay!" I heard Brogus call out, struggling to keep his voice down. The light from the beacon in Brogus's office partly illuminated the reception area. I grabbed the doorknob with one of my puffily gloved hands and pulled hard. Locked.

I clumsily took hold of the knob with both thermally protected hands and tugged furiously, ready to tear the damn door off its hinges. Then I felt Reggie's hands on my shoulders. "Clay," he rasped. I immediately noticed that something in the quality of his voice had changed. A minute earlier—had it even been a minute since we entered his office, since I first laid eyes on my dead lover?—he had been sobbing desperately. "Clay," Brogus said again, his big, beefy hands pressing down on the shoulders of my parka. "Claaaaaaay . . ." His voice now was steady, calming.

"Open the damn door, Reggie," I said. I stood perfectly still, my hands on the knob. I did not turn to face Brogus.

"Just be cool, Clay."

Even as my capacity for rational thought was slowly recovering, I felt my body responding, surrendering, to this new quality in Brogus's voice, this sudden, soothing authority. The fact was only beginning to sink in that Reggie might have just killed Jenny. Yet, I knew, on some subterranean level, that, right here, right now, in the incoherence of this moment, I would do whatever Reggie Brogus told me to.

* * *

When you are in a crisis, the structure of time seems to change, now truncating, now elongating, suddenly spiraling, then smoothing itself out again before altering shape with your next seizure of fear or rage, guilt or suspicion. The moment of recognition, when I saw Pirate Jenny's lifeless face—eyes and mouth wide open, just as they had once been at the ecstatic apex of orgasm, frozen in the very same expression in the shock of death—was an excruciating infinity. After that, the flow of time gets a bit choppy.

I am sitting on a plastic chair, one of those deep-bottomed, metal-legged chairs I always associate with dentists' waiting rooms, in the reception area of the Afrikamerica Studies Department. Reggie Brogus offers me a small paper cup filled with water from the cooler near the part-time secretary's desk. I drink, my gloved hand trembling. There is a window behind the secretary's desk, outfitted with Venetian blinds. The blinds are closed. The light from the beacon I found in my garage, the beacon that now rests on the desk in Reggie's office down the short hallway, casts blue shadows in the reception area. Reggie is crouched before me, on one knee, like a quarterback in the huddle. The dim light plays trickily on the thick lenses of his glasses. Though I know he is staring steadily at me, I cannot quite see his eyes. My mind is a jumble of questions. By now, I have lost any sense of this being a story I am covering. Yet I revert to asking questions, falling back on reportorial habit as a way of seeking coherence. Brogus is calm. In fact, he is cool as shit.

"What happened, Reggie?"

"I walked into my office late tonight and found this body."

"Why are you wearing a warm-up suit?"

"I went out for a run. I came by the office to pick up my laptop."

"You run? Like for exercise?"

"Only in the middle of the night, when no one can see me. I get embarrassed."

"And you just walked into your office . . . at what time?"

"I don't know. One-thirty. Two?"

"And found this . . . body?"

"Yes."

"Do you know this *girl*?" I hear my own voice squeak on the last word.

"No." Reggie pauses. I cannot see his eyes. "Do *you*?"

A logical question, but not one I was expecting. I hesitate and know that Reggie is aware of my hesitating. "No. . . . Um, I don't know. I mean, I don't *know* her, but . . . I think I've seen her around. I think she's a student."

Brogus crouches before me. He does not flinch. This man who less than half an hour earlier—at least I think it was less than half an hour— had arrived at my house a near-psychotic wreck now speaks with an air of command. He seems to have gained confidence from my discombobulation. "You listen to me, brother. Listen to me good. I don't know this girl. I never touched her. I did nothing. This is a setup. I don't know what we are dealing with here, Clay, but this is some serious shit."

Reggie reaches out and puts his hand on my shoulder. He seems to be gathering strength, steeling himself against the magnitude of his ordeal. And this is where it happens: this is the moment when I believe him. A young woman I cared about was dead in Reggie's office with Reggie's suspenders twisted around her neck, yet I believe Reggie, profoundly, utterly, when he tells me he is innocent. Later, I will doubt him. Many times, in the very near future, I will be certain that he murdered Jenny. But at this moment—when it counted most—I am positive that Reggie is telling the truth.

"So how," I ask, "did this girl wind up here?"

"I don't know, man. I don't fucking know. All I know is I ain't never even seen this bitch"—I wince at the word and wonder if Brogus notices—"before. Somebody planted her in my office."

"Who?"

Brogus paused, then seemed to choose his words carefully. "I think, my man, that what we are dealing with here is a hydra-headed beast. A hydra-headed beast. It ain't any one person. That's not how they come at you. This is a confluence of forces."

"You suspect a conspiracy?"

"You just used that word, not me."

"But what do you think?"

"Clay—you know my history. And you know that, given my history, anything is possible."

The old Brogus bragadoccio was returning. Even now, Reggie could not contain a certain gloating pride in his own specialness. But I, for the first time since I had met him in the flesh, was as impressed by Reginald T. Brogus as he was by himself. At last I could see in this obese, middle-aged, bald-headed black Republican, the traces of the young revolutionary. I finally, fully succumbed to his power, his charisma.

"What do you wanna do?" I asked.

"I need your help, brother man. I need to know what you're willing to do."

"All right."

"Will you help me move this body?"

"Move it where?"

"I don't know. Maybe we could put it in your car—"

"No way!"

"And drive out to the lake—"

"Fuck no!"

"Lemme finish, man, we could dump—"

"Forget it, Reggie. Lemme get the fuck outta here!"

"Okay, okay, okay, relax, brother man, relax. I need you to keep your head now. Lemme lay Plan B on ya. I need you to drive me out to the airport."

"Why don't you drive yourself?"

"My car's in the shop, man, you know that!"

"I forgot."

"Can you do it?"

"What?" I was starting to feel a bit spacey, light-headed.

"Drive me to the airport!"

"Aw, shit, Reggie." The instinct to flee was returning. But part of me, most of me, I know, was mindlessly swept up in this drama, in the sheer, horrific, unreal exhilaration of it. Experientially, I was in a completely new place. But Reggie Brogus had been here—or someplace like it— before. Maybe I gave in to him as the uninitiated explorer gives in to his veteran guide as they plunge into the most mysterious and dangerous terrain. Looking back, of course, there are all sorts of things I could have said, all sorts of things I could have done, should have been thinking, would have said or thought or done if only I had the wisdom all the people who were not in my immediate situation always seem to have. Ah, yes, reasonable conclusions, quick responses to a crisis they were not actually in themselves: people always know what you should have done—what *they* would have done if they were you—as they hear your story. But this is what I said to Brogus: "You're gonna catch a plane dressed like that?"

Brogus tilted his head slightly and now I could see his bulbous eye-balls in the streaky light bouncing off his glass lenses. He continued to speak calmly, as if, presented with this insane dilemma, he had, through quick calculation—and with a well-honed urban guerrilla élan—arrived at the shrewdest plan of action. "I have a change of clothes in my office. I have a reservation on the six a.m. to Cleveland at Arden Airfield. From there I'm supposed to go to Washington to give the President's Day Address at the Foundation for American Virtue. I'm not going to make it to my speaking engagement. I'm goin' underground. I know how to do this. I've done it before. But I need a ride to the airport."

I was beginning to feel woozy, stoned by the weirdness of all this. I lamely suggested the obvious, the obvious suggestion I'd made before. But this time I knew Reggie would reject it. And I knew I would resign myself to giving him a ride. Still, I did say, one more time: "Reggie, don't you think we oughta call the police?"

Brogus, crouched on one knee before me, bowed his head solemnly, as if he were waiting to be knighted. "Clay," he whispered. He raised his head again. "We don't have much time. It'll take me five minutes to change into my clothes. Then I need you to drive me to Arden Airfield. That's only twenty minutes. I need you, Clay. This is brother to brother. Help me, brother. Help me."

Say what you will about me. It would have taken a better or wiser man than Clay Robinette to say no to Reggie Brogus that night. And Reggie must have known that. Why else would he have called me, of all the people in Arden, Ohio, in his most desperate hour? I cannot say I acted against my better judgment. I simply didn't think about it very carefully. Reggie Brogus asked for my help. I gave it to him.

*   *   *

My parents were nice, integrating folks, proud to call themselves Negroes instead of "colored people." Dad was (still is) a dentist. Mom was (still is) in what I guess you would call arts administration. My little brother and I grew up in a comfortable apartment in a brownstone in Philadelphia. Through most of my childhood, my parents did a lot of entertaining. They were particularly close with four or five other Negro couples who they always referred to as "the gang." It's funny to think that, back in those days, the members of the gang were pretty much the same age I am now. Even then they seemed like especially earnest, idealistic people. Hell, they were contemporaries of Martin Luther King, Jr. It was their generation of Negroes that was running the civil rights movement, smashing barriers, changing America. The gang was always debating. Should the movement be more focused on legal or economic issues? How did racial problems in the South differ from those in the North? How long would it be before the United States elected a Negro president? Would racism ever be eradicated from America? If so, when? Maybe by the year 2000? Would we really have to wait *that* long?

I used to stay up late sometimes when the gang was around, sitting just outside their circle, cross-legged on the wall-to-wall, deep shag carpet, in my bathrobe and pajamas, pretending to be absorbed in my comic books, my toys and games, but more focused on the grown-up conversation. Don't get me wrong: the gang wasn't a philosophical society. They drank, smoked, and got loud, listened to Motown and Stax records, danced the twist, played cards, and cracked dirty jokes I didn't understand. But I loved listening to their debates. Sometimes they sounded more like strategy sessions on how to build their lives, raise their young families in a world they were helping to reinvent. Though they often disagreed on specific points, the members of the gang were thoroughly likeminded, united in their belief in nonviolent protest, in the promise of integration.

After April 1968, all bets were off.

* * *

Mom and Dad kept the forbidden texts at the top of the wall-length bookshelf in the high-ceilinged study. Did they really think I wouldn't climb the ladder, as they did, to get a look at their collection of Sexual Revolution literature, the how-to-increase-your-pleasure manuals, the scandalous, popular novels of the day filled with the sort of explicit detail and profane language respectable American writers of only a few years earlier had always left out? My folks were constantly encouraging my brother and me to "use our library," to look things up in the dictionary or the encyclopedia or the musty old history books they cherished. Did they really think I would be deterred from climbing the ladder and perusing the forbidden texts as well?

It must have been sometime in 1969 that I first laid eyes on Reggie Brogus, up on that top shelf.

For more than a year, "the gang" had been disintegrating. Ever since April 4, 1968, When They Killed Dr. King—as my parents and their friends always referred to the assassination—the once-friendly debates had turned into nasty confrontations, furious tirades. Everybody was pissed off. Their optimism about the future had changed to a bitter fatalism. The faith in integration was replaced by a sense that white and black Americans could never peacefully coexist. Their belief in nonviolence had been irrevocably refuted by the violent death of their leader. The murder of Bobby Kennedy two months later only hardened them more. Anger was one thing all the members of the gang now shared. They were united in their rage. Yet they took that rage out on one another. They screamed in each other's faces about the need for violent revolution. They were no longer Negroes. Now they were black. But they were still irredeemably bourgeois. Much as they might have liked to, they were not going out and leading any bloody uprisings. So they lashed out at each other. The accountant called the lawyer an Uncle Tom. The nurse accused the high school principal of "trying to be white." The dentist said the sales executive was a hypocrite. The psychologist damned the arts administrator for not befriending more black people from the ghetto. One or another of the couples in the gang—or sometimes one person alone when a husband and wife turned on each other—usually wound up storming out of the party, slamming the front door behind them.

They shouted at each other about Malcolm X. I was just beginning to learn who he had been. A separatist, not an integrationist like Dr. King. A Muslim, not a Christian. A black nationalist who believed not in nonviolence, but in fighting back. Because Malcolm X had been assassinated, like Dr. King, he seemed to hold a special place in the gang's hearts. They may have disagreed with him when he was alive but now they yelled that Malcolm had seen reality for what it was. He was a martyr, a prophet. The gang could agree, however tempestuously, on Malcolm X.

There were other names, the names of younger black activists, people younger than my parents and their friends, that provoked more hostile arguments. Names connected with the Black Panthers, Black Power: Huey Newton and Bobby Seale, Stokely Carmichael, H. Rap Brown, Eldridge Cleaver, Reggie Brogus. I used to get most of the black revolutionaries all mixed up. But Reggie Brogus definitely stood out in the gang's shouting matches. Brogus, some said, was not a real revolutionary at all—he was a terrorist. Others argued that he was a con artist, a copycat, "a crazy nigga." Brogus was just what the movement needed, someone would yell, because he scared the shit out of white folks. But Brogus seemed to scare the shit out of a lot of black folks, too. Of all the revolutionaries, Brogus was clearly considered the most dangerous.

So dangerous, in fact, that he warranted a place on the shelf of forbidden texts. Standing atop the ladder, browsing through my parents' selection of sophisticated smut, I was startled to see the name "BROGUS" written in black block letters on the white spine of a slender volume. My parents never stashed political books up on the sex shelf. I remember feeling a sharp intake of breath when I pulled out the book and saw the photo on the jacket. I tottered on the ladder, shocked to find myself staring down the barrel of a pistol, a pistol pointed straight into the camera, aimed straight at *you*, with the same menace that the gaze of the man holding the pistol was aimed straight at you: the huge, bugged-out eyes in the dark face, a face so dark and eyes so immense, with lots of white all around the black pupils, the image was almost like an old racist caricature. Only this cartoon minstrel had gone psycho-guerrilla. There was no stupidity, no eagerness to please in those bulging eyes, but a broiling intelligence, and a fervor, a look that conveyed this man would pull the trigger because he just could not stop himself from pulling the trigger. Instead of a big, accommodating, white-toothed grin, this black face wore a twisted, tight-lipped scowl. Muscled like a linebacker, the man seemed to be busting out of his camouflage shirt. He wore a black beret atop his head. Just above the beret, written in jagged black letters on a white background was the title: *LIVE BLACK OR DIE!* At the bottom of the book jacket, at about the level of the pistol-pointing revolutionary's navel, were the words: *A Militant Manifesto.* I wasn't quite sure what that last word meant. Only when I opened the book did I see, on the title page, the author's full name: REGINALD TIBERIUS BROGUS.

The book was a beat-up and cheaply produced paperback. The pages looked as if they'd been banged out on a manual typewriter, then shrunk and copied. I was so excited by this find that I couldn't read the book chronologically. I started skipping randomly around the hundred or so pages, my eyes quickly scanning the paragraphs looking for the juicy bits. Here at last was the work of Reggie Brogus! The most dangerous revolutionary, the "crazy nigga" whose views were so incendiary they frightened other black radicals. What I read was more apocalyptic than political. There were no ten-point programs, no practical agenda I could perceive. It was more a violent poetry, unreasonable, delirious with rage. Brogus wrote of an inexorable force called Blackness and if you were not Black by birth then you must choose to make yourself as Black as possible. Even if you *were* born Black but were somehow not Black enough, you must become Blacker. Or be put up against a wall and shot. He wrote rapturously of waves of Black people from other nations overrunning America. He called for mass public executions of white males. He advocated the rape of white women by Black men in order to (1) make up for the rape of Black women by white men during slavery and (2) to ensure a Blacker populace. Yet he opposed interracial marriage. Black men should marry Black women exclusively. White women were only to be raped. I read the whole book in patches, feeling, by turns, thrilled and baffled. *LIVE BLACK OR DIE!* was lunatic, genocidal bloodlust, a sex-filled, often incoherent, usually irrational, racial revenge fantasy. I was hooked.

It was 1969 and I was a well-brought-up, eleven-year-old middle-class kid. To say I regarded Reginald T. Brogus as a role model would be ridiculous. I knew I would never be a man like him. But staring at his photo on the book jacket, I felt the pangs of abstract infatuation. I can't call it hero worship because Brogus was not a hero. He was something so much better, so much cooler, so much Blacker, than that. He was an antihero.

*   *   *

"Who do I look like?" Reginald T. Brogus fumed. "Yesterday's fool?"

He sat beside me in my dark blue Volvo—the safe, solid family car—bundled in his bulky, gray down jacket, a furry hat with earflaps, slightly askew, atop his head. Instead of his warm-up suit—I could smell it, stale and cold-sweaty, stuffed in the overnight bag that rested on the backseat of the car—Brogus now wore an ill-fitting blue pinstripe business suit and red suspenders. His Hermes tie—patterned with cutesy little elephants—was also askew, twisted around his neck, the folds of which

bloated at the pinching collar of his starched white shirt. A laptop computer, zipped up in its black canvas carrying case, rested on Brogus's
massive belly. He rhythmically, absentmindedly stroked and scratched
the scraggly black and white hairs of his beard as he spoke. He seemed to
be talking to himself as much as to me, veering between plotting his
escape and cursing his enemies.

"It is now 3:09," Reggie said. "Arden Airfield opens at 5 a.m. My flight
to Cleveland is at six. Where I go from Cleveland is the question. . . .
Fuck these motherfuckers! Who the fuck they think they dealin' with?
Tryin' to frame *me?* You wanna mix it up with Reggie Brogus? All right,
motherfucker, bring it on! . . . But today is Monday, a holiday. I doubt
anyone will go by the Afrikamerica Studies office today. That means no
one will find the body before Tuesday morning at the earliest. That gives
me a twenty-four-hour jump. Twenty-four hours of lead time. That's an
advantage. Must be exploited. . . . The cowards! Spineless, gutless, dick-
less, ass-licking, sniveling little faggots! You wanna pull some Amateur
Hour bullshit like this on me? On *me?!* I will crush them into the filth that
spawned them! . . . It is now 3:11. How much longer till the airport?"

The Volvo was zipping along, headlights beaming, slicing through the
darkness. I clutched the steering wheel, looking out at the flat earth,
the broken white line stretching endlessly before me in the center of the
road, the cold, hard expanses of winter-barren fields. This was farm
country. It was all there was in the thirty miles between Arden University and Arden Airfield. I saw the shadowy outlines of barns and houses,
far off in the distance, on either side of the road. The occasional grain silo
loomed in the vast night sky, then disappeared behind me. My mind had
entered a neutral zone, the half-distracted, half-purposeful state of a
man running an ordinary errand. Yes, I was just dropping a friend off at
the airport.

Like images from a dream you can't quite remember, the sight of the
body in Reggie's office flashed now and then across my mind. It was not
Jenny. Driving in my semitrance, I had convinced myself that the body
was not Jenny's body, the face not Jenny's face. I had been dreaming of
Pirate Jenny when Brogus woke me with his phone call almost an hour
earlier. That was it. I could not remember the dream, but I was still

groggy when we entered Reggie's office and, seeing the face of the poor dead girl, I must have superimposed Jenny's face over it. But it was not Jenny lying strangled on the couch. It couldn't have been.

I didn't know how long I had been driving in this semitrance, listening to Reggie in the half-interested way I might have listened to the car radio, thinking I just had to drop him off at the airport, then I could turn around and soon be back where I belonged, home in my bed. But the farther I drove, the more my neutral state of mind gave way to a specific fear: the fear of being seen, of the headlights of another car, particularly of a police car, appearing out of the darkness in front of me.

"Clay!" Reggie snapped.

"What?"

"How much longer till the airport?"

"I don't know. We can't see the control tower yet. When you can see the control tower in the distance, it's five miles or less."

"All right. Say we get to the airport at 3:20. That gives me an hour and forty minutes to stand outside."

Brogus paused and I could feel him staring at me. I kept my eyes on the road.

"I won't ask you to stay with me, though," Reggie said. "Just leave me there. I'll be all right. It's cold out there, but, shit, this ain't nothin' compared to Russia. I spent the winter of '78 in a safehouse in Leningrad. No heat, no fucking hot water. Now *that* was cold! Man, Russians are some backward motherfuckers!"

I felt a twinge of illicit thrill again. Here I was, in flight with Reggie Brogus, the erstwhile fugitive and exile, on the run again. But dread quickly extinguished my excitement. I was coming out of my semitrance. What the hell was I doing?

"Cointelpro," Reggie growled. Then he said it louder, to make sure I heard him. "Cointelpro."

"What?" I asked. I thought, perhaps, he'd said something in Russian.

"CO-IN-TEL-PRO," Reggie pronounced impatiently.

"What's that mean?"

"Counter Intelligence Program!" Reggie barked. "J. Edgar Hoover's program to destroy the Black Power movement. Never mind how much those clowns were doing to destroy *themselves* already—without FBI assistance! But Cointelpro was a system of disinformation, dirty tricks and double agents, infiltration—assassination! I've tangled with these sons of bitches before, Clay! I know whereof I speak. These motherfuckers have scores to settle with me. Shit goin' back twenty years. These motherfuckers don't never forget. They waited for the opportunity. And this is how they're comin' after me."

I spotted the darkened control tower, alone against the purplish sky. I could feel a certain clarity returning to my thoughts. Seeing the face of that girl in Reggie's office—the face I had imagined to be Jenny's—was like getting kicked in the head. I had been, in a way, knocked out. I was only really "coming to" right now. I felt a rage bubbling up inside me. I was furious with Reggie Brogus, who I suddenly remembered might very well be out of his mind, but even more furious with myself: Here I was enabling a possible—hell, a probable—murderer in his escape. I was making myself a fucking accessory to homicide!

"You never even heard of Cointelpro," Reggie sneered. "You gotta know your history, Clay. You gotta know it if you're gonna help exonerate me. . . . Hey, I see the control tower!"

Feeling calmer than I had all night, I pulled the car over to the side of the road, onto a bumpy, frozen field. We were still a good four miles from the tiny airport. I clicked off the headlights, shut off the engine.

"What the fuck are you doing?" Brogus hissed.

"You killed that girl, didn't you, Reggie?" I said in a voice so cold it surprised even me. Brogus was silent. With the headlights off, we were sitting in almost complete darkness inside the car. The sky outside seemed to be lightening, changing from purple to pearly blue-gray. The only thing punctuating its emptiness was the black silhouette of the control tower. I heard the wind gusting outside the Volvo's windows. Brogus didn't make a sound.

"I know how it happened," I continued in my glacial tone. "It was sex that just got a little too rough, right? This was just some girl you were fucking. It was just a game. You'd played it before. Like in that kinky Japanese movie, *Realm of the Senses*. Choking the person, getting them right to the brink of asphyxiation increases the intensity of the orgasm.

That's the game, right? You'd done it before and she was really into it. Hell, it was her idea, right? And tonight you just got a little carried away. It was an accident. The poor girl died. But it wasn't murder. It was . . . I don't know what . . . involuntary manslaughter. Right?"

"Is that what you think?" Reggie's voice sounded as cold as mine.

"Reggie, there's a naked dead girl in *your* office with *your* suspenders tied around her neck. What the fuck else am I supposed to think?"

"This ain't about sex, Clay. It's about politics."

"Yeah, right, Reggie. First you say the cops are behind it and now it's the CIA."

"FBI. Cointelpro was an FBI operation."

"Well, whatever the fuck it was, I'm not buying it, Reggie. Why the hell would they plant a body in your office?"

"To get rid of me, Clay!" Brogus's voice was turning panicky and desperate again. "Because I know too much."

"Stop it, Reggie."

"I'm serious, man. This is what I have to tell you. This is the story. This is what you have to report! I have specific information, Clay. Information they don't want to get out. Tapes! Documentation! Classified files!"

"About what?"

"About what happened in Memphis," Brogus said solemnly.

Memphis? The first thing I thought of was Graceland, Elvis Presley's home. "Where?" I asked.

"Memphis, Tennessee," Reggie intoned. "The Lorraine Motel. April 4, 1968. Dr. King's assassination. I have the MLK files, Clay. I know what really went down in Memphis."

Call me an idiot. Call me anything you want. But Reggie Brogus had managed to do it to me again. Half of me thought he was a raving madman, but the other half of me was suckered. Like a journalistic Pavlov's dog, I started salivating at the prospect that there might actually be a scoop in here somewhere. "You have these files in your possession?"

"Not with me now," Brogus said, clutching his laptop computer tighter against his belly. "They're in a safe place. But these motherfuckers know I could go public with this information at any time. I have concrete, irrefutable, documentary evidence of the government conspiracy to murder Dr. King. That's why they want my ass in jail. Or in a fuckin' electric chair! I'm tellin' you, Clay, this shit they put in my office is a setup!"

I decided that this was no time to weigh Brogus's credibility. A police car could appear on this lonesome road at any second and I would be sitting here in a getaway car, registered in my name, with the prime suspect in a homicide. I stared at the black silhouette of the Arden Airfield control tower, far in the distance.

"I'm goin' underground, Clay," Reggie rasped. "But you've got to cover this. Uncover it! Think of it this way, brother man. You could be sitting on one of the stories of the century! You might even win a Pulitzer Prize for this!"

Reggie overplayed his hand there. The dog stopped salivating. "Reggie," I said, the coldness returning to my voice, "I can't drive you any farther. The airport is about four miles away. Start walking."

"You're not gonna drive me the rest of the way?"

"No, I'm not."

Brogus sucked his teeth loudly. "Ain't that a bitch? We get all the way out here and now you gonna put me out on the road."

"Start walking, Reggie."

"Yo, Clay, man, you owe me. You *owe* me!"

Now I felt the hate, the hate I would feel for Reggie Brogus again and again. What was he doing, bringing up my debt to him? If I did indeed "owe" him anything. Was it a deeper suspicion that ignited the hate? Maybe that *was* Jenny in Brogus's office? Did he know her? Had Reggie fucked her, too? Did he know she was the woman he'd caught me with? Did he know it was Jenny that night, despite her brilliant disguise? But no, that couldn't have been Pirate Jenny's body in Brogus's office. Still, there *was* a body in Brogus's office. And this fat slob had the nerve to talk to me about what I owed him!

"Get the fuck outta my car, Reggie."

Brogus was silent for a long time. Finally, he said, "So it's like that, huh?"

"Yeah."

Reggie pulled his overnight bag from the backseat. "I understand. You got a wife and children to protect. Thank you for taking me this far. I appreciate it. I'll never forget it, brother. I hope you believe in me. Will you remember what I told you tonight?"

"Yes," I said, as coldly as I could manage.

"Will you try to find out what you can?"

"I'll try, Reggie."

"Thank you, Clay."

Brogus opened the door and I felt a blast of frigid air. He stepped out of the Volvo. I heard him zip up his down jacket. I expected him to close the door. Instead he leaned down and stuck his head into the car. "Don't sell me out, Clay," he said.

"I won't," I said suddenly, reflexively.

Brogus softly closed the car door. I heard him walking away, his footsteps crunching on the hard, frosted soil. I turned on the motor, clicked on the headlights. Brogus was glaringly illuminated now. I saw only the back of him, the furry hat, the gray down jacket, the blue pinstriped pants and black shoes, the overnight bag strung over one shoulder, the laptop strapped across the other. He did not turn around to look at me, did not seem surprised by the sudden flash of the headlights. There was something sort of pitiful about this large round mound trudging away, into the night.

I took firm grip of the steering wheel, turned the car around, and headed back to town. The fear had taken over now. All I wanted was to make it home without being seen, without another car passing me. I looked at my watch. It was 3:23. I cannot think of any other time when I wanted so desperately just to be home, in my bed, with my arms around my wife.

CHAPTER 3

PENELOPE WAS STILL SNORING LIGHTLY when I got back home. I undressed quickly in the dark, then slipped into bed. My wife was the heaviest sleeper I'd ever met. Except when it came to the voices of our children. I'd seen Pen snooze through ringing alarm clocks, loud music, and relentless pneumatic drilling outside her bedroom window. But if one of the twins woke up in the middle of the night and, from their bedroom down the hall, even softly called out "Mom . . . ?" Pen would snap awake, instantly alert and on the case, ready to handle anything. I could tell that, in the time I had been away with Brogus, Penelope had not stirred. I felt drugged with exhaustion. I wrapped my body around hers. My thermal underwear rubbed cosily, comfortingly against the flannel of the men's pajamas she liked to wear. I nuzzled my nose in her curly hair and took in her delicious, uniquely Penelope scent. Her lovely snore gently rattled.

Penelope hated the fact that she snored. "It's not very feminine," my very feminist wife would say. Since, of course, she was always asleep during it, Pen wanted to know what her snoring sounded like, how loud it was. I'd provide her with examples of grotesque honks and snarls and gurgles and say she sounded a bit like that, only louder. But Pen knew how much I actually loved her snoring. It gave me a strange solace, the intimacy of cuddling up to my wife and listening to the soft rhythmic purr of her breathing while she slept. It meant my darling was resting well, our children were safe in their beds.

The red digits on the bedside clock radio glowed 3:42. Exactly one hour and fifteen minutes had passed since Reggie Brogus woke me with his phone call. Back home, in my bed, the entire episode began to feel like a bizarre dream I'd just had. As I drifted into unconsciousness, I thought that none of it—not the phone call, the talk in the kitchen, the discovery of the body in the office, the drive to the airport—could really have happened. I felt that very precise relief one feels when realizing, on the border of sleep, that a particularly nasty nightmare was just a product of your imagination, nothing you would have to contend with when you got out of bed. I felt tranquil, reassured, soothed by Penelope's lullaby snore. Nothing would harm us. All was well with the world.

*   *   *

I like to say that Penelope Law and I had a self-arranged marriage. Strange as it may seem, we both had a feeling when we met, at age twelve, that we would, even *should,* someday get married. I was in the seventh grade at the oh-so-prestigious Dreedle Prep. She was in the same year at Dreedle's sister school, located directly across a courtyard on the suburban Philadelphia campus, the Hadley Girls' School. Despite its wealthy, Waspy reputation, Dreedle-Hadley fancied itself a progressive institution. Pen and I were part of a minority population that made up 15 percent of Dreedle-Hadley's student body. As soon as we spotted each other on the schoolbus—me in my Dreedle blue blazer, white shirt, plaid tie, khaki pants, and moccasins, she in her Hadley white blouse, blue tie, plaid pleated skirt, short white socks, and loafers—we knew. It wasn't love at first sight. Many more years would pass before we actually fell in love. What we experienced at age twelve was something much more practical, a feeling of commonsense inevitability. Someday we would be married. It was just obviously going to happen. Like I say, I know this sounds strange. But Pen and I would talk about this as adults and confirm that, back in pubescence, we felt the exact same rightness, the exact same quality of fate, about each other.

It was the fall of 1970. In November, the black members of the school's upper classes, the sophomores, juniors, and seniors, took over the administration building. What a blast! They were brazenly emulating college students of the day. The Dreedle-Hadley confrontation, however, was notably tame. The black kids didn't carry any weapons. And the headmaster, the headmistress, and all other members of the adminstrative staff peacefully surrendered the building. I was bitterly disappointed that, as a mere lower-schooler, I was too young to take part in the takeover. I heard of how the black upperclassmen pasted the walls of the authorities' offices with posters of Che Guevara, Huey Newton, Angela Davis, and, of course, Reginald T. Brogus, pointing his pistol straight into the camera. The takeover lasted about forty-eight hours. Finally, the students and faculty negotiated a settlement. There had been no need to call in the cops—no swinging billy clubs, no clouds of tear gas. Though I had been left out of the action, I definitely benefited from it. The following school year, uniforms were banished, the boys' and girls' schools were merged, and a whole raft of new courses, including Black Studies, was initiated. Revolution was fun!

Penelope became one of my closest friends, but we were never High School Sweethearts. She dated other Dreedle-Hadley guys, I dated other girls. Still, we always shared this unexpressed understanding. I never had the sort of raw, horny fantasies about Pen that I had about other girls. When I fantasized about Penelope, it was always about the wedding we might have, or the sort of house in the country we might someday own. Daydreams of bringing our newborn baby home from the maternity ward. After high school, I enrolled at Cornell in upstate New York. Penelope went off to Berkeley in California. We occasionally wrote each other, sometimes got together over the holidays. By the time we graduated from college in 1980, we still had not had sex together. We didn't need to. Because we had our unofficial pact. When it was time to get serious, we would be ready for each other. There was no way Pen and I would not tie the knot.

*   *   *

Sometimes one era begins before the previous one has ended. For me, the Conservative Age began with the election of Ronald Reagan—the embodiment of right-wing malevolence—as president of the United States in November 1980. The Liberal Age did not end until one month later when John Lennon—my favorite Beatle, the committed, iconoclastic, radical one who sang "Give Peace a Chance"—was gunned down by a deranged fan outside his Manhattan apartment building. Lennon's assassination was for me the same sort of psychological turning point that the assassination of Dr. King was for my parents and their gang. But Lennon's murder did not inspire rage or a lust for revolution. Coupled with the ascendance of Reagan, it left me feeling depressed, powerless. The times they were a-changin' for the worse. People were suddenly wearing their hair short, dressing for success, turning apolitical. I noticed that expressions from the business world—"That's just the bottom line!"—and the military—"Get with the program!"—were creeping into everyday conversation. The world had grown harder, meaner, colder. And there wasn't a goddamned thing I could do about it.

In the spring of 1981 I was living in Greenwich Village and working at my first job, an internship with the new, glossy weekly magazine *A Bite of the Apple*. One morning at the office, an item on the Associated Press wire caught my eye. Reginald T. Brogus had been apprehended in Paris and extradited to the United States to face federal conspiracy charges. It had been years since I'd heard Brogus's name. According to the article, he had been in hiding since April 1974, when members of his so-called terrorist cabal—officially named Blackness as a Revolutionary Force, or BAARF—bungled a bank robbery in Detroit. In a wild shootout in the bank's parking lot, two police officers and three members of BAARF were killed. Apparently, there had been a plan to take the loot, commandeer a helicopter, and drop the stolen money over the poorest ghettos in Detroit, to send millions of greenbacks raining down on the inner city. While Brogus had not been one of the ski-masked, rifle-wielding robbers, he was believed to be the mastermind of the scheme. For seven years, Brogus had eluded U.S. lawmen, fleeing first to Cuba, then making his way to Angola, Algeria, Turkey, the Soviet Union, and finally Paris, where he was busted while sipping a glass of Bordeaux and munching a slice of Camembert cheese in a sidewalk cafe. He was now in a maximum-security prison in Michigan, awaiting trial.

I told my editor that I thought the capture of this revolutionary fugitive would make a terrific story for *A Bite of the Apple*. "Reggie Brogus!" the editor snorted. "He's a has-been!"

Back in those early days of my journalistic career, I believed that editors actually knew what they were talking about. So, even after my internship ended and I embarked on a successful run as a freelancer, I never followed up on the Brogus story. Over the next three years, I never stumbled across another news item about Reggie Brogus. I didn't know how his trial had turned out, or if the case had even gone to trial at all.

Then, one day in September 1984, my old editor at *A Bite of the Apple* had a package sent to my apartment by messenger. It was a book with a sheet of yellow legal pad paper clipped over the cover. "Maybe now is the time for a story on this guy," the editor had scrawled on the paper. I remember feeling a sharp intake of breath when I pulled away the note and saw the photo on the jacket. There was a chubby, self-consciously distinguished-looking black man, holding a pipe to his lips. He wore a powder blue shirt with a button-down collar, a blue-and-white polka-dot bow tie, and red suspenders. His salt-and-pepper hair was thinning and he sported a neatly trimmed beard. Were it not for the enormous, froggy eyes, staring directly into the camera from behind thick, old-fashioned black-framed glasses, I would not even have recognized the man as the great antihero of my youth. Just above his balding head, written in an elegant cursive script was the title: *An American Salvation: How I Overcame the Sixties and Learned to Love the USA.* At the bottom of the jacket, at the level of the author's potbelly, was his name: Reginald T. Brogus.

The book was a slickly designed hardcover, brought out by a major publishing house. I was so stunned by Brogus's new image that I couldn't read the book chronologically. I started skipping around the two hundred or so pages, my eyes quickly scanning the paragraphs, looking for clues to this shocking transformation. So far as I could tell the book was a right-wing screed, a furious denunciation of government welfare programs, affirmative action, abortion rights. Brogus condemned left-wing activists, cursed the Black Power movement of which he had once been a leader, denigrated poor blacks as lazy, shiftless parasites. He was full of praise for Traditional American Values, lauding such men of principle as Herbert Hoover, George Wallace, and Ronald Reagan. Rather than concerning themselves with their black heritage, "American Negroes," Brogus wrote, should emulate the white people who had made this country great.

I hurled the book against the wall. What *was* this shit? A parody, an attempt at satire, a practical joke? What on earth had happened to Reggie Brogus? Had he been deprogrammed, brainwashed, born again? It was not as though I had considered the revolutionary Brogus of the sixties some kind of honorable icon. But at least that Brogus was challenging the establishment, threatening the power structure. This new Brogus was simply a mouthpiece of that establishment, a tool of that same power structure. Did he really believe what he was writing in *An American Salvation*? Had he really believed what he had written in *LIVE BLACK OR DIE!*? Perhaps Reggie Brogus had never held a true conviction in his entire life. Perhaps he was nothing more than a craven opportunist, changing his views to fit the fashion of the times. Or maybe he really had undergone an ideological conversion. Why did I find that the scariest possibility of all?

I phoned my editor and told him I would never, ever, write anything about Reginald T. Brogus.

*   *   *

Penelope and I married young, younger than any of our friends. She called me the day she moved to New York in the spring of 1984. She was about to start a job in the human resources department of a large insurance company. I told her I'd always found that an ambiguous, vaguely ominous term, "Human Resources." Basically, Pen explained, she recruited minorities, dealt with employee complaints, and tried to make sure that everybody in the company, regardless of race, sex, color, or creed, was treated fairly. It sounded like honorable work, I said. "It's just a job," Penelope said. "It's not my life. So—are you seeing anybody?"

I was, but that didn't matter. I quickly jettisoned my girlfriend of the moment. Pen and I were ready for each other. We had both had our fair share of relationships—with partners black, white, and other. We were sick of dating. There was also, in 1984, a palpable fear of herpes in the air. It seems quaint now, the terror of a few painful genital warts. But back in those days, AIDS was still considered a gay disease. In any event, Pen and I had had our sexual adventures and were ready to make good on our unofficial pact. The wedding took place on Valentine's Day, 1985.

The twins were born exactly eight months later. Pen and I were both twenty-seven years old.

What makes a good marriage? Some say opposites attract. But that was certainly never the case between Pen and me. We shared the same race, the same middle-class background, the same hometown, the same easygoing temperament and sense of humor. We even looked alike, so much so that, back in high school, people sometimes thought we were brother and sister. And when it came to sex, we were perfectly, even ecstatically, compatible. At least in the early days. Forget *looking* at other women. During the first four years of our marriage, I didn't even *fantasize* about having sex with anyone other than Penelope. The fact was I didn't think anyone could satisfy me sexually as much as Pen did. I knew older guys who often cheated on their wives. But I never felt the temptation—not in those first four years.

Then came my public disgrace. Exposed as a fabricator of quotes and sources, unable to find any publication that would hire me to write an article, rapidly going broke, with a wife and two infant daughters to support (well, partially support, anyway, since Pen always made more money than I did), I took to drink. I became a late afternoon barfly at Babson's, a buppie watering hole on the Upper West Side. One day, an old college pal of Penelope's walked into the joint. Jasmine was a big, buxom gal with honey-toned skin, caramel-colored, straightened hair, and wide, ginger-hued eyes. As usual, she was showing off her formidable cleavage. Jasmine had always looked, to me, like a giant piece of candy. She embraced me as if I were a long-lost brother, then propped herself on the barstool next to mine and ordered a whiskey sour. Jasmine was a flirt by nature. I don't think she knew how to talk to a man without hinting that she was available. I had never been attracted to Jasmine— until that day in early 1989.

I was drunk and horny as a hare when we left the bar. Jasmine linked arms with me and led us to her nearby apartment. Next thing I knew she was sprawled naked on the bed, in all her voluptuous, confectionery glory, exhorting me to help myself. And, Lord, how I wanted to! But you know what? I couldn't. The image of Penelope's face, and of her lithe brown body, kept flashing across my mind. I was physically incapable of indulging Jasmine. After an hour or so of concerted effort, we both felt embarrassed, ashamed. I don't know which of us was more apologetic. I went home to my wife and daughters, worried that Penelope would somehow be able to guess what had happened, that she would take one look at my face and know that I had attempted to betray her. But if Pen noticed my shame that night she probably attributed it to my ongoing career crisis.

So cheating on my wife, I decided, was a physical impossibility. Nothing I would ever be capable of. Two years after my encounter with Jasmine, after we had moved to Arden, Ohio—but before I met Pirate Jenny—Pen and I, in bed one night, talked abstractly about infidelity. I told her that if I ever learned she had been with another man, I would be so depressed I'd probably just curl up in the fetal position and die. I asked what she would do if she found out I'd been with another woman.

"I'd track the bitch down," Penelope said, "and strangle her."

*   *   *

The suburban jazzy theme music of the *Huck Blossom Show* faded out and the host's long, pale, horsey head filled the screen. In his folksy-but-educated Carolina cracker accent, he delivered one of his typical introductions, saying that his first guest tonight needed no introduction. The camera cut to Reginald T. Brogus, wearing a crisp white shirt, gray pin-striped suit jacket, and a yellow "power tie." I was always amazed by how fat Reggie Brogus had become. He was ripplingly muscled on the jacket of *LIVE BLACK OR DIE!* in 1968, somewhat chubby on the jacket of *An American Salvation* in 1984. But over the past seven years, as his political views lurched more to the right, his body had seemed to expand correspondingly.

"That's the guy," I said to Penelope. My wife and I were curled up together on the living room couch. It was early April 1991, eleven o'clock at night. Amber and Ashley were alseep, but Pen and I were staying up later than usual to see on television the man Dean Jerry Shamberg had just hired for a Visiting Professorship in the Afrikamerica Studies program, an appointment that would begin in September.

"This guy was in the Panthers?" Penelope asked incredulously.

"No, he had his own group, Blackness as a Revolutionary Force."

"Were they the ones who kidnapped Patty Hearst?"

"No, that was the Symbionese Liberation Army."

"What's Symbionese?"

"I forget. But Brogus wasn't one of them."

"But he fled the country?"

"He was on the run for seven years. But he returned to the States in the early eighties, the charges against him were eventually dismissed, and he became a right-winger."

Penelope frowned at the screen in her effort to recognize Brogus, to distinguish him from the other former militants she vaguely remembered. "Is he the one who ran for Congress or the one who started hawking his homemade barbecued rib sauce?"

"Actually, Brogus ran for Congress *and* hawked his own homemade barbecued rib sauce. He was the Republican nominee for a House seat in Michigan back in '86. Fortunately, he got clobbered by the Democrat. Then he went into the soul food business and wound up declaring for bankruptcy. Now he's on TV all the time. He's on those Sunday morning shows where men sit around in a circle and scream at each other. Then he pops up on these polite little late night pseudo-intellectual chat shows. And then, whenever anything that might qualify as a Black Issue comes along, he appears on the news to give his opinion about it."

"That's just for his freak value," Pen said. "He shouldn't be on TV at all. He should be trotted around the countryside in a circus caravan. SEE the bearded lady! SEE the two-headed dog! SEE the black conservative!"

"Yeah, and in five months he's going to be my colleague."

I felt Pen shudder in my arms. "Why?" she asked.

"Marketing."

On the TV screen, Huck Blossom and Reggie Brogus sat near each other at a round wooden table, surrounded by utter darkness. That was the Huck Blossom set. People talking against a black background, a conversation in a void. Brogus was cheerily thanking Blossom for having invited him to a delightful dinner party recently. Blossom magnanimously thanked Brogus for thanking him. This was the sort of exchange I'd seen more and more of lately, a talk-show guest and a talk-show host ostentatiously chumming it up on the air, letting the audience know that they had a relationship off the air, that they were part of a privileged little celebritocracy to which *you*, the viewer, would never belong.

Huck Blossom leaned toward Brogus, furrowing his brow. "Let's talk about Los Angeles. We have all seen, in the last two weeks, grainy video footage of LAPD officers beating an unarmed black man, mercilessly, with billy clubs. And apparently without cause—"

"Was it without cause?" Brogus interjected.

Huck Blossom seemed surprised, but at the same time a bit pleased, by Brogus's question. "Well, to all appearances, it certainly seems as if the police behaved with excessive brutality toward a black man who was—"

"Who was what?" Brogus challenged. "Unarmed? How could they be sure he was unarmed? They stopped him because he was driving erratically. And let's not forget, this Rodney King had a record. We all know that a disproportionate number of young black men are in prison or somewhere in the judicial system. How were these L.A. peace officers to know that this Rodney King might not have been a dangerous violent criminal? He wasn't cooperating with them. And they had to get him to submit. But there is no reason, given their day-to-day experience with the black male criminal element why they should have assumed this Rodney King would be some sort of gentle, law-abiding citizen."

"Okay, okay," Huck Blossom said. He was bouncing excitedly in his seat now, but still leaning forward, furrowing his brow even more strenuously, and trying to suppress a smile. "But wouldn't you say that if police are naturally suspicious of black males that that is a little bit, well, maybe, unfair?"

"Unfair?" Brogus repeated, putting a sarcastic spin on the word. "It's hard to argue with statistics, Huck." Reginald T. Brogus leaned back in his chair, unbuttoned his suit jacket. As the gray pinstriped jacket fell open, Brogus looped his thumbs around the bands of his suspenders. "As John F. Kennedy once said," Brogus intoned, leaning back-, flaunting his red-white-and-blue, stars-and-stripes decorated suspenders, "'Life is unfair.'"

*　　*　　*

Is this a memory or is it a dream? Pirate Jenny sits across from me in the brightly lit coffeehouse. Her wild orange hair tumbles over her shoulders. She smiles sadly at me, her slightly slanted eyes glittering. She still has her fresh, unfinished face, the features not yet set and dried, still the face of an adolescent, not of a woman in full. She wears a red sweater with a big, loopy cowl neck. I am nervous. I don't want to be here, don't want to be seen with her.

"I have a present for you," Jenny says.

She holds it in her hand, offering it to me. Her hand, with the flat, black computer disk lying on its white palm, seems to float above the small, round, fake marble table.

"It's my diary," Jenny says. "I want you to have it. I want you to know my secrets."

The black disk, with no label on it, nothing indicating its contents, seems like some sort of evil talisman. I try to push it away, but, somehow, I cannot. Jenny's hand continues to float above the table, the flat black disk emanating invisible rays.

"I want you to know my secrets," Jenny says.

"With knowledge comes responsibility," I say. "And I don't want that."

"It's too late," Jenny says, feline eyes glittering.

The disk has disappeared, but I know that, somehow, it is now in my possession.

"Now you're the guardian of my secrets," Pirate Jenny says.

*　　*　　*

"Are you sick, baby?" I heard my wife say. "You're sweatin' like a sharecropper."

I opened my eyes and saw Penelope sitting on the edge of the bed. I felt as if we had just been reunited after a long separation. She looked so beautiful to me, with her mahogany skin, almond eyes, and lustrous, curly black hair. She was wearing the black cashmere sweater I had given her for our seventh wedding anniversary three days earlier and crisply ironed blue jeans. Penelope softly pressed her hand against my forehead.

"I think you've got a fever, Clay."

I turned my head and looked at the bedside clock radio. It was 9:29.

"How do you feel, baby?" Penelope asked, her voice sounding worried.

"I love you so much, Pen," I said sleepily. "Do you know that? I love you so much."

Penelope smiled. "I think you're delirious. Maybe you should stay in bed today."

"I have an eleven o'clock class," I said, surprised by the weakness of my own voice.

"No, you don't. Today's President's Day. No school. Remember? I'm taking the girls to Toledo."

Right. We all had the day off. Pen was taking Amber and Ashley to visit a museum and see the Ice Capades. I was to be left alone to catch up on grading papers and maybe put in some work on the screenplay I was supposed to be writing.

"We have to go now, sweetie," Penelope said. "Don't force yourself to get up if you don't feel well. Okay? We should be home around six-thirty. Okay?" Penelope rose from the bed. "I'll call to check in on you this afternoon. All right, honey?"

"I love you," I said groggily.

"I love you, too, Clay."

*   *   *

Dexter, as was his wont, was drinking from the toilet. He sat, delicately poised, with his hind paws clinging to the edge of the seat. He leaned forward, extending a sleek black front leg, reaching down ever so carefully, as if testing the temperature of the water, then abruptly ducking his head and, with a quick flick of the tongue, lapping up a drop, then another, and another. Dexter then turned and looked at me, the expression in his silver eyes at once guilty and shameless. *"Yow,"* he squeaked.

Dexter always said the same thing but its meaning was always a matter of context, of subtle inflection. At this moment my interpretation of Dexter's *yow* was: "Yes, I know I'm not supposed to drink from the toilet but, damn it, I *like* drinking from the toilet so what are *you* gonna do about it?" But as he saw me preparing to pee, Dexter hopped off the bowl and scampered out of the bathroom, tossing a casual *"Yow!"* over his shoulder, as in "Later, man."

And I thought: Dex: Wasn't he somewhere in that weird dream I had last night?

I spent most of President's Day in a state of suspended reality. That is to say, since I felt unsure whether the episode with Reggie Brogus had really happened, I decided not to make a judgment on whether or not it had happened at all. I would simply have to wait to find out if there really had been a body in his office, if I really had helped him flee Arden, Ohio, or if I'd just dreamed the whole incident. By the time I dragged my ass out of bed at 11:30, I no longer felt feverish. I showered, dressed, consumed a pot of coffee and a bowl of Special K. I then commenced with several hours of mindless puttering. It's amazing how much of this sort of thing one can do in an average-sized American home. I puttered about the study, arranging and rearranging shelves of books, files of records, piles of paper. I puttered about the master bedroom, reordering the clutter in the closets. I puttered about the kitchen, loading the dishwasher, alphabetizing the spice rack, changing the naked bulb that hung from a rubbery cord in the pantry, unloading the dishwasher. I puttered about the living room, picking up toys and fluffing throw pillows. I turned on the television and channel-surfed, figuring that if there really had been a murder on the Arden University campus, I'd find some urgent news bulletin about it. After half an hour of zapping through soap operas, game shows, and talkfests, I decided that no news was good news. I then remembered that, today being a holiday, no one would have discovered the body in Brogus's office yet—if indeed there was a body in Brogus's office to be discovered.

Finally, around 4:00, I decided to go by my office in the English Department. I could have taken our second car, the tiny Honda, but instead opted to ride my bike. The temperature had risen about twenty degrees and a morning rain had washed away the ice that coated everything the night before. As I pedaled toward campus, the sky was a dingy, mop-water gray. Entering the quadrangle, I rolled past the Mathematics building. It looked bleak and uninhabited. Was there really a dead, naked body in there? I saw a few students walking across the quadrangle, but, for the most part, the campus had an eerie, evacuated feeling.

The English Department occupied a pleasant, white clapboard house on the north end of campus. I chained my bike to the outdoor rack and entered the building. No one, it seemed, had been inside the place over the long weekend. My small office was a mess. Looking at the stacks of unread, ungraded student essays on my desk, I knew I didn't have the energy to tackle them. I turned on the computer and called up the file for my script. I stared at the words on the screen:

ELEGY FOR A HITMAN

By Clay Robinette

That was as far as I'd progressed on my screenplay. I shut off the computer, suddenly feeling tired and overwhelmed by melancholy. I cleared some books and papers off the threadbare couch and stretched out. Maybe I was coming down with the flu. Or something. I was drifting somewhere between sleep and wakefulness when the vision of Pirate Jenny returned.

She is sitting there in the brightly lit coffeehouse, wild orange hair tumbling, green cat's eyes aglitter. "I want you to know my secrets," she says beseechingly. Then she pulls at the collar of her cowl neck sweater, revealing her flesh to me. I see her bare alabaster skin. There is no bra strap. Just a red, raw scar, like a rope burn, descending from her collarbone, toward her left breast, which remains concealed by the sweater. "Look," Jenny says, her voice impassive. "Now will you read my diary?"

I bolted upright on my office couch. This was no dream. It had really happened. I had not wanted to see Jenny that afternoon—When was it, late November, early December?—at Cafe Bellafiglia, but she had insisted. I had worked so hard to put Jenny out of my mind, to erase our entire—What to call it? Relationship? Affair? Compulsion?—time together from my memory bank, that I hadn't even been sure if this meeting had taken place. But it had. And Jenny had indeed shown me her scar, she really had handed me a black unlabeled computer disk. But I had never read it. I had put it . . . where? What the fuck had I done with Pirate Jenny's diary?

* * *

Jenny must have considered herself irresistible. Physically, I had, up to a point, found her impossible to resist. But she must have thought that even if I had, finally, mustered the willpower to reject her body, I would never be able to resist her mind. I would never be able to stop myself from exploring her secrets. Or maybe she thought that out of sheer human curiosity, or a reporter's natural voyeurism, I would be eager to read her diaries. What she didn't realize was that once I was through with a lover, I was no longer all that interested in what she thought about things.

Back in New York, in the days before Penelope and I finally hooked up, I had a misbegotten three-month relationship with an emotional live wire of a young woman who, in the weeks after our breakup, mailed me several letters, no doubt detailing, in each one, everything that was wrong with me. Or maybe not. Maybe her letters were self-critical, or maturely analytical. Or erotic, vitriolic, melancholic. I have no idea because I never read any of them. As soon as I realized a letter was from this woman Marcy—even if she had not put down her return address on the envelope, I recognized her handwriting on my address and on the occasions when she had typed my address, the absence of a return address tipped me off to the fact that Marcy had probably sent it—I tossed it in the trash without opening the envelope, let alone reading its contents. Marcy finally phoned. "Haven't you been getting my letters?" When I told her I had thrown them away without reading them she first refused to believe me, then decided I was even more of a "bad person" than she had thought. At least she stopped sending me letters.

So I was not naturally inclined to peruse Pirate Jenny's diaries, even after she had so provocatively advertised them to me. But what the fuck had I done with that disk she had thrust upon me?

Forget puttering about. For two hours that Monday afternoon, I *ran-sacked* my cramped little office in the English Department, spilling the contents of drawers out onto the floor, flinging through shelves. I came across dozens of computer disks, but every one of them had a label on it. I suddenly wondered if Jenny's diary disk was also labeled and I simply had a distorted memory of its being naked. I then examined every disk I'd found, reading each label. None gave any hint of bearing Jenny's diary. Now I was certain that it was a black disk I was searching for, a black disk that bore no label.

I was still functioning in a state of suspended reality. My obsession was with a little piece of metal, encased in plastic. I had managed to disconnect it from the idea that there might be a dead body—and that the body might belong to Jennifer Wolfshiem—in an office across the campus. I was not thinking in terms of evidence. I simply invested every bit of my emotional and intellectual energy into the search for this little disk. Where would I have put a computer disk I had no interest in reading? Had I just thrown it in the trash like Marcy's old letters? After my exhaustive search, I was certain the disk was not in my office. What the fuck had I done with it? Had I brought it into my home?

By the time I started bicycling back to my house at 6:30, night had fallen. Lights were coming on in dormitory windows, students were returning from the short holiday. Rolling past the dark mass of the Mathematics building, I began to feel feverish again. Maybe, I thought, I should call Pirate Jenny, just to make sure she was all right. But no. I had never phoned her before. To do so now might be asking for even more trouble. Maybe, I thought, I should call Brogus and hear him laugh at the bizarre dream I had had about him and the body in the office. Or maybe I should call the police? Pedaling away from the campus, through the suppertime gloom of Arden's suburban streets, I realized that, whatever it was that had happened the night before with me and Reggie Brogus, I must reveal it to no one.

*   *   *

"Hey, Clay, it's us, it's about six-thirty. Are you there . . . ? . . . No, okay, baby, you must have gone to the office after all. Sorry I didn't call earlier.

You looked so sick this morning I figured you might spend the day in bed. Anyway, hope you're feeling much better, hope you're being productive. I don't know when we're gonna be home. The traffic is nightmarish, everybody coming back from the long weekend, I reckon. Your children were bouncing off the car windows but I think they're burning each other out now. I have to say, the backseat smelled really stinky. I thought maybe you had left some running shoes back there. Anyway, we stopped at a McDoodoo's for dinner. Just got here, the girls are waiting in a long line so I have to go. Just wanted to let you know I doubt we'll be home before eight, then it's straight to bed for the girls and probably for me, too, I'm beat. We had fun, though. But I know you'd prefer a root canal to Holiday on Ice. Anyway, you've got the A-girls for an appointment with Beauty and the Beast . . . yes, them again . . . on Saturday afternoon. Don't forget: I'm doing a workshop in some other town, I forget which, that day. Okay, Clay, you've got to suffer through a lonely bachelor dinner tonight, but if we're not home by, say, eight-thirty, I'll give you a call. Who loves ya, baby?"

I erased Penelope's message from the answering machine and went into the kitchen. The familiar scratching noise began. I opened the pantry door and looked down at Dexter. *"Yow,"* he said, meaning "Feed me." I scooped some meaty cat food into a bowl for Dex, popped a frozen individual serving of lasagna into the microwave for myself. I ate in front of the big color television in the living room, something Pen never allowed me and Amber and Ashley to do. I zapped across the airwaves, giving in to the narcotic pull of the medium. I spaced out, went numb, my mind sponging up the images. No news of Brogus or dead bodies on the Arden campus. I did come across several items about this Bill Clinton character. Now, it turned out, he was not only a philanderer but a draft dodger. An unworthy candidate for the presidency, the talking heads said. No chance of winning the Democratic party nomination, let alone getting elected next November, they pronounced. Dead in the water. I assumed they were right, though I had dismissed the Arkansas governor weeks earlier when I learned his campaign theme song was "Don't Stop Thinkin' About Tomorrow" by Fleetwood Mac. What a weenie.

I started speculating again. I know it may seem incomprehensible but I was not focused on the memory of the body on the couch or Reggie Brogus's whereabouts: Had he really gone "underground"? (And what did *that* mean? Was he on a raft at this very moment, braving choppy waters on his way to Cuba?) Nor was I thinking about the danger I may have placed myself or my family in by assisting a fugitive and not reporting a crime. I was obsessed only with finding this little piece of metal and plastic, this black unlabeled computer disk.

I turned off the TV and rushed to the study, where I had so assiduously puttered a few hours earlier. I meticulously flipped through the freshly ordered stacks of dozens of multicolored computer disks, all of them labeled with some notation indicating some content other than Jenny's diary. And I wondered: If I had brought home a computer disk that I did not want anyone else—my wife, say—to sneak a peek at, would I leave it conspicuously unlabeled? Of course not. I would, instead, give it a decoy label, indicating that its contents were innocuous, inherently boring, or, at the very least, of no interest to anyone but me. "NOTES FOR ESSAY, 9/24/91." Something like that. I booted the desktop and carefully, methodically, began loading each innocuously labeled black disk, just to see if Jenny's diary popped up onscreen. I had just finished all the labeled black disks and, wondering if maybe I'd remembered the color wrong, was starting on a pile of labeled, dark blue disks when I heard the Volvo pull into the driveway. I looked at my watch: 8:39.

*　　*　　*

One hour later, Penelope and I were snuggling in bed, the flannel of her men's pajamas rubbing cosily, consolingly, against my naked skin. We had just bathed together, but she still felt cold and had to put on the pajamas. I was trying, under our down comforter, to warm her up. The kids had been totally zonked when I saw them, wrapped around each other in the backseat of the Volvo. (It *was* a bit stinky. I apologized to Pen for having left a pair of my sneakers back there over the weekend, not mentioning the lingering stench of Reggie Brogus's warm-up suit.) I took Ashley in my arms, Pen picked up Amber, and we carried the sleeping children up to their room. Getting each of them out of their day outfits and into their nightclothes as they squirmed and muttered sleepily, I was reminded of their babyhood, when Pen and I would each take a child for changing, or dressing, and, after their weaning, of course, feedings. We were always careful to alternate daughters on a regular basis. We didn't want our twins in any way assigned His and Hers. Amber and Ashley had grown so independent in the past couple of years that Pen and I had stopped this sort of maintenance. So I got a nostalgic kick out of us putting the girls to bed after their busy day. From the moment I had seen Pen and the girls huddled in the Volvo in the driveway, I had gone into my benevolent husband-father mode. Cuddling with my wife, after our sweet, steaming hot herbal bath together, I felt protected, and I felt like the protector. We were—this family—a world unto itself.

I caressed the flesh beneath the flannel pajama shirt, relished the feel of the skin that was squeezed over the elastic rim of the pajama bottoms.

"Don't pinch my fat," Pen said.

"That's not fat," I said. "It's just fatty deposits."

"Same difference," Pen said as she wriggled her hips.

"I like 'em," I said, sliding the pajama pants down her smoothly wriggling thighs. "I love you forever, Pen."

"I love you forever, Clay."

We made the most beautiful, intimate kind of love I have known, the profoundly married kind. Penelope fell asleep before I did. As I dozed off to my wife's gentle lullaby snore, I knew that nothing could harm us. All would be well with our world.

CHAPTER 4

TUESDAY, FEBRUARY 18, 1992—9:09 a.m. The sun shone brilliantly but the air was tingling cold. Riding my bike toward campus, I felt prepared for anything. Far in the distance, I could already see the crowd around the Mathematics building. Rolling down the asphalt walkway, getting closer and closer to the scene of the crime, I saw a red light spinning silently atop an ambulance. I saw people clustered around a white van that I first took to be another ambulance, until I spotted the ACTION NEWS logo on its side. There were blue-clad cops everywhere. I locked up my bike in the parking lot behind the Math building. *Be cool*, a voice in my head repeated over and over. *Whatever happens, just be cool.*

Wading into the crowd, trying to work my way to the front of the building, I had a disturbingly familiar sensation. It was that ticking collective anticipation one feels walking into an arena just before a much-hyped concert or sports event, or milling through the hordes of people gathered in Times Square at, say, 11:45 on New Year's Eve, awaiting the countdown. The crowd around Arden University's Math building was made up overwhelmingly of students, bundled against the cold and buzzing excitedly. Certain words kept bubbling up as I jostled my way through the heavy overcoats, the down and leather jackets:

"Dead . . . girl . . . body . . . naked . . . strangled . . . raped . . . nude . . ."

I almost tripped over heavy cables snaking along the walkway. I turned around and saw a tall, heavily made-up woman with a beaky nose, electric blue eyes, and a rigid blond helmet of hair. She wore a navy blue overcoat with black velvet lapels and held a microphone to her lips.

A cameraman edged forward as students politely stepped out of his way, moving in closer to the reporter.

"Details are sketchy at this time, Rex, but I can tell you there are a lot of very frightened young students at Arden University this morning. Isn't that right?"

The reporter stuck her microphone in the face of a frizzy-haired, freckle-faced student who didn't look in the least bit frightened. In fact, the girl wore an odd little half-smile as she leaned into the mike and spoke with a practiced banality: "You just never think that something like this could happen here."

I pushed my way toward a little platform and a lectern crowned with microphones that had been set up just outside the front doors of the Math building. A press conference seemed imminent. Suddenly the crowd surged forward, nearly knocking me to the ground. The doors of the front entrance opened and, as police pushed back lunging photographers and TV camera crews, two emergency medical workers carried out a stretcher with a white sheet draped over it. The crowd stared, mesmerized, as the men in white hurried past and a gusty wind kicked up. The lumpy outline of the body seemed to press against the fluttering white sheet. As the paramedics slid the stretcher into the back of the waiting ambulance, I was not even thinking about who might be under that white sheet. I began to feel the way I would guess a lot of people in the crowd felt: like I was watching all this on television.

Be cool. Whatever happens, just be cool.

"Talk about putting a college on the map, eh, old bean?"

I turned my head and saw Roger Pym-Smithers standing beside me, leering. He wore a long, black overcoat and a stylishly battered, floppy black fedora. He leaned forward on the balls of his feet, his hands stuffed in the pockets of his tweed trousers. Roger was a professor of British history and, though he had lived in America for more than a dozen years, he liked to underscore his Englishness by using expressions like "old bean," which I had never heard leave the lips of any other person, English or not, but which reeked of some sort of Edwardian Oxbridge clubbiness that was intended either to impress or annoy Americans. I always thought that Roger must have been a handsome "bloke" back in Swinging London, but he had gone somewhat to seed over the years. He had developed a red, jowly drinker's face (Roger considered himself quite the connoisseur of fine French wines), and his gray eyes were turning a bit rheumy in middle age. Roger had sharply arched eyebrows and he had seemed, of late, to be subtly combing the thin hairs at their peaks, causing them to flare out devilishly. Though a lot of Arden faculty members couldn't stand Roger Pym-Smithers, I'd always sort of liked him. And, even at this moment, I appreciated his sardonic wit. When, for instance, he spoke of "putting a college on the map," he was quoting Dean Jerry Shamberg who constantly spoke of the need to do just that with Arden University.

"Nothing like a little murder to garner some publicity, don't you think?" Roger said in his posh "public school" accent, leering extravagantly.

Be cool. Be cool. Whatever happens, just be cool.

"Murder?" I said, staring quizzically at Roger. "Are you serious?"

The leer disappeared from Roger's face, and he suddenly looked stricken. "You mean you don't know?" I shook my head. "Bloody hell. Kwanzi and I got a call early this morning. Come."

Roger took me by the arm and led me out of the swarm of people, to a little patch of yellow grass near a corner of the Math building, on the edge of the crowd. The day before, during my President's Day of suspended reality, I had given no thought at all to Roger Pym-Smithers or to his wife, Kwanzi Authentica Parker. Kwanzi was a righteous, kente-clothed sister who had taught at Arden University for twelve years. It was Kwanzi who had come up with the whole notion of an Afrikamerica Studies program. Before Brogus arrived on campus the previous semester, everyone had assumed that when Afrikamerica Studies ended its two years as a "pilot program" and became a full-blown department, Kwanzi would be named its chairperson. The chair was Kwanzi's to lose. But in recent weeks, Dean Jerry Shamberg, celebrity-loving, controversy-craving Dean Jer, had been floating Brogus's name for leadership of the program, a program that Brogus had infamously suggested renaming

American Negro Studies. Professor Kwanzi Authentica Parker—who had publicly, vehemently opposed Shamberg's hiring of Brogus in the first place—was, understandably, pissed. To Kwanzi, Reginald T. Brogus was the vilest sort of race traitor.

Roger and I stood face to face on the patch of yellow grass. "I really shouldn't be facetious about this. Kwanzi's really quite distraught. Let me give you the facts as we know them. At around six this morning, Pops Mulwray entered the Afrikamerica Studies suite and found the body of a young woman. She was murdered. She was completely naked. And, perhaps most interestingly, given the location of her corpse, she was white."

I looked Roger in the eye, trying to reveal nothing more than a horrified but detached curiosity on my face. "Fuck."

"That's what Kwanzi said."

We were both startled by the sudden whine of a siren. As the crowd parted, the ambulance carrying the body slowly moved along the walkway. Once there were no more people in its path, the ambulance sped away across the quadrangle, siren wailing. *Okay,* I thought, *a white girl was murdered but that doesn't mean it was Pirate Jenny. It could have been anybody. The face you saw was bruised, the features distorted. You thought it was Jenny but probably Jenny is gonna come walking up to you any minute now, with that brazen, knowing look in her eye.*

"Anyway," Roger continued, "Shamberg rang us up about half-past seven. Kwanzi's in the Maths building right now with Shamberg, Pops, and the police. And, as you can see, the media have been alerted."

"Damn," I said. "And did they find any sort of murder weapon in Brogus's office?"

Roger's rheumy eyes flashed, and I immediately realized my slip. Roger stared intensely at me. "What did you just say, old bean?"

Shitfuckmotherfucking stupid fuck . . . Just be cool, Clay. Just be cool.

"I said did they find a murder weapon in Brogus's office?" I repeated.

"Yes, quite right, old bean," Roger said slowly. "Only I didn't mention Brogus's office. I only said a body had been discovered in the Afrikamerica Studies suite."

"Oh . . . well . . . just moving through the crowd, I heard everybody buzzing about Reggie Brogus. I figured whatever was going on, it must have something to do with him."

Roger Pym-Smithers leered at me, the moist-looking little hairs at the peaks of his eyebrows flaring devilishly. "You wouldn't happen to know where Professor Brogus *is*, would you, old bean?"

"If you do, you'll stand to collect a one hundred thousand dollar reward," I heard a nasal male voice say. I turned and saw Andy Chadwick standing behind me on the patch of grass. "Reggie Brogus has a price on his head! Can you believe this?"

Andy grinned. A gangly twenty-four-year-old with oily dark blond, dandruff-flecked hair, and acne scars on his cheeks, Andy Chadwick, as usual, had something (What was it this morning? It looked like maybe a bit of spinach) wedged between a couple of his front teeth. He wore tortoise-shell glasses and a rumpled beige trenchcoat over his brown corduroy suit. He had a pencil tucked behind his ear and a spiral-bound notebook sticking out of his breast pocket. Two years earlier, Andy Chadwick had been a student of mine in a feature-writing class. Today, he was the star reporter for the *Arden Oracle,* the town's daily paper. I knew that Andy had been frustrated in his job. He felt he was made for bigger and better gigs. I have to say, the kid did have talent. And, by looks alone, he would have been a perfect fit for the *New York Times.* But he was young and inexperienced and all the best entry-level spots at the most prestigious newspapers went, according to Andy Chadwick, to women and minorities. He made this claim without rancor. He just wanted to let you know that his failure to land a plum job was no fault of his own. He would just have to pay his dues on a small-potatoes paper like the *Arden Oracle,* racking up clips and waiting for the big break, a major league story, to come his way. On this brilliantly sunny, tingling cold February morning, Andy Chadwick could not contain his glee. He stood on the patch of yellow grass, looking first at me, then at Roger Pym-Smithers, then back at me, shaking his head and grinning, that green sliver of spinach squished between his teeth.

"How often does a story like this drop in your lap? Huh, Clay?" Andy seemed awed by his good fortune. And how could I not relate to him?

About thirty or so hours earlier, when I drove Brogus up to this very building, expecting to see some coke that had been planted in his office, I felt much the same way. "I'm gonna make my bones on this story," Andy Chadwick said, employing the Mafia term for a first kill. "I'm gonna make my fucking bones on this story."

"Well, that's jolly good for you, Andy, but it doesn't help that young girl very much, does it?" Roger said scoldingly—and, given his own earlier wisecracks about the murder, hypocritically.

Andy Chadwick just looked at Roger and sneered. "It's a journalist's thing. You wouldn't understand." Andy turned his attention to me. "I've just been in the building. I've seen the chalk outline of the body. The yellow police tape."

"Did you see the body?" Roger asked.

"Not yet. I'm gonna try to get into the autopsy."

"But do you know if she was found completely nude?" Roger inquired.

"She was wearing a pair of socks," Andy said in a low, ghoulish voice. "And she had a pair of Brogus's suspenders tied around her neck."

"Suspenders?" Roger said uncertainly.

"Braces," I said, remembering that, in England, "suspenders" were what Americans call "garters."

Roger nodded. "And Brogus has vanished."

"The FBI is here," Andy burbled. "They're leading the nationwide manhunt. Meanwhile, the investigation in Arden is being run by . . ." Chadwick paused for effect . . . "Patsy DeFestina. They choppered her down here from Toledo." Andy paused again, this time somewhat reverentially. I didn't understand.

"Who's Patsy DeFestina?" I asked.

Andy dropped his jaw and gawked at me in awkwardly exaggerated disbelief. "WHO is Patsy DeFestina?"

"Really, Clay," Roger chimed in, "even I know who Patsy DeFestina is."

"The former nun, current superstar crimefighter," Andy Chadwick said, as if he were reciting a subheadline. "Famous for putting rapists and killers of women behind bars. Patsy DeFestina has been profiled on 20/20, Clay!"

"Musta missed that episode," I said.

"Well, I just met her! She's way cool!"

"Did you gentleman know," Roger Pym-Smithers pronounced, "that back in England I have something of a reputation as an amateur sleuth?"

"You should be in on this story," Andy said to me.

"No, I didn't know that," I said to Roger.

"Very similar circumstances. A don at my college had been throttled in his study. Through a rather ingenious bit of deduction, I helped Scotland Yard solve the crime. It's too complicated to go into now, but I'll explain the whole case to you someday. I'm quite well known for this in the U.K."

"You don't say," I said.

"Clay!" Andy snapped. "Now is the time for you to write a piece for us!" Chadwick had been pestering me for a year to contribute something to the *Arden Oracle*. I had always politely declined, saying I was still too embarrassed by my professional disgrace to publish right now, rather than telling Chadwick the truth: that the *Oracle* was far too pathetic a rag for even a discredited hack like me to want his work in. "Come on, Clay," Andy wheedled. "You know a great story when it bites you on the ass!"

"I thought this was *your* golden career opportunity," Roger said to Andy.

"It is! But I'm covering the crime story, the gory details, the manhunt. We need somebody to cover the human element. The effect that a trauma like this has on other students. And what about the victim? What was *her* story? I know your stuff, Professor Robinette. Nobody could write a piece like that as well as you. Nobody in *this* town."

"Well, who *was* this girl, anyway?" I said, trying my best to sound hard-boiled. "Do we even have a name for her?"

"I forget," Andy said. He pulled out his notebook and started flipping through the pages.

I suddenly felt as if I were hovering above this scene, like I was up on a balcony, looking down on the patch of yellow grass, leaning my upper body over the railing, feeling a vertiginous dread, feeling my feet leaving the floor, tipping over . . .

"Jennifer Esther Wolfshiem."

. . . closing my eyes, falling, falling.

"Waaaaaauuuuurrrrrggggggggh!" The anguished scream forced me to open my eyes. "No!" a young woman shrieked. "No! Nooooooo!"

"What the fuck?" Andy Chadwick said. He pulled his pencil from behind his ear and plunged into the crowd.

"Are you all right, old bean?" Roger said. "You looked like you were about to swoon."

I could feel my body swaying. I rubbed my eyes. "Sorry. It's just that . . . I knew that girl. She was . . . a student of mine."

Roger gave a solemn nod. "Hmm. Name sounds familiar to me as well. I think I may have had her in my course on the Victorians. . . . Were you two very close?"

I stared into Roger's filmy eyes. He looked genuinely sympathetic. I swallowed hard. "Depends on what you mean by close."

Roger and I were no longer on the edge of the crowd. The roiling mob had engulfed our little patch of grass. Looking around, I saw more of everybody—more students, more cops, more camera crews. Roger and I were pulled away from each other by all the jostling bodies. "I'll speak with you later," Roger called out before disappearing into the throng.

I almost turned and went home. I had the sudden impulse to go back to bed, to hide under the covers. But I knew it was too late. What I needed now was information. I pushed my way through the crowd, moving toward that platform and lectern that had been set up in front of the Math building, hoping a press conference would begin soon. Just as I reached the edge of the platform, Andy Chadwick came lunging at me. He put his arm around my shoulder and brought his face close to mine. "That girl who screamed," Chadwick said, "she's Wolfshiem's roommate. Someone had just told her the news." Andy's stale coffee breath made my nose quiver. I tried to push him away, but we were squeezed together tight by the crowd, like rush hour commuters in a subway car. "She might be worth talking to for your story. I wrote down her name and address."

"Can we have some quiet, please?" Dean Jerry Shamberg's voice boomed. I looked up and saw the head of Arden University standing at the lectern. A small cluster of people, including Kwanzi Authentica Parker and Pops Mulwray, stood with him on the platform.

"You shoulda heard Shamberg in the Math building a little while ago," Chadwick snorted in my ear. "He was freakin' out. 'We're hemorrhaging!' he says. 'We're hemorrhaging! We've gotta stop the hemorrhaging!' Outraged parents were already calling, mostly from Manhattan, of course, saying they were gonna take their spoilt little brats outta the school, they were so worried about their safety now." Andy giggled. "Let's see how Dean Jer spins this one."

"People . . . ? Could we just have a little bit of quiet, please, people?" Whatever his behavior had been in the Math building, Jerry Shamberg was certainly not freaking out now. He stood solemnly at the lectern, tapping on a couple of the microphones to check if they were working, waiting for the crowd to settle down. Shamberg was a sturdily built, bronze-skinned man of fifty who clearly spent a lot of time at the gym and the tanning salon. With his close-cropped, thinning gray hair and a tonsorially correct goatee, he looked as much like an aging Hollywood executive as a university dean. The most peculiar thing about Shamberg was that he always seemed to look at you sideways. Even now, at the lectern, he tilted his head to the left, but his eyes drifted to the right. As he scanned the crowd, slowly turning his head to the right, his eyes slid leftward.

"Today, we as a community, are coping with a tragedy." The crowd was silent but the clicking and whirring of cameras continued. "There really isn't much to say right now. Our thoughts and prayers are with the family of Jennifer Wolfshiem. And all efforts are being made to find out exactly what happened and who was responsible for this heinous crime."

As Dean Jer droned on about the loss we all felt, his head and eyes shifting and sliding in counterpoint, my gaze fell on Kwanzi Authentica Parker. She stood just a few feet away from Shamberg on the platform, staring forthrightly out at the crowd. Like everyone else on the platform, Kwanzi wore no hat or coat. She was resplendent in a flowing, dazzlingly colorful African robe, her hair arranged in a cornucopia of tightly twisted little braids. I had heard some black folks in Arden describe Kwanzi as light-skinned but that's not how I saw her. There was an autumnal cast to Kwanzi's skin, a burnished tone that evoked her Cherokee ancestors. It occurred to me that Kwanzi's complexion was precisely the one sought by Jerry Shamberg and his fellow sun lamp worshipers. Standing on the platform in the bold sunshine, plaited head held high, eyes staring righteously, Kwanzi seemed incandescent with pride, with satisfaction. Her detested rival, Reginald T. Brogus, was on the run, wanted for murder. Whatever damage this incident might heap on the Afrikamerica Studies program, Reggie Brogus was gone for good. Her contempt for him had been, in a perverse and dramatic way, justified. Maybe, I realized, Kwanzi was not, as her husband Roger Pym-Smithers had described her this morning, "quite distraught." Maybe Kwanzi was actually happy.

"But today," Dean Jerry Shamberg proclaimed, "we do not just mourn a victim. We celebrate a hero. Out of this tragedy, we are reminded of the true spirit of Arden University. Pops, come over here."

Pops Mulwray, bony and stooped over, trembling slightly but still exuding his own certain elegance in his green Arden University custodial staff uniform with "Pops" sewn in cursive gold lettering above the breast pocket—like a dark brown Duke Ellington in coveralls—shuffled up to the lectern. Dean Jer threw his arm around Pops's shoulders, held him tight.

"Pops Mulwray is seventy-nine years old. He has Parkinson's disease and he doesn't get around so well anymore. But Pops has worked at Arden U. for thirty-seven years. And he still loves putting in a good day's work. He arrived at the Math building at six o'clock this morning, to go around from office to office, tidying up just in case people had come in over the long weekend. It was Pops who stumbled upon Jennifer this morning. And though he can't talk much anymore, though it's painful for him to get around, Pops Mulwray made his way to the campus police station and brought officers back to the scene of the crime. That, my friends, shows the true spirit of Arden University. Pops Mulwray—we salute you!"

The crowd applauded enthusiastically. I had to hand it to Jerry. By one gesture he had shown interracial solidarity with a black member of the Arden staff in the midst of a potentially explosive racial situation and, at the same time, given the audience something to feel good about, their applause for the old black man offering a "positive" emotional outpouring. Pops Mulwray, for his part, stood glassy-eyed and trembling at the lectern. He seemed bewildered by all this clapping. He waved limply, then shuffled back into the cluster of people on the platform.

Andy Chadwick giggled in my ear. "Yeah, but how does Dean Jer know Pops didn't kill the girl himself?"

I scowled in annoyance at Andy. He looked embarrassed, then started scribbling furiously in his notebook.

"And now," Shamberg said, sounding like a master of ceremonies, "I'm going to turn the podium over to Detective Patsy DeFestina . . ."

"Here she is!" Andy yelped.

On the platform, a uniformed police officer set a small footstool in front of the lectern. As a tiny, middle-aged woman mounted the footstool, the clicking of cameras suddenly exploded in volume. The strange racket of all those shutters in the crowd made me think of a jungle alive with the chirping of exotic insects hidden in the tall grass. Just as the tiny woman leaned toward the array of microphones and opened her mouth to speak, reporters started yelling and flailing their arms.

"Patsy! Patsy! Patsy! Detective DeFestina! Over here! Hey, Patsy!"

I had noticed Detective DeFestina earlier, in the cluster of people on the platform, but figured she was some university administration official—maybe a PR person—I'd never met. She wore wide, seventies-era, rectangular eyeglasses with a clear plastic frame, a red-and-black checked jacket over a brown turtleneck, black slacks, and sensible shoes. Once I discovered her identity, it did occur to me that this woman had the asexual aura of a nun dressed in civilian clothes. But I would never have pegged her for a cop.

"No questions," DeFestina said firmly but politely, raising a tiny, doll-like hand to quiet the crowd. "I will be holding a joint news conference with the FBI later but at the moment I can answer no questions . . ."

DeFestina kept talking, but I had stopped really listening to her. I knew she was just recounting the details of what little was known at this time. As DeFestina prattled on, I scrutinized her face and demeanor, pricked up my ears to her accent rather than to the words she spoke. And I stood there baffled, stumped in the rarest of ways. What *was* this

Patsy DeFestina? White? She had an Italian name, yes. Her skin was certainly lighter than Kwanzi's. And far lighter than Shamberg's permatan. But did I not detect an olive shade to DeFestina's complexion? So was she black? She certainly didn't "sound" black. She had a pleasant, flat Ohio accent, with wide, twangy vowels—a voice that was more regional than racial. Or maybe she was a mulatto? Her short brown hair, cut in a perfectly nondescript style, did seem to kink a bit in places. And weren't those full lips, and that round little nose of hers, signs of black blood?

Don't get me wrong. I didn't *care* what Patsy DeFestina's ethnicity was. What bothered me was that I couldn't tell. Ordinarily, I could detect the presence of Afroid genetic coding in a person's face on sight— instantaneously, and with infallible accuracy. Well, let's just say if a person was half-black anyway, I could always spot it. Maybe, I thought, the fact that I suspected Patsy DeFestina might have a black parent was proof that she did. On the other hand, if I had learned that both the detective's parents, and all four of her grandparents, had been white, it would not have surprised me. Standing at the foot of the platform, staring closely at Patsy DeFestina, I didn't know what the fuck she was.

"That's all, folks," DeFestina said in a congenial but no-nonsense tone. "I got work to do. So long."

As she turned away from the microphones, the reporters erupted. In the aural mishmash of questions screamed, one word relentlessly jumped out and pounded against my eardrums:

"BROGUS!—BROGUS!—BROGUS!—BROGUS!—BROGUS!—"

Patsy DeFestina spun around to face the microphones again. She pointed to a reporter. "What did you ask?"

"Is Brogus your only suspect, Patsy?" a male voice bellowed importantly.

DeFestina paused and eyed the journalist carefully, pitilessly, from behind her windshield glasses. "Until the sick murderer of this young woman is found . . . everybody is a suspect."

My blood ran cold. Everyone in the crowd was stunned by the sudden steely menace in Patsy's voice. If I had had to face Sister DeFestina in an elementary school classroom, I was sure it would have traumatized me for life. The idea of facing Detective DeFestina in an interrogation room anytime soon scared me so much I wanted to puke.

As DeFestina hopped off the footstool, the press snapped out of its momentary stupor and started shouting questions at her again.

"BROGUS!—BROGUS!—BROGUS!—"

The uniformed cop picked up the footstool and rushed after Patsy DeFestina, who had already hopped off the platform and was striding, with startling velocity on her stubby little legs, back into the Mathematics building. The reporters continued braying. Until a husky voice rang out:

"I am Professor Kwanzi Authentica Parker, Chair of the Afrikamerica Studies program."

As the crowd quieted, Kwanzi stood glaring at us all from behind the bouquet of microphones. I wondered if any of my colleagues on the Arden faculty had noticed that Kwanzi had just promoted herself to a position that did not yet exist.

"As an African living in America," said the New Jersey–born Kwanzi, "I would hope that the laws of this country will be respected by those of you in the media . . . Innocent until proven guilty. That is the law of this land." Kwanzi's voice resonated with indignation. She exuded a certain majesty up there on the platform, glaring indignantly, her little corkscrew braids quivering slightly in the breeze. "Let there be no rush to judgment. I repeat: *Let there be no rush to judgment.* We are *all* victims today. Even a member of our community who stands accused is a victim today. We in the Afrikamerica Studies program regret the loss of life that has taken place. But we insist that fairness and justice rule in the investigation of this matter. God bless you all. Thank you."

As Kwanzi stepped away from the lectern, murmurs rippled through the crowd. I can't say what anyone else was thinking at that moment but I was amazed that Kwanzi seemed to be . . . well, if not defending, then sticking up for the rights of, Reggie Brogus, a man she passionately despised. Perhaps, in a situation like this, racial loyalty mattered more to Kwanzi than Brogus's racial betrayals. Had I been governed by a similar impulse when I drove Brogus almost all the way to Arden Airfield?

The crowd continued to buzz, nobody seeming sure exactly how to respond to Kwanzi's remarks. Suddenly, one person started applauding vigorously. I saw Roger Pym-Smithers standing in the crowd on the other side of the platform. "Well said!" Kwanzi's husband shouted, frantically slapping his palms together. "Hear, hear! Very well said!"

Others in the audience began applauding, but with a pitterpat timidity. Dean Shamberg stepped up to the mikes. "Well, that just about wraps things up for now. The Women Student's Union has announced that a candlelight vigil will be held for Jennifer Wolfshiem on this spot tonight at eight o'clock—"

"Hey!" Andy Chadwick nudged me in the ribs. "You should cover that, Clay!"

As Shamberg made announcements about the rescheduling of Math classes in other buildings, the crowd began to disperse. I was able to put a little space between me and Chadwick. The young reporter stood grinning at me, that remnant of last night's spinach still wedged between his front teeth.

"Just do a piece on the mood on campus." Andy ripped a page from his notebook and handed it to me. "That's the name of the girl who screamed, Wolfshiem's roommate." He stopped grinning. "Seriously, Clay, this could be a good thing for you. I'm going back to the newsroom now. Can I tell my editor you'll write something for tomorrow's paper?"

"Let me think about it," I said. "When do I have to let you know?"

Andy Chadwick reached into his trenchcoat pocket and pulled out a crumpled business card. I laughed lightly as he handed it to me. "Did you use this card as a Kleenex, Andy?"

"Call me before noon," he said. "I'm off to make my bones."

As Andy walked away, Kwanzi glided up to me in her billowing, technicolor gown. We embraced for a long moment. Kwanzi smelled, as always, of cocoa butter. She gently pulled away from me but kept her hands on the shoulders of my parka. "Brother Clay," she sighed.

"How are you, Kwanzi?"

She closed her eyes and nodded. "I'm coping." She opened her eyes. "The spirits are helping me to cope with all this."

Roger Pym-Smithers stood behind Kwanzi, staring rapturously at the back of his wife's head.

"This could be a major problem for the program, huh?" I said.

"My concern isn't with the program right now. It's with Reggie."

"I thought you hated his guts."

"Oh, Clay," Kwanzi said softly. She took my right hand in both of hers.

"Kwanzi doesn't think Brogus did it, old bean," Roger said.

"You don't?"

"I'm getting some very powerful vibrations about this case," Kwanzi said.

"Kwanzi's really quite psychic," Roger confided.

"I never hated Reggie," Kwanzi said. "I felt he was a troubled brother who had lost his way, lost touch with who he was. You know, Clay, Reggie Brogus really meant something to black people."

"Yes, I know."

"But you're too young to *really* know. You hear about all the dramatic, violent stuff but Blackness as a Revolutionary Force made a real difference in the lives of a lot of people. Nobody ever talks about the free lunch programs BAARF provided to inner-city children."

"Wow," I said. "I've never heard you talk this way about Reggie before."

Kwanzi smiled beatifically at me. "I'm channeling so many different things right now, my brother. But one thing I'm certain of: Reggie didn't kill that white girl."

"How do you know?"

"I can't tell you how I know. It's information I'm receiving spiritually, from another plane. But trust me: Reggie didn't do it."

"Okay."

"Kwanzi's never wrong about this sort of thing, old bean. She really is quite psychic."

Kwanzi did not acknowledge Roger. She stroked my hand and stared into space. "The killer is close, though. He's very close to us."

Kwanzi was starting to give me the creeps. "I think I better go," I said.

"Are you writing about this, Clay?" Kwanzi asked.

"Did Roger tell you I might do an article for the *Oracle*?"

Kwanzi stared wide-eyed at me. "Roger didn't tell me anything about that."

"It's true, old bean, I didn't mention a word of it."

"This is something I intuited." Kwanzi laid her right hand against my left cheek. "Be careful, Clay. The spirits are watching out for you. But you have to be careful."

"I'm sorry, Kwanzi," I said, forcing a chuckle, "but you, er, you're really sorta creepin' me out here."

"Just be careful, Clay," Kwanzi said, her hand pressed against my cheek, her voice solemn yet serene, brown eyes shining. "You may be in grave danger."

CHAPTER 5

YOU ONLY RECOGNIZE A STRANGER the second time you see him. The first time, you might not even notice him, not consciously. That was the case with the tall black man in the aviator shades. I had barely seen him in the swirl of people in front of the Math building, just after the press conference an hour earlier. In the millisecond that I registered his presence in the crowd, taking in his dark suit, white shirt, red tie, black trenchcoat, the ramrod-straight bearing, hands seemingly clasped behind his back, the aura of bland, watchful menace of a Secret Service agent protecting the president at a campaign rally, sunlight glinting off his large, shaved head, his somehow noble-looking, walnut-toned face impassive behind the dark green-lensed Douglas MacArthur–style Ray-Bans, I wondered who he was, then turned my attention to Andy Chadwick, instantly forgetting the imposing brother in the sunglasses. I might never have thought of him again had I not seen him standing outside Reggie Brogus's apartment building, in exactly the same pose, seemingly staring straight at me as I sat in my tiny Honda across the street. I recognized him immediately. And I knew he had to be FBI.

Like a lot of other professors in the humanities, I canceled all my classes that Tuesday out of respect for Arden's slain sophomore. Unlike a lot of students and faculty, I did not savor this extra day off after a holiday weekend. I was, after all, on assignment. Though I had not given Andy Chadwick a yes or no answer, I knew I would write some sort of article for the *Arden Oracle*. I knew a piece in that local birdcage-liner would do nothing to enhance my career. But I was no longer thinking about the New York glossies. Maybe I just needed to throw myself into reporting to make some kind of sense of what has happening to me. Or to try to discover who had killed Jenny. I had told Reggie I would find out what I could, but I had no interest in exonerating Brogus that Tuesday morning. Kwanzi had spooked me with her psychic vibrations about Reggie's innocence. Even though I'd always considered Kwanzi a little bit wacky, I myself had believed Reggie innocent for that critical moment in the Afrikamerica Studies suite. Now I didn't know what to believe about Reggie. I didn't know what to think or to feel about Jenny. And I damn sure didn't know what to make of myself. So I just set out to get a story.

I went home, traded my bike for the Honda, then took a spin around Arden, Ohio. I talked to students, teachers, shopkeepers, the mayor, the wino who hung out in front of the 7-Eleven on Main Street. And with everyone I sensed this chilling disjunction between what they said they felt—shock, sorrow, anger, disbelief, sympathy for the victim's family—and what they actually seemed to be feeling: not just a morbid excitement, but a sort of civic pride. They spoke of the need to come together as a community, "to show what Arden is made of," but they also seemed to gloat over the fact that this gruesome murder had happened *here* even as they said they never would have thought it *could* happen here. Everywhere I went in town, there was a vaguely festive atmosphere.

One could even detect an abashed party mood behind the wrought iron gates of Woodland Oaks Terrace—a cluster of identical three-story apartment houses with red tile "Spanish-style" rooftops ("Sophisticated Splendor in Suburbia," trumpeted advertisements for the complex) that Penelope had dubbed "the yuppie projects"—where Reginald T. Brogus had lived during his abbreviated stay in Arden. Cops and camera crews and titillated neighbors roamed the lawn in front of Reggie's unit. I was about to get out of the Honda, to do a few more spot interviews with ordinary citizens, when I recognized the tall black man in the black trench and aviator shades, his attention, it seemed, focused on me. I could faintly see a wire hanging out of his right ear, disappearing behind his thick neck. His face remained impassive, immobile, as he nodded, slowly, twice, continuing his intimidating surveillance of me. Was someone talking to him in his earpiece? Was anybody else checking me out? His hands still clasped behind his back, the agent took a step forward on

Brogus's lawn. He looked as if he were about to approach my car, to question me. I drove away before he could.

*   *   *

"Jen? All I can say is she was really, *really* . . . nice." Brittney Applefield paused, then said again, almost gravely, "*Really nice.*"

"Could you, maybe, be more specific?" I asked.

Brittney Applefield sucked on her lower lip, seemed to concentrate. "You know, she just did a lot of nice things. And even though she wasn't, like, American, I think she was from Europe or someplace, maybe even, like, Berlin, she was just a really nice person. A *really* nice person."

Brittney was pretty darn nice herself, with her short gamine haircut, plump cheeks, and Disney chipmunk smile. Resting her head against fluffy white pillows, Brittney still managed to smile a lot. She could have been the host of an early morning TV show, this chirpy Brittney Applefield, doing her best to make you just feel sorta good getting up to face another tedious day of your wretched and meaningless job. As such, she was nothing even remotely like Jennifer Esther Wolfshiem—or at least the Pirate Jenny I knew—and I couldn't imagine what the shrewd, daring young woman I had known would have seen in this little whitebread cheerleader. The one time I had been in this house before, Jenny told me her roommate—or "flatmate" as she said—was away. At no other time had Jenny mentioned this girl. But Brittney Applefield had shrieked—publicly—in pain and horror when she learned of Jenny's murder.

"I'm going to be speaking at the candlelight vigil tonight," Brittney said.

"Really? I was amazed that the students had organized something like that so quickly. I mean, people only learned of what had happened to Jennifer a couple of hours ago. In my day, it would have taken at least twenty-four hours for a candlelight vigil to be organized."

"I guess Jen just had a lot of friends," Brittney said chirpily.

No she didn't and you weren't one of them. Don't you even know that Pirate Jenny hated people like you?

"She was just a really nice person," Brittney added, scrunching up her pixie face. "She had a really good heart."

And a first-rate mind, too, but you wouldn't have noticed that, would ya, Brittney? And she spoke five languages fluently while you blunder along in one and she wrote like a dream and was recklessly curious and had a worldly/ otherworldly look in her eye and gave spectacular head . . .

"What did you say your name was?" Brittney asked.

"Clay Robinette."

"*Professor* Robinette? Jen talked about you all the time!"

"Really? What did she say?"

"Just that you were really, *really* nice."

Obviously, this interview was going nowhere. It was with some trepidation that I had driven up to Jenny's place, a quaintly shabby row house on a block of quaintly shabby row houses rented out almost exclusively to Arden University students. Had I seen any police or media people in front of the building I would never have gotten out of the Honda. Jenny and Brittney rented the two-bedroom apartment on the second floor. As a young student who identified herself as Brittney's friend Caitlin welcomed me into the living room, I can't say the place felt familiar. The one time I'd been in this apartment it had been at night, the lights were out, and I'd barely glimpsed the shadowy living room as Jenny escorted me to her bedroom. Caitlin introduced me to two other preppy white girls, Brooke and Becky, who were there "to provide moral support" to Brittney. I wondered where the students Pirate Jenny had liked so much—Euphrasia and Tamika, Yolanda and Shereena—were. But then, those sisters had never seemed to crave Jenny's company when she was alive. Why would they come to her place to mourn her death?

Caitlin told me Brittney was in her bedroom, resting, but when I explained I was a reporter she encouraged me to knock on the door. "I'm sure she'd be happy to talk to *you!*" Caitlin said perkily.

Walking down the uneven wooden floor of the hallway, I saw a yellow police tape, emblazoned with black letters reading DO NOT CROSS, stretched across the closed doorway of what I knew was Jenny's bedroom. When exactly had the cops been here? And were there still any of them lurking about? I considered slipping into Jenny's room but quickly thought the better of it. Instead, I knocked on Brittney Applefield's door and entered her world of niceness.

"I know one thing I can tell you about Jen!" Brittney suddenly squealed.

"Yes?"

"She was writing, like, all the time. I think what she really wanted was to be a writer. Had she lived, I think she would have followed that dream." Brittney paused. "Do you think that would be a nice thing for me to say—at the candlelight vigil? That thing about following her dream?"

"Oh, yes, very nice. Can you tell me, do you know if Jenny kept a journal?"

"You mean like a diary?"

"Yeah."

Brittney Applefield started sucking her lower lip again, evidently deep in thought. Three brisk taps on the bedroom door broke her concentration. "Come in?" she said with that interrogative inflection American women like her often gave to simple declarations.

"Brittney?" A fiftyish woman with waist-length gray hair and a deeply creased face tentatively stepped into the room. "My name is Sara? The university health office sent me? I'm your grief counselor."

I politely excused myself, leaving Brittney and Sara to share together. Softly closing Brittney's door behind me, I stood still in the hallway. There were no longer any voices in the living room. It seemed that Caitlin, Brooke, and Becky had departed. I took a few cautious steps down the hallway, the wooden slats of the slanted floor creaking beneath my Timberland boots. I stopped in front of Jenny's bedroom door. I could hear the muffled voices of Brittney and her grief counselor but there was no other sound in the apartment. I pulled my thick, thermal gloves out of the pockets of my parka, slipped them over my hands. Reaching under the yellow tape that was tacked to the wall on either side of the entrance, I took hold of the doorknob. Turn. Click. The door slowly swung open. I squatted, ducked under the flimsy police barrier, and stood upright in Jenny's bedroom.

The room was ablaze in hard white winter sunlight, burning through the closed, curtainless windows. The only other time I had set foot in this room, it had been bathed in candlelight. I had not realized what a stark and minimalist space it was, decorated with only a few pieces of black furniture—desk, four chairs, shelves—and a bare futon on the sloped hardwood floor, the white walls naked save for a poster from a New York Public Theater production of *The Threepenny Opera*, with a portrait of the Latino actor Raul Julia as Mack the Knife, staring at you in hollow-eyed malevolence. Taking a few, lumbering steps into the center of the room, I felt a shiver of guilt, like someone returning to the scene of his crime. My crime, though, was not against Jennifer Wolfshiem. It was against my wife and our children. The impulse to stay and take a good look around was only fractionally larger than the impulse to get out of there at once. I looked at the black, state-of-the-art CD player with its large black speakers. The black shelf nearby contained about fifty CDs, mostly classical and rap. I lumbered over to the desk, looked at the sleek, gray laptop on the black surface, its lid closed. A clear plastic case of disks sat beside the computer. The disks were all black. I began to feel a bit dreamy again. I watched, with a strange sense of detachment, my right hand, in its heavy black astronaut glove, moving slowly in space toward the plastic case full of computer disks. I saw my thermally protected index finger—it seemed like an alien, probing instrument—flip open the case.

"Hey!" a female voice barked behind me. "You're not supposed to be in there!"

Be cool. Be cool. Whatever happens, just be cool.

I turned around and faced the open doorway. On the other side of the yellow tape suspended across the entrance stood Detective Patsy DeFestina, wearing a black-and-white plaid overcoat and black earmuffs. Behind her was a hulking, beet-faced, blue-uniformed cop.

"Excuse me," I said. "I just wanted to take a look a—"

"I know *you!*" DeFestina said. "You're Clay Robinette!"

I struggled not to gulp before answering, "Yes."

DeFestina eyed me steadily from behind her windshield glasses. "Have I been dyin' to talk to *you!*"

*   *   *

Detective Patsy DeFestina, it turns out, was a fan of mine. She called herself a "magazine junkie." Not only did she remember all sorts of articles I had published over the years—book reviews, travel features, celebrity profiles, you name it—but she could actually recite lines I'd written—and long forgotten—to me. "You're a very fine prose stylist," she enthused.

What can I say? It may sound pathetic, but I was hugely flattered. Instead of arresting me in Pirate Jenny's bedroom, DeFestina was stroking my ego. I told her I was reporting on the murder for the *Arden Oracle* and asked if she would like to be interviewed. The diminutive detective smiled and said, "I can give you half an hour."

We sat in a booth at Ned's Coffee Cup, a gritty, blue-collar diner. My pocket-sized recorder was propped on the table between us, the tape inside slowly rolling. Patsy, explaining that she had not had a chance to eat breakfast this morning, was merrily chowing down on runny eggs, butter-soggy wheat toast, and fat, greasy slabs of bacon. I nursed a mug of Ned's nasty, steaming brew and wondered how tiny Patsy—who insisted that I call her by her first name—processed all that cholesterol she consumed. Seeing her squat little body up close, I also wondered if Patsy suffered from some mild form of dwarfism. And even speaking directly with her, subtly examining her pudgy, vaguely olive-tinted face across the formica tabletop, I still could not figure out what Detective DeFestina *was:* black, white, or other?

"I'm so glad you're gonna be back in print," Patsy said as she mopped up what was left on her plate with a ragged morsel of toast. "Of course, I read about your little scandal a while back."

"Oh, yeah," I said, taking a sip of Ned's special house blend, which had a consistency not unlike that of motor oil. "That was all blown out of proportion."

"Sure it was. I mean, we all stretch the truth a bit now and then."

"Well, I don't know if I'd say I—"

"The important thing is to move on, you know what I mean? When I heard you were teaching at Arden, I thought, 'Good for him!' Who needs that New York rat race, you know what I mean?"

"I know what you mean."

"And I always hoped that someday I'd get a chance to come down here from Toledo and we might meet. And now look what happens! I'm sitttin' here in Ned's Coffee Cup being interviewed by Clay Robinette! I ask you: Is this life a wondrous feast of serendipity or what?"

At that moment, I decided Detective DeFestina must be white. "So, Patsy, let me ask you about this case."

Patsy soaked up the last smear of egg from her plate, popped the last damp crust of toast into her mouth. "Shoot," she said, chewing.

"I'm interested in how you got involved in this case. You received a call in Toledo this morning?"

"Exactly. My friends here in the Arden police department knew this sort of thing was right up my alley. But let me say that the men and women of the Arden police force were perfectly capable of handling this situation on their own. As any police officer knows . . ."

I zoned out as Patsy rattled off a string of platitudes about competent cops, the dedication of law enforcement officers, the spirit of cooperation that everyone brought to this investigation, yamma-lamma-ding-dong. Damn, she was smoother than a politician. And it occurred to me that Patsy DeFestina might very well run for mayor of Toledo or governor of Ohio someday if she was as famous and admired as I'd been led to believe. But was she a Republican or a Democrat?

Finally, Patsy stopped talking to take a gulp from her mug. "Mmmm, that's good coffee."

"You said an interesting thing this morning, Patsy: that everyone is a suspect."

"Theoretically, yes."

"But there's always a *prime* suspect, isn't there?"

"Certainly. And I'll tell ya something, not to say more than I should about this case, but just generally speaking, ninety percent of the time, the guilty party is the most obvious person. Now, that's the opposite of the movies where the killer is always the *least* obvious person. But in real life, it's the most obvious. Ninety percent of the time anyway."

"And what about the other ten percent?"

"The other ten percent of the time, it's the *second* most obvious person."

"So are you saying there's a ninety percent chance that Reggie Brogus murdered this girl?"

"I did not say that, Clay." Patsy maintained her congenial, chatty tone. "Now don't go putting words in my mouth."

"But Brogus is the most obvious person in this case. Wouldn't you say that?"

"No comment."

Patsy's voice had turned frosty. But I didn't let up.

"If Brogus is the most obvious, then who is the second most obvious?"

Patsy stared long and hard at me, her eyes like black buttons behind those outsized, rectangular glasses. She didn't seem like so much of a fan of mine anymore. I don't know what made me press her the way I did. I just couldn't stop myself.

"Off the record?" Patsy said finally.

"Sure."

Then Patsy did something no other interview subject of mine had ever done. She reached over and turned off my tape recorder. Leaning forward in her red, plastic seat, she then placed her elbows on the table and folded her little doll's hands.

"Of course Brogus is the most obvious person. But Brogus isn't my immediate concern. He's for the FBI to deal with. They're running the manhunt and they'll catch him, too. He could be anywhere in the country by now. But it's the FBI's task to find Brogus, the most obvious person. So my job, here in Arden, is to find the second most obvious." The steely menace that had stunned the crowd in front of the Math building was back in Patsy's voice. I began to feel nauseated again. "Let me stress that I am saying all this off the record. And if you print it, I'll deny it. Understand?"

"Understood."

"Good." Patsy took another swig of coffee. "So let me ask *you* a question, Mr. Reporter. Do *you* think Brogus did it?"

It was getting harder to hide my nervousness but I had to try. Returning Patsy's even stare, I said, "I have no idea."

"Maintaining your journalistic objectivity, huh?"

"I guess you could say that."

"It's a disgusting scenario, don't you think? Assuming Brogus was involved with that poor girl. Violence and murder aside, it's absolutely unconscionable, a professor taking sexual advantage of a student. Don't you agree?"

"Well, what if there was a relationship of, you know, mutual consent?"

"Mutual consent!" Patsy scoffed. "When you're talking about an older man in a position of authority and a young innocent girl, mutuality and consent have nothing to do with it. It is a brazen abuse of power! Do you know how old that Wolfshiem girl was? Nineteen! When you're talking about a professor and a girl that young, it's even worse than abuse of power. It's practically child molesting!"

"Now, Patsy, I don't know about that, I—"

"Well, I *do* know about it. I've been putting sexual monsters behind bars longer than that poor Wolfshiem girl was alive. And as far as I'm concerned, any grown man who would take advantage of a girl that young ought to have his dick chopped off!"

Microscopic droplets of sweat prickled across my forehead. "You feel very strongly about this."

"You got that right!" Patsy downed the last of her coffee. When she spoke again, her voice seemed to have dropped an octave. "And I'll tell you another thing. The fact that Brogus is black and this girl was white only makes matters worse."

"What do you mean?" I said warily.

Patsy's plump lips curled in the faintest of smiles. "You know what I mean. I *know* you know what I mean. You know how folks think."

At that moment, I decided Patsy must be black. Or at least a mulatto.

"How was everything today, Patsy?" a jolly voice said. I looked up and saw the obese, ruddy waitress waddling up to our booth, a spherical, glass pot of coffee in her hand. "Can I warm your coffee for you?"

"Sure can, Nan," Patsy said. "Everything was just super. Tell Ned his coffee gets better every year!"

"How 'bout you, sir?" the waitress asked, swinging the pot my way.

"Please," I said, not wishing to offend. Watching the unctuous brew streaming into my cup and feeling the last mugful fermenting in my gut, I knew I would pay for this politeness later.

"Terrible thing, isn't it?" the waitress said, with the peculiar half-smile I'd seen on the faces of so many Arden residents this morning.

"You're tellin' me," Patsy said.

As the two women delighted in their shock and disbelief, I tried to figure out how old Patsy was. Forty-five? Fifty-? Sixty? Did she look young for her age, or old? It was impossible to tell. And what about her sexuality? She had left the convent, but had she maintained her vow of celibacy? Did she have sex with other cops? Was she a lesbian? Or an onanist? Should I ask her?

"So where were we?" Patsy said as the waitress, having cleared the table of everything but our coffee cups and my idle tape recorder, waddled away.

"You never answered the second half of my question," I said, thinking *Don't go there!* but knowing I had to. "If Brogus is the most obvious person, who is the second most obvious?"

Patsy gave me her black button stare again. "We still off the record?"

"Until you say we're not."

Patsy took a long, pensive sip of her coffee. Then, with both hands, she delicately placed the mug back down on the table. I wondered how Patsy wielded a gun with those elfin hands.

"I don't know, Clay," Patsy said in a confidential tone. "I just feel like somehow I can trust you."

I gave a faint nod. Patsy was not the first interviewee to say something like that to me. And my air of trustworthiness was, I think, one of the things that made me a reporter. Not that I did anything so special. I just gave the impression of really listening to people. And I had learned long ago that the average person was so rarely truly listened to that she/he would say just about anything to anyone who actually seemed to be paying attention. My neutral expression was pleasant, inquisitive, and completely nonjudgmental. For some reason, people felt they could tell me their secrets. Don't ask me why, but it had always been this way. Nobody could ever really tell exactly what I was thinking.

"Lemme put it this way, Clay," Patsy continued, "you have to ask yourself some basic questions. For instance, if Brogus didn't commit this crime, then someone with access to his office had to. So, you ask, who else had keys to the Afro-American Studies suite?"

"Afrikamerica Studies," I said, correcting her.

"Whatever," Patsy shot back. "And of those people who had keys, who had contact with this Wolfshiem girl? By the way, you don't have keys to the suite, do you?"

"No," I said, a bit too eagerly. "Not at all."

"I didn't think so." Patsy took another sip of piping hot slime, set the mug down with almost surgical care. "But there is someone, someone other than Brogus, who had access to those offices and who had a relationship with the dead girl. Do you know of a Tyrell Williams?"

Without taking a moment to consider the unfamiliar-sounding name, I quickly answered "No."

"He was a file clerk in the Afro-American Studies Department. It was his work-study job. Not that he showed up very often. Anyway—"

"T-Bird!" I exploded.

I had not recognized "Tyrell Williams," but the image of that sullen young man, slouched in his chair in my classroom, baseball cap turned backward atop his head, jaws languidly rotating as he popped his chewing gum, eyes radiating boredom and contempt, had suddenly sprung up in my brain and I called out his nickname like a contestant on *The $20,000 Pyramid* screaming a synonym.

"So the name rings a bell, after all," Patsy said.

"Sure," I said, quickly regaining my composure. "I had him in a course last year."

"Well, this so-called T-Bird seems to have flown the coop. Of all the people with access to Brogus's office—except, of course, Brogus—this Tyrell 'T-Bird' Williams is the only one we haven't been able to find. Nobody has seen him on campus since Friday night."

"Really?" I said as casually as I could. Meanwhile my mind was spinning: T-Bird, T-Bird, T-Bird, T-Bird . . . Of course it was T-Bird! How could I not have thought of that insolent little punk before? T-Bird: my student, my rival.

"We'll find him, though," Patsy said, her voice steeling again. "I deal with kids like him every day. God only knows how someone like him got into Arden U. But it happens, you know. Quotas. Arden is required to take a certain number of in-state students each year. And in-state minority students. This T-Bird is from Impediment. Do you know that town? It's just south of here."

"No," I said, shaking my head, trying to keep my facial expression neutral, inquisitive, nonjudgmental.

"Affirmative action." Patsy grimaced. "I hate to say it, but a lotta kids get into these schools where they just don't belong. You take a kid like this T-Bird. Black, fatherless, mother on welfare. Born into some crime-infested ghetto. Surrounded by street gangs, drug dealers, pimps. You know how we describe Tyrell's ilk in my profession? Life expectancy of a match. That's what a kid like T-Bird has: the life expectancy of a match. Yet, with his basement-level grade point average, his subbasement SAT scores, this kid gets into a fine school like Arden U. A place where, really, he has no business being."

Now I was confused. If Patsy were white, I doubted she would blurt out such a racist statement to me. If she were black, or even half-black, then this sentiment made her just as much of a right-wing zealot as Reggie Brogus. Either way, I should have felt offended. As a firm believer in affirmative action, I should even have been outraged. As someone who had encountered far more dumb-ass white kids than dumb-ass black kids during my five-plus semesters at Arden University, I should at least have told Patsy DeFestina that she didn't know what the hell she was talking about. But T-Bird Williams really had been a terrible student. And he struck me as someone who might very well be a dangerous hoodlum. Even as I wanted to challenge Patsy on her conservative bias, I had to admit that, in this case anyway, she was right. And I was ready to believe that T-Bird had killed Jennifer Wolfshiem.

I heard a sudden electronic bleating. Patsy pulled a mobile phone from her jacket pocket. "Yall-o," she said. "Yep. . . . Really? . . . Gotcha . . . All right. Be there in a jiff." Slipping the phone back into her jacket, Patsy explained that she had to get back to work. She apologized for not being able to finish the interview. I was, of course, as magnanimous about it as I could be.

Out on the sidewalk, a police car was waiting for Detective DeFestina. The beet-faced cop I'd seen her with in Jenny's apartment sat behind the wheel. Already bundled in her black-and-white plaid overcoat, Patsy wrapped her furry black earmuffs around her head. A fierce wind gusted and I pulled up my bushily lined hood. Patsy stared up at me.

"Interesting," she said. "I found a strange fiber on the carpet in Brogus's office this morning. I wondered what the heck it was. Just a fine, hairlike strand, a funny beige kinda color. I don't know, I have an eye for these sorta things. I'm built low to the ground, you know what I mean? Anyway, I had it sent to the crime lab for analysis. But now, I see that it was very much like the lining in the hood of your parka."

"Really?" I said hoarsely.

"Who knows?" Patsy said. "Maybe our killer was wearing a coat like yours."

Patsy raised her arm. I reached down. My right hand engulfing hers, we shook. "Hope we get to meet again," I lied.

Patsy DeFestina smiled. "Count on it."

CHAPTER 6

THE CAMERAWORK WAS CLUMSY, the black-and-white image on my TV screen sharpening, then blurring again, in and out of focus. Whoever was holding the camera seemed to be fidgeting about. From time to time, the camera would swing and focus on the back of someone's head before returning to the image of the muscular black man with the huge Afro, dressed in prison clothes, his wrists locked in handcuffs. I assumed that, at the time, cameras were banned from courtrooms and the documentarian was trying to conceal his device. Off-camera, a white man's voice whined, "The defendant Reginald T. Brogus—"

"Mkwame Obolobongo."

The camera swung wildly, zeroing in on the bald, bespectacled, black-robed judge. "What did you say?"

"My name is Mkwame Obolobongo." The camera swung back to the prisoner, his dark face morphing in and out of focus, huge black-and-white eyeballs glowering at the judge.

Off-camera, the judge wheedled, "It says here your name is Reginald Tiberius Brogus and this proceeding—"

"That is my slave name," the prisoner intoned. "You will address me by my African name: Mkwame Obolobongo."

"In my courtroom I will address you any way I please, Mr. Brogus."

"Mkwame Obolobongo." The black man stood tall, hands chained in front of him, his head held high, tilted slightly back. He exuded arrogance, power, a pure and raw charisma.

The crowd of spectators in the courtroom started murmuring. The camera swung over to the judge, who furiously banged his gavel.

"Order in the court! Order, I say! You are charged here as Reginald T. Brogus!"

"Mkwame Obolobongo!"

"And if you persist in this name game I will further charge you with contempt of court!"

"I am Mkwame Obolobongo!" the prisoner shouted as the camera swung back and locked in on him. Two uniformed court officers appeared in the frame, converging on the prisoner.

"Your name is Reginald T. Brogus!"

"My name is Mkwame Obolobongo!"

The gavel banged frantically off-camera. "You are hereby charged with contempt of court!" the judge shrieked. "Take him back to his cell! Get that nigger out of my sight!"

Now the crowd erupted in cries of indignation. As the court officers dragged him away, the prisoner twisted violently in their grip, kicking, snarling, screaming "I AM MKWAME OBOLOBONGO! I AM MKWAME OBOLOBONGO!" Even after he had been hauled out of the courtroom, I could hear his strangled howl echoing: "I am Mkwame Obolobongooooooooooooooooooo . . ."

Now I heard the stilted voice of a contemporary newscaster. "The judge's racial slur in this 1971 proceeding helped lead to a dismissal of the weapons charges. Brogus was once again a free man."

The image on the TV changed. The cinematography was just as shaky, but the footage now was in color. Two rifle-toting men in black leather jackets and black ski masks ran across a parking lot. They ducked behind a van. Gunshots popped in the background. The camera abruptly swung around and trained on the body of a police officer lying prone on the gray asphalt. His blue cap lay upside down, somehow forlornly, on the ground beside him. I had seen this clip before. It was the scene of the bank robbery in Detroit, the 1974 heist that went horribly wrong and set Reggie Brogus on the lam for the next seven years.

"I remember that," Mrs. Henderson said just as the disembodied voice of the newscaster began describing the action. "I was livin' in Deetroit at the time."

Mrs. Henderson's ample girth was nestled in a corner of the living room couch. A copy of the *National Enquirer* lay open in her lap. When I walked in a few minutes earlier, Mrs. Henderson—our sitter-cook-all-purpose and indispensable five-afternoons-per-week helper-around-the-house—had actually shushed me, so absorbed was she in the five o'clock news. Standing beside the couch, watching the broadcast, I could smell the chicken Mrs. Henderson had fried for our dinner tonight. Penelope and I considered Mrs. Henderson a godsend. We met her our first week in Arden and immediately responded to her air of gentle but intimidating, churchgoing elderly black lady authority. The twins loved her and were at their best behavior when she was around. She picked them up from school every day and made sure they did their homework. Seeing how Mommy and Daddy deferred to the baby-sitter, Amber and Ashley knew instinctively that they couldn't act up with Mrs. Henderson. While she addressed us as Clay and Penelope, we could never bring ourselves to call her anything but Mrs. Henderson.

"Do you think Reggie Brogus killed that girl, Clay?"

"I don't know, Mrs. Henderson. I really don't."

As the newscaster spoke of a "political conversion," a quick sequence of clips flashed by on the TV screen: Brogus, now bloated and wearing a business suit, shaking hands with President Ronald Reagan; Brogus shaking hands with President George Bush; Brogus shaking hands with Senator Jesse Helms; Brogus shaking hands with General Colin Powell; Brogus in a commercial for "Reggie's Real Deal Barbecue Sauce," taking a bite out of a gigantic spare rib, smacking his lips and saying to the camera "That's good eatin'!"

"The press done already tried, convicted, and sentenced the man," Mrs. Henderson said. "I've seen lynchings in my day, you know. I think it's a damn shame."

"I hear ya," I said. I did not tell Mrs. Henderson that I had just spent the afternoon in the newsroom of the *Arden Oracle* writing an article that basically tried, convicted, and sentenced Brogus.

A shot of Arden Airfield appeared on the screen. The control tower loomed against the bright blue sky. A fleet of tiny so-called commuter planes idled on the tarmac. They were not even jets, these little propeller-driven craft with front doors that dropped down like wall-imbedded Murphy beds to create the short staircase you had to climb to get into the plane. Whenever I had to fly out of Arden Airfield—which provided service exclusively to locations within the state of Ohio, mainly Cleveland, Columbus, and Cincinnati—I had found myself rediscovering religion, praying as I rarely did anymore, begging the Lord to please let this flimsy hunk of tin make it safely to my destination.

"Brogus had a reservation on a six a.m. flight to Cleveland at Arden Airfield yesterday morning," the newscaster's voice said. "But he never showed up to catch his plane. This leads some investigators to believe that Brogus may still be at large in the Ohio area."

"He didn't catch the plane?" I whispered.

"Say what?" Mrs. Henderson said.

The autumn-toned, Cherokee-cheekboned head of Kwanzi Authentica Parker, haloed by squiggly little braids, filled the screen. Her name appeared in white letters, just below her chin, and just below the name, the title she had created for herself this morning: Chair of Afrikamerica Studies. A pink hand shoved a microphone in her face.

"I like *her*," Mrs. Henderson said. "She's been on TV all day. At least *some* colored folks are stickin' up for Reggie Brogus."

I grunted and stared at the TV screen.

"I think we all just need to let ourselves grieve," Kwanzi said, frowning at the reporter. "But I do have a special message." Kwanzi tilted her head and stared directly into the camera. "Reggie . . . my brother . . . if you're out there . . . and you're watching . . . Please come home. Nobody's gonna do you any harm. We just want to get at the truth . . ." Kwanzi's eyes turned glassy. "Please come back, Reggie. . . . We believe in you . . ."

"Weird," I said, as Kwanzi began to choke up.

"Say what?" Mrs. Henderson said.

The TV screen displayed a grainy black-and-white head shot of Reggie Brogus. Beneath the photo was that familiar American expletive, in big, black block letters: WANTED.

"The Federal Bureau of Investigation," the newscaster pronounced, "is offering a $100,000 reward for information that might lead to the apprehension of Reginald Tiberius Brogus. We remind you that this man is still at large and may be armed and dangerous."

Staring at the screen, thinking of the shaven-headed brother in the black trenchcoat and the aviator shades standing ramrod straight on Reggie's lawn, I remembered Brogus's fevered rant in my Volvo in the wee hours of Monday morning: Cointelpro . . . Counter Intelligence Program . . . The files on the assassination of Dr. Martin Luther King Jr. on April 4, 1968, in Memphis, Tennessee . . . Scores to be settled . . . And I wondered: What if Reggie had been telling the truth?

* * *

The memory is hazy at best. I know it was summer and I know I was still in college so I would guess it happened in 1978 or 1979. My parents had already been divorced for a couple of years and I had agreed to accompany Dad to a Robinette family reunion in Luckett, Tennessee. My brother, who must have already started at UCLA by then, somehow weaseled his way out of attending the celebration and Dad must have arrived down South a day or so before I did. He picked me up at the Memphis airport for the drive to Luckett. "I want to make a stop along the way. I need to show you something," my father said cryptically.

I remember the mood better than I do the physical details. It was a gray and muggy afternoon. My father and I stood alone on the sidewalk, facing the Lorraine Motel, which I recall being painted pink and aquamarine. I think it was the second-floor balcony Dad pointed to. "That's where they killed Dr. King," my father said. "He took it in the neck."

How many times had I seen the famous black-and-white photo? The small group of black men, all pointing up and across the street as MLK lay at their feet in a puddle of blood. I remember the eerie, unreal feeling I had seeing the real thing, the actual balcony of the actual motel in its faded, once-festive colors. In the parking lot, just below the balcony, adding to the air of strangeness, was a wide-bodied, clunky-looking car with decorative fins, a midsixties model that seemed to have been left exactly where it was a decade earlier. I turned around and looked at the row of bleak, reddish-brown brick buildings across the street, one of which the men in the photo must have been pointing to.

"The shot must have come from over there," I said.

"Evidently," my father replied.

We were silent for a long time, standing there on the deserted sidewalk in the clammy, humid air. Dad just stared at the motel, slowly stroking his trim little mustache with thumb and forefinger. I had never in my life seen him look so sad. "What was the name of the guy who shot him?" I finally asked, already knowing the answer but wanting to impress Dad with my knowledge. "Wasn't it James Earl Ray?"

"Ray confessed to the crime," my father said, still not looking at me. "They—the so-called authorities—picked him up in London two months after the assassination. A white racist just as you'd expect. He eventually pleaded guilty. So there was never any trial. Now Ray claims he didn't do it."

"Do you believe him?"

My father continued to stare, transfixed, at the balcony. He shrugged with a hopelessness so profound I felt like crying. After a while, he said, "You know, the bullet that struck Dr. King didn't match Ray's rifle."

"No, I didn't know that."

"It's a very little-known fact. But don't expect to read about it in the press. Nobody wants to report that stuff. Because then you'd have to go into the questions of who *did* kill the man . . . and why."

"What do you think, Dad?"

"I think we'll never know." After another long pause, my father said, "Doesn't really matter anyhow. The man is dead. That's what matters. And so much died with him that I don't think folks will ever comprehend it, ever be able to face it." There were tears in my father's eyes now. And in mine. "The loss," Dad said quietly. "The loss."

*   *   *

I had just said good-bye to Mrs. Henderson. It was about 5:30 and Penelope wouldn't be home until six, so I thought I'd enjoy a half hour of

Quality Daddy Time with Amber and Ashley. Walking upstairs, I could already hear the music through the closed door of the girls' room, the familiar female voices, the black Queens street accents, the famous horny exhortation:

Ah, push it!
Push it good!

Oh my God! What were my daughters doing listening to a raunchy Salt 'n' Pepa song?! Amber and Ashley were only six years old! . . . I bounded to the top of the stairs, raced down the hallway, and flung open the door. I saw my daughters, identical twins, little replicas of their mother with their delicately shaped, long-lashed eyes, rich, deep brown complexions, and curly mops of shiny, jet black hair, standing in the center of the bedroom, facing each other, hands on their hips, thrusting their little pelvises and singing along with the music blaring from the outmoded cassette recorder that used to belong to me but now belonged to them, their shrill little voices chanting: "Push it *so* good!"

"Hey!" I shouted.

Amber and Ashley suddenly stopped their lewd gyrations. For a second they both looked up at me in shock. "Daddy!" they shrieked in unison. While Ashley ran toward me and leapt into my arms, Amber quickly turned off the music, then skipped over and wrapped herself around my midsection. The three of us toppled onto one of the narrow beds, the girls giggling maniacally, uncontrollably, bouncing, flailing, squealing, squirming in and out of my arms, excited to see me but more thrilled, I sensed, by being caught doing something they knew was naughty. Before I could stop myself I was laughing crazily, too, laughing at the antic glee of my little girls, laughing to release all the excruciating tension of this day, laughing in the giddy pleasure of the rare emotion that, at this time in my life, I shared with Amber and Ashley and, perhaps, nobody else: a pristinely unconditional love.

Finally, we all settled down. The twins knelt on the springy mattress, my body sprawled between them. Amber, the older one by thirteen minutes, the somewhat shrewder, more keenly intellectual, ever-so-slightly quicker-on-the-uptake one, the one who had rushed to turn off the raunchy tune, was on my left; Ashley, the little bit more openly affectionate, infinitesimally more impulsive and intuitive one who had immediately jumped into my arms, was on my right. I had an arm wrapped around each of them. I tried my best to put on a stern parent tone as I spoke.

"What was that music you were listening to?"

"Salt 'n' Pepa!" Ashley squealed.

"Yes," I said, "but do you know what they're singing about?"

"They're singing about *dancing*, Daddy!" Amber said in a tone of exaggerated exasperation.

I sat up straight on the bed. "Does your mother know you have this tape?"

"Mommy bought it for us!" Ashley said.

"She did?" I yelped. "Didn't it have a warning sticker on it?"

"A what?" Amber asked impatiently.

I looked over at the cluttered table where the cassette recorder rested. But the object that suddenly seized my attention was the near obsolete Macintosh computer that sat beside it, a hand-me-down to the twins from Pen. I'd forgotten the kids had a computer of their own.

"Do you use that Mac much?"

"Sure, Daddy," Ashley said. She hopped off the bed and ran over to the table.

"We have to ask you something, Daddy," Amber said, sounding more like a stern parent than I did.

Ashley hurried back over to the bed, showing me an array of brightly colored computer disks, fanning them out like a hand of playing cards. The labels on the disks displayed familiar cartoon characters and TV puppets offering lessons in spelling and arithmetic.

"We love the computer!" Ashley bubbled. "You wanna see how it works?"

"That's okay, sweetie. I use the one downstairs."

"Daddy," Amber said, "we have a question for you."

"Do you girls ever use any of the disks that Mommy and I keep in the study?" I asked Ashley, ignoring Amber.

"Nope," Ashley said.

"Because there's a disk I'm looking for. I seem to have misplaced it. It's a simple black disk without a label."

"If it doesn't have a label that means there's nothing on it," Amber said. "It might not have even been formatted yet."

"That's right most of the time, honey," I said to my eldest daughter. "But this disk is formatted and it does have something on it."

"But how do you know what's on it if it doesn't have a label?" Ashley asked.

"Well, that's the problem, sugar. One of my students gave me this disk, but she forgot to put a label on it."

"That's silly," Amber said.

"Do you want me to look for the disk, Daddy?" Ashley said.

"No, that's okay. I don't think it's in the house, but if you do happen to come across it—"

"Daddy," Amber snapped, "are you going to answer our question or not?"

"What question?" I asked, finally giving Amber my full attention.

Her dark brown eyes bored into mine. "Did Uncle Reggie do it?"

I was stunned. It was stupid of me, but somehow I had imagined my daughters would be ignorant of the one subject everybody in town was talking about. I paused for several seconds before falling back on one of my traditional responses to the twins: "Ask your mother."

*　　*　　*

My wife was angry with me. The fact that she had not changed out of her tweedy business suit and into more comfy homey clothes for dinner was a sure sign. Since moving to Arden, Penelope had made a lucrative living as a freelance diversity consultant. She offered courses—varying from Saturday workshops to monthlong programs—on how best to integrate women, minorities, and the physically handicapped into white male-dominated corporate environments. Penelope had instructed top executives, middle managers, and administrative assistants in multicultural awareness, sensitivity training, and transpersonal interfacing techniques at accounting firms, insurance agencies, high-tech companies, and retail chains all over Ohio. During those weeks when she didn't have an on-site gig somewhere, she locked herself in our guest room and banged away on her laptop, revising the handbook she had been writing—but had not shown a page of to me—tentatively titled *Making Diversity Pay Off for YOU!*

When I had called Penelope at her current place of employment—an agribusiness company in nearby Mulchville, Ohio—from the *Arden Oracle* newsroom that Tuesday afternoon to tell her I was working on the campus murder story—she'd already heard about the crime and Reggie Brogus's disappearance on the radio—the immediate response was a mystified pause on the other end of the phone. Finally, her voice laced with irritation, Pen said, "Why?" Somehow I managed to deflect the question and apologetically explained that I would have to go back out after dinner to report on the candlelight vigil for my campus mood article. After another long silence, Penelope said, "Okay. You can explain this to me at dinner."

But during the meal, I was scared to mention anything about the article. Amber had wasted no time in following my earlier instruction to her. "Mommy," she said sternly as she took her seat at the dining room table, "did Uncle Reggie do it?"

I could see Penelope's whole body stiffen. She had always hated that the girls called Brogus that. "Amber, a terrible tragedy has taken place in our community," Penelope said in a patient but scolding tone. "A young woman has lost her life in a very awful way and that is not dinner table conversation. We can discuss this later if you like but not during our meal."

"But Mom-meeeeeeeee," Amber whimpered.

"You heard me, young lady. Now, how was your day at school?"

"Something really funny happened!" Ashley trilled.

She excitedly began recounting the incident—something involving an obnoxious boy in their class and a tray of fingerpaints—and Amber quickly joined in. I'm ordinarily a pretty astute listener to my daughters' anecdotes but on this evening I was utterly lost in my own head. I didn't really hear what the girls said. I just saw the joy on their faces as they told their story to Pen, who listened attentively, asked pertinent questions, and encouraged elaboration. I had a melancholy sensation, a feeling that had become increasingly common when I was with Pen and Amber and Ashley, a vague isolation, an undercurrent of outsiderness. Was it a gender thing? Was it just natural that I felt a little bit left out of their special aura of intimacy since I was the only male in the house? Don't misunderstand me. I'm describing an almost imperceptible degree of alienation, not a lessening of love. I still *lived* for these three human beings.

So maybe it was my betrayal of them that made me feel cut off. My little tryst with Jenny had broken a bond with the three most significant people in my universe. They didn't even know it. And I could not bring myself to contemplate what might happen if they found out.

*　*　*

"He's a monster," Penelope said. After dinner, the girls had retired to the living room to watch a syndicated *Cosby Show* rerun and Pen and I went to the kitchen for a pot of decaf. She did not mention his name but, of course, I knew my wife was referring to the man who had sat with me at this very kitchen table about forty-one hours earlier while she snored obliviously upstairs. "He's an entertaining, celebrity monster. That's why you're drawn to him. He's a monster who celebrates, revels in his monstrosity. But, you know, there's only so far you can take this stuff. Even if you're a grotesquely mediagenic monster who reporters are infatuated with."

"What about Amber and Ashley?" I said. "They're infatuated with Reggie and they're not reporters."

"They're six years old. Children are always susceptible to the attractiveness of monsters. Grown-ups are supposed to know better."

Sitting across from me in her smartly cut suit and fake pearls, Penelope wanted to shame me with her maturity. Yes, she had always seen through Brogus. Why hadn't I? But had I *not*?

"So you think Brogus did it?" I asked.

"That's beside the point."

"Whoa!"

"Clay," my wife said severely, leaning toward me across the table, "why are you writing about this?"

Could I tell Penelope how rattled I was after my interview with Patsy DeFestina? Could I tell her how sure I had been that T-Bird Williams had murdered Jenny but how when I walked into the *Oracle* newsroom and felt the Brogus Fever I suddenly realized that it *must* have been Reggie—with the body in his office and his suspenders twisted around its neck—who had killed Jenny and if he had, then I had helped a murderer escape and even if he hadn't, I had failed to report a felony— which might be a felony itself—and whether anybody caught Brogus or not I had to do anything I could to keep this whole mess away from *me*, to cover my own tracks? Could I tell Pen about how I didn't write what I perceived—the subtle gloating, the civic pride, the quasi-erotic titillation—in the responses of Arden residents to the killing, but wrote instead a manipulative tearjerker about a community that earnestly considered itself in grief: an article made up entirely of authentic quotes but which was, nonetheless, a lie? Could I tell her how perversely psyched I was to go to the candlelight vigil tonight to soak up a little more ghoulish schmaltz for tomorrow morning's newspaper? Could I tell her how I'd even managed to squeeze out a box on Detective DeFestina, a nice little obsequious item—complete with a flattering, iconic photograph that the *Oracle* kept on file and ran whenever Patsy was in the news—quoting the celebrity supercop's platitudes about the teamwork of the heroic law enforcers who would crack this case, not saying that Patsy thought there was a ninety percent chance that Brogus was guilty, but, behind every sentence of my carefully crafted journalese, conveying the idea—in both the DeFestina box and in the mood-on-campus piece—that, yes, it was Brogus who did it? Maybe Penelope was right. Maybe Brogus's guilt or innocence was beside the point. But let the world think he—the celebrity monster—was guilty. I would help them think it. Just so long as no one turned their attention to *me*.

Could I tell my wife how I felt like I was cracking up? Could I confess the whole ugly business to Penelope, the person who knew me best?

What do *you* think? I gave a hapless shrug and said, "It's a good story."

We both heard the sudden, insistent scratching. I rose from the table and opened the pantry door. Annoyed by my wife's annoyance with me, I lashed out at the cat. "If you don't want to get trapped in the pantry, stop falling asleep in there all the time!"

"Yow," Dexter said, a laconic "Fuck you, buddy." He bounced haughtily over to his bowl of fishy cat food.

Penelope glanced at her wristwatch. "You better go or you'll be late." She pulled a copy of the *Wall Street Journal* from the leather bag at her feet and started reading, consciously ignoring me.

I grabbed my parka from the hook on the wall and headed for the back door. Turning the knob, I found the door, once again, unlocked. I sucked my teeth, loudly, in irritation. Having grown up in Philadelphia and having spent nearly a decade in Manhattan, I was conditioned to lock doors behind me. Whether entering or leaving my home, I automatically locked a door as I closed it. When we lived in New York, Penelope had always done likewise. But since migrating to the heartland, my wife had become deliberately lax about basic household safety. The merry residents of Arden, Ohio, prided themselves on leaving their doors unlocked. This was a town where neighbors didn't think twice before tapping on your unlocked door and walking right into your home. It gave me the creeps. But Penelope didn't mind. She embraced these strange suburban ways and, by her example, encouraged our daughters to do the same. "Pen," I said with a weary sigh, "how many times do I have to say it? We don't live in Mayberry, RFD."

Pen sipped her coffee, read her newspaper, continued to ignore me.

"You know," I said, "a woman was murdered in our safe little community and they haven't caught the killer yet. You might take that into account."

Seeing my wife's shoulders suddenly tense up, I knew I'd struck a nerve. "Point taken," she said.

For a city boy like me, the streets of suburban Arden always seemed too dark at night. Fortunately, we had a streetlamp near our house, but just outside its cone of light a long dark expanse of sidewalk and road stretched until the next streetlamp, the next, faraway cone of light. I was standing in my driveway, zipping up my parka, when I spotted the fender and hood of the Lincoln Town Car, sitting in the gloom just outside the radius of the nearby streetlamp. I could make out two silhouettes in the front seat of the car. I knew, instinctively, that one of the figures belonged to the man I'd seen on Brogus's lawn. I climbed into our Volvo. As I started the engine, I saw the headlights of the Lincoln come on. I backed out of the driveway and headed down our street, Maplewood. The Lincoln followed me to Pirate Jenny's candlelight vigil.

CHAPTER 7

"WELFARE IS SLAVERY!" REGINALD T. BROGUS thundered. "Affirmative action is slavery! Political correctness is slavery!" Brogus prowled the wooden platform, eschewing the podium, holding the cordless microphone close to his lips, moving his three-hundred-pound bulk with a natural athlete's languid grace, a limber dancer trapped inside the lardy body of a junior-league sumo wrestler. The jacket of his seersucker suit had been casually tossed across the lectern. His blue-and-white striped pants were held up by navy blue suspenders decorated with kelly green dollar signs. After a half-hour of nonstop, rapid-fire patter, Brogus seemed to be reaching a perfervid, rhetorical crescendo, occasionally mopping the rivulets of sweat that cascaded down his face with a white, balled-up handkerchief. "These are worse forms of slavery than our ancestors lived with! They are enslavements of the mind! Of the spirit! Black people have got to let go of this slave mentality! It must be abolished! We need a New Abolition! And I am a New Abolitionist!"

September 1991. Reggie Brogus's first lecture as a Visiting Professor at Arden University. Big white letters spelled out the name of the course on the green chalkboard behind Brogus: DON'T WORRY, MAKE MONEY: THE AMERICAN NEGRO AND THE PROMISE OF DEMOCRACY. While the suite of offices for professors in the Afrikamerica Studies pilot program was located in the Mathematics building, courses were conducted half a campus away in Hexler Hall, which belonged to the History Department. And while those classes were typically held in small seminar rooms—enrollment in Afrikamerica courses averaging about fifteen students—Brogus's debut performance was held in one of Hexler's largest lecture spaces. Astonishingly, for an "Afram" course, half the seats in the ampitheater-style hall were filled. Even more shockingly, half of the two hundred students in the auditorium were white. Ordinarily, there were no white students in Afram courses at all.

"Supply and demand," Dean Jerry Shamberg had said to me forty minutes earlier, as a steady stream of students made their way into the lecture hall. We sat together in the tenth row, stage left from the platform and podium. Dean Jer caressed the salt-and-pepper goatee that had sprouted on his face sometime during the summer vacation. "That's all education is. If people do not want to get taught a certain subject, it won't get taught. That's the simple logic, the invisible hand, if you will, of the intellectual marketplace."

As he spoke, his head tilted ever so slightly away from me, his eyes seemed focused on something just beyond my right shoulder. One of the irritating things about talking to Shamberg was the distracted air that went along with his sideways glance. You—or, at least, I—never had his undivided attention. He talked at you, gave you his spiel, but your responses didn't always seem to register with him. As we waited for Brogus to arrive, Dean Jer was offering his rationalization for why he had not yet decided whether to make Afrikamerica Studies—which was just beginning its second year as a pilot program—a full-fledged department.

"Fewer than half the black students on this campus will ever take an Afram course," Shamberg said, his gaze now shifting and seeming to focus on something over my *left* shoulder. "And that's with black kids making up only ten percent of the student population here. Compare that to the Women's Studies program. Half the student population here is female. Even with only half of them ever taking a Women's Studies course, that's a quarter of the undergraduate Arden market buying the product! When you compare that to only five percent of the total market buying Afrikamerika Studies, the question of whether or not to make it a full department is a no-brainer. It's simply not cost-effective. Un-lesssssss . . ." Shamberg paused and stared into space for a long moment. Then, picking up the train of thought he had seemingly lost, continued: "Unless you have a crossover success. A black professor who can bring in white students, thus capturing a larger market share."

Shamberg's eyes were darting about now, scanning the gathering crowd. "I have to say, the signs this morning are encouraging. Like it or not, Reggie Brogus is a star."

They gathered in segregated clusters, a pack of four or five white students here, a group of five or six black students there. I saw kids of both races who looked like nerds, others who were clearly jocks, young lovers holding hands, rebels with nose rings, polished, most-likely-to-succeed types. But whatever the individual image, whatever fashion statement any one student was making, they all adhered to an unwritten racial seating code, blacks with blacks, whites with whites. Shamberg and I were the only interracial pairing in the lecture hall and no one sat anywhere near *us*, not out of any ethnic bias but simply because Dean Jer was the head of the university and students, as they often will, seemed afraid of getting too close to such an authority figure. No one but Jerry and me occupied the tenth row on the right side of the auditorium and the four rows in front of us and behind us—even as other sections of the hall filled up—remained empty.

"Awright!" a high-pitched voice cried. "This nigga gonna teach me how to make some *moe*-NAY!"

I turned and saw T-Bird Williams in the center of the auditorium, laughing and slapping high fives with a group of eight or so other black students as he took his seat among them. As far as I was concerned there were only two types of student. And ethnicity—black, Wasp, Jewish, Asian, Latino, whatever—was not among the distinguishing characteristics. The two types of student, in any given class, were those who took the course seriously, and those who didn't. Tyrell "T-Bird" Williams exemplified the latter breed. I had had him in my creative nonfiction class one year earlier. He showed up for about half the sessions and was a powerfully negative presence in each one he attended, slouching in his seat, smacking his gum, looking around the classroom with an air of nonchalant disdain. When I would ask him a question, try to get him involved in the class discussions, he would just shrug his shoulders and give an insolent grunt. He turned in only two of the four papers I had assigned and those were obvious rush jobs, sloppily put together, riddled with spelling errors and typos. I wanted to flunk him. But the course I taught was an undemanding one and the lowest grade I had ever given anyone at that point was a B. I won't deny that, even though he had shown nothing but contempt for me and my class, I cut T-Bird some slack because he was black. I knew from an autobiographical essay he had turned in that he came from a poor, inner-city background. He had written of seeing people shot and stabbed to death on his street. Lord knows he had enough obstacles in his life without me dragging his already low grade point average into the gutter. So I gave him a B. And T-Bird actually went to the head of the English Department to complain that he deserved a higher grade. But the B remained unchanged.

"So let's say Brogus is a hit and next year Afrikamerica Studies is one of the hot departments," Shamberg said, his gaze meeting mine for a second before sliding away again. "Then maybe you and I could reopen negotiations."

"We never *opened* negotiations, Jerry."

For the past two years, Shamberg had tried to get me to teach classes in the Afram pilot program, in addition to my journalism and creative nonfiction courseload. But I had always said no, giving the excuse made ubiquitous by fired coaches, chief executives forced to resign, and politicians wimping out of campaigns: "I want to spend more time with my family." But Shamberg knew there was no way I was taking on more work without getting paid a lot more money.

"Okay," Dean Jer said, as we sat together in Hexler Hall, surrounded by seats no student dared to occupy. "Name your price."

Knowing that Reggie Brogus was making double my salary in his one-year appointment, I decided to play it cagey. "I don't know if you can afford me, Jer."

"Don't go breakin' my heart, Clay. Our endowment can only stretch so far. Listen to me . . ."

At that instant, I stopped listening to Shamberg. I didn't know when the girl had come in and taken the seat. She seemed to have just appeared, alone, three rows in front of us, a few places closer to the lecturer's platform. It was the tumult of burning red hair that first caught my attention. Then, as Dean Jer prattled on—he seemed to be saying something about budgetary constraints—she turned around and fixed me with a brazen stare. "Striking" would be one way of describing the young woman but let me be more honest and say she was downright weird-looking: pale, translucent skin, oddly slanted, asymmetrical green eyes, cat's eyes, and a bony, angular face that still had that certain unfinished, adolescent softness to it, but also a slyness, a cruelty, an androgynous alien quality, an early David Bowiesque sensuality. The girl stared brazenly at me—and I stared straight back at her—for an eternal moment. Finally, she turned to look at the platform and all I could see was the fiery mane tumbling over the back of her seat.

"Yoo-hoo," Dean Jer cooed. "Oh, Claaaaaaaay? Earth to Claaaaaay." Shamberg never gave you his full attention but he noticed immediately if yours had wandered. I looked at Jerry, he looked at the crimson-haired girl, then looked back at me. "I have just two words for you, Clay: sexual harassment. Touch a student and your academic career is over. That's what it's come to these days."

"Who's touching?" I said indignantly. "I'm just looking."

"Even *that* can be dangerous! Did you hear about the old professor in New Hampshire last year? He was fired, lost his tenure and his pension, for allegedly undressing students with his eyes! That's what the girls accused him of: *undressing them with his eyes!* Now the geezer's life is ruined. I ask you, my man: What is this nation coming to? I mean, having affairs with students is one of the great academic traditions! There was a time when boffing your professor was considered a crucial part of any ambitious young woman's sentimental education. Christ almighty, two of my wives were former students of mine! The rules have changed on us, Clay. And in just the past five years! Why, back at the College of the Dunes, I rarely hesitated to give a fine young coed a pat on the rump. Nothing sleazy, mind you! A simple gesture of paternal affection. Now I live in fear."

"Well, I don't," I said smugly. "I've always been a good boy. Do you know that I've never once cheated on my wife?"

For perhaps the first time since I'd known him, Jerry locked eyes with me. He stared long and hard, seemingly speechless, his mouth hanging open, a look of helpless bewilderment on his face. Finally, he said, "Are you shittin' me?"

Suddenly, a deep-voiced chant arose in the lecture hall.

"Reh-GEE!—Reh-GEE!—Reh-GEE!—Reh-GEE!—Reh-GEE!—"

Looking around the auditorium, I noticed it was only white males doing the chanting. I spotted Brogus descending the steps, black leather briefcase in hand, heading for the podium.

"I had no idea Brogus had so many young fans," I said.

"They all know him from the *Rash Knoblauch Show*," Shamberg said. "He's a regular guest."

"Who's Rash Knoblauch?"

"Talk radio guy. Arch-conservative. Huge following."

Brogus set down his briefcase on a table in front of the chalkboard. As the chanting faded out, Brogus pulled the mike from the podium and walked to the edge of the platform. He began quietly.

"Ladies and gentlemen, we are a little more than eight years from the new millennium. America has won the cold war. Communism is dead. Capitalist democracy rules the planet. We have the privilege of living in the world's last remaining superpower, victorious in the Gulf War, the envy of all other civilized nations . . . and yet, Negroes are *still* whining."

At this, the majority of the black audience—myself included—let out one huge noise, a combination groan of disgust and cry of protest. Many white students laughed and a few applauded. A smattering of blacks in the house joined them. Brogus continued, his voice rising.

"Because they don't see that we stand on the edge of the promised land! America is realizing her glorious potential. The end of race as we know it! The blessed institution of interracial marriage will white out the color line, making us not a darker but a lighter nation, one in which the only thing that will matter is the only thing that *should* matter: How much money you make! The pursuit of capital will bring equality to all! I see a day when Americans will be judged not by the color of their skin but by the content of their financial portfolios! When society will be ruled by a simple standard: What do you bring to the table? A time when the only color that matters is green! A day when black people will be able to join hands with our white brothers and sisters and sing: Rich at last! Rich at last! Thank God almighty, I'm rich at last!"

From my tenth-row perch I checked out Brogus's colleagues in the Afrikamerica Studies program. Front row and just off-center sat Arthur and Matilda Davenport. Meticulously groomed, ineffably classy, the Davenports had been semiretired the past couple of years. For two decades, from 1952 to 1971, Art and Matilda had been the only black professors at Arden University. They had been generalists, he in American History, she in American Literature. Throughout the 1970s and 1980s, as more black professors came to Arden, stayed for a few terms, then took off for warmer if not necessarily greener pastures, Art and Matilda each taught a special course, he in Afro-American History, she in Afro-American Literature, as part of their respective mainstream departments. While they had since given up their other courses, they continued to teach the black history and lit classes, only now as part of the Afrikamerica Studies pilot program. My wife and I always enjoyed Art and Matilda's company. We were honored to be invited to their fiftieth wedding anniversary celebration in June of '91, where the Davenports danced a mean jitterbug. Now, watching Reggie Brogus in Hexler Hall, the Davenports wore perfect poker faces. They both sat up straight, their expressions alert, attentive, and utterly unreadable. I can't say I knew Art and Matilda intimately but I would guess they were unfazed by the likes of Reggie Brogus. I had the feeling they had seen all manner of proselytizers in their day and regarded Reggie as just another curiosity. I do know that since Shamberg had hired Brogus, the Davenports were talking more seriously about taking full retirement and sailing around the world after the '91–'92 school year.

Next to Arthur and Matilda sat Xavier Lumbaki, the professor who put the "Afrika" in Afrikamerica Studies. Born and raised in Dakar, Senegal, now a citizen of Paris, France, and graduate of the Sorbonne, Xavier taught a course called History of the African Continent. His specialty was colonialism. Xavier and his French wife, Aurore, had arrived in Arden the same time as my family and I did, in September '89. We became fast friends. We were about the same age and Xavier, who was at Arden on a three-year teaching and research fellowship, looked at America with a bemused and fascinated—and not unaffectionate—anthropological eye that I appreciated. His wife, however, a twelfth-generation Parisian, detested the U.S.A., particularly its antismoking ordinances, which she found obsessive, even though she herself did not smoke. Penelope and I were among the few couples Xavier and Aurore socialized with during their first year. Then, in the fall of 1990, when Aurore gave birth to Nathalie, she and Xavier went into baby shock. Pen and I saw a lot less of them, but, having gone through the experience—squared—we understood. Watching Xavier Lumbaki watch Brogus, chin in hand, a somewhat puzzled smirk on his face, I knew that, even though Xavier would probably return to Paris with his wife and daughter when his fellowship expired at the end of the school year, there were certain entertaining cultural oddities about America that he would someday, nostalgically, miss. Brogus would probably rate as one of them.

Just behind Xavier sat Kwanzi Authentica Parker, sporting a towering multicolored African headdress and matching gown. She seemed to be smoldering in her seat, glowering at Brogus as he rambled on about such heroes as George Washington and Richard Nixon and the common values that made America "the greatest nation on the face of the earth." Kwanzi's husband, the British historian Roger Pym-Smithers, sat beside her, with his jowly, raspberry face, eyebrows flaring devilishly, frequently cupping a hand and whispering in his wife's ear. Since arriving at Arden in 1980, Kwanzi had taught courses in Black Consciousness, elusive, catchall classes with ever-changing reading lists comprised of social theory, history texts, polemical tracts, self-help books, poetry, and novels. What the courses actually amounted to were bull sessions where black students could vent all their racial frustrations, anxieties, and self-justifications under the sympathetic guidance of a gregarious professor. Kwanzi's students adored her. And Professor Parker, who had never had children herself, expressed a maternal affection for the black students who consistently sought her out for advice, "like I'm some mammy with twenty teats," Kwanzi liked to say with a laugh.

Kwanzi was far less popular with Dean Jerry Shamberg. She complained that he didn't take her seriously. For nearly twenty years, Kwanzi had been what academics call A.B.D.—all but dissertation. Meaning she had done all the coursework to earn a doctorate in Black Studies from Craven University in Craven, Delaware, but she had never received a Ph.D. because she still had not finished writing a two-hundred-page dissertation. In the early seventies, Kwanzi had gone to live in London, believing she would be more inspired to write there. After eight years, she returned to the States with an English husband but no finished dissertation. Kwanzi had changed her thesis topic a dozen times, had begun and abandoned a number of other long projects—a few biographies, articles for scholarly journals, a book on African spirits, the inevitable novel—and, as of 1991, had yet to publish a single word. I had been at dinner parties where Kwanzi talked all night about things she would like to write. She just hated actually writing.

"You gotta shit or get off the pot," I'd once heard Shamberg say of long-term A.B.D.s. He could tolerate teachers like me or Brogus who had never attended graduate school but had had careers in what he termed "the civilian sector." But he did seem a bit contemptuous of people who had signed on to pursue a doctorate, then dithered for years, or decades, over a dissertation. Kwanzi had always suspected that Shamberg wanted to fire her. She also had theories for why he didn't dare: because she had been at Arden six years longer than Dean Jer and was one of the few black female professors on the faculty; because her husband Roger Pym-Smithers, who had followed her to Ohio from London, was an accomplished and tenured member of the History Department; because Kwanzi had been pushing Shamberg to create an Afrikamerica Studies program and—as much as he might look down on Kwanzi—Dean Jer had to know that multiculturalism was hot, cutting edge, the expanding academic field of our time.

During Afrikamerica Studies' first semester as a pilot program in 1990, Kwanzi Authentica Parker and Jerry Shamberg maintained a wary partnership. He seemed to like the idea of having such a department, but he didn't particularly want Kwanzi to head it. As the undeclared but presumptive chairperson of the program, Kwanzi proved to be a flustered and less-than-competent administrator. Still, she was full of pride. The program had been her brainchild and she believed she was doing a fine job of running it. Then, in April 1991, Shamberg announced he was hiring Reginald T. Brogus to teach whatever he felt like teaching in the program. Rumor had it that Kwanzi and Dean Jer actually engaged in a screaming match over the hiring. Kwanzi thought she should be the one to decide who would or would not teach in the program. Shamberg reminded her that he was her boss. Kwanzi threatened to resign. Shamberg told her to go right ahead. Kwanzi, thinking that her resignation might have been Shamberg's ulterior motive in hiring Brogus, stayed at Arden, hanging tough. But she cursed Shamberg and Brogus to everyone she encountered.

Now, as she sat in the second row during Brogus's debut lecture, Kwanzi squinted her eyes, scrunched up her nose, and pursed her lips as if the man speaking before her were a gigantic, unsightly, reeking turd. Meanwhile, Roger, who had been shaking his head and rolling his eyes throughout Reggie's performance, was whispering furiously in Kwanzi's ear. Brogus had actually seemed to win over the majority of the audience, blacks as well as whites. Perhaps to these students who had spent most of their politically cognizant lives in the Reagan-Bush era, there was something inherently appealing about Brogus's money-worshiping rhetoric. After all, even T-Bird Williams had seemed psyched about the theme of this course. But then Brogus started his diatribe about the "slave mentality" and you could feel a collective squirm in the lecture hall.

"I am a patriot," Brogus said, the "p" in his self-description echoing spittily in the cordless mike he held too close to his lips. "And that is why I fight for the abolition of the slave mentality. Let me read you something . . ."

Brogus hurried to the table in front of the chalkboard. The clunk of the microphone as Reggie set it down on the table echoed in the hall. His back to the audience, Reggie bent over the table and one could hear his amplified rifling through the books and papers in his briefcase. What one saw was this huge seersuckered butt. Reggie had only remained in this position, seeming to salute the audience with his monumental cheeks, for a short while, but it was just about two seconds too long, giving you just enough time to notice how the material at the seam down the middle underside of the pants was stretched to the ripping point, a flash of fire engine red underwear poking through, giving you just enough time to find—secretly, only to yourself—the sight of Reggie bent over quite funny when—

"PPPPFFFFFFGGGHHHLACHTPPPPFFFFFLLLLLLLL . . ."

The simulated fart noise, something I associated more with a junior high school gymnasium than a university lecture hall was so startling, so unpleasantly rude and immature, and, yet, so well timed with Brogus's flaunting of his big butt, so realistically fartlike while obviously, grotesquely, loudly exaggerated as it reverberated in the auditorium that even the more mature, serious students and a couple of professors— Xavier Lumbaki and me, to be precise—couldn't stop themselves from laughing. And one cluster of eight or so students was cackling hysterically, screaming and clapping their hands. T-Bird Williams rose from the center of the group and took a bow.

Professor Brogus was not amused. He had whirled out of his butt-waving stance the instant the noise erupted. Now he stood at the edge of the platform, pointing at T-Bird and yelling into his microphone: "Go ahead and laugh, slave! 'Cause that's what you are! Nothin' but a slave!"

"And you a big, fat ugly muthafucka!" T-Bird called out.

While a good part of the audience, mostly black, laughed and cheered T-Bird, many more students, mostly white, booed him vigorously. But Reggie, yelling into the microphone, drowned out everyone else.

"You may not *think* you're a slave 'cause you ain't toilin' in the fields. You got it easy here in a college where you can hang out and not crack a book and be a clown with half your tuition subsidized by hardworking American taxpayers! You think 'cause you don't have an iron chain around your neck—like LeVar Burton in *Roots*—you can't be a slave. You got it too good for dat! But most slaves had it good, too, you know. It wasn't all whips and chains like on *Roots*. Read the slave narratives. Most of them enjoyed life on the plantation! And they had affection for their masters! Look at Tom Jefferson and Sally Hemmings! It wasn't slaves that started the Civil War. They didn't want slavery to end just as you don't want *your* slavery to end. They didn't want to take on the white man's burden. 'Cause slaves had it easy!"

"THAT'S ENOUGH!" Kwanzi Authentica Parker shrieked, springing upright from her second row seat. She was overwrought, arms stretched out in front of her, her hands clutching at the air as she continued to scream at Brogus. "Have you lost your mind, Reggie Brogus? To say that slaves had it easy? Are you mad? Are you really going to diminish and distort the four-hundred-year atrocity of slavery? What you're saying is completely ahistorical!"

"Read the slave narratives," Reggie said calmly.

"I *HAVE* READ THE SLAVE NARRATIVES!"

"Then you know what I'm talking about," Brogus said with a smug flourish.

"I don't know what in the hell you're talking about because *you* don't know what in the hell you're talking about!" Kwanzi paused as black students applauded her. When she spoke again, it was in a more subdued but still tortured voice. "What did they do to you, Reggie?"

"Nobody did anything to me, sistuh," Reggie said firmly, his lips brushing the microphone. "I saw the light."

"You used to mean something to black people."

"I got wise."

"How did they get you to betray us?" Her voice was earnest, but Kwanzi was all too aware of the audience watching her. Kwanzi was, as always, *on,* milking the theatricality of the moment, every bit as melodramatic as she was sincere. "How did they take you away from us?"

"I was always true to myself," Brogus said flatly.

"Well, I, for one have had enough of your lies for one morning!" Kwanzi said, her voice rising brassily. She turned to face the aisles of spectators. "I would urge all people of conscience in this hall, black and white alike, to join me in a walkout of this lecture. To walk out on this man, this charlatan, as a sign that we will show zero tolerance for racism on this campus!"

Now Roger Pym-Smithers sprang out of his seat, standing beside his wife and slapping his palms together. "Hear, hear!" Roger barked. "Well said! Very well said!"

"You goddamned right!" T-Bird Williams shouted. He was already leading his entourage up the stairs and out of the auditorium.

There was a chaotic mingling of boos, whistles, cheers, and applause in the hall. Half the auditorium seemed to be standing now, but it was impossible to tell who was leaving and who was just up on their feet making noise. I saw the top of Kwanzi's headdress, bobbing majestically above the crowd, as Professsor Parker climbed toward the exit.

"Racism?" Reggie Brogus shouted into his mike. Standing near the edge of the platform, feet planted solidly, Reggie looked as stubbornly immovable as a sequoia. "WHO is being racist? WHO is being small-minded, prejudiced against new ideas? Anybody in this room who wants to close their minds, who wants to stick to their slave mentality, you can follow that lady on outta here! But anyone who believes in free-dom of speech, in the free expression of ideas, in the glory of American democracy, is stayin' right here with me!"

Now the deep-voiced chant rocked the house: "REH-*GEE!*—REH-*GEE!*—REH-*GEE!*—REH-*GEE!*—REH-*GEE!*"

I glanced at Jerry Shamberg as clusters of people streamed out of the auditorium, others stood clapping and chanting, and the rest sat in their seats, looking—like Art and Matilda Davenport and Xavier Lumbaki down in the front row— somewhat perplexed, but definitely intrigued. Dean Jer was craning his neck, twisting his head to and fro, eyes darting, trying to take in all the action, wearing an enigmatic little smile. At the end of the exodus, Brogus had held on to about half the audience. Of those who remained, about two-thirds were white, one-third black. As the crowd calmed down, Shamberg settled back into his seat. He gave me one of his sideways looks. "Interesting, huh?"

Standing on the platform, mike held to his lips, Reggie Brogus, with a pro's sense of timing, said quietly: "Now where was I?"

At this, the crowd burst into a new round of applause. I cast an eye three rows in front of me, eager for a glimpse of the flame-haired girl with the brazen stare. But she was gone.

CHAPTER 8

A THOUSAND POINTS OF LIGHT flickered in front of the Mathematics building. The night was cold but nearly windless. Pulling into the parking lot behind the building now felt queasily routine. As I stepped out of the Volvo, I looked for the Lincoln Town Car. The black sedan had trailed me from my home to the edge of campus but veered off and disappeared down the road just as I had turned to enter the parking lot. So maybe the car hadn't been following me at all.

I could hear the crowd stirring, the amplified chords of a guitar. Walking quickly past the side entrance I had used with Brogus, I nearly bumped into Pops Mulwray as he was leaving the Math building. Pops had seemed a bit distracted, maybe a little foggy-headed, as he shuffled through the doorway in his green custodial jacket and matching baseball cap. He gave a startled hoot as we almost collided. His head jerked up and I saw a sudden fear in his eyes.

"Sorry, Pops," I said, patting the old man's shoulder reassuringly. "I almost knocked you down. I don't know what the hell I'm running for."

Pops gave a weak smile. The whites of his eyes were yellow. He mumbled something and lightly touched the sleeve of my parka. With some effort, he turned around and locked the door.

"It's been a long day for you, huh, Pops?"

Pops nodded. "Oh, yeah," I heard him say faintly.

"You get some rest, man," I said. "Ya hear?"

"Thank you, son." At least that's what I think I heard Pops say. I shook his knobby hand, he shuffled off in the direction of the parking lot and I headed for the vigil.

For someone who was a loner in life, Jennifer Esther Wolfshiem had acquired a whole lot of friends in death. They swayed slowly to the music, this multitude of fresh-faced white kids, clutching their white and yellow candles, some of them linking arms and singing tunelessly along. A makeshift concert stage had been erected in front of the Math building. Onstage, a grungy, reed-thin student with his hair hanging in his eyes strummed the guitar and warbled into the stand-up microphone:

Oh, I seen fire and I seen rain,
I seen sunny days that I thought would never end,
I seen lonely times when I could not find a friend,
But I always thought that I'd see you, baby, one more time again . . .

"Fire and Rain"? A James Taylor song? At Pirate Jenny's memorial? Didn't anyone here actually know this woman? Didn't they know she would have wanted a Brecht-Weill song played at her service? Or maybe "Fuck Tha Police" by Niggaz With Attitude, which she, quite rightly, considered the great political song of its day? And who was this dork with the guitar? Had he ever even met Jenny?

A girl with purple pigtails, mouthing the words to "Fire and Rain" the whole time, placed a candle in my hand and lit its wick with the flame from hers. I noticed a gun-metal gray apparatus behind the singer: two tall poles, one on each side of the stage, joined at the tops by a crossbar. Hanging by rings from the crossbar was what appeared to be a rolled up carpet, or canvas or screen. As guitar boy whined through the song's fadeout, a young woman fiddled with one of the poles. Suddenly the enormous banner unfurled. And there was the face of Pirate Jenny, in black and white, two stories high.

Denial, my wife liked to say, is the strongest force in human consciousness: "Each of us, just to get through a day, has to deny the fact that we're gonna die. If you can't deny that one huge fact, you go crazy and/or, probably, you die. So the thing that keeps you going, the basic psychic engine that keeps you humming along is this daily denial of the inevitability—made worse by the inherent unpredictability—of death. After that, all other denials are easy."

I wasn't sure I agreed with Penelope and we sometimes enjoyed debating the point but as I watched the banner unspool and saw this giant image of Jenny, I recognized the extent to which I had been in thrall to denial, ever since denying it was Pirate Jenny on the couch in Reggie's office, refusing to believe it, telling myself I'd imagined it. Now I was prepared to deny any involvement with her at all. And in pursuing my ridiculous little newspaper story today, I had, in my mind, in my memory and imagination, denied Jenny a measure of her humanity. I abstracted, obliviated her. I was writing a piece about what people felt about what had happened to her, but had deliberately avoided writing a piece about *her*. And, in denying her, had felt no genuine pity. I had pitied myself, agonized over the situation I had put myself in. But I had allowed myself no feeling for Jennifer. I couldn't bear to feel for her. Couldn't bear to think about what it must have been like for her, to die the way she did.

*   *   *

What you have to understand is that this whole Jenny thing (I refuse to call it an affair) happened on the periphery of my life. I was never paying all that much attention to it. Do you want to know what was really pre-occupying me in September and October of 1991? Well, first Ashley and then Amber caught chicken pox. They each missed two weeks of school—with one overlapping week—and were miserable-happy in that way of children who have a temporarily debilitating but none-too-threatening malady. Meanwhile, Penelope was having problems with some young crypto-racists who had hired her for a diversity workshop at a high-tech company in McGrath, Ohio. She also thought Mrs. Henderson was getting too bossy, telling us how we should raise the girls (me, I was happy to take any advice that was proffered). And Pen worried about not having enough time to work on her diversity handbook, which she was sure would pay for the twins' college education—if she could only finish and publish it.

And I was contemplating my failure, scratching and peeling the scab of my disgrace. I rehashed mistakes, pondered how I could have handled things differently. I considered means of redemption. Maybe I could write a noble biography of some noble person. I brooded over a screenplay, since that, everybody seemed to know, was the way for a writer to get rich. I wondered what courses I might teach in the Afrikamerica Studies program and tried to guess how much more Dean Jerry Shamberg would be willing to pay me to teach them. I fretted over the decreasing frequency of sexual intercourse between my wife and me. One morning, Penelope had actually laughed at my budding potbelly as I stepped out of the shower. And I was, it must be said, increasingly fascinated by Reginald T. Brogus during those weeks of September and October '91. I was thirty-three years old and wondered, more analytically than regretfully, if I was already past my prime.

These were the problems at the center of my life, not my encounters with the weird-looking redhead who had so boldly scrutinized me at Brogus's first lecture and who, two days later, walked into my office in the white clapboard house that was the home of the English Department.

* * *

"You don't know Pirate Jenny? *Seeräuberjenny?* She's a character in a song in *The Threepenny Opera.* You must know it: Bertolt Brecht and Kurt Weill. Jenny is this insignificant little woman who dresses in rags and washes the glasses and makes the beds in a cheap—How do you say it in English?—*fleabag* hotel in some seaside town. The men, the customers, they treat her just like dirt. They drink and taunt her and throw her the occasional penny as a tip. Then one night, the men in the hotel bar hear screams from the harbor. They are scared. But Jenny just stands behind the bar, washing her glasses and smiling. And nobody knows why."

She took a long drag on her clove cigarette, exhaled languorously, filling the air in my untidy office with a spicy, nose-tickling aroma. I had offered her the chair on the other side of my desk. She preferred to sit on the couch. I cleared away small stacks of books and papers to make a space for her. She was unlike any student I'd met at Arden. First of all, she was wearing a microscopic black dress that your average Arden woman might wear to go for a weekend clubbing in New York but would never walk around campus in on a Wednesday afternoon. Then there was her whole manner. Direct, self-possessed, precocious. No other undergraduate who had come into my office to get acquainted or discuss their work had ever spoken to me with such a complete lack of deference, entirely as an equal. And none had ever spoken with such a sultry and mysterious accent. I guessed she was European but I could not discern a distinct nationality. Finally, she did something I could not even imagine any other Ardenite I had met doing, at least not during office hours with a professor. She asked me for an ashtray. I didn't have one. I offered her a coffee-tarnished styrofoam cup. She fired up a clove cigarette.

"A ship with eight sails and fifty cannons has arrived at the harbor. The pirates lay waste to the village. They burn down every house but the cheap little fleabag hotel. And the townspeople wonder: did some important person live in this place? And out steps Jenny, the pathetic little washerwoman at whom they mocked and jeered. And the towns-people say, No, it can't be *her!* The ship with eight sails and fifty cannons runs its flag up the mast and the pirates round up all the town folk and bring them, in shackles, to Jenny, the pirate queen. And they ask her: which ones shall we kill? Everyone is silent as they wait for the answer of Pirate Jenny, her decision on who will die."

She took another hit of clove, fixed me with her crooked, naked gaze.

"And Pirate Jenny says: the lot of them!"

She suddenly sliced a hand through the air, a sword lopping off a head, and sang: *"And as the first head rolls, I'll say: hoppla!"*

She broke into an indulgent, deep-throated laugh. And she kept laughing, cracking herself up, pausing to suck on the clove cigarette, then laughing some more as she continued to stare at me with her green, Picasso eyes. It was then that I realized this young woman might be crazy. My attraction to her swelled.

Let me be clear: when it came to my sexual life, there had been only two categories of women: (1) Penelope; and (2) everybody else. When people asked me what my "type" was, I always answered "Penelope." She was the standard by which all other women were judged. Looks, brains, temperament, whatever: every woman I encountered from age twelve onward was measured by the degree to and direction in which she varied from the Penelope standard. When it came to what I loved, Penelope was it, the sui generis embodiment. During those years I waited for Pen to come back East so we could make good on our secret, unspoken marriage pact—the whole first half of my twenties—I dated all "types" of women. But I did have a few particularly intense encounters with women who were Penelope's opposite, like that woman Marcy who kept sending me letters after our breakup: neurotic exotics, anorexic shizophrenics; artsy, small-breasted, unreliable, pale. In that sense, the young woman in my office was, for me, a throwback.

She told me she was a writer. Not that she "wanted to be" or was "trying to be" one. Just: "I am a writer." She said she was interested in taking my creative nonfiction course but she did not know what "creative nonfiction" was. I told her I didn't either. She said she wrote all the time. Maybe what she was writing fit the bill. I asked her what she wrote about.

"Myself, of course."

She pulled a sheaf of pages from her knapsack, handed it to me. I read the laser-printed title page aloud.

"'Perceptions of a Languid and Bittersweet Tuesday Afternoon' by Pirate Jenny. I assume that's you."

"My *nom de plume.*"

"And how did you come by that?"

"You mean you don't know?"

That's when she launched into her synopsis of the song, after which she couldn't stop laughing her young madwoman's laughter. And I was, for whatever reason, perhaps unreasonably, enchanted.

"So you must identify with this character, this Pirate Jenny," I suggested.

"Ugh!" she cried. "*Identify* with the character! What is this supposed to mean? It's like that complaint people in this country say all the time when talking about books and films and theater: 'I don't *care* about the characters.' What a ridiculous thing to say. And what does it mean? Do you *care* about Mack the Knife? Of course not! Nobody *cares* about Iago or Lady Macbeth or Stanley Kowalski. They aren't nice people! They aren't role models! They're monsters, distorted pieces of humanity. That's what makes them great fucking"—the way she pronounced the word, it sounded like *foo-king*—"characters! Yet people say this thing, 'I don't care about the characters,' or 'I *can't* care about the characters,' like it's some kind of intelligent analysis. It is so wildly subjective. And yet they act as if their not-caring is the fault of the artists rather than some basic deficit of human empathy on *their* part. Critics on TV, students in classes, reviewers in newspapers, they practically scream their lack of feeling, they are so strangely smug about it: 'I DON'T *CARE* ABOUT THESE CHARACTERS!' Like they don't *care* about that panhandler so let him freeze to death on the sidewalk. Or they don't *care* about women and children in Iraq—but evidently they *do* care about oil—so why not slaughter a hundred thousand of them? Who *cares?* How proudly stingy people here are with their caring! And I suppose to *care* you must *identify.* So, no, I can't say I care about or identify with Pirate Jenny. It's beside the point."

"But you took her name for your pseudonym. That must signify something."

She blew a pungent cloud into the air, stubbed out her clove cigarette in the bottom of the styrofoam cup. "Unless," she said, "it signifies nothing."

Her real name, the name on her birth certificate, anyway, was simply Esther Wolfshiem. Her father, a West German diplomat, had chosen it. But her mother, an American who, I gleaned, was significantly younger than Herr Wolfshiem, insisted that their child have a more "normal-sounding" name. So Frau Wolfshiem always called her daughter Jennifer. The family had lived all over the place: Berlin, Beijing, New York, New Dehli, Paris and Panama, Geneva and Johannesburg. Jennifer Esther had finished high school in Brussels, Belgium. After one year at Georgetown University, she had transferred to Arden. She said she couldn't stand living in Washington, D.C. She added that her father was currently based there.

"And where is your mother?" I asked.

"In Hell," Pirate Jenny said. "If you're a Catholic—and she always claimed she was—that's where you go when you commit suicide."

I was stunned by the sudden, casual revelation. Jenny pulled out another clove cigarette.

"I'm sorry," I said.

"I used to be," Jenny said. And here is where she finally showed her age. The self-conscious callousness of her comment, the forced, "I'm over it" hard-boiled tone of voice, the studied nonchalance with which she then lit her cigarette revealed her late teenage aching vulnerability. I remembered a friend of mine from college, a beautiful girl of rare talent who started a rock band called Shatterproof People. This girl, Esme, had had a nightmarish family life but she always had to convince herself, and others, that it had not gotten to her, that the emotional agony would never break her, that she was shatterproof. Of course, Esme eventually shattered. She put herself back together and, later, was shattered again. I hadn't heard from her in years. I assumed she had recovered once more and knew by now that there *are* no shatterproof people. Pirate Jenny, in September 1991, was still pretending to be indestructible. But her mother's death was, obviously, an almost unbearable, open wound.

I told her I had to go teach a class (true) but that I'd be happy to read the story she had given me (a lie). She told me she had scheduling conflicts that prevented her from taking any of my classes. But she wondered if, maybe, I would be willing to act as her academic adviser—every new student at Arden University was required to have one. No student had ever asked me before. I said okay. The rules said we had to meet for at least half an hour, once a week. My office hours with students were always in the afternoons. She said only evenings were convenient for her. I said okay. She suggested Wednesdays, at 7 p.m. I said okay. I knew I'd catch hell from Penelope about that. I didn't care.

We shook hands and said good-bye, see you next week.

"I hope you like the story," Pirate Jenny said. "It was inspired by you."

"Perceptions of a Languid and Bittersweet Tuesday Afternoon"—as I discovered late that night, reading it in my study at home, after Pen and the twins had gone to bed—was a five-page set piece about a man and a woman, naked and evidently postcoital, lying in a bed. It was a gorgeously written, opulently detailed work, full of grandiloquent descriptions of the feeling of sweat on skin and sheets, the sight of motes of dust floating in sunlight slanting through Venetian blinds, the smell of sex, the sounds of the street outside, and the black cat watching everything in a corner of the bedroom. There was a heartbreaking sensuality about the piece. The author had it. Even if it was still underdeveloped and raw, she had it: the gift.

The piece was written in the first person. The narrator called herself Pirate Jenny. The nude, brown-skinned man sleeping at her side, the man who had, she wrote, deeply "pleasured" her, was called Clay.

*   *   *

Like I said, all this Pirate Jenny stuff was peripheral to what I considered my real life. Still, I found myself looking forward to those Wednesday evening office hours. At seven o'clock on any Wednesday, the English Department headquarters was—save for Jenny and me—deserted. As night fell earlier each successive Wednesday that September, our meetings felt more and more intimate, even illicit. Not that "anything"—as the euphemism goes—had "happened." I was supposed to be guiding her choice of curriculum, to help her map out a career path. Instead, we sat there talking about literature, music, cinema, the lives of artists we liked, the different countries she had lived in. I had given her a very basic, dry critique of "Perceptions." I said nothing about the character sharing my name, but I did tell her that "pleasure" was not a verb.

"Oh, but it is!" she said.

Neither of us ever brought up the subject of her mother and I rarely mentioned my family. Jenny often spoke of her father, though I remember her mixed tone of affection and contempt for the man better than any specific thing she ever said about him. While Jenny always sat on the couch, I remained in the chair behind my desk. Every Wednesday evening, the air was dense with the smell of clove cigarettes and the humidity of a seemingly pheremonal level of sexual attraction.

Looking back, I wonder if I was somehow testing myself, seeing how far I could go in this weekly flirtation without taking the next step. I once read that Mahatma Gandhi, as a way of purifying his spirit and strengthening his will, used to lie in a bed with nubile, naked girls and force himself not to touch them, to resist temptation. Well, I certainly wasn't willing to put myself through the Gandhi test. But I think those after-sundown sessions with Jenny did amount to a sort of deliberate contest I arranged between the spiritual, that is to say, my conscience, and the physical, that is to say, my dick. For several weeks, I was as close to Gandhi as I'll ever get.

*　　*　　*

"Jen was just one of the nicest people I ever met," Brittney Applefield said, feedback distorting her chirpy voice as she stood on her tippytoes, speaking into the stand-up microphone at the candlelight vigil. "I don't know how else to say it. She was just incredibly nice."

The blown-up black-and-white photo on the banner behind Brittney was from Jenny's International School yearbook. As always, it was the look in Jenny's eyes that was most unsettling. There was a discomfitting frankness about her photo: no smile, no studious seriousness, no hopeful gaze into the future. Just that bold, stripping-down appraisal, that shamelessly inquisitive stare. Just beside the rectangular photo was a slogan in bold black block letters against the white canvas background: STOP THE VIOLENCE!

"Jen really wanted to be a writer," Brittney said. "Had she lived I think she would have followed that dream."

Brittney paused. The bulk of the audience finally took its cue and began applauding. Brittney flashed her cartoon rodent smile and left the stage. Sunshine Radisson walked up to the mike wearing no coat, only a gray sleeveless T-shirt, with black jeans, and black leather boots. A layer of stubble seemed to be growing on her pale, shaved head. Sunshine had been a grim, hectoring presence at just about every campus rally this year. "It's time to stand up, people!" she shouted. "It's time to speak out against the abuse of women on this campus!"

The crowd roared. I don't know what Jenny's relationship with Brittney Applefield was like. Maybe Brittney knew her better than I ever could have. My guess was that Jennifer had answered Brittney's advertisement for an apartment share and they had a polite, passing-in-the-hallway-on-the-way-to-the-toilet-or-out-the-door acquaintance. I don't know if Jenny knew Sunshine Radisson *at all*. I do know that she was aloof about all campus causes. I was sure Jenny never saw herself as a victim. But that is exactly what she wound up becoming. Did that make me a victimizer?

*   *   *

"Have you ever read this? I got it from the library. Nobody had checked it out in fourteen years!" Jenny, sitting on the couch in my office on a Wednesday evening in late September, pulled the slim, well-thumbed book from her black knapsack, held it up for me to see. "This guy used to be brilliant!"

There was young Reggie Brogus, pointing his pistol in my face, the title in jagged letters above his head: *LIVE BLACK OR DIE!*

"An artifact of a forgotten age," I said.

"It's meant to be a polemic," Jenny said excitedly, "but it's more like an improvisational monologue. It's really a precursor of rap, only it doesn't rhyme."

"You may have noticed Reggie's changed his tune of late."

"Of course—I saw you at that lecture of his. But do you know him, personally?"

"We just had lunch yesterday."

"Really? Do you think maybe you could arrange a meeting between the three of us?"

I shifted uncomfortably in my chair. "Why don't you just go to his office hours?"

"I tried. There's a waiting list a mile long."

"Damn. Reggie."

"This whole Blackness thing. You know, for someone like me, this is all very fascinating."

Race had come up in conversation before. At one of our earlier meetings, Jenny had contended that the U.S. capital was more racially polarized than Johannesburg: "Washington is something like eighty percent black. Yet, almost all the white people live in one quadrant of D.C.—the most prosperous one—and almost all the black people live in the three other sections. Even Johburg is more integrated than that!"

She was baffled by what she called the "social apartheid" on the

Arden campus. "Yet, everybody seems happy with it. The black kids regard the white kids with total disdain. The white kids imitate the black kids constantly, their clothes, their expressions of speech—yet they are terrified of them. The fashion thing is very funny. You know, somehow a black man with a shaved head is very attractive while a white man with a shaved head always looks like a convict who murdered his entire family with an ax."

Jenny had occasionally broken the cafeteria seating taboo, joining a group of four black students who regularly ate together. I knew two of the girls: Euphrasia and Tamika. I had had them both in journalism classes and they were excellent students: bright, energetic, always engaged. I gave each of them an A. They and the two other members of their crew, Yolanda and Shereena, did not exactly shun Jenny. They accepted her at their table, Jenny believed, because she, unlike white American kids, was obviously not afraid of them. But they also let her know, through the myriad cruel and subtle ways cliques have, that she would never be part of their circle. I told Jenny she shouldn't be surprised or hurt by such exclusionary tactics. Those four girls were linked by experiences in this country that Jenny could never know.

"But, you, Professor Robinette, you are not a separatist, are you?"

"No. I'm a realist. And I just recognize the American reality."

"This Brogus fellow," Pirate Jenny said, looking at Reggie's first book, turning it over in her hand, seeming to examine it as if it were indeed a rare specimen, a lunar fossil, "I should like to meet with him, to discuss his ideas."

"I can tell you right now, he would disown any idea he espoused in that book."

"You won't arrange a meeting, then?"

"Let me think about it. So what are you writing?"

"A work of reportage: Life in the Black Ghetto."

"Which black ghetto?"

"Impediment, Ohio. Do you know that town? Just an hour from here. I have been there twice on research."

"By yourself?"

"No, I have a guide. He is from there. The first time we went, he told me he would show me pimps and *ho's*. I thought he was speaking of gardening tools. I expected to see all these gangstas carrying hoes, you know, like they were some new type of weapon. But I interviewed some pimps and some *whores*. The second time, I went to a crackhouse!"

"Are you serious?"

"Quite."

"Your guide took you there?"

"Yes."

"And who is this guide of yours?"

"T-Bird Williams."

"T-Bird!"

"Do you know him?"

"Yeah, I do." And then, before I could stop myself, before I could conceal my feelings, I blurted out: "Are you seeing him?"

Jenny stared right through me. She took a drag on her clove cigarette. Exhaled. *"Seeing?"*

"You know what I mean."

"I've *seen* him several times." Jenny looked me up and down. I felt exposed. "Are you jealous?"

"No," I said curtly. I looked at my watch. "Our half hour's almost up." Ordinarily, we spent at least thirty minutes more than our university-designated minimum time together in my office. "Do you mind if we cut it short a bit early this week? One of my little girls has the chicken pox. I need to get back to my family."

"All right, professor." Pirate Jenny shot me her ultralascivious, sex-ray look, a bad yet effective imitation of Lauren Bacall in *To Have and Have Not.* "I won't tell anybody."

"Tell anybody what?"

Jenny packed up her knapsack and, without another word, left.

*   *   *

Even though, the following Wednesday, both my daughters were ill with the blistery virus, and Penelope had canceled important business appointments to be home with the twins all day, I still went to the white clapboard English Department headquarters for my weekly rendezvous with Pirate Jenny. By 7:10, she had still not shown up. The telephone rang. It was Jenny calling, wanting to know if I'd mind coming by her place for our meeting tonight. She was expecting an important phone call from her father, who was visiting South Africa, and didn't want to miss it. I suggested we skip tonight's meeting.

"If that's what you really want," Jenny said reasonably. "But my flat-mate is away tonight. I have the apartment all to myself. We'd be able to meet in perfect privacy."

"What's the address?" I asked.

Driving to Pirate Jenny's house in the blue Volvo, I veered between denial (she doesn't want to have sex with me; this is just a harmless mentor's housecall.) and fear (what if, given that this girl obviously wants to have sex with me, I can't get it up, like in that humiliating encounter with Jasmine two and a half years ago?).

Jenny was holding a candle when she opened the door. She wore only a black silk Chinese robe. "I seem to have blown a fuse. You wouldn't know how to fix it, would you?"

"No idea."

"Let's go to my room. There's something I want to show you."

I followed her down the corridor, felt the slope of the hardwood floor beneath the soles of my Rockports. There was a fragrant steam in the air, as if Jenny had just taken an herbal bath. We entered her candlelit bedroom. The second she closed the door, we were all over each other, the sexual tension of the past several weeks bursting in a twirling, tumbling, clothes-tugging fury. In seconds, we were both naked on the bare futon on the warped floor. The sex was like Hobbes's description of the seaman's life: nasty, brutish, and short. Also sweaty, grunty, and fast. Exuberant, exultant, almost out of control. I would never be so cocky as to claim to *know*, but my guess is that her orgasm was as explosive as mine. Afterward, we collapsed on the thin Oriental mattress.

We didn't say much. Jenny offered me a swig from a plastic bottle of designer water. She lit up a clove cigarette. We cuddled. I don't know what she was thinking about. But I can tell you what *I* was thinking about: my alibi. There was no way I could return to my home later than expected, smelling like pussy. Penelope wouldn't catch the telltale scent when I walked in the door, but she certainly would when we got into the bed together. Unless I did something about it. I decided that after I left Jenny's place, I would go to the campus gym, put in ten minutes on the Stairmaster, then take a shower before I returned home. That way I would have a perfect excuse for my tardiness, one Penelope could not argue with since she thought I could use some exercise anyway what with my laughable budding potbelly. And there would be no vaginal aroma to give me away. That's what I was thinking about staring at Pirate Jenny's peeling ceiling as she finished her clove cigarette. Then we fucked again. Maybe just to see if the second time would be as volcanic as the first. It was. Soon after we collapsed again, I said I had to go.

Fully clothed, standing at her door, I gave Jenny a sloppy, sensuous kiss good-bye. I wondered if she felt this was the start of something. I had already decided it was the end of something. We had fed the beast, satisfied the curiosity. Now would come the difficult part. Whether Jenny knew it or not, it was time to move on. Somehow or another, I was going to have to extricate myself from this situation. Call me a shit if you like. All I can say in my defense is that I am nothing but a man.

Stepping out onto the sidewalk in front of Jenny's building, I saw the shiny brown team jacket across the street. It took a moment for me to focus my gaze on the young man wearing it, his back against a lamppost, arms folded across his chest, red baseball cap turned backward atop his head, eyes glaring at me. T-Bird watched me as I unlocked the door and got into my car. As I pulled out of the parking spot, I wondered if he would confront Jenny, question her on what I had been doing in her apartment, sniff the still-moist futon, slap her around a bit. Maybe come looking for me with his 9-mm semiautomatic loaded, trigger finger itchin'.

I parked on the walkway in front of the gym. As I stepped out of the Volvo, my muscles were tensed. I was ready for some kind of an ambush. But there was no sign of T-Bird. I went into the gym, opened my locker, changed into my Cornell Intramural Track & Field T-shirt and shorts, my New Balance running shoes, and put in my ten minutes on the moving staircase, just enough time to work up a stinky sweat. As I showered and dressed, I braced myself for a confrontation with T-Bird. No, I figured, he wouldn't just shoot me right off the bat. Maybe there would be some subtler means of intimidation first. I would just have to talk to him, man to man. Explain that I had no interest in stealing his woman. I had my wife and family to think about. Jenny was nothing to me. Less than a ho. Well, maybe I wouldn't say *that*. But T-Bird was nowhere to be seen as I left the gym. I revved up the Volvo, headed home, freshly scrubbed, confident that my wife, busy tending our ailing daughters, would have no idea what I had been up to this evening.

I spotted the shiny brown jacket again as I pulled into my driveway. T-Bird stood directly across the street from my house, leaning against the hood of a Nissan Z. Standing in my driveway, looking right at him, I considered crossing the street and giving him the monologue I had rehearsed in my head. But I decided against it. Ignoring T-Bird, I went into my home, locked the door, drew the curtains. I don't know how long T-Bird Williams stood out there on the street, but he had gotten his message across: he knew where I lived.

*　*　*

Sunshine Radisson had become the de facto emcee of the candlelight vigil, introducing one female student after another who told her personal story of being date raped. Perhaps that was, more or less, what had happened to Jenny. Maybe sex with T-Bird had gotten just a little bit too rough. Still, I wondered what this confessional parade had to do with the painful human specificity of Jennifer Esther Wolfshiem. I doubt anybody else did. They had turned Jenny's horrific tragedy into a story about *themselves*. But then again, in my own way, so had I.

Once the last student victim had been applauded for sharing her experience, Sunshine led the crowd in the song, the song I had sung with my parents on marches when I was a little boy, the song that, whatever its origins, had come to define a heroic moment in the history of *our* people. And I wondered what it could possibly mean to all these pink-skinned kids with their flickering candles. Had it taken on a special contemporary significance for them in February 1992? Or did they think this was just the song you were supposed to sing at a demonstration, no matter what the cause? The only black person in the crowd, I moved my lips faintly but I could not full-heartedly join Sunshine Radisson and her thousand-strong choir as they sang "We Shall Overcome."

*　　*　　*

I would like to tell you that I was tortured by guilt in the days after I had sex with Pirate Jenny, that I despised myself for my craven and ugly act of adultery. But that was not the case. The isolation I would feel from Pen and the twins would happen gradually, subtly, incrementally. The weekend after my tryst with Jenny, I felt no awkwardness whatsoever with my wife and children. My main concern was actually T-Bird and whether he was now stalking me. But I hadn't seen him since he lurked outside my house Wednesday night. I didn't expect to hear from Jenny until our usual office hours, the following Wednesday. At which time, I planned to give a polite little speech explaining why we could no longer see each other. I was constantly revising my remarks and rationalizations in my head that weekend. And all the while, I nursed a perverse sense of self-satisfaction. Yes, indeed. For just that one evening, I had managed to cheat on my wife. No Mr. Floppy this time! I'd finished what I'd started. So there was no need to test my machismo any further. I certainly didn't want any problems with T-Bird. So I would kindly, maturely, break things off with Pirate Jenny.

Or would I? We'd gotten away with an illicit fuck this time. Why wouldn't it work again? Maybe T-Bird, discouraged by my obvious superiority to him, had already dropped out of Jenny's life. So why not continue the illicit fucking? Surely, Pirate Jenny was game!

That first weekend of October 1991, I decided that, as far as Jenny was concerned, I would keep my options open. But then, late Sunday night, Penelope turned on the radio.

*　　*　　*

Clarence Thomas was Reggie Brogus's kind of guy. A once-liberal black conservative. Young: forty-two. Well educated: Yale Law School. Tested: as chairman of the Equal Employment Opportunity Commission in the

Reagan administration. In July 1991, President George Bush nominated Clarence Thomas to succeed Thurgood Marshall, who was retiring after serving twenty-four years as the first black U.S. Supreme Court justice. Marshall was a giant of historic proportions, the man who had spear-headed the postwar civil rights movement when, in 1954, as a lawyer for the plaintiff, he argued and won the *Brown vs. Board of Education* school desegregation case before the Supreme Court—the body on which he would someday serve with distinction—by a vote of 9–0. My wife and I were among the majority of African Americans who were disgusted that a relatively inexperienced, right-wing black man who opposed affir-mative action, welfare, abortion rights, and much of the entire liberal agenda of the past generation would be nominated to take the place of a champion of the left like Thurgood Marshall. Reginald T. Brogus, on the other hand, called Clarence Thomas a New Abolitionist.

After hearings before the Senate Judiciary Committee, Thomas seemed well on his way to winning confirmation as the second black Supreme Court justice. But on the night of Sunday, October 6, 1991, the name Anita Hill was broadcast on the American airwaves. Hill was a former colleague of Thomas's at the EEOC and she had just publicly accused him of sexual harassment in the workplace.

"BUST-*ED!*" Penelope screamed joyously.

The twins were already in bed. Pen had been sitting cross-legged at the coffee table, looking over her notes for a diversity workshop she would be conducting the next morning. I was stretched out on the couch reading a terrific Don DeLillo novel. Pen had just turned on the radio, which was always tuned to National Public Radio, when the bulletin about the allegations came on. Thomas's confirmation was suddenly in jeopardy. Anita Hill would have to appear before the Senate Judiciary Committee to detail her charges. Now my wife was on her feet, dancing a merry little jig at Thomas's bad news. I had to tell her to calm down, lest she wake the girls. Like Penelope, I hated Clarence Thomas with every fiber of my being. But I wanted to see him defeated, rejected by the Senate for a seat on the Supreme Court, because of his abhorrent political and social views—not because he may have made a clumsy pass at a woman in the office. If that was what had happened.

I was sitting up on the couch now and Pen was crouched beside one of the stereo speakers, listening to the NPR report. "They still haven't said what Anita Hill *is*," Pen said. "What is she?"

The news bulletin ended and the station returned to the jazz program. "Unless we missed it," I said, "they didn't mention her race."

Penelope, still crouching by the speaker, seemed lost in contemplation. Finally, Pen said, "If she's black, Uncle Thomas has a chance. If she's white . . . he *daid*."

There was no longer any doubt as to what I had to do about Pirate Jenny.

*   *   *

"You are afraid," she said. "I can feel it."

"Yes," I said. "You can say I'm afraid of hurting my wife and family."

"Don't be so puritanical. So bloody American. I'm not talking about *marrying* you! I just want to be intimate. In the most enjoyable way. Why can't you think of it as purely recreational? Nobody gets—how do you say?—*bent out of shape* about this in Europe."

"We're in Ohio, Jenny."

My Wednesday night let's-call-the-whole-thing-off speech was not going as smoothly as I'd planned. Jenny seemed to actually like me. I liked her, too. But still.

"If I was black, you wouldn't be so scared, I betcha." She fixed me in her asymmetrical eyelock. I felt like I was melting under the green laser beams. "You're just like T-Bird. He wants to fuck me, but he is afraid to be seen with me in public, in broad daylight."

"Actually, it's the opposite with me, Jenny. I don't mind being seen with you in public. So long as we are exclusively teacher and student. I just don't want to fuck you. For all the reasons I've just explained."

"Coward." Tears glistened in her eyes.

"And I don't think we should continue in this advisorship program."

"I would never *report* you, you know. I'm not gonna *report* you."

"I don't know what you're talking about."

"Can't you please talk to me like a human being?" She seemed on the brink of an emotional outburst. I didn't know what to say.

I remained silent.

Jenny got up and walked out of the room. She left my office door hanging open. I thought I'd never see her again.

*   *   *

"It has been said that children should bury their parents. . . . Parents should not bury their children. . . . And so I speak to you in a most terrible state of emotion."

After the final refrain of "We Shall Overcome," Sunshine Radisson said she would close the evening with a recording of an answering machine message that "Jen Wolfson's" father had left on her—Sunshine's—answering machine that afternoon. The voice was startlingly old-sounding, weary and bone-dry. The man seemed, at times, to be groping for words in English.

"Esther and I . . . lost . . . her mother . . . only . . . not too recently. . . . And it was, as you might imagine . . . a very sad thing."

The sound of the man swallowing reverberated in the cold night air. Maybe he had paused to take a sip of water. Or something. No one in the crowd moved. All the banalimentality of the candlelight vigil had been demolished by the excruciating voice of this old man.

"And now . . . for me . . . to lose . . ."

We listened, entranced, stomachs knotted, to the stretches of staticky white noise echoing on the tape in the gaping pauses between the words. Maybe, for the first time, I truly, marrow-deeply, recognized Pirate Jenny as somebody's child.

"*Meine . . . liebste . . . Esther . . .*"

The old man's voice broke off. There was a click. And then, an echoing dial tone. Tears were streaming down my face. Whoever it was had killed Jenny, I felt I could kill the killer myself.

CHAPTER 9

"BITCH SHOULDA KEPT HER MOUTH shut!" Reggie Brogus said, slurring the words as his own mouth, at the moment, was filled with beef. "I'll tell you what the *real* deal was: back in the eighties, sistuh wanted bruthuh all for herself. She had designs on him, but he wasn't studyin' *her*. And when he went and married the fat white bitch instead of nice little black Anita, nice little black Anita couldn't handle it. She waited to get her revenge. If she couldn't have the alpha black male for herself, she would destroy him publicly. Don't you see? This was attempted payback for his rejection of her! But the forces of good—as they have a way of doing in America—triumphed over evil!"

Brogus was eating a steak the size of my foot and offering his simultaneous commentary on the Clarence Thomas–Anita Hill clash. It was mid-October 1991 and Thomas had just been confirmed for his seat on the Supreme Court by the slimmest Senate majority since the Civil War. A couple of days after my breakup talk with Pirate Jenny, Penelope and I joined a huge chunk of the American populace watching Anita Hill's testimony before the fourteen white men who comprised the Senate Judiciary Committee. We watched with a lurid fascination as Hill told of the lewd comments Thomas made to her back when they worked in the same office: his reveries about the porn star Long Dong Silver, his bizarre sighting of pubic hairs on his can of Coke. As Hill told her story, Pen kept talking to the television, egging her on: "All right, girlfriend, now give us the real dirt. What did he *do* to you?"

But Anita Hill had no more serious charges to make.

"He never even touched the bitch!" Brogus cried, a sirloin particle flying from his mouth. "He made a few jokes! Big fucking deal!"

We were sitting in a booth in The Meat Locker, a dark, brick-wall-and-wood-beams highway steakhouse a few miles from the Arden campus. Lunch here with Reggie Brogus—this was my third in four weeks—was beginning to feel like a ritual.

"Well," I said, pausing between bites of my jumbo charburger, "Thomas *was* the head of the EEOC. He was supposed to be enforcing workplace sexual harassment codes, not breaking them."

"This is war," Brogus said, ignoring my comment. "This is what the book I'm writing—*The New Abolition*—is all about: the ideological battleground. Hearts and minds. The war of ideas. The obsolete American left tried to defeat Clarence Thomas and failed! Folks can scoff at Clarence Thomas. They can scorn his company, sully his name, spit in his face. But my boy is gonna be sittin' on the YOU-nited States Supreme Court until the day he dies! Ain't gonna be but one Negro sittin' in that room tellin' them eight white folks, the people who decide the Law of this Land, what to think about black folks and that one Negro is gonna be Clarence Thomas—God willing, for a long time to come!"

Reginald T. Brogus had sought me out, dropping unannounced by my office one September afternoon, saying we had mutual acquaintances in New York (but unable to remember their names), remarking that Dean Jerry Shamberg had spoken admiringly of me and inviting me to lunch. Climbing into Brogus's orange BMW that breezy afternoon, I hoped that no other black professors—most of all, Kwanzi Authentica Parker—spotted me with this pariah of the African American faculty. I was glad he was taking us to a restaurant away from campus, where there would be less chance of our being seen together. I would never have been bold enough to break the unofficial ostracism and propose lunch to Brogus. But I was far too beguiled by the antihero of my youth to have said no when it was Brogus doing the inviting.

"I can talk to *you*," Brogus said after he'd known me for about fifteen minutes. "I can see you're a highly intelligent young man. Cats like you make me feel good about the future of the race."

Even though I regarded the contemporary Reggie Brogus as a right-wing clown, I couldn't help but feel a certain grudging esteem for him. Because he had lived so much more intensely than I ever would. He was a man of extremes. Someone who had *taken.* Someone who had imposed himself. In my life as a hack I had encountered a handful of famous people like Reggie, irradiated by their own sense of destiny, so convinced of their unique significance that—even if you were unconvinced—you had to be impressed by the monumentality of their conviction. During our lunches, I always had to resist the urge to interview Reggie, to pummel him with questions. Better, I felt, just to let him talk.

"You see, Clarence is onto something that the rest of us Negroes need to learn: that there ain't gonna be but a few of us at any one time in any of the rarefied environments where we need to be. Where we need the right kind of *minds* to be!"

Reggie took a long thirsty swig from his frosted mug of beer. He had tucked a red-and-white checked napkin under his collar, to keep his shirt and tie and suspenders dribble-free. He set down the mug, then dabbed his lips with the checkerboard bib. He speared another cube of bloody, oozing beef with his fork, stuffed it in his mouth, began talking again as he chewed.

"Imagine if you were up for tenure and some crazy bitch wanted to stop you from gettin' it 'cause you had told her some dirty jokes. A grown-up black woman. Some bitch you never even fucked! Never even *tried* to fuck!"

I remembered Jenny's words the last time I'd seen her, the almost scornful tone, mocking my not-so-secret fear: "I'm not gonna *report* you."

"And all she had to do was keep her mouth shut. Shit, Clarence mighta felt grateful to her and helped her gain passage into some of them oak-paneled rooms he gets to hang out in, those enclaves where the real power is. Instead Anita Shrill tried to destroy Clarence's career diggin' up old stories to scare the white folks. All outta petty feminine jealousy! But look who's sittin' up in the associate justice's chambers and whose career—ANITA'S— is totally fucked up! It's like Moms used to say: If you stir up old shit, it'll stink!"

Reginald T. Brogus liked quoting his Moms. She had been a postal clerk—"One of the few truly necessary government jobs," as Reggie liked to say—in Slackerton, Michigan. Reggie's father—"a common hoodlum" in his son's words—was killed in a knife fight three weeks before

Reggie was born in November 1942. Bethel Brogus was a tough, strap-swinging single mother, the only person in the world Reggie seemed truly to love. She was retired now, living somewhere down South, "chewin' tobacco and watchin' Oprah—that's my Moms," Reggie said fondly.

Brogus talked a lot about his childhood, depicting it in the nostalgic glow of a ghetto Norman Rockwell. "Yeah, we lived on the hardscrabble side of the black side of town, but we were never *po*. We were working class. You dig? We *worked*. And all the black folks I grew up around *worked!* In the post office, on the assembly line, on the back of a garbage truck. Folks worked, man. There was honor in that! Human dignity! Now, you know I don't mean to put down your family, Clay, but your parents were part of the professional class, not the working class. They had *professions*. All my Moms ever had was *work!*"

Stickball, Fourth of July barbecues, humble Christmas presents: Brogus never tired of recounting his boyhood memories. And he enjoyed talking about the times in which we lived and the sunshiny future of global markets and technological marvels. He was nearing fifty, he said: "Time for a man to take stock." Yet Brogus seemed reluctant to talk of the one period of his life I really wanted to know about. How did the fun-loving but well-behaved rustybutt Slackerton boy become the Mau-Mauing militant, then metamorphose into the patriotic scoundrel munching his meat across the table from me? What happened between stickball and golf balls? How had he made the transition from tossing Molotov cocktails at the New York Stock Exchange in 1969 to sipping gin and tonics at the Century Club in 1991? Yes, he had written about his ideological conversion in his second book, *An American Salvation*, but the portions of that collection of essays I had managed to read before hurling it across the room had seemed peculiarly impersonal. If *LIVE BLACK OR DIE!* was indeed a nihilistic proto-rap, then *An American Salvation* was its rhetorical rebuttal, a passionate sermon promoting conservative values. What was missing was any description of the emotional process that must have been a part of his political transfiguration. I wondered if Brogus was as much of a mystery to himself as he was to me.

Every once in a while, Brogus would make a tantalizing reference to his revolutionary past. "Look, I said, '*Oigame, Fidel!* You're wasting these beautiful stretches of beach! You should bring back the casinos! Havana could be the Vegas of the Caribbean. But *you* stay in charge. Beat those imperialist scumbags at their own game! You could be the first capitalist/communist dictator!' This was back in '75. But did he listen to me? Fuck no. He just laughed and sucked on his damn cigar."

For the most part, though, the names Brogus dropped were those of TV and radio talk-show hosts he knew, authors and columnists, politicians and campaign consultants, current and former diplomats, magazine and book industry bigwigs, think tank heads: the New York–Washington media circle jerk. Reggie was an insider and he wanted me to know it.

"I once believed, like a lot of deluded people back in the day, that power flowed from the barrel of a gun. But now I know it emanates from the lens of a television camera. With one appearance on the *Huck Blossom Show*, I reach more people than I ever did waving my piece and screaming 'Kill Whitey!'"

At the beginning of the twentieth century, the great African American intellectual W. E. B. Du Bois believed that a Talented Tenth of blacks would serve as leaders, social pioneers, and role models for the rest of the race. Near the end of the century, Reginald T. Brogus believed that Du Bois's figure was way overblown.

"It's more like the Talented *Ten!*" he proclaimed. "When you're talkin' real, actual power, not sports and entertainment power—I'm talkin' not *Michael* Jordan power but *Vernon* Jordan power, not Michael Jackson but Colin Powell power—there ain't gonna be but ten Negroes at any given time who really possess it. Clarence Thomas just joined that elite."

Reggie harpooned the last gristly bit of steak fat on his plate, popped it in his mouth, washed it down with the dregs of his beer. Most of the lunchtime crowd in The Meat Locker had gone. Reggie stared at me with his bullfrog eyes, silently. I was just beginning to feel unnerved when he said, "Do you think you could be one of the Ten?"

"Me? Is that a joke?"

"Hey, I know you fucked up as a journalist. But now you can repackage yourself as an academic! Why the hell you think I'm spending a year in fucking Ohio? That visiting professor credential just adds to my cachet as an intellectual. There's no telling how far a media-savvy black academic could go in the nineties. And you: clean-cut, well-spoken. White folks love you, Clay. You know how to talk to 'em. How to make 'em feel comfortable. A lotta white folks are still scared of me 'cause of all my crazy radical baggage. I still have to overcome that. They don't know that even then, back in the sixties and seventies, I was serving the country I love."

Reggie continued to stare at me, unblinking. I didn't know what he meant by that last statement.

"But, you, Clay. You're too young to have that kind of baggage. You should join the Afram program. Hell, man, you could even become head of the department. Instead of that walking, talking anachronism Kwanzi! Then use your title to get back in print, to get that pretty face of yours on TV. Lemme introduce you to some people next time you're in New York. I'll hook you up, brother man. I am totally serious about this. I think you have the potential to be one of the Ten."

I laughed. "What if I don't want to be?"

"Say what?"

Reggie cocked his head and squinted at me. I seemed to have offended him. I struggled to find the precise words for what I wanted to say.

"I mean, I've always thought that black writers, black thinkers, if you will, ought to, you know, challenge the establishment."

"Challenge the establishment?" Brogus repeated incredulously. "Why the fuck would you wanna *challenge* the establishment when you can *be* the establishment? Damn it, Clay, I thought you had some sense! Don't tell me you're just another bourgeois hypocrite! I know you fancy yourself a liberal but you don't also have to be a fool! Just what exactly do *you* do to challenge the establishment, Mr. Suburban Homeowner?"

Now I felt embarrassed. "Not much, I guess."

"Hmmph! Not a goddamned thing is more like it!"

Reggie was attacking me but somehow I didn't mind. I sensed a fraternal affection in his tirade. And he was right: I had never fought for or against anything in my life. I'd never stuck my neck out for any cause. I couldn't even say I was a particularly good citizen. I did no volunteer community service, gave to few charities. I voted regularly, always for Democrats. I obeyed the law. I tried to look out for my wife and kids. That was about it. Yet Reggie Brogus seemed to sense something special in me. Maybe he was right. Maybe I *did* have the potential of a Talented Tenner. Maybe, I thought, I should keep an open mind about Reggie Brogus. After all, he seemed to be exceptionally well connected. And he networked across the board, not just with right-wingers. Would it be such a bad thing for him to introduce me to some of his friends? Maybe Penelope and I should have him over to dinner?

"You've got to make the best of the gifts the Good Lord gave you, Clay." Reggie's tone now was less scolding, almost tender. "You owe it to yourself. You owe it to your people. To all Americans. There's a lot to be said for the power of ideas. As the spokesman for the right ideas, you could attain unimaginable levels of personal power." Reggie grinned. "And the pussy that comes with power." Reggie licked his lips, then dabbed them with the stained and greasy checkerboard bib. "You would not *believe* how much pussy I've had in the seven years since I published *Salvation* and became a modern media figure. Man, I had more white girls throw themselves at me in the *week* after my first appearance on *Larry King Live* than I did even during the *en*-tire Summer of Love back in '67! Celebri-*tee*. It's the ultimate aphrodisiac. I tell you, man, I gotta credit the old-timesy feminists for one thing: almost every American woman today goes down! You know, I'm old enough to remember the day when you used to have to *beg* a bitch to suck your dick. And sistuhs were the worst!" Reggie suddenly put on a high-pitched, indignant voice. "'Nigga, is you crazy? I ain't puttin' that thing in my mouth!'" Reggie returned to his normal baritone. "But today, they all go down. I'll tell you, though, there's still one big difference between black and white girls. And I bet you can tell me what it is."

Reggie paused. I laughed and shrugged. "I've been married a long time," I said. "You'll have to educate me."

Brogus leaned across the table, took a quick glance around the nearly empty restaurant—as if he were wary of eavesdroppers—then focused his bugged-out eyes on me and said: "White girls swallow."

*   *   *

I recognized her immediately. She had a huge, kinky Afro and deeply tanned complexion. She wore a black turtleneck, black jeans and boots, and a camouflage jacket. A machine gun hung from a strap around her neck and a gold ring glittered in her left nostril. Her skewed green eyes were laughing. "Hi, Jenny," I said.

She made a disappointed face. "How did you guess it was me?"

"Who else would be coming by my office at 7:30 on a Wednesday night?"

It was Halloween Eve. Three weeks had passed since I had seen Pirate Jenny. I had stayed away from my office the previous two Wednesday nights, worried that she might show up and try to start something. I let my wife believe, however, that I was holding my regular adviser's conference those two weeks and used the period of 6:45 to 8:15 as a window of private time, driving out to The Meat Locker, taking a seat at the bar and reading a book as I downed a beer or three. But at 7:00 p.m. on Wednesday, October 30, 1991, I entered my office in the English Department's white clapboard house, sat down at my desk and waited. I told myself that I would work on my screenplay. Or maybe catch up on grading papers. But all I did was wait. Not waiting *for* Jenny, really, but waiting to see if she would or would not come. Her absence would reveal as much as her presence. Her absence would mean that she had realized—as *I* had and hoped *she* had—that we could not continue sexual relations. What her presence would mean was more difficult to know. But I had to find out. Placing myself in my office at that hour on that night was an act of calculated recklessness. I had already failed my moral midget's version of the Gandhi test. And I knew—at least, I truly thought—that I did not want to get more sexually involved with Jenny, however intense the attraction between us might still be. Maybe I just missed her, missed talking to her. Missed the attention, the ego boost. So I sat in my office for a half hour, waiting. I thought it was as likely as not that Pirate Jenny would walk in the door. What I did not expect was that she would appear in the guise of a black militant.

Jenny thrust a fist into the air. "Power to the people!"

"I hope you're not wearing shoe polish on your face," I said. "I've never been one for minstrel shows."

Jenny lowered her arm in abrupt dejection. "Oh, you're no fun at all!" She closed my office door, plopped down on the couch. "I just spent a week in Johannesburg with my father, who's over there either trying to speed up the dismantling of apartheid or slow it down, I can't always be sure which, and I happen to tan exceptionally well." She tossed her head, setting the Afro wig wiggling. "I thought you'd like me like this."

"I don't know. It's a bit like the white guys with the shaved heads. Or white girls with dreadlocks."

"Yes, but I am actually *passing* tonight!" Jenny giggled. "Do you know three black students—total strangers—waved and said hello to me in the last half hour? *That's* never happened before!"

"Acceptance at last."

"I thought maybe *you* would accept me now."

"Why?"

Pirate Jenny laid down her fake gun, took off her camouflage jacket, pulled a pack of clove cigarettes from one of the pockets. I handed her the small black plastic ashtray I had bought after our first meeting. "You know, I was thinking of how America is in many ways the exact opposite of Germany. In Germany everything is forbidden—except that which is permitted. In America everything is permitted—except that which is forbidden. So many unwritten codes in this country. And it is the unwritten codes that are the most severe."

"I don't know if I follow you."

"Perhaps you, Professor Robinette, are permitted to have affairs with black students but are forbidden from having affairs with white students."

I watched Pirate Jenny as she lit her cigarette, took a long drag, exhaled theatrically. I found her, in her Halloween costume, to be, in equal measure, ridiculous and erotic.

"I think you need to get to know America a little better," I said. "An affair with any student of any race is definitely *verboten.*"

"Yet interracial relationships are a special taboo. Everybody just *says* that they aren't."

"You're wrong. Look at this campus, look at the Afram program. Xavier Lumbaki is married to a white woman. A Frenchwoman, anyway."

"Yes, and he is widely, if very quietly, resented for it."

"He is?"

"Didn't you know that?" Jenny said with a needling little Where-have-you-*been?* tone in her voice.

"Well, no one resents Kwanzi Authentica Parker," I said. "And she's married to a white man. Whiter than white, even. He's English."

"Yes, but Kwanzi absolutely despises white *women.*"

"How do you know all this?"

"How do you *not* know it?"

Now Jenny was pissing me off. "Enjoy your Halloween," I said.

Pirate Jenny stubbed out her cigarette in the ashtray. She slowly rose and walked around to my side of the desk. I remained in my seat. She stood six inches in front of me, her black-sweatered breasts at my eye level. "Trick or treat," she said.

"Trick."

Pirate Jenny dropped to her knees.

All I really heard was my own moaning echoing in my ears. The sound of the front door of the house opening and closing, the heavy footsteps on the thin carpeting in the corridor outside my office: they were barely audible beneath my accelerated gasping. I was lost in sensation, pants around my ankles, body jerking, swimming in her mouth, my hands full of kinky wig, my eyes wide open, staring at the closed door of my office. Had one of my colleagues in the English Department come by to do a little after-hours paper grading or screenwriting or to retrieve a forgotten briefcase? My wave was crashing just as the unmistakable baritone sounded in the corridor.

"Yo, Clay!"

My office door swung open and there stood Reggie Brogus. I immediately shut my eyes.

"Oh, shit!" I heard Reggie say. "Sorry."

The door slammed. I saw a crazy strobe effect inside my tightly shut eyelids, felt a seizure in my veins, felt my life pouring out of me, streaming down a soft canal.

*   *   *

"Just call me your Uncle Reggie!" Brogus roared joyously, bouncing one of my daughters on each of his massive, cushiony thighs, a jolly black

Santa Claus in early November. Amber and Ashley squealed with delight. Who would have guessed that Reginald T. Brogus would be such a charmer of children? But from the moment he walked in the door, Brogus had wowed the twins with his quarter-behind-the-ear-style magic tricks, funny faces, and affectionate ticklings. Less than seventy-two hours after he had barged in on Pirate Jenny going down on me, Brogus was our family's Saturday night dinner guest. And after thirty giggly minutes in their company, Reggie was telling the twins to treat him like he was my brother.

It had taken a lot of persuading, and social horse-trading, to get Penelope to allow Reggie Brogus into our home. She finally relented when I agreed to escort her to an upcoming business function that promised to be painfully dull *and* to invite Xavier and Aurore Lumbaki to the Brogus dinner as well. Penelope thought she might detest Brogus so much she would be unable to speak to him. She even considered hiding the twins from such a malevolent influence, maybe sending them to spend the night with Mrs. Henderson. But when the twins overheard that Mom would be making spaghetti carbonara, their favorite dish, they insisted on being included in the dinner party.

I phoned Xavier at around 6:00 Wednesday evening, an hour before I would arrive at my office to await Pirate Jenny. He said he and Aurore would love to come to dinner the following Saturday. I called Reggie, got his answering machine, left an invitation. About an hour and a half later, he blundered into my office and quickly blundered out. What did Reggie see? Me writhing in my chair, of course. But what did he see of Jenny? Probably just an Afro bobbing up and down behind my desk. When I arrived home after my session with Jenny, Pen told me Brogus had called to say he would be happy to come to dinner. He had asked to speak with me. She told him I was at my office. He said he might drop by there to say hi to me.

"Did he?" Pen asked.

I had a split second to decide whether to tell my wife the truth— or to lie.

"No," I said.

I did not hear from Brogus again until he rang the doorbell Saturday at 6:00 sharp. I had considered calling him—but what would I say? "Don't mention to my wife that you caught me getting a blow job in my office"? Make him complicit in my lie, ask him to compound it, to say he had not come by my office at all? I decided to do nothing, to wait and see how Reggie comported himself at the dinner party. Xavier and Aurore bowed out late Saturday afternoon, saying their daughter Nathalie had come down with a fever. This put Penelope in even less of a hospitable mood when Brogus showed up. The bottle of wine and bouquet of flowers our guest offered failed to defrost my wife. And Brogus's instant rapport with the twins seemed to chill Pen even more. As for his manner with me, I wondered if I was mistaken but doubted I was: Reggie Brogus showed a new and obvious respect, flashing me secret, meaningful glances, full of admiration. During dinner he told my girls what an accomplished and intelligent man their father was. He told Penelope how much he had learned from me in the past few weeks: about getting along at Arden U.; about the concerns of our generation; about the unique rewards of contemporary family life. I didn't know what the hell Reggie was referring to. But it was clear I had risen in his estimation. I felt a twinge of guilty pride.

We were just digging into the chocolate layer cake I had bought for dessert when Ashley asked, "Do you have any children, Uncle Reggie?"

"No, I haven't been blessed with any yet," Brogus said.

"Have you ever been married?" Amber wanted to know.

"Nope."

"Why not?"

Reggie was taken aback. "You're quite an inquisitive little girl, aren't you?"

Amber just stared at him.

"Well," Reggie said sheepishly, "I've traveled a lot in my life, which isn't real conducive—real good for—raising a family. And I never met the right girl. Just my bad luck. I never found a woman who could really measure up to my mother."

Looking across the dining room table, I saw Penelope roll her eyes in Gimme-a-break aggravation. Reggie had fully launched into one of his worshipful odes to Moms when Pen interrupted him in the tone of a sarcastic D.A. cross-examining a witness: "And when did you last see your *Moms?*"

Reggie continued to address the twins more than Pen or me. "I last saw Moms back in February. She came up to Washington to see me receive the Citizen of the Year Award from the Foundation for American Virtue." Brogus seemed to lose himself in the memory. "My Moms and I were the only Negroes at the awards banquet. We were seated at a table with one of the top deans at Harvard University and the editor of the *New York Times Book Review!*" Reggie paused to let us all take in the grandeur he was describing. The twins were riveted to their new "uncle." Reggie continued, in awe of himself. "Imagine! There I was, a little black boy from Slackerton, Michigan, with my old black Moms, sittin' next to people like *that!* . . . I tell ya . . ." Reggie was getting misty-eyed. "I finally felt like I really . . . belonged. Like I could say . . . I *am* somebody. A *real* somebody. And I was just so happy my Moms was there to see it."

Reggie was fighting back tears now. Ashley rose from the table, grabbed a box of Kleenex from a nearby shelf and offered it to Reggie. He smiled and pulled a tissue from the box. As Reggie removed his black-framed glasses and blew his nose, Amber stroked his shoulder consolingly. I looked at my wife across the table. She sat staring at Brogus, narrow-eyed, frozen with contempt.

After dessert, a perfunctory handshake from Penelope and whiny, reluctant farewells from the twins, Reggie stood with me in the driveway, complaining about all the trouble his brightly colored vintage BMW gave him. Then, lowering his voice, he said, "You da man, Clay."

I smiled. "Awwww . . . *you* da man, Reg."

"Uh-*uh!* You the one got it all figured out. Domestic bliss with wifey and the kiddies *and* . . ." Brogus stared at me, grinning and shaking his head. "But I was cool, though, wasn't I? At dinner tonight. I didn't blow your cover. I didn't give *nothin'* away, did I?"

"No, you didn't."

"Your secret's safe with me, brother man. . . . Just tell me one thing . . ." Brogus leaned closer to me, spoke in a whisper. "Did she swallow?"

I still did not know exactly what Brogus had seen. Did he think it was a black or a white girl sucking me off behind my desk? I played it coy, giving Brogus a sideways look and saying, "What do *you* think?"

Brogus broke into gaudy laughter. "You da MAN, Clay!"

I chuckled weakly. "'Night, Reg."

He got into his car, rolled down the window, stuck out his head. "Just remember, brother man . . . You *owe* me!"

*   *   *

It wasn't until a week or so after Halloween Eve that I began to hate myself. Naturally, I cut off all communications with Jennifer Wolfshiem after Brogus caught us in the act. I kept away from the office the following Wednesday evening. I stayed at home, telling Pen that my freshman had found another adviser, one more suited to "his" academic needs. I avoided both Jenny and Brogus, deliberately failing to answer messages they left on my voice mail. Thursday evening I went to the gym to put in some time on the Stairmaster and only when I got back home did self-loathing grab me by the balls. Penelope greeted me at the door with that fretful look she wore when she had bad news to report. "Magic Johnson has AIDS," my wife said.

Actually, the star of the Los Angeles Lakers had only been found to be HIV positive. But on November 7, 1991, that seemed like a certain death sentence. I turned on the TV and watched Magic announce his retirement from the National Basketball Association. Since the retirement a few years earlier of the greatest living American, Julius Erving—b.k.a. Dr. J—from my hometown Philadelphia '76ers, L.A.'s Earvin Johnson had been my favorite player. A five-time champion, the happiest of warriors, a magnificent fluke of nature (who had ever heard of a 6 foot 9 *point guard?*) who combined an astonishing power—those pinpoint-accurate full-court one-bounce passes—with a gasp-inspiring sleight of hand with the ball that earned him his perfect nickname, Magic was still near the top of his game. Just a few months earlier he had played in his ninth NBA finals in twelve years! Now I imagined him, in another year's time, being wheelchaired onto the floor of the fabulous L.A. Forum, a purple-and-gold Lakers cap sagging on his thin-skinned skull, the press oohing and aahing about his always-winning, now skeletal, smile. I sat on the couch, fighting back tears, watching the news reports that night. Magic hailed from the neighboring state of Michigan and the media was mourning him—though he was still the picture of health—as a native son. The obituaries were being readied. Magic was a goner. He was also the first demonstrably straight, non-drug-injecting male celebrity I knew of to come down with the virus. A black man my age. A married father.

Only then did I worry about the fact that I had not used a condom with Pirate Jenny. The notion of latex protection had occurred fleetingly to me in Jenny's bedroom, not at all when she went down on me in my office. Having spent my bachelor years in the oblivious twilight of the sexual revolution, I had, in fact, never worn a rubber in my life. But I had also, until Pirate Jenny, never betrayed my wife.

What a filthy bastard I was! Endangering the life of Penelope, the mother of our children, for some cheap teenage pussy! The next morning I went to the University Health Services office and, under the most discreet circumstances, took an AIDS test. I asked the medical examiner not to mail the results to me. I would come back to the office in person, in a week's time. I almost wept with relief when the results were negative.

Still I wondered if there was something seriously wrong with me. What perversity led me into these (self-) destructive situations, these obvious, carelessly camouflaged traps? I considered therapy. But I had heard that all the best shrinks in Arden, Ohio, were also members of the medical school faculty and I didn't want to risk bumping into my therapist while strolling across the quadrangle. So I deleted the Pirate Jenny file from my memory. It wasn't difficult. After all, she had only been peripheral to my real life. I did, however, take the time to mosey by the records office. I pulled the Wolfshiem dossier. I was pleased to see that the space following ACADEMIC ADVISER on the front of the folder bore the name of a woman I'd never heard of.

*   *   *

As you may have noticed by now, I have a knack for blotting life's most unpleasant events from my mind. Perhaps you share this trait with me. Maybe you can understand that when I picked up my office phone five or six weeks after I'd last seen Jenny, I didn't even recognize her voice. Yes, it must have been mid-December. She wanted to meet for coffee.

"In a public place," Jenny said. "That way you won't have to worry about me jumping you."

I was in denial even as we sat across from each other at the small, round fake marble table in Cafe Bellafiglia, a precious little latte and capuccino joint on University Boulevard, acting as if the meeting was not important, trying to forget it as it happened. I didn't want to be there, didn't want to be seen with her. I only agreed to this meeting to appease her. I didn't want some possibly unstable young student I'd fucked angry with me. "Hell," I thought, looking at her crooked emerald eyes under the bright lights of the coffee shop, the pale skin that had lost its Johannesburg tan, "she isn't even pretty."

I tell her I can't stay long. It's a Saturday and I need to do Christmas shopping for my children.

"Okay," she says meekly. Pirate Jenny still has that bold look in her eye, but she has changed since I last saw her. The sassy attitude is gone. She seems exhausted, emotionally wrung out. Something has happened to her. I don't know what. I don't want to know. Don't want to think that I might be the cause of her depression. After five minutes of strained small talk, Jenny blurts out, "I think about you a lot. Do you think about me?"

Now, for the first time, I really *see* Jenny, the shattered young girl, the one whose mother abandoned her in the most brutal way. I do not want to hurt her, but I know I must.

"No, Jennifer, not really," I say apologetically. "You know, with my course load and a busy family life, I've just got too many other things on my mind."

The comment does not seem to have registered with Jenny. She just smiles sadly at me. "I have a present for you," she says, her voice sounding almost drowsy. I wonder if she is medicated. Jenny takes something from out of her black knapsack, offers it to me.

Did I take the black, unlabeled disk from her hand?

"It's only a diary of the last few months. Since I arrived at Arden."

Did I pick it up after she laid it down on the table before me?

"I want you to know my secrets."

Did I put it in the pocket of my parka? In my briefcase? Was I even carrying my briefcase that day?

"Now will you read my diary?"

Pirate Jenny pulls at the cowl neck of her scarlet sweater. I see the raw, red scar on her flesh. Good God, I think, did she do this to herself? Or did someone else do it to her? Am I supposed to be titillated, worried, horrified, curious, outraged, jealous?

As it is, I just want to get the hell out of there.

Jenny puts her collar back in place. "You care about me, Clay, don't you?"

"Of course, I do, Jenny." I smile, desperate to lighten the mood. "Even if I don't *identify* with you."

Jenny smiles her sad smile back at me. "I have to go powder my nose."

I wait until I see her disappear into the women's room. I leave five bucks on the table to pay for our drinks, then walk briskly out of the coffeehouse. I will never see Pirate Jenny alive again.

*   *   *

"Brogus has been sighted in Mississippi!" Andy Chadwick hooted. The young reporter was ecstatic, grinning, a niblet of creamed corn mashed between his two front teeth. "I'm catchin' the next flight down there!"

Tuesday, February 18, 1992—11:45 p.m. Old-timers at the *Arden Oracle* said there hadn't been this sort of a buzz in the newsroom since "they shot JFK," back in '63. I had come straight here from the candlelight vigil a couple of hours earlier to put some finishing touches on my campus mood article. I was on my way out the newsroom door, a copy of tomorrow morning's *Oracle*, literally hot off the presses, tucked under my arm, when Chadwick came running up to me with the latest. He asked if I wanted to go on the manhunt with him. I told him I had classes to teach. He asked if I would consider writing another article for the *Oracle*, maybe "an in-depth profile of the Wolfshiem girl. What was she like before she was dead?"

I told Chadwick I was resuming my journalistic retirement.

"We miss you already. I loved your little Patsy DeFestina item. And, hey, Professor. That piece you wrote tonight. The part about the candle-light vigil . . ." Chadwick, still displaying his corn-studded grin, raised an index finger to his right eye. "Tears, man. Tears."

So Brogus had fled South. Maybe, I wondered as I drove home through the deserted streets, Reggie had gone to hide out with his Moms. Did anybody know Bethel Brogus's precise whereabouts?

Near the end of this bizarre day I could not stop thinking about the Patsy DeFestina Theory of Homicidal Probability and how it related to this case, to wit: (1) there was a ninety percent chance that Reginald T. Brogus, who everyone knew was the most obvious person, had killed Jennifer Esther Wolfshiem; and (2) there was a ten percent chance that Tyrell "T-Bird" Williams, who very few people knew was the second most obvious person, had committed the murder.

If Brogus had done it, he *must* have known who Jenny was, her connection to me. He lied when he told me he didn't. She must have sought him out. But she might *not* have told him that she was the woman he'd caught me with in my office, or else he wouldn't have shown me her corpse on his couch. But what if he *did* know we'd shared the same lover? Had Jennifer gone to the Afrikamerica Studies suite to meet with Brogus, maybe late Sunday evening, for one of the sort of after-hours office hours she had enjoyed with me? Did Brogus, when there was nobody else around, ravish Jenny on his muddy pleather couch? Did he like to tie her up with his suspenders? That scar on Jenny's chest, the one she showed me at Cafe Bellafiglia in December: Had *Brogus* done that to her? Had he bound her in his office again, last Sunday night, or Saturday or even Friday night, gone out of his mind and strangled her? And then had the gall to come to *me* to help him out of his predicament?

No. That didn't make any sense. As much as I hated Brogus at this moment, as much as I had breathed the fumes of hate in the air, the bur-bling, toxic mob hatred of the *Arden Oracle* newsroom, even though I had written articles that insinuated Brogus's guilt in their every line, I real-ized that Reggie killing Jenny, then coming to me, didn't make sense.

So, I thought as I pulled into the driveway of my home on safe, pleasant Maplewood Road, it had to have been T-Bird! Maybe Jen came by to see him as he diligently performed his file clerk duties over the holiday weekend. Maybe the kooky, sex-mad kids just couldn't stop from going fuck-wild in the Afrikamerica Studies suite. Maybe they did it in every office, finally making their way to Reggie's couch, T-Bird indulging himself with the suspenders hanging in Brogus's closet, getting a bit freaky on Pirate Jenny, leaving her body there for Reggie to discover a day or so later, fleeing the Mathematics building in a panic, getting out of town. It wasn't some government conspiracy that "planted" a body in Reggie's office. It was just a horny boy from the 'hood, the same one Brogus had called a "slave." I wondered if Brogus had ever run into T-Bird in the Afrikamerica Studies suite. If he had, he probably wouldn't even have recognized him.

I turned off the headlights, shut down the engine, sat alone in the shadowy stillness of the Volvo. One thing seemed certain: Jennifer was fucking Reggie Brogus or T-Bird Williams or both of them. Somehow, I didn't mind the idea of T-Bird fucking Jenny. But the notion of Reggie with his flabby paws on her filled me with disgust. What secret was it that Jenny had wanted me to know? If I had taken the time to read her diary, would I now know who had been doing her, who had killed her? What the fuck had I done with the disk? I finally decided that I must have thrown it in the trash—maybe even in a sidewalk wastebasket—the very day Jenny gave it to me.

I was still sitting in the Volvo when the black Lincoln Town Car came slowly gliding down Maplewood. As it passed through the cone of light cast by the streetlamp, I saw, through the tinted glass on the passenger side, the ghostly features of the face: the high, walnut forehead, downturned mouth, barely visible behind the dark, misty window, and the eyes (the agent was not wearing his aviator Ray-Bans at midnight): big, drooping, haunted, like the eyes of that wretched soul in the Edvard Munch painting, *The Scream*. Only after I saw the taillights of the Lincoln fade into the blackness down Maplewood did I feel brave enough to get out of the car and hurry into my house.

*   *   *

Penelope was pretending to be asleep. I knew it as soon as I stepped into our darkened bedroom. Because she was doing her fake snore. I had to smile. Pen, unconscious as she always was during the real thing, could not manage a credible imitation of her lullaby snore. I stretched out beside her on the bed, still fully clothed. My wife's snore tonight was, when compared with her authentic one, comically artificial, like something out of a Max Fleischer cartoon.

"You can't fool me, Snoozy," I whispered in Penelope's ear.

She opened her eyes. "How do you always know?" Her voice was wide awake.

"Because only *I* know your real snore."

"And what does that sound like?" Pen asked for the thousandth time.

I offered my usual catalog of grotesque honks and snarls and gurgles. As always, Pen laughed and pounded me softly with a fist. "You sound like that," I said. "Only louder." We were both laughing giddily now, at our corny, ancient joke.

"I'm sorry I was grumpy earlier," Pen said.

"I was the grumpy one."

"I just don't know how to feel. . . . But I keep thinking how terrible it must have been for this girl. And I keep thinking of her as a *girl*. Not as a contemporary of mine. Do you know this girl was nineteen? That's right between our age and the twins."

"It is?"

"They're six. We're thirty-three. That girl was thirteen years from middle childhood and fourteen years from whatever it is we're in. Early middle age?"

"Wow. I never thought of it that way."

"Did you write a good story? Why don't you get undressed and come to bed?"

"I did. I will."

I stripped, peed, brushed my teeth. Slipping into the bed I was surprised to find that my wife was, like me, naked. We cuddled, nuzzled, cooed, and squeezed. There was always such comfort in this delicious flesh, this body I knew almost as well as my own.

"Did you know Jennifer Wolfshiem?"

I didn't know exactly when but at some point earlier in the day, I had anticipated that Penelope would ask me that question and I had an answer prepared. It was a risky gambit of a reply, what journalists call a nondenial denial. For instance, whenever a public figure who has come under a cloud of suspicion says to a reporter's inquiry "I won't even dignify that with an answer," that public figure is, invariably, guilty of whatever it is he has been accused. He has offered a classic nondenial denial. He has not admitted his obvious guilt, nor has he exposed himself as an obvious liar. And he takes the risk that the reporter will not probe any further. I gave Pen my nondenial denial and hoped she wouldn't press me.

"Baby, there are eight thousand undergraduates at Arden University," I said lazily. "I can't know them all."

Instead of saying "That's not what I asked you," Pen shrugged in my arms and said, "I just thought maybe."

We snuggled some more, then Pen said, "I didn't find the disk."

My heart skipped a beat and I wondered if Pen, her body entwined with mine, felt it. "What?" I said faintly.

"Amber told me about the disk you were looking for. Black. No label. I looked in the guest room, through all my shit. I didn't find it."

"Oh. Thanks." I held her even tighter. "Are you sleepy?"

"No."

"Neither am I."

We made love with a sudden, desperate hunger, as if it were for the last time.

CHAPTER 10

2/19/92

CLAY: DO NOT SELL ME OUT! HAVE YOU FORGOTTEN WHAT I TOLD YOU
IN THE CAR? WHAT THE REAL DEAL IS! YOU MUST UNCOVER THE TRUE
STORY! DO NOT FORSAKE ME BROTHER! PLEASE!!! DO NOT SELL ME
OUT!

brogus@arden.edu

I stared, dumbstruck, at the message on my computer screen, read it
again and again as if it had been written in some secret code I had to
decipher. But the words could not be any plainer. I slowly wheeled backward in my swivel chair, away from the desk. I looked around the office,
afraid, almost as if I expected Reggie Brogus to pop out of the closet or
crawl out from under the couch. But wasn't Brogus supposed to be in
Mississippi? That's what it said on the TV this morning. So how could he
have sent me this electronic message? You have to remember, this was in
the early days of email. I rarely received any and had never even sent
one myself. There was no cheery, robotic voice in my computer bleating
"You've Got Mail." Occasionally somebody—usually Dean Jerry Shamberg—would call me and complain that I didn't check my emailbox
enough. When I did remember to check I always found it either empty or
occupied by two or three messages that had languished unread for days,
or weeks. I don't know what made me check this Wednesday morning.
But I did.

"YOU MUST UNCOVER THE TRUE STORY!"

It took a minute for me to recall that Brogus could have sent this electronic mail from anywhere, even if his address indicated Arden University. Suddenly, I remembered the laptop computer Brogus cradled against his belly as I drove him toward Arden Airfield.

"DO NOT FORSAKE ME BROTHER!"

Still, as I wheeled forward in my chair, close to the screen again, rereading the urgent, anguished words, Brogus's message felt more and more creepily like a call from the netherworld, from beyond the grave. Though Reggie was still alive, wasn't he? Last I'd heard, he was.

Damn. I had been doing a fairly good job of pretending that this was just an ordinary Wednesday morning. I woke up at nine, as I usually did on Wednesday mornings, an hour after Pen and the girls would have left the house. I showered, dressed, had a cup of coffee and watched the local news on the tiny four-inch-screened black-and-white TV that sat on the kitchen table but was only ever watched by me. Sports. Highway traffic conditions. Footage of bloodhounds, tethered to white men wearing flat-brimmed Smokey the Bear ranger hats and carrying shotguns, trawling through Mississippi swamplands in the hunt for Reggie Brogus. I watched blankly, as if the story had nothing to do with me. Weather report: bitter cold, gray skies, likelihood of a snowstorm late in the day. Driving the Honda toward campus, on my way to the English Department, I thought about the journalism class I was scheduled to teach at eleven o'clock. The Arden community had returned to normal. Not a TV crew or a police car in sight. I parked behind the white clapboard house, entered my office at 10:15 a.m. and *just happened* to check my email.

"PLEASE!!! DO NOT SELL ME OUT!"

Did Reggie suspect that I would betray him? Had I not already betrayed him with my insinuating journalese in this morning's *Arden Oracle*? And what about this "true story" of his? How the hell was I supposed to find out if Reggie had been telling the truth about the Martin

Luther King assassination files? I was no *investigative* reporter. Sure I could write a gooey campus mood article, but I wasn't Bob fucking Woodward! What the hell did Reggie want from me? If he was innocent, why did he flee? And where did he get off asking me not to forsake him? I'd already stuck my neck out driving him almost all the way to Arden Airfield. (And he didn't even catch the plane he had plenty of time to make! So how did he get to Mississippi—hitchhiking?) And as for selling him out—I hadn't breathed a word to anybody about what I knew. I had let Brogus suck me into this madness and here he was hectoring me to get more involved trying to validate some wacko conspiracy theory. Fuck Brogus!

I had broken into a clammy sweat. I could feel my flannel shirt sticking wetly, itchily, to my skin. I was breathing hard now. I erased Brogus's email, shut down my computer. I needed fresh air. As I rose from the chair, I felt a dizzying rush. I grabbed my parka and nearly stumbled to the door. Outside the English Department house, on the hard yellow lawn, I stood bent over, hands on my knees. My breathing began to stabilize. The stinging cold air felt good in my lungs. Finally I stood upright.

I spotted it right away, across about thirty yards of flat yellow lawn, parked on Liberty Drive. The black agent sat on the passenger side of the Lincoln Town Car, his window rolled down. Even though there was no sun shining in the industrial-gray sky, the bald, high-browed man was wearing his aviator Ray-Bans again. And he seemed to be looking straight at me. But this time I was unafraid. I started striding across the lawn toward the black sedan. I wasn't even thinking about what I would say to the agent. I just wanted to confront him. Was I mistaken, or did I detect a trace of fear—or maybe shock—in that leathery face as I got closer and closer to the car? I saw him turn his head to the driver.

"Yo!" I called out.

As the engine revved up, the window on the passenger side of the Lincoln quickly rose, the agent's bleak face disappearing inch by inch behind the smoky-tinted glass. I was almost close enough to touch the car now, reaching out to grab the door handle, when the Lincoln pulled away from the curb. And I actually started to run after it! There I was chasing the Lincoln down Liberty Drive.

"Yo!" I screamed again.

The Lincoln picked up speed, but so did I, chasing that damn car for two blocks. But as I saw the black sedan turn the corner at Liberty Donuts and take off down University Boulevard, my sprint turned into a lope, deteriorated to a jog, and finally broke down into a heavy-footed plod until I stopped in front of the dreary old pastry shop with its giant dusty beige plastic donut perched above the glass doorway. But I wasn't looking at Liberty Donuts. I was peering into the distance, trying to find the Lincoln Town Car, which had merged into the busy, fluid traffic on University Boulevard. I heard the sharp, sudden rap of metal against glass. I turned and saw Kwanzi Authentica Parker sitting in the donut shop, banging her multiringed fingers against the window, then waving anxiously, beckoning me to come inside.

*　　*　　*

"I know you don't believe in the spirit world, Clay," Kwanzi said, a bit resentfully, "but this is just further proof that there are no coincidences." She sat across from me, bundled in a black overcoat, a kente-printed kufi atop her head. A half-eaten jelly roll, a steaming, styrofoam cup of tea, and a copy of the *Arden Oracle* sat before her on the small plastic table. "I've been wanting to talk to you all morning. Then I'm sittin' here in Liberty Donuts, the first time I've been in here in *years*, thinking of *you*"—and there you appear, running down the street, coming to *me!*"

"Actually, Kwanzi, I was running after a car."

"You were *ostensibly* running after a car," she intoned, her voice fraught with the importance of secret meanings. "But you were *really* running to see *me.*"

I knew there was no contradicting Kwanzi when she was in her omniscient psychic mode. Her eyes took on a spacey, beatific look while her voice dripped with all the portentousness of Vincent Price in some Roger Corman horror picture. "So," I asked, "what was it I was running here to talk to you about?"

Kwanzi raised the cup of tea to her lips, closed her eyes as she sipped. Even across the table, the smell of cocoa butter on her skin was powerful. She set down the cup and fixed me with her wide-eyed stare. "Clay," she said heavily, "I read your story in the *Oracle* this morning." She paused. Maybe she wanted me to ask what she thought of my work. I didn't. After a moment, Kwanzi continued. "Well, I just wanted to know . . . Why didn't you interview *me?*"

"You?"

"Or anyone else in the Afrikamerica Studies program?"

"Well, I know all of you. I thought it might be awkward if—"

"Do you know how many interviews I gave yesterday?" Kwanzi said, cutting me off. "At least five TV stations, even more radio, including NPR, *and . . .*" Kwanzi gave a long, single blink, then said proudly, huskily, "this morning, the *New York Times* called for my comments on the case."

"Wow," I said tonelessly.

"It just strikes me as strange that I should be left out of the local paper. Roger agrees with me." Kwanzi often did that, tacking on the opinion of her husband, the British historian Roger Pym-Smithers, as if to validate her own.

"Sorry, Kwanzi, I guess I just didn't—"

"I should have been included," Kwanzi said, the indignation rising in her voice. "Especially when you wrote about this evil little dwarf!"

"You mean Patsy DeFestina?"

"That woman," Kwanzi said through clenched teeth. "That woman is . . . *ruthless.* Absolutely ruthless. Roger thinks so, too."

"Really?"

"You should have seen the way she treated Art and Matilda Davenport!" Kwanzi was talking rapidly now, furiously. "Grillin' 'em—an old married couple—like they were some kinda criminals. Everybody! Ol' Pops Mulwray, the Lumbakis, Mabel the part-time secretary. DeFestina was barkin' at everybody like she was some kinda damn pitbull! She knew better than to take that tone with me, 'cause she could tell just by lookin' at *me* that I don't play that shit. But even when she's trying to be polite, she's still a fucking bitch. I told her Roger and I had both been away for the long weekend. I was at a conference in Chicago and he was at a conference in New York. I *told* her this! So did Roger! But don't you know that bitch still made us show our plane tickets, to prove we didn't get back to Arden 'til Monday night. And all yesterday morning she was in my face: 'Who's got keys? Who's got keys? Who else? Who else? Who else!'"

"Keys?"

"Keys to the Afram suite. Actually it's just one key. But Patsy kept harassing me about who else might have had access to the suite. She wanted to interrogate every single person who had ever had a key. Even after I wrote up a list she was like 'Who else? Who else? Who else!' I just wanted to *smack* her."

"Well, Kwanzi, one could say she's just doing her job."

"You defend her?"

"Well, not exactly. I just—"

"Now it's T-Bird Williams she's after. First everybody wants to string up Reggie Brogus, now it's T-Bird! Did you hear about this? Young brother was a file clerk in the department. Nobody's seen him on campus. The poor boy's probably terrified. Probably he saw the news and thought, 'I'm a young black man—I bet they gonna try to pin this on me! I better hide!' Now there's a lynch mob lookin' for him!"

"So you don't think Brogus *or* T-Bird is guilty?"

Kwanzi paused for a long moment. "I don't *think* T-Bird is guilty. But I *know* Reggie is innocent." The distant, clairvoyant look returned to Kwanzi's eyes. "What if I told you that the body," Kwanzi said slowly, Vincent Price-ishly, "the body in Reggie's office . . . had been *moved* there?"

"Did the spirits tell you this?"

"No, Clay. The police know very well that the body was *moved* there."

"How do you know the police know this?"

A thin smile crept across Kwanzi's face. "Did you know that, back in England, Roger has quite a reputation as an amateur sleuth?" Kwanzi pronounced the word not in the American way ("ama-*chur*") but with a posh English accent—a hard T sound ("ama-*tur*")—like her husband's.

"So he told me."

"Well, Patsy the Pitbull knew about this case Roger had helped Scotland Yard crack back in the sixties. So when she questioned him—he's my husband, after all, so of course he has a key to my office and of course since he has a key to the Afram suite, Patsy DeFestina just had to question him—she got all chummy, knowing his reputation and shit and little Patsy may have let slip more than she intended to. Speaking collegially, as she was, to her fellow sleuth."

"And she said the body had been moved there?"

"She said it was obvious." Kwanzi gave another long, single blink.

"So . . . this was a setup?" I said tentatively.

"Mm-*hmm*," Kwanzi hummed affirmatively. She took another sip of her tea. "I know folks may think it strange that I've come to Reggie's defense as I have. But I remember what Reggie Brogus *was*. And so do a lot of other people. I loved Reggie for what he *was*. But a whole lotta folks hate him for it. You used the word *setup*. Well, if this was a setup, then I think somebody is tryin' to get back at Reggie, to punish him, for what he *was*."

I nodded slowly. "Cointelpro."

Surprise flashed in Kwanzi's eyes. "What did you just say?"

"Cointelpro," I repeated. "Counter Intelligence Program."

"Of course, of course," Kwanzi said. "What do you know about it?"

"Well . . . I had lunch with Brogus a couple of times and he . . . er . . . he seemed to think that there were people in Cointelpro who might . . . uh . . . I don't know . . ."

"Want to do him harm," Kwanzi drawled portentously. "Even now."

"Um . . . yeah."

We were both silent for a long time. I didn't know what to say. I kept thinking about the black agent in the black Lincoln Town Car. I considered telling Kwanzi about him but knew I shouldn't.

"You know what they say happened to Reggie, don't you?" Kwanzi finally said. "Word on the street was that after he was apprehended in Paris and extradited back in '81, Reggie was placed in solitary confinement. He was in a boxlike cell filled with bright lights and a surveillance camera. Twenty-four hours a day. He couldn't turn the lights off. He slept, used the toilet, whatever, in this tiny, brightly lit room. He never knew if it was day or night. He wasn't allowed any visitors, not even a lawyer. He had no books, no newspapers, no television, no radio. They kept him in that cell for a year, Clay. Who *wouldn't* have cracked? After that year in solitary, well, Reggie was a zombie. . . . That's when they went to work on his mind. They gave him all kinds of psycho-pharmological medications. Electroshock therapy. Rumor had it he was even subjected to neurosurgery. That's how they got him to reject his past, to deny what he *was*. And made him into the creature they wanted him to be."

"Jesus."

"He never told you any of this?"

"No."

"I don't even know how much of it he would remember," Kwanzi said. "Anyway, it's just a rumor. But there might be some folks out there who figure brainwashing wasn't enough. They want Reggie dead."

"And you suspect Cointelpro?"

"Clay, I don't know if Cointelpro even exists anymore." Kwanzi sighed, blinked slowly again. "Frankly, I suspect it was the *pigs*. Maybe some of Ohio's finest decided they didn't want the likes of Reggie Brogus—remembering the old Reggie Brogus, what he *was*—in their communi-*tee*. So they decided to, as you say, set him up. That's why I don't trust that DeFestina bitch one goddamned bit."

"You really think the cops would go to that much trouble," I said, "to punish Brogus for his sins of the past?"

Kwanzi stared out the window. "I don't know, Clay," she said wearily. "I just don't know." After a moment, she added: "Roger doesn't agree with me."

"Oh, no?"

"No. He's convinced this was a crime of passion. Committed by someone who knew both the girl *and* Reggie—intimately."

"Well, then, T-Bird might qualify. But I don't know how intimately he knew either Brogus or the, uh, Wolfshiem girl."

"By the way, Clay . . . Roger says *you* knew her."

"Um, yeah, briefly."

"She was a student of yours?"

"Not a student, really. I didn't have her in a class. I was her temporary academic adviser for a couple of weeks in September." I felt like I was doing a good job of sounding matter-of-fact. "She was an interesting young woman. Very, er . . . nice."

Kwanzi was getting all spacey-eyed again. "Roger says you were very upset upon hearing the news."

"Well, of course."

"Roger said that you said that you and the girl were very close."

"I did?"

Kwanzi gave a solemn nod. "It's obvious from your article in the *Oracle* today that you felt some personal . . . *attachment.*"

The way Kwanzi said the word, slathering it with innuendo, made the hairs on the back of my neck tingle. "Yeah," I said warily. "So?"

Kwanzi lowered her head, stared into her styrofoam tea cup. "So . . . how are Penelope and the twins?"

I felt almost as if this was a trick question. "They're fine," I said cautiously.

"Didn't you and Penelope have an anniversary recently?" Kwanzi asked, her tone turning more casual and chatty.

"Number seven," I said, still looking for some kind of a trap.

"And you haven't felt the seven-year itch yet?"

"If I did, I wouldn't scratch it."

Kwanzi hooted with laughter. I smiled but still felt on my guard. "I know how you feel, my brother," Kwanzi said, shaking her head sympathetically. "Marriage. It's about so much more than sex, don't you think?" Kwanzi spoke with an Oprah-like piety. "Security. That's what marriage really is. Emotional security. Look at me and my husband. I know Roger isn't the love of my life. I *had* my crazy passion—before I met Roger Pym-Smithers. But I just feel so secure with him. Because he loves me so much. Do you know that Roger was the first man who ever told me he loved me? All the men who came before Roger—the men I think of as the loves of my life—never told me they loved me. It makes me sad sometimes that it had to be a white man to be the first to profess his love for me. He said it the night we met. He told me that he had experienced what the French call a *coup de foudre.* A thunderbolt. Love at first sight. And he feels the same way today. Roger loves me to death. He would do anything for me. I *know* that. I have that security. Before Roger, I was just a vagabond. A bohemian, if you will, but no better than a vagabond. After I met Roger, I knew what it was like to be loved. To know that your phone bill and your electricity bill would be paid. To know that your checks wouldn't bounce. To know that you wouldn't come home and find that the landlord had put your furniture and your clothes out on the street 'cause you were three months late with the rent. To know that you will always be loved and taken care of. That's what marriage means to me. Do you know that when we got married, Roger said he would never, ever hurt me, intentionally or unintentionally?"

I wondered how you could promise never to do something "unintentionally"? I wanted to say "That doesn't make any sense." Instead, I smiled and said, only vaguely sarcastically, "What a guy."

"And I know you would never do anything to hurt Penelope, would you, Clay?"

"Kwanzi," I said impatiently, "what are you getting at?"

She took a sip of her tea, made a sudden bitter face. "Colder than I thought," she said, setting down the styrofoam cup. "Actually, Clay, there was something else I wanted to talk to you about."

"Yeah?"

"About a year and a half ago, when we opened the Afrikamerica Studies suite, we had a soul food party there. Do you remember?"

"Of course."

"At that party . . . didn't I give you a key to the suite?"

"Why would you have given me a key? I don't teach in the program."

"Yes, but I had hoped that you *would.* I just seem to remember having an extra key and giving it to you as a goodwill gesture, to say you were always welcome in my department."

"I don't remember that at all," I said truthfully.

"Take a look on your key chain."

"What?"

"Please. It's a very unusual-looking key. Very modern."

Now I felt certain that Kwanzi was wrong. I pulled the ring of a dozen keys from the pocket of my black courdoroy pants. I set the cluster of keys noisily down on the table.

"There it is!" Kwanzi said instantly.

Sure enough, there was a very odd key on my ring. It was smooth all around, without the ragged, teethy ridges my other keys had. The surface of the flat, oblong piece of metal had five or six little pockmarks on it. Kwanzi reached into her pocket. She placed an identical key next to the weird one on my ring. I sat there, my mouth hanging slightly open, staring in stupefaction at a key I had become so accustomed to seeing in my hand and feeling in my pocket that I had long ago stopped even noticing it. In a year and a half, I had never even used it.

"Well, my brother," Kwanzi said, "next time you see your friend Patsy DeFestina, *she* might be the one interviewing *you*."

"Yeah," I whispered.

"Clay," Kwanzi said softly, "is there anything you want to tell me?"

I picked my key ring up from the table, put it back in my pants pocket. "Yes," I said, struggling to recapture my matter-of-fact tone. "I have a class at eleven. I think I better go."

I waited for Kwanzi while she paid her bill at the cash register. As we stepped out into the gray and cold, Kwanzi said, "I know what you told Roger on Boxing Day."

"What?"

We stood face-to-face on the sidewalk in front of Liberty Donuts. "The night after Christmas." Kwanzi pulled up the collar of her overcoat, continued to stare spacily. "When you and Penelope came over for dinner. I know what you told Roger."

Now I was mad. I could feel a surge of blood in my face. "Kwanzi—I don't know what the fuck you're talking about."

A car horn honked suddenly, obnoxiously. I turned and saw a patrol car pull up to the curb on University Boulevard. The window on the passenger side was rolled halfway down. Two sets of little fingers appeared, curling over the edge of the window. Then Patsy's tiny head, furry black earmuffs wrapped around it, popped into view. "Good morning, Professors!"

"Well, hello, Detective DeFestina!" I said as brightly as I could manage. I turned back to look at Kwanzi. I saw her walking away, striding briskly down University Boulevard.

"I'm afraid that woman doesn't like me very much," Patsy said.

I walked over to the patrol car, leaned toward the window. "Well, this is a terrible ordeal for people in the Afrikamerica program."

Patsy nodded her little head. I detected a real sympathy in her black button eyes, glimmering behind the clunky, rectangular panes of her glasses. "What are you doing right now?" she asked. "I want to invite you somewhere."

At that moment, I forgot all about the class I was scheduled to teach in five minutes. "Where?"

Patsy grinned elfishly. "We're going on a T-Bird hunt. Come along!"

*   *   *

Patsy DeFestina was merrily monologuing along in her pleasant, colorless Ohio accent—inflections as flat as the fallow farmland that stretched out before us, vowels as wide as the infinite gray sky above—as the patrol car sped south toward the town of Impediment. Sitting in the backseat, I could not even see her as she spoke and wondered if Patsy was able even to see over the dashboard.

"You were too kind to me, Clay. Really," Patsy had said, soon after I'd stepped into the car, not even thinking anymore about my eleven o'clock journalism class—or, for that matter, the classes I was scheduled to teach at one or three or four o'clock. "You know, I've dealt with the press a lot," Patsy said, her bland but cheerful voice rising from below the headrest of the passenger seat, "but yours was one of the nicest stories about me I've ever read. And you know what they say: Flattery will get you everywhere! Ain't that right, Larry?"

Larry, the beet-faced, blue-clad cop I'd seen Patsy with before, was driving. He emitted a gravelly chuckle. This would be his response to most of the detective's comments as she rambled indefatigably on, Larry playing a kind of amiably gruff, nonverbal Ed MacMahon to Patsy's garrulous Johnny Carson.

"And I thought you were very fair in your treatment of Reggie Brogus."

"Did you?" I said.

"Absolutely. You didn't mention him much, but you didn't condemn him either, the way so much of the media has. You know, making him out to be the big, scary nigga who raped and killed the poor little white girl. The usual racist crap!"

Now I *knew* Patsy had to be black—at least biracial. No white cop would say something like that. Yet Kwanzi, just a little while earlier, in Liberty Donuts, had repeatedly called Patsy a bitch. I hadn't even bothered to ask Kwanzi what she believed Patsy's racial background to be. It seemed obvious that Kwanzi thought Patsy was white, a white racist. And Patsy had just told me twenty-four hours earlier that there was a ninety percent chance that Brogus was guilty. Yet, according to Kwanzi, Patsy knew that the body had been moved into Reggie's office. Why would Brogus, if he had murdered Pirate Jenny someplace else, drag her into his own office? It made no sense. So T-Bird Williams was definitely the killer. He had murdered Jenny—maybe accidentally—then dumped her body in Reggie's office, to set up the man he had taunted as a "big fat ugly muthafucka." Was that what Patsy had deduced? Was that why we were going to a city an hour away—*on a T-Bird hunt?*

"Check it out," Detective DeFestina said. "None of Brogus's white conservative buddies has had anything to say about this crime, or the manhunt. That talk radio guy, Rash Knoblauch—he refused to discuss the matter on the air! But they'll turn on him sooner or later. Whether he killed the girl or not. Ain't that right, Larry?"

Larry grumble-chuckled.

"Not that I'm some kinda bleeding heart liberal!" Patsy hastened to add. "I love this country!"

"So do a lot of bleeding heart liberals," I said. It was the last word I would get in for a long time.

"You know why I love this country?" Patsy asked, answering her own question in the next breath. "This is the only country in the world where a person such as myself, who happens to be a woman. Who happens to be . . . ethnic. Who happens to be height-challenged . . . could, through playing by the rules and—let's be honest—having a string or two here and there pulled on her behalf . . . become a police detective. And, if I may say so myself, a role model for millions. Only in America! Ain't that right, Larry?"

"Grmrrffrrfff."

"You know, it's like I said to Barbara Walters . . ."

Patsy was off on a solipsistic soliloquy about faith and discipline and the burdens of being a role model and maintaining simple values. I pretty much tuned her out. I stared out the window as the scenery changed from ageless rural to contemporary anywhere: the billboards, the megastores, the multiplexes, the empty "developments"—prefab roadside neighborhoods of twelve or twenty identical houses—the long stretches of scrubby, uninhabited flat earth as we approached the outskirts of urban Impediment. I noticed the curious glances of other drivers as they passed us. With a sudden surprise, I realized that they had no idea I was a reporter on a story. They must have thought I was in custody. Why *wouldn't* they, seeing a youngish black man in the back of a police car?

I had to stifle a laugh at the perversity of my situation, sitting in the back of a police car, with my new best friend Patsy DeFestina and her squinty-eyed goon Larry, on our way to track down Tyrell "T-Bird" Williams, who had been seen walking the mean streets of Impediment that morning. Like most African American men, I had naturally distrusted, not to say detested, the police. Yet here I was sucking up to Patsy DeFestina. Because, somehow, I thought she could lead me to the truth. I could not believe—as Kwanzi did—that the local police would have set up Reggie Brogus by planting a naked corpse in his office. I figured regular cops were far too stupid to pull off anything as complicated as that.

I was still rattled by my encounter with Kwanzi in Liberty Donuts. Seeing the key to the Afrikamerica Studies suite on my ring was disturbing enough. But Kwanzi had really freaked me out, and pissed me off, with her cryptic little comment about what I had "told Roger" last December 26th. What the hell was she referring to? Penelope and I had gone to their house for dinner. Roger kept opening one bottle of wine after another. Kwanzi eventually got tired and went to bed. Pen went home. But I hung out a while longer, boozing it up with Roger and talking about . . . what? Certainly I hadn't confessed my little tryst with Jenny to him. I wasn't *that* damn drunk! Yet Kwanzi seemed distinctly suspicious of me. Had her sleuthing husband deduced that maybe *I* had killed Jenny?

"This town is a graveyard," Patsy said as we drove past the boarded-up textile factories and abandoned tenements of Impediment. "And it used to be a thriving city. There was a white side of town and a black side of town. You had comfortable folks and poor folks on both sides of town. Now there's just one side of town and it's black and it's *po'*."

Patsy continued to talk as a staticky voice screeched on the police radio and she didn't stop yammering even as Larry picked up the receiver and muttered answers to the scratchy questions coming at him. Ignoring Patsy, Officer Larry and the incomprehensible radio squawk, I stared out the window at Main Street, Impediment. What seemed to have once been a busy commercial district was now, except for a few clusters of homeless black men, deserted. The banks, department stores, coffee shops, and drugstores had all been closed down, surrendered. A couple of bars, an X-rated cinema, a pawnshop, a check cashing joint, and a liquor store were the only places open for business. I heard Larry mutter something about "Mandrake Towers" before hanging up the radio receiver.

Larry turned off Main Street. I could feel the cop car pick up speed as we drove down an avenue of dilapidated row houses, some of them with rusted tangles of junk on their scraggly lawns.

"Do you agree?" Patsy's voice projected, somewhat impatiently, from below the headrest in front of me.

"I beg your pardon," I said.

"Clay, I get the feeling you're not listening to me. Back when I was Sister DeFestina I would have had to crack you on the hand with my ruler—right on the knuckles, so you'd feel that sting of wood on bone."

"Yikes. Sorry."

"I was talking about mysteries," Patsy said.

"Okay."

We drove past a graffiti-smeared sign welcoming us to Mandrake Towers. We had entered a world of concrete, a labyrinth of pinkish cement block edifices, each six stories high and lined with long and narrow vertical strips of window.

"I have this theory that most mystery novels would be better if they were written from the perspective of the criminal rather than the perspective of the person trying to solve the crime. You know what I mean? It's much harder to get away with a murder than it is to nail a murderer. The culprit's efforts to cover up the crime are so much more fascinating to me than the uncovering. Do you agree?"

"Um, I don't know," I said lamely.

Larry expertly maneuvered the car through the concrete alleyways between the buildings. Every once in a while, we would exit the labyrinth and drive through an open square decorated in the center with a bare, gnarly-limbed tree planted in a huge concrete pot, before entering the concrete maze again.

"Roger Pym-Smithers agrees with me," Patsy said. "I met him yesterday. Do you know him? Fascinating man. Back in England he has quite a reputation as an—"

"There he is!" I screamed. The words had leapt from my mouth, almost involuntarily, the moment I spotted the shiny Cleveland Browns football team jacket, the red Cleveland Indians baseball cap, turned backward atop the young man's head. T-Bird was standing in a group of about five guys near one of the potted trees in the center of one of the rare open spaces in this project. Larry was driving so fast that we had passed T-Bird and his homeys and reentered the labyrinth between buildings before his brain caught up with my sudden cry. Larry turned on the siren, then whipped around the next narrow corner, and the next, zooming back to the square where I had seen T-Bird.

"Whoopeeeee!" Patsy screamed above the wailing siren. "Hey, Clay, this is just like that show COPS, isn't it?"

Suddenly, I heard the piercing whine of another police siren not far away. As we tore through the empty square—T-Bird and his boys had quickly scattered—the other cop car passed us, on the opposite side of the potted tree, zooming in the opposite direction. My heart was pounding in my throat. I felt something unfamiliar, a violence, almost a bloodlust, churning inside me. Just as we were about to reenter the concrete maze, I saw the shiny flash of brown polyester through the broken glass doorway of one of the buildings.

"STOP!" Before Larry had even finished grinding the car to a halt, I had spilled out of the back door, rolled twice over the concrete tiles in front of the building, clumsily righted myself, and stumbled through the broken glass doorway into the darkened lobby. I was feeling my way along a wall, searching for a light switch, when the wall suddenly seemed to break open, yellowish light bursting through the widening crack. T-Bird sprang from the shadows of the lobby and disappeared into the shaft of light. The elevator doors were already closing again when this bizarre force inside of me, this eager rage I had never known before, hurled my body forward. As I swished across the threshhold, feeling the sliding door on each side of my body brushing the burly shoulder fabric of my parka, I heard the voice of Patsy DeFestina ringing in the blacked-out lobby behind me: "CLAY—DON'T!"

Now all was tumbling, fumbling, banging fury. T-Bird and I were alone, trapped in the shakily climbing elevator. I had lunged right into his body in a crunching Ronnie Lott–like tackle. We were both bouncing off the slick walls of the elevator that shined like aluminum foil, wrapped around each other like boxers in a clinch. At one point, I had my arms around T-Bird's midsection, my hands groping wildly, his belly, his chest, searching for a gun, trying instinctively to disarm him, just in case he was armed.

"What the fuck's the matta witch you, nigga!" T-Bird screamed, twirling madly, slamming my body, and his own, against the flimsy, quivering elevator walls. "You crazy? You crazy fuckin' faggot!"

"You killed her," I mumbled, spinning blindly, the hood of my parka twisted around my head, acrylic hairs of the bushy hood lining bristling in my nose, my mouth, but still mumbling, my hands groping T-Bird's writhing torso, "You killed her!"

I am crazed, but coherent. I know that T-Bird is not carrying a gun. And from the pounding of his fists, I know that I am at least as strong as he is. The elevator stops with a jolt. I feel a hand on my face, underneath my hood. A fingernail scratches the surface of my eyeball. I fall to the floor, hear the elevator doors slide open. I tear the bearish parka from my body. Staggering out of the elevator, I see T-Bird at the top of a short flight of black metal stairs, pushing against a black metal door. As I stumble up the stairs, the door opens. T-Bird has disappeared. A single ray of sunlight, penetrating the thick mass of charcoal gray clouds, shining through the doorway at the top of the stairs, blinds me. I blunder onto the rooftop. My left eye burns. Creeping step by step along the soft asphalt surface of the rooftop, looking warily all around, squinting through my scratched left cornea, I see no sign of T-Bird.

Then I look down and notice T-Bird's red cotton baseball cap lying at my feet, the racist caricature of a grinning Native American's head—the "Indians'" mascot—sewn above the bill. Beet-faced Larry bursts onto the rooftop, gun drawn. Patsy pops up right behind him, holding a pistol that seems enormous, clutched as it is in her tiny hands. "Get down, Clay!" she barks. I do not move. Two more cops appear, bounding gracelessly across the rooftop, guns clutched in both hands, turning this way and that. "Clay, get down!" Patsy shrieks again.

I see T-Bird now, sprinting along the edge of the rooftop, not all that far from me. His head is bare, his hair braided in zigzagging cornrows. I don't know where he thinks he's running to.

"Halt!"

I turn and see Officer Larry pointing his gun straight at T-Bird.

"He's unarmed!" I scream.

"Halt!" Larry yells again.

I hear the single firecracker pop of Larry's gun. T-Bird stops running. He is clearly not hit but he stops, a bit too abruptly, turning to face the shooter—who has obviously missed his target—twirling awkwardly on his left ankle, losing his balance at the edge of the rooftop.

"He's unarmed!" I scream again.

I see the bumbling, almost comic look of surprise on T-Bird's face as he tumbles backward, his feet leaving the surface of the rooftop. His arms are flailing, his face contorting strenuously as he falls. The soles of his bright white hightop sneakers are the last things I see before T-Bird disappears over the edge.

*   *   *

I got sick. Up on the roof, I collapsed. I didn't faint. I don't think I lost consciousness. But I was knocked flat on my ass by a sudden, attacking fever. I was burning up but trembling at the same time. The same sensation I had had after reading Brogus's email in my office—only far worse.

I had trouble breathing. There was no sign of Patsy DeFestina. Where had she gone? The scene before me, a mass of cops on a rooftop, began to swim ever so subtly. My left eye hurt like hell. Next thing I knew I was lying down, stretched out in the backseat of a police car, sweating all over, shaking violently. I heard sirens outside, a multitude of voices. In my mind's eye, I kept seeing T-Bird, the look of tragic slapstick surprise on his face as he tumbled backward: the strangeness of seeing him before my eyes, grimacing, flailing, then, a second later, seeing nothing but gray sky where his body had been. And the words kept sounding in my head: *You . . . killed . . . him.* I threw up on the floor in the back of the police car and that must have been when I passed out.

*   *   *

"Clay, you awake? It's me, Patsy. Hey, there ya go. That's quite a blood-shot eye you got there. Ouch."

I slowly sat up. I was startled to find myself wrapped in a threadbare blanket. I was sitting on a couch in a small, completely nondescript, dimly lit office. Through the one small window in the room, I saw that night had fallen.

"You're in the Impediment police station, it's six-thirty," Patsy said, answering my first two questions before I even asked them. She sat beside the couch in a hardback chair, her feet just barely touching the floor. "Could you say something please?"

"Something please," I croaked. I still felt somewhat delirious; hazy and abstract.

"Good. Now listen up. Tyrell Williams didn't survive his fall. It's a real shame, a terrible accident. Larry fired a warning shot—into the air— the kid got scared and tripped."

"Life expectancy of a match," I said bitterly. "Right, Patsy?"

"These things happen." The steel had returned to Detective DeFes-tina's voice. "What you need to know is this: I kept your name out of it. The press has got onto this incident already. Do you understand me, Clay? *I kept your name out of it.* Only a few people—and none of them reporters—know that you were with us on that rooftop. I protected you."

"What if I don't want my name out of it? What if I want to report what I saw in the newspaper?"

Patsy stared beadily at me from behind her windshield glasses. "It's a free country," she said. "But I have a few more bits of information to share with you. If you really feel like writing another article. They found sperm in Jennifer Wolfshiem's body. And it wasn't Reggie Brogus's sperm. The feds had DNA samples of Brogus from back in the early eighties. They'll be taking a sample from the dear departed Tyrell, too, but I'm beginning to get the feeling that it isn't *his* sperm in the Wolfshiem girl either."

My nausea returned. I remembered the sight of Jenny's naked body on the couch in Reggie's office. I saw T-Bird tumbling off the roof. Jenny and T-Bird. Two nineteen-year-olds, both dead. And me, bound up in both their deaths. I felt the hot sting of a tear in my scratched eye.

"And lemme tell ya another thing," Patsy continued. "I got a call from someone at Arden University late this afternoon. Seems *you've* got a key to the Afro-American Studies suite, Clay. And I'll tell ya something else. There's a rumor goin' 'round that you knew the Wolfshiem girl—and possibly in the biblical sense. And get this, Clay. We just got the printout listing all the calls Reggie Brogus made on his mobile phone. The last call he made was at 2:27 last Monday morning. And guess where Brogus called: *your* house! He talked to somebody there for about a minute and a half. Ain't that peculiar?"

I was ready to break down, to crack, to confess all. "Patsy," I said hoarsely, "I can explain everything."

"Save it. This has been a long day for me, too, you know. I've arranged for an officer to drive you back to Arden. I could arrest you right here, right now. But I don't know, Clay, for some reason I still like you. Go home to your family. I'd imagine you've got a lot of explaining to do to your wife. You might also want to talk to a lawyer. Try to get a good's night sleep and report to the Arden police station at 7:00 tomorrow morning. Ask for me at the front desk. Bring your lawyer if you like. You're gonna be in for several hours of questioning. Blood tests, fingerprints, hair samples. Like I say, Clay, I like you. But if I find out you were responsible for what happened to that girl, I will see to it that you are tried, convicted, and sentenced to death, and I'll pop open a bottle of Champagne at your execution. Tonight you've got the benefit of the doubt. Go home to your wife and children. But be at the police station tomorrow at seven a.m. sharp. If it's 7:01 and you're not there, I'll be comin' to get your ass."

CHAPTER 11

BEING AMERICAN, I HAD ALWAYS assumed that the English holiday, Boxing Day, had something to do with fisticuffs.

"Actually, old bean," Roger Pym-Smithers corrected me, "it has to do with Christian charity. In olden times something called the Christmas box was placed in the local church. The townfolk deposited coins in it and this 'dole of the Christmas box' or 'box money' was distributed to the needy on December 26th. Hence, Boxing Day."

Ordinarily, Penelope, the girls, and I were in Philadelphia on the day after Christmas, visiting Pen's parents, my mother, or my father and his second wife. But we decided, just for a change, to spend the entire Christmas season of 1991 in Arden, Ohio. When I bumped into Roger, walking across the quadrangle on the last day of the semester, and told him we'd be spending the holidays in town, he said we "simply *must*" come over for dinner on Boxing Day.

"It's a bit of a tradition in our home," he explained in his upper-crust Etonian accent, "my feeble way of keeping in touch with my *roots*, as Kwanzi puts it. Not that I go about distributing alms to the poor, mind you. I usually just cook a pheasant and bake a mince pie. And it's usually just Kwanzi and me. But we would be pleased to have you and your lovely wife . . . *chez nous*."

Roger Pym-Smithers had a knack for making just about everything that came out of his mouth, even a dinner invitation, sound all wry and sardonic. He leered and waggled his thin, steeply arched eyebrows, the moist-looking hairs at their peaks curling up like tiny devil's horns. I'd always found Roger to be amusing company, and it had been a long time since I'd seen Kwanzi Authentica Parker, so I immediately said yes. Of course, I should have checked with my wife first.

"Ten o'clock and I'm outta there," Penelope said as we drove to Roger and Kwanzi's place at about seven on the evening after Christmas. "I'm telling you my exit strategy right now, so don't try to coax me out of it when I'm ready to leave." Pen was the one behind the wheel of the Volvo tonight and she let me know that the car would be going with her when she left to pick up Amber and Ashley at Mrs. Henderson's house. "If you wanna hang out late with Monsieur Le Connoisseur, feel free. But you'll have to walk home. It's not that far."

"Yes, dear," I said.

We had only dined at Roger and Kwanzi's once before, when we first arrived in Arden two years earlier, and Pen had not enjoyed herself that night. "I like Kwanzi," Pen said afterward. "And I don't dislike Roger. It's just that there's something claustrophobic about them, like they've spent too many years on top of each other in their musty house. I mean, they're very hospitable. You just get the feeling that, at any second, a dinner with them could turn into *Who's Afraid of Virginia Woolf?*"

My wife also did not like the fact that I got totally shitfaced at that gathering in the fall of '89. Roger had converted his basement into a vast wine cellar and he insisted that we sample his collection. He and Kwanzi could really put the stuff away. And I did a pretty good job of keeping up with them, bottle for bottle. Penelope was not supposed to be the designated driver that night but that was what she became when she had to pour her drunken husband into the passenger seat.

"Try to be home by midnight," Pen said two years later as we drove to the Boxing Day dinner.

"I'll try, sweetheart," I said with a false plaintiveness. "But you know it's hard to resist Roger when he puts on that English charm."

"Yuck." Pen cringed.

*　　*　　*

So what did I remember of that night, December 26, 1991?

I remembered thinking how odd a couple Kwanzi and Roger were—the spiritual soul sister from the Jersey projects and the eccentric aristo-

Brit with the hyphenated last name—yet how perfectly well suited they seemed to each other. They lived in a Tudor-style house that was quaintly attractive on the outside but chaotically cluttered and generally uncared for, unloved, on the inside. Nevertheless, Kwanzi and Roger seemed content in their messy, book-strewn home, a house shared by two professors but that had the provisional feel of a graduate school dormitory. I did not get the sense of domestic weirdness that my wife detected in Roger and Kwanzi's company. They seemed, to my eyes, to have the easy rapport of a lot of long-married couples who had managed to remain genuinely fond of each other, genuinely comfortable with one another, over the long haul. Still, there was something a little bit sad about them. Was it the absence of children? Kwanzi had once told me that she and Roger had deliberately decided not to have kids. "We were just so in love with each other," she had said over lunch in the faculty cafeteria one day, "and in love with our lifestyle, we didn't think a child would fit in." She shrugged. "Now it's too late."

I remembered the Boxing Day dinner conversation being pleasant and convivial. We talked about the Soviet Union—which had just been dissolved by Mikhail Gorbachev the day before. We talked about the wildly controversial new Oliver Stone movie *JFK*, though none of us had seen it. And from there it was an easy segue to the favorite topic of both Kwanzi and Roger: the sixties. Or, more precisely: The Sixties and How Incredibly Great They Were and How Tragic It Is That YOU Were Too Young to Really Share the Experience. We ate the pheasant—good if a bit too gamy for my palate—and the tasteless, gummy mince pie. We discussed food and travel and I remembered feeling relieved not to be talking about Afrikamerica Studies and office politics. And we drank: a bottle of Beaujoulais, a Burgundy, a Bordeaux; and then it was on to the wines of Roger's favorite French region: the Côtes du Rhône.

"Ah, the nose, *the nose!*" Roger exulted, bending forward and sticking his bright pink proboscis right into his glass of red wine. He inhaled deeply, then raised his head again. His eyes remained closed, the trace of a smile on his face. Clearly, he was a man transported. "The bouquet soars from the glass," he said, eyes still closed, nostrils aquiver. "Ah, Gigondas! One can smell the robustly endowed tannins. Oooh la la, the aromas . . ." Roger's nose wrinkled . . . "peppery . . . herbaceous . . . opulent and heady . . ." He slowly opened his rheumy eyes. "Smoked sausage . . . leather." He took a long, indulgent sip from the glass. His ruddy jowls wiggled as he sluiced the wine in his mouth. I saw his throat undulate as he swallowed. "And the flavors: full-bodied, voluptuous . . . chewy."

"Chewy?" I said. "A *chewy* liquid?"

Roger sniffed around the rim of his glass. "Come to think of it, there's even a hint of roasted peanuts in the nose."

"I'd hate to have roasted peanuts in *my* nose!" I broke into compulsive giggles, tickled by my own adolescent wisecrack. I was already pretty drunk at this point and found what I had just said to be utterly hilarious. I couldn't stop laughing at my own bad joke. And the more I tried to stop, the harder I laughed.

"Are you takin' the piss out of me, old bean?" Roger shouted good-naturedly. "Are you takin' the piss?"

Kwanzi smiled. "That's British for: 'Are you poking fun at me?'" she explained.

I was still laughing too hard to talk.

"Go ahead," Roger guffawed. "Take the piss. Haw-haw-HAW!"

Penelope shot me a dirty look, then glanced at her wristwatch. "Thanks for a great evening," she said, "but I've got to go pick up the girls."

"You're not leaving already!" Roger protested. "We haven't even sampled the Château neuf du Pape!"

Penelope, of course, hadn't sampled a drop of anything alcoholic. "Clay might want to stay and have another tasting, but I gotta go."

Roger, Kwanzi, and I stood in the doorway of the Tudor house and waved good-bye to Penelope as she backed the Volvo out of the drive-way. I could tell by the last stern glance my wife gave me that I damn well better be home by midnight. Back inside, Kwanzi said she had a headache and went upstairs to the master bedroom. Roger and I, mean-while, retired to the study. I was feeling rather wobbly as I plopped down in a cushy, purple velvet armchair.

"I'm glad you could stay, old bean," Roger said as he uncorked another bottle of wine. "I've been wanting to have a little chat with you. For quite some time now." He focused his filmy gray eyes on me. "It's about Reggie Brogus."

*   *   *

Nearly two months later, on the night of February 19, 1992, I struggled to remember where my drunken conversation with Roger Pym-Smithers had gone from there. I stared out the window of the police car as it zoomed past the strip malls, headed for the farmland and on to the pleasant little college town I called home. It was a black cop, Officer Daniels, a brother about my age, behind the wheel. We said nothing to each other during the ride, but the silence felt in no way tense or hostile. I had no idea what Daniels thought of me or what had happened to T-Bird. I didn't want to know. I had plenty of other things to think about.

Like, for instance, a lawyer. Whenever I had needed one before, I had called my father in Philly and he called his attorney Frank Tatum, a former civil rights lawyer who, since leaving the movement in the early seventies, had run a lucrative private practice counseling a black middle-class clientele. But how could I bear to talk to my Dad *or* Frank Tatum in this situation? I'd have to find somebody else. On the other hand, I wouldn't be able to keep the mess I'd made of my life a secret from my parents or from the rest of the world for very long.

And in less than an hour, I would be confessing everything to my wife. I would have to start by telling her about Pirate Jenny: "It wasn't really an affair, sweetheart, just two quick fucks on her futon and a blow job in my office." Then, on to Brogus: "Sure, I gave him a ride to the airport. What are friends for?" Finally, I would tell her about this afternoon: "Yeah, I led the cops in chasing a young black man to his death. Sorry!" I tried to imagine how Penelope would react but it was impossible. We were in uncharted waters here.

I pressed my forehead against the cop car window. I felt like crying but was too embarrassed to do it in front of Officer Daniels. It was too painful for me to think of how much I was about to hurt my wife. I was going to have to dwell on another aspect of this catastrophe. That was when I remembered Kwanzi's cryptic little taunt outside Liberty Donuts this morning: "I know what you told Roger on Boxing Day." I started trying to piece together the entire dinner party. Up until the start of my private drunken conversation with Roger in the study, after Pen had gone home and Kwanzi had gone to bed, I could not remember saying anything provocative, revealing, or dangerous. But what the fuck had I said to Roger in the study?

"Where would you like me to let you out, Professor?" Officer Daniels asked.

We were approaching South campus. At first, I thought I'd have Daniels take me to North campus, to my office in the English Department. That way, I could retrieve my briefcase, check my email (just in case I'd received another message from the number one fugitive in America), write and post an apology for all the students I had stood up today, then get in my tiny Honda that I had parked behind the white clapboard English Department headquarters this morning and drive home to destroy my wife and family.

But just as the police car was passing the Mathematics building on South campus, I heard the rising chant. "I'll get out here, please."

Walking across the parking lot behind the Math building, I was struck by the power, the rich and defiant timbre of hundreds of black voices, the sheer anger in the chant: "NO JUSTICE—NO PEACE! NO JUSTICE— NO PEACE! NO JUSTICE—NO PEACE!"

The demonstration was taking place in the exact same spot as Jennifer Wolfshiem's candlelight vigil the night before. I was walking rapidly now, drawn to the chanting. Approaching the side entrance of the Math building I saw—just as I had twenty-four hours earlier—Pops Mulwray, in his green custodial cap and jacket. Only tonight he was entering rather than leaving the building. And he was carrying a brown paper sack that appeared to be filled with groceries. Swinging open the door, Pops turned and looked right at me as I strode toward him. He quickly looked away and hurried inside. Walking past the side entrance, I heard Pops bolt the door shut. I thought little of it.

"NO JUSTICE—NO PEACE! NO JUSTICE—NO PEACE!"

I had never seen so many black Arden students gathered together in one place. They were not holding candles but thrusting their fists into the bone-chillingly cold night air, their chant resonating throughout the quad: "NO JUSTICE—NO PEACE! NO JUSTICE—NO PEACE!"

A huge canvas banner, two stories high, was displayed on the makeshift concert stage in front of the Math building, illuminated by bold, blue-white floodlights. On the banner were the words TYRELL WILLIAMS 1972–1992 and a blown-up version of T-Bird's high school yearbook photo. He looked terrific in his cap and gown, smiling proudly, the tassel dangling from the slanted mortarboard atop his head. At that moment, I felt the same pain in the marrow I had felt listening to the voice of Pirate Jenny's father at the candlelight vigil. Tyrell Williams had also been somebody's child. Now he was some parent's loss, a mother's grief. And it was my fault. Were it possible to die of shame, I would have dropped dead right then and there.

Squeaking, staticky feedback filled the air, drowning out the chanting crowd. Only then did I notice the group of people onstage. Kwanzi Authentica Parker, dressed in her black overcoat and kufi, was adjusting the stand-up microphone and causing the ear-stinging screech. She was surrounded by five or six black student activists, her colleagues in the Afrikamerica Studies program—Xavier Lumbaki and Arthur and Matilda Davenport—and the four girlfriends Pirate Jenny had tried to hang with: Euphrasia, Tamika, Yolanda, and Shereena. There was only one white person standing on the floodlit stage. In fact, he seemed to be the only white person in the entire five-hundred strong crowd in front of the Math building. It was Roger Pym-Smithers, wearing his floppy black fedora and a black overcoat that seemed to match his wife's.

"I ask you again," Kwanzi's husky, amplified voice rang out, "Why did T-Bird have to die?" I realized I must have arrived right in the middle of her speech. "I guarantee," Kwanzi said, "you won't read any weepy stories about the death of T-Bird Williams in tomorrow's newspaper. But that's all right, y'all. 'Cause this is not a time for sorrow. It is a time for rage!"

The crowd exploded in cheers.

Kwanzi looked blissed out, smiling beatifically, eyes shining in the blue-white floodlights, as the applause washed over her. She waited until the noise died down before continuing: "We must let the world know that T-Bird Williams did not die in vain! We must see that those responsible for this young man's death pay the severest price!"

With that, the chanting erupted again: "NO JUSTICE—NO PEACE! NO JUSTICE—NO PEACE! NO JUSTICE—NO PEACE!"

I stood among the crowd, bushily lined hood over my head, hands thrust in the pockets of my parka. The deadly shame I had felt minutes ago was giving way to a bizarre sense of bemusement. It occurred to me that if this crowd of my fellow African Americans knew what had really happened in Impediment early this afternoon, they might lynch me right here.

"I promise you," Kwanzi intoned, "I will get our message out all across this country." She gave a slow, single blink, then continued proudly: "Later tonight, I will be catching a plane to New York City. Tomorrow morning I will appear live on the nationally televised program *Rise and Shine America!* And I will be speaking out for justice. Justice for Reggie Brogus. Justice for T-Bird Williams. So be sure to get up early tomorrow—or at least set your VCRs. The show comes on at six-thirty in the morning. Check it out, y'all!" Kwanzi paused, as if waiting for a big crowd reaction. There was only a smattering of applause. Kwanzi looked panicked for a moment. "Okay," she said, "now I'd like to turn the mike over to the best friend of African Americans on the *entire* faculty of Arden University: Roger Pym-Smithers!"

"Who?" I heard several students behind me say.

Roger stood close to the microphone stand, clutching the thin metal rod with both hands and wringing it anxiously as he spoke. "I just want to say, well, I think it's . . . Kwanzi asked me to speak tonight . . . because . . ." The crowd now was utterly quiet. Roger's eyes darted about nervously. "As a white member of the faculty . . . I feel it must be said that . . ." Roger seemed to be gaining confidence. His voice grew stronger, less hesitant, though he continued to wring the mike stand. "I think it's outrageous that people are always trying to make the blacks out to be violent. I mean, we—white men—we're the bloody savages! Not *you* people! Not you blacks! I mean, where I come from, in Europe, we've been slaughtering each other for thousands of bloody years! I mean, look at bloody Yugoslavia for Christ's sake!"

Roger paused. The crowd responded with a profound and excruciating silence.

Kwanzi quickly pushed her husband away from the microphone. "Well said!" she cried. Kwanzi vigorously slapped her palms together. "Hear, hear! Very well said!" There was a lukewarm trickle of applause among the students. "Very well said indeed!" Kwanzi cheered. Roger smiled and waved shyly to the audience.

I turned and started jostling my way through the crowd. I could hear Kwanzi's voice ringing out behind me. "Now I'd like y'all to join me in an old, old protest song. We used to sing this back in the sixties, before y'all was even born. But the words might be familiar to you. Just follow me. One . . . two . . . three . . ."

As I parted from the crowd and walked farther away across the quadrangle, heading for the English Department on the other side of campus, I was stirred by the sound of those five hundred black voices singing "We Shall Overcome." And my heart, like Kwanzi's, was back in the sixties. My mind, however, was back on Boxing Day.

* * *

"There is a coup afoot," Roger Pym-Smithers said, managing to sound at once ominous and sarcastic. "Rumors of one, at least."

I took a long, luxurious sniff of my glass of Château neuf du Pape. "Mmmmm," I said. "Black currant . . . burning autumn leaves . . . a splendiferous hint of toejam."

"I am serious," Roger said, sounding only half-serious. "You're friends with Reggie Brogus, aren't you?"

I slumped deeper in the cushy velvet armchair. The study of Roger and Kwanzi's house had the same tousled, dusty feel of the rest of the place but with more of a touch, in the old-fashioned chairs and furniture, of a grandmotherly parlor. I could feel my mood sliding from pleasantly drunk to unpleasantly drunk. "You know, old bean," I said to Roger, "I've had to have so many conversations about Reggie Brogus this past semester that he's the last person I feel like talking about right now."

"Indeed! That's how we all feel. Yet we *have* to talk about him. Because he imposes himself! That's part of his sinister genius! It's what made him a charismatic leader in the sixties and such a menace today."

"I think you overrate him."

"Well, certainly you know him better than I do." Roger leered at me, eyebrows flaring devilishly. "You know him better than anybody on this campus."

Now I was irritated. "Roger, I had lunch with the guy a couple of times and I've hardly seen him since early November."

"So he didn't say anything to you about renewing his residency for another year? About Jerry Shamberg offering him an extension—and a raise?"

I almost choked on my wine. "A raise!"

"Heads of departments always get a raise."

"You don't think—"

"That is the scuttlebutt, Clay. I thought you could enlighten us on its veracity."

"Reggie Brogus as head of Afrikamerica Studies?"

"American *Negro* Studies," Roger drawled, his voice all ominous-sarcastic. "Brogus apparently wants to rename the program."

"This I had not heard."

"Really?" Roger sounded as if he doubted me, but I was telling the truth. What reason would I have to lie? "Well, there's bound to be a shake-up," he said. "The Davenports will be retiring at the end of next semester and Xavier Lumbaki is returning to Paris. If Brogus does not return next year, that would leave Kwanzi as the only professor in the program. If that were the case, I doubt Dean Shamberg would make Afrikamerica Studies a full-fledged department. But if he *is* going to continue with the program, then regardless of whether Brogus stays or not, regardless of whomever else is teaching in the program, Kwanzi Authentica Parker damn well deserves to be the chairman! It's her bloody department!"

Roger had lost his customary air of ironic detachment. I could see the raspberry color in his jowls deepening. "You're right," I said.

"You agree with me?"

"Of course."

Roger beamed. "Jolly good!" He took a satisfied gulp of wine. "Well, that brings me to the next rumor going around: that you, Clay, might be joining the Afrikamerica Studies Department next year."

"Did Dean Jer tell you that?" Roger just leered at me. I wondered if he actually waxed and combed his eyebrows to get them to stick out the way they did. "Not so," I said.

"But if it were so, if it were you, Kwanzi, and Reggie teaching in the department next year, you would support Kwanzi as chairman, yes?"

"Chairperson," I said.

"Oh, don't be so bloody American! What I need to know is: Could we count on you to be in Kwanzi's camp?"

"Yeah, sure, fine," I said irascibly. I downed the last bit of wine in my glass. Roger quickly leaned over to refill it. "One for the road," I said.

"Another question, if I may, old bean. Do you happen to know of a Trevor Bledsoe III?"

"Sure, I know Trevor."

Roger was referring to the head of Africana Studies at Vymar College in Vymar, Massachusetts. He must have been somewhere between Reggie's age and mine, a smooth and affable brother who was popping up more and more in newspaper profiles and opinion journals and on *The Huck Blossom Show* as an authority on race. Reggie had once told me I should model myself after Trevor Bledsoe III. Though Trevor was neither as bombastic nor as conservative as Brogus, Reggie still considered him a "spokesman for the right ideas."

"You've met him?"

"A couple of times. In New York."

"And?"

"He always seemed like a decent enough guy. A bit full of himself, but a decent enough guy."

"Well, that *guy*, as you say, might be joining the Afram department next year and he will no doubt be in Reggie Brogus's camp! They might even become *co*chairmen of the department! Word has it that Shamberg and Brogus have both been wooing Trevor Bledsoe III with promises of money, status, and perks if he comes to Arden. Apparently, Trevor has become quite the media darling. I had lunch with Shamberg last week and he says that in New York everybody's always talking about Trevor and Reggie, Trevor and Reggie, Trevor and Reggie. Kwanzi's sick to death of hearing about the both of them. The other night they made a joint appearance on *The Huck Blossom Show* and Kwanzi started shrieking. 'Trevor and Reggie again! What are they: lovers?' I thought maybe she had a point."

"I'm pretty sure Reggie's a hundred percent hetero, Roger, and as for Trevor Bledsoe, he's got a wife and a couple of kids."

Roger was leering his ass off now. He poured himself another glass of wine. "Back when I was a young assistant professor in England, I joined a club, a somewhat exclusive one. And I soon realized that a lot of the more distinguished members were buggering each other. This was an all-male club, of course. Well, one evening, the club chairman said to me that the following Thursday, or whatever, was the annual banquet to which women were allowed. A sort of Ladies' Night, as it were. He encouraged me to bring my girlfriend. I said I would. But I asked him, 'What do the homosexual members of the club do on Ladies' Night?' And he said, 'Why, they bring their *wives*, my dear boy, they bring their *wives.*' Haw-haw-HAW!"

I had a good laugh myself. "Another great English tradition," I said.

"Oh, not just English, old bean. I think we are speaking now of a generational sense of propriety. Those distinguished gentlemen at my club understood the basic hypocrisy of society, of matrimony. They understood the duality of human nature and the necessity of wearing social masks. My generation, we tried to do away with the masks, to do away with social hypocrisy of any sort! Openness was our ideology. Everything out of the closet! And I'm not just speaking of homosexuality now. I couldn't possibly speak from experience. I am, as you say, one hundred percent hetero. I'm talking about any kind of sexuality. My generation was for bringing all of it out of the closet! We did not understand, as the generation before us understood, the usefulness of closets." Roger took a pensive, melancholy sip of wine, then fixed his rheumy gaze on me. "And what of *your* generation, Clay?"

"What of us?"

"How does your generation deal with the inherent hypocrisy of matrimony? Do you wear masks, separate a private self from a public self? Or do you lay it all out in the open—your so-called infidelities?" Roger was beginning to slur his words.

Spacing out in my drunkenness, I saw Pirate Jenny, her naked body writhing beneath mine, on the futon, in the candlelight, her eyes wide open, mouth a perfect O as she came. It had happened less than three months ago, but it already felt like an odd, half-remembered dream.

"So, how many?" Roger asked.

"What?"

"How many? How many women have you fucked?"

"Ever? I don't know. I'd have to stop and count."

"I don't know precisely how many women I've had either," Roger said. "I stopped counting after one thousand."

"Wow," I said tonelessly.

"Of course, most of my conquests occurred in the sixties and seventies. Things were so much simpler then. Ah, you just don't know what you missed, old bean. You were simply born too late."

"You were one randy bloke, eh, Rog?"

"But it wasn't just me. It was everybody of my generation—blokes *and* birds! You should have known Kwanzi back in London in the seventies. I'm sure she took part in *far* more orgies than I did!" Roger sipped his wine and waggled his eyebrows, a paunchy, middle-aged satyr. "We've both mellowed quite a bit. Though I still engage in some extracurricular activity. Did you know I keep a flat in New York?"

"No, I didn't."

"Well, I do. Why do you think I'm always flying off to New York? I have quite a little fan club in the so-called Big Apple."

"Does Kwanzi know?"

"About the flat? Of course she knows. As for my fucking other women: she knows, but she doesn't know. We generally follow a don't-ask-don't-tell policy. As Kwanzi says . . ." Roger switched to a startling, shrill voice: "'Honey chile, I don't *wanna* know, jes' so long as you wear a condom!' Haw-haw-HAW!"

I smiled tightly but couldn't bring myself to laugh. Roger's imitation of Kwanzi sounded nothing at all like Kwanzi. Not only was it gratingly falsetto while Kwanzi's actual voice was husky, throaty, but Roger's impersonation had a grotesque, minstrel show quality about it. He sounded like Butterfly McQueen playing the ignorant slave in *Gone with the Wind* who screams "I don't know nuthin' 'bout birthin' no babies!" Was that how Roger thought his wife sounded?

"But what about *you*, Clay?" Roger said, returning to his normal tone of mocking insinuation. "Surely, you and your lovely wife must have some sort of . . . understanding?"

"No, we're not that sophisticated."

"Come, come now, old bean. I'm sure you're a man with a secret. Probably *many* secrets. Anyone who talks as little about himself as you do must have *lots* to hide." Though my glass was only half-empty, Roger filled it almost to the rim. I did not protest. It was awfully good wine. "I think we're the same," Roger said, settling back into his armchair. "I see that dangerousness in you. Like me, you're drawn to the *forbidden*."

"Oh, really."

"Really. I am by nature a breaker of taboos. For instance, of the more than one thousand women I've fucked, do you know that at least ninety percent of them have been black?"

I was as skeptical as I was surprised. "Roger, are you saying that you've slept with nine hundred black women?"

"Oh, *at least* nine hundred. In fact, I haven't slept with a white woman since 1969! There's just something about *your* women, old bean. And I'm not just talking about black *American* women. I've traveled all over the African continent. And I can't even count the number of times I've been to Jamaaaaaaica, *mohn!*"

I was experiencing one of those moments in life when you most need to have a powerful retort to a comment you have found somehow vulgar, repulsive, but you are so shocked by the vulgarity and repulsiveness that you are at a loss to find the appropriate comeback. At that moment, all I could think to say was "Well, good for you, Roger."

"But you, Clay. Certainly you feel the attraction to the forbidden. Surely you must look at these luscious young students and feel the temptation. Especially with the white girls. The forbidden."

I was flabbergasted, but too numb-drunk for it to register in my face or manner. I thought of Pirate Jenny again, her nude legs wrapped around mine, bucking wildly. "You know," I said. "America is in many ways the exact opposite of Germany. In Germany everything is forbidden—except that which is permitted. In America everything is permitted—except that which is forbidden."

Roger leaned forward in his chair, a twinkling of recognition in his eyes. "To coin a phrase, old bean," he said. "To coin a phrase."

"Listen, man," I said, feeling suddenly agitated, fired up. "You wanna know about my generation, I'll tell ya about my generation. We respect our commitments. Okay? I'm committed to Penelope. For life. And there isn't a goddamned thing in the world that will ever change that."

Roger actually looked wounded. He slumped back in his chair. "Don't you think *I'm* committed to Kwanzi?" he said hoarsely. "Old bean, I am completely and utterly committed to Kwanzi, till the bloody end of our days!" Roger began blinking rapidly and I feared he was about to cry. "I *love* her, Clay," he rasped. "I would do anything for Kwanzi. No matter how many other women there are." He spoke haltingly now, a painful catch in his voice. "And even if . . . it isn't sexual . . . between me and Kwanzi anymore . . . it might be again someday. . . . But I would do . . . anything . . . for Kwanzi. Do you hear me?" A tear rolled down Roger's face. "*Anything.*"

This was getting way too intense for me. I set my glass of wine on the floor. "Sorry, Roger, but I gotta get going. If I'm not home before midnight, Pen's gonna . . ."

Roger quickly raised a palm. "Say no more."

Standing in the doorway of the Tudor-style house, back in my parka, ready for the long walk home, I held out my hand to my host. Instead of grasping it, Roger took hold of my shoulders and lunged toward me. He kissed me once on each cheek, like a European. "Good night, old bean," he said. "And give my best to your lovely wife."

Lumbering drunkenly down the sidewalk, I heard Roger close his front door behind me. I pulled on my thermal gloves and wiped Roger's slobber from my face.

*   *   *

So what the fuck had I *"told"* Roger Pym-Smithers on Boxing Day? Nearly two months later, walking across campus, from the T-Bird Williams demonstration to the English Department, I had pieced together my entire talk with Roger in his study that night and could not think of a single incriminating thing I had said. I remembered now that I'd found Roger pretty offensive that night. Maybe that was why I had blotted the conversation from my memory. Since I generally liked Roger I didn't want to remember his distasteful comments. Probably, I also didn't want to imagine what might have been going through his filthy mind when he looked at my wife—a beautiful black woman.

There was a distinct bite in the night air and the vacuumlike feeling that precedes a major snowstorm. I spotted my Honda parked behind the English Department house. All the lights in the house were out. I unlocked the front door, stepped into the receptionist's area. Without really thinking about it, I decided not to turn on the lights. I had no problem making my way down the darkened corridor to my office. Turning the key in my office door, I wondered if I would find another email from Reggie Brogus in my computer. Pushing the door open, reaching for the light switch on the wall, it occurred to me that Brogus might very well have been captured by now. Then the overhead light clicked on and I froze in my office doorway, unable to move or speak.

He sat in the chair behind my desk, cocking his high, noble, walnut-toned head. Even though he had been sitting in the dark at 8:30 p.m., the agent still wore his green-lensed aviator sunglasses. His black trenchcoat was buttoned up to the collar. I immediately sensed that there was also someone behind me. The feel of a hard piece of metal pressing against the back of my parka, jabbing right into my spine, instantly confirmed my suspicion.

"Good evening, Professor," said the man sitting behind my desk, his voice a mellifluous basso profondo. "You're coming with us. Don't ask where we're going because I'm not going to tell you. But I *can* tell you right now that you will either survive this night . . . or not. The choice is yours."

CHAPTER 12

"WHERE IS HE?"

My interrogator sat across from me at a wooden table, a sort of picnic table. Even in the shadowy orange firelight, he refused to take off his MacArthur-style shades. I was sitting on a hard low stool, my wrists in handcuffs, behind my back. We were sitting in a barn, illuminated by a kerosene lamp. I had no idea where exactly the barn was located. We had not driven far, but I was unable to view the scenery. Right after the agent greeted me in my office, someone behind me pulled a black sack, almost like an executioner's hood minus the eyeholes, over my head. There were three of them altogether, the bald-headed black man and two guys I had not even seen. My hands were locked behind me and I was whisked blindly down the corridor of the English Department house, gripped firmly under each arm by unseen hands, pushed through the front door out into the biting cold. I heard a car door open. A huge hand, fingers spread, came down with a ferocious pressure on the top of my head, forcing me to bend my knees. I was shoved into the car. No one said a word during the short drive. The goon with the enormous paws stayed in the backseat with me. The other goon must have been driving, with the boss man, as usual, in the passenger seat. Bizarre as my situation was, the most curious thing to me was that I felt completely unafraid. Mainly, I was pissed off, emboldened by rage. My fever had broken. The strange bloodlust I felt chasing T-Bird had returned. But now I was bound and blindfolded. There was nothing to do in the back of the Lincoln Town Car but seethe.

Soon I felt the car rolling over bumpy, frozen earth, slowing to a halt. I was shoved out into the cold. I heard a door creak open in front of me. Even with the black sack over my head, I was overwhelmed by the odor of large, thick-hided animals, the sharp smell of hay. I was pushed down onto the stool. The sack was taken off my head and I found myself looking at the bleak-faced agent. "You fellas wait out in the car," he said in his James Earl Jones as Darth Vader voice. I heard the door close behind me. I couldn't help but feel a bitter amusement at the cozy, rustic setting. It was just me and the boss man now. I stared hard at him, silently, my fury smoldering.

"I'll ask you one more time," he bellowed. "Where is he?"

"Who the fuck are you?" I said.

Boss man cocked his walnut head. I could not see his eyes but I knew they were registering surprise. He smirked and said, "Special Agent Guffin."

"Special Agent of the FBI?"

"Something like that. Does it matter?"

"I just want to know who to name when I press kidnapping charges."

Guffin let out a low, rumbling laugh. "Presumably after your trial for first-degree murder, Professor. And that's only assuming you survive this night. Now, let's cut the bullshit. Where the fuck is Brogus?"

"Gee, Mr. Special Agent," I said, oozing sarcasm, "I thought the FBI said he was in Mississippi."

Guffin just stared at me from behind his dark green lenses. After about half a minute he leaned forward and folded his hands on the picnic table. "Answer my question, boy."

"I thought the FBI was offering a reward for information on Brogus. A hundred thousand was the figure I heard." I was looking right into Guffin's face. I barely noticed him unfold his hands. "Now," I continued, "if you wanna open negotiations—"

I saw it only peripherally, the open palm flying in space, a millisecond before impact. I was blinded again, my neck twisting violently, the whole left side of my face burning. After a moment I raised my head, a tiny flame sizzling in each pore of skin on the left side of my face. My vision began to refocus.

Guffin sat before me, his hands folded on the table again. "That time, I slap you like you was my bitch. Next time, I'm gonna hit you like a man. Now where the fuck is Brogus?"

"Are you from Cointelpro?" I said, as the fire in my face died down. I knew I might be beaten. I believed I might even be killed. But I didn't care. If I had stopped to think about it, I'd have thought I was losing my mind. But I did not stop to think—a sign, perhaps, that I had *already* lost my mind. I just wanted some answers.

"Say what?" Guffin growled.

"I know what the real deal is. Reggie tangled with you motherfuckers before, back in his radical days. You thought you had him beat, brainwashed. But somehow, some way, Reggie got hold of some files. The top secret files on Martin Luther King's assassination."

Guffin was staring at me, his eyes concealed, slack-jawed. Obviously, I knew more than he knew I knew.

"You knew Reggie might go public with this info," I continued, my confidence swelling. "So you had to neutralize him. Somehow, some way. So you killed that girl and planted her body in his office. To frame him for murder. I assume the cops looking for him will just shoot him on sight now, huh? Shoot first, shoot to kill, ask questions later. Get Brogus out of the way. Then retrieve those files. Keep the truth a secret. Ain't that right, Guffin?"

The special agent slowly closed his mouth. He took a deep breath, then said, "Is that what he told you?"

"More or less."

"That Cointelpro, Brogus's old nemesis, was out to destroy him?" Guffin spoke slowly, carefully, as if he were trying to grasp a difficult concept. "That he had tangled with Cointelpro before?"

"Yeah."

"That's what he told you?" With a delicate, almost painful, deliberateness, Special Agent Guffin raised his hands to his face. He gingerly removed his sunglasses, then pressed the thumb and forefinger of his left hand against his closed eyes, rubbed them hard. "You poor stupid fuck," I thought I heard him mutter.

I leaned forward, hands locked behind my back. "What?" I said.

"BROGUS *WAS* COINTELPRO!" Guffin exploded.

I recoiled on my low, hard stool, almost tumbling off it as Guffin lunged at me, his head only inches from mine, his enormous, haunted brown eyes screaming in his haggard face. We must have remained suspended like that for several seconds, me leaning back, Guffin practically mounting the picnic table, madman eyes screaming. Finally, Guffin fell back in his seat and I straightened up on my stool. Guffin closed his eyes, rubbed them hard with his knuckles, then said it again, his voice low and hot: "Brogus *was* Cointelpro."

I could feel the atmosphere in the dimly lit barn decompressing. The rage between Guffin and me subsided. But my curiosity now, my need to know, was stronger than ever. "Tell me," I said quietly.

Guffin was silent for a long time, pressing his fist against his eyes. "That nigga was like my blood," he finally said. "Like a little brother to me." Guffin paused again and I was afraid he wouldn't continue.

"Go on," I said gently.

"I recruited him right out of college," Guffin said, slowly lowering his hand from his face. The lamplight flickered in his glassy eyes. "U. of Michigan. Class of '64. The president had just been killed and you knew there was a danger the whole country might crack up, have a nervous breakdown. And it did." Guffin nodded his head. He did not look at me. He stared fixedly into the kerosene lamp, as if reading his memory in the flame. "Reggie Brogus helped set things right. He was a true patriot. One of the great ones. He set a standard for self-sacrifice that has never been matched. Certainly not by any other colored agent. And not by most of the white boys either. Self-sacrifice short of death, that is. But Reggie risked being cut down in the line of duty. Risked it many a time. Let's give the man his due."

"Are you saying," I practically whispered, "that Reggie Brogus was never really a radical? That he was a government agent from the start?"

Guffin let out a bitter little laugh. He still did not look me in the eye. "What year were born, boy?"

"Nineteen fifty-eight."

"Yeah, young folks is stupid. They always are. Except for Reggie. He always knew the score. Knew what mattered. Understood what this country is all about."

"What do you mean?"

"What do I *mean?* I mean that between 1964 and 1974 a lotta crazy niggas was tryin' to burn this great country of ours down to the ground. And a lot of oh-so-well meanin' ofays was stupid enough and starry-eyed and guilty-conscienced enough about black folks to stand back and let 'em do it, to hand 'em the gasoline to pour on the flames! The radical black element had to be destroyed before it destroyed America. All decent black folks knew that. But a lotta white folks can be awfully naive about black folks. Especially back then. White folks had to be made to see just how fuckin' crazy the Black Powermongers were. And the Black Powermongers had to be assaulted from the outside and poisoned from the inside. Reggie Brogus was one of the great poisoners. He was undercover, man: deep, *deep* cover. Even today, almost nobody knows that the Brogus who posed on the jacket of *LIVE BLACK OR DIE!* was a fraud. A fraud designed to scare the shit outta white folks and to divide black folks. And guess what? It worked! We won!"

I remembered pulling Reggie's first book from the top shelf in my parents' library in 1969, remembered how it shook me to the core. "The militant manifesto," I said softly, still bewildered by Guffin's outpouring, "was a fraud?"

Guffin's low, wicked laugh rumbled. "Brogus and me, we wrote that book one drunken weekend at Quantico. And, you know, neither one of us ever saw any royalties from it. But *I* never bitched about it."

"What about the bank robbery in Detroit, in '74? That was staged?"

Guffin winced. He still had not looked at me. "Like I say, Brogus was deep, deep cover. That robbery was for real. But Reggie didn't plot it and he wasn't at the scene of the crime. Anyone who was payin' attention would have noticed that every time Brogus had been arrested, he was released on some technicality. We made sure of it. But that bank heist was totally fucked up. We lost two peace officers that day. But the radical black element lost *three* of its comrades. That was Reggie's last serious gig. After that, we got him out of the country and kept him underground for the better part of ten years. He's been completely on his own since 1984. And, frankly, I don't see where he's done too damn badly for himself." Special Agent Guffin lapsed into another long silence, continued to stare into the kerosene lamp.

I, meanwhile, was having trouble digesting all this. "Blackness As a Revolutionary Force?" I murmurred.

"BAARF? Reggie thought that one up, that's true. But his African name, Mkwame Obolobongo—that one was mine." Guffin laughed bitterly again. "Mkwame Obolobongo. Shit, even *Reggie Brogus* wasn't that motherfucker's real name. I can't even remember what his real name was."

"So Brogus wasn't brainwashed after he was arrested and extradited to the States?"

"Brainwashed? That motherfucker couldn't *wait* to get back home. And he came back to us a fuckin' hero, man. Everybody in domestic intelligence respected Reggie Brogus. And we made sure he was treated well overseas, too. We brought him in after seven years and for the next three years he kicked back and took it easy, at government expense, on government property. How you think he got so fuckin' fat between '81 and '84?"

"And after '84 he was on his own?"

"We cut him loose. That was what he wanted. He wasn't a lifer, like me. That boy always had something special. I saw it back in '64."

"So the right-wing Reggie Brogus who wrote *An American Salvation*, that was the true Brogus all along?"

"That motherfucker never changed," Guffin said wistfully.

"And these files Brogus told me about," I said, a bit tentatively. "On Dr. King's assassination. What's that all about?"

Now Guffin looked me directly in the eye, his death mask face scowling in the flickering lamplight. "Let me tell you something, boy. Dr. King was a great man. But he lost his way. I love him for fighting for the constitutional rights of our people. But in the last couple years of his life, he began to succumb to the radical black element. He started talkin' that commie trash about redistribution of wealth. He was rabble-rousin' against Vietnam—a war that *had* to be fought! Organizing a so-called

Poor People's Campaign! Dr. King wanted to turn America into Russia! Like a lot of the best black American minds of the twentieth century— I'm speaking now of Du Bois, of Robeson—he was on the wrong side of the great question of the times. He was a commie simp! As a civil rights crusader, he was a great man. But he had served his purpose. He had to die when he did."

"So the FBI killed him."

"Of course the FBI killed him! Everybody knows *that*, nigga!"

"So what about the files Brogus has?"

"Files?" Guffin shook his head and laughed. "What's he got? Transcripts of tapes of Dr. King fuckin' white women in hotel rooms? Who cares? Those tapes will be made public in 2027. That's the law."

"Brogus says he has the raw data on what really went down in Memphis, when Dr. King was killed."

Guffin looked down at the table, fiddled with his sunglasses. "Do you know your history, boy?" he said in his low growl.

"Sometimes," I said.

"Do you know what Dr. King was doing in Memphis in the spring of '68?"

"Yes!" I said, like an eager pupil. "He was supporting a strike by black sanitation workers."

"Garbagemen!" Guffin bellowed. He lifted his Ray-Bans from the table, carefully hooked them around his ears. "Do you know what Reggie Brogus was doing in Memphis in the spring of '68? Dr. King's nonviolent marches were disrupted by violence, violence instigated by young black thugs. Well, Reggie Brogus was one of the ringleaders of those young black thugs. This was about six months before we published LIVE BLACK OR DIE! He was down there in Memphis on the day Dr. King got whacked, getting ready to cause some more disruption, to show what sort of chaos King's brand of radicalism would lead to."

"So Brogus, or whatever his name is, was working to thwart Dr. King?"

"Thwart?" Guffin spat out the word. "Destroy!"

"And you were part of it."

Guffin grinned, his eyes concealed once more behind his dark green shades. "Lemme ask you, Professor: What the fuck do you think Martin Luther King Jr. would be doing today, in the America of the 1990s? He'd be a fuckin' nobody! A fat, white-haired, sixty-something old has-been preachin' about the Promised Land. A jive-ass, sorry-ass chump. Instead, he's an American icon, a deity of the Republic. 'Cause he died at thirty-nine. Just six years older than Jesus. The man's birthday is a damn holiday. Just like Jesus. And just like Jesus, ain't nobody really listens to what the man had to say. But, like Jesus, Martin Luther King, Jr., has his purpose. Like Jesus, he's better off worshiped dead than alive. I loves my Jesus! And I loves my Dr. King! Just like every other American. Just so long as all you remember is I HAVE A DREAM! And forget that radical crap he espoused, forget that he was rabble-rousin' the fuckin' garbagemen, tryin' to overthrow the democratic capitalist system that is the envy of the entire fuckin' world! Don't you see, boy? Dr. King alive was dangerous. Dr. King dead is safe."

I sat on my stool, awestruck. Looking at Guffin, I felt I was staring into the face of unfathomable evil. "And Brogus? Is he more dangerous to you alive than dead?"

"Lemme tell you something, boy, I will not be blackmailed. Not by anybody."

"Blackmail?"

"What the fuck you think Brogus is doing with these King files? He has threatened to make them public unless he gets paid twenty million dollars for his service to our government. One million dollars for each year he was on the team! That fat, greedy motherfucker!"

"A true capitalist."

"Don't get wise with me, boy! You don't know what you've got yourself mixed up in here! Brogus is a crazed fucking paranoid schizophrenic who is willing to humiliate this nation before the eyes of the world, to expose me, to expose himself, to degrade the King family with these files! That motherfucker would attempt to extort twenty million dollars from the people who nurtured him, protected him, and gave him the foundation to be the celebrity he is today. That greezy fat fuck is trying to blackmail me! *Me!* Well, I'm not havin' it, boy. Now where the fuck is Brogus?"

I paused, wanting to make sure that I answered in a calm, even voice. "I don't know."

Guffin reached into his trenchcoat pocket and pulled out a large gun. He pointed the weapon, I believe it was a 9-mm semiautomatic, directly in my face, inches from the tip of my noise. "Where the fuck is he?"

"I honestly don't know."

"DON'T YOU FUCKING LIE TO ME, BOY!"

Now I was scared. I heard the drowsy braying of large barnyard animals. There was a sudden knock behind me, the sound of the barn door creaking open, the wind gusting outside. "Everything all right, Mack?" I heard a white-"sounding" voice say.

"The professor here is being a bit . . . uncooperative," Guffin grumbled. "Let us demonstrate for him our powers of persuasion."

*   *   *

I don't know when I surpassed my threshhold for pain, when the barrier was shattered, transcended. I could feel the blows land, but they no longer hurt. There was a thudding resonance within my body after each hit. But I was beyond pain now. As I could not see, I never knew from which direction the next fist would fly. Back in the barn, as Guffin pointed his gun in my face, the black sack was placed over my head again. Another short drive in the Lincoln. Then I found myself standing out in the icy night air, the fabric of the executioner's hood itching against my face. Someone pulled my parka from my shoulders. I could feel it bunched around my wrists, which were still in the handcuffs, locked behind my back.

"Where is he?" Guffin asked, his voice coming from a few feet in front of me.

"I don't know," I said through the black sack.

POW! The first shot was to my right kidney. I bent over, wheezing.

"Where the fuck is he?"

I slowly straightened up. "I have no reason to lie to you, Guffin," I managed to say between gasping breaths. "I honestly don't know where Brogus is."

BAM! The second blow—it must have been the ham-fisted goon hitting me—caught me upside the head, just above my already scarred left eye. Perhaps that was when I entered a heretofore unknown realm of consciousness, feeling the blows but feeling no pain. No physical pain, that is.

Let them kill you, the voice inside my head said. *You deserve to die.*

"Where is he?" Guffin bellowed. He asked the question over and over, but I was no longer answering. It was hard enough just to breathe. I was punched in the stomach, slammed in the solar plexus, bashed across my brow. I was staggering blindly about, but I remained on my feet.

Good! This is what you deserve. Let them kill you. They killed Pirate Jenny. Now let them kill you. You killed T-Bird. His innocent blood is on your hands. Two young people dead. Because of you. It is only fair and just that you should die. Die!

I just did not want to get kneed in the balls. I was beyond ordinary pain. I was a blind, wheezing, staggering wreck. But still I dreaded that unique, howling, hollowed-out excruciation that followed a knee to the testicles. I no longer cared if I lived or died. I just didn't want to get kneed in the balls.

Die, you worthless piece of shit! Let them kill you. You're a failure. A coward. A loser. A traitor to your family. Who the fuck could ever care about a character like you? Just die.

I toppled to the ground. I felt the sack torn from my head. I felt frozen needles of grass prickling in my face. All I saw was blackness. Suddenly, a cold piece of metal was pressed against my temple.

"Where is he?" Guffin's voice was all echoey, rubbery, like a recording played at ultraslow speed.

Go ahead and shoot. Please.

I see a white hand in the blackness, Pirate Jenny's alabaster palm, offering the black, unlabeled computer disk, as if on a platter. "Take it, Clay," I hear her say. "Take it now." The hand and the disk dissolve. Then I see my little girls in the void. Their sweet, identical faces are sad as they wave good-bye to me. They recede, gradually, into the blackness, as if they are disappearing down an invisible road. Amber and Ashley are still waving to me as their faces, getting smaller and smaller, are swallowed up by the void. I hear the click of the gun pressed to my temple and I know I am about to die.

Forgive me. Everybody. Please forgive me.

*   *   *

The wet tickle of snowflakes on my face awakened me. I very slowly sat up. My left eye was swollen, throbbing, and completely closed. Fat, white flakes cascaded from the dark sky and clung to the yellow blades of grass. I saw my parka sprawled on the ground in front of me. There were no longer any handcuffs around my wrists. I tasted blood in my mouth. A sticky sensation in my underpants made me wonder if I'd peed on myself. I looked at my watch. Ten minutes to midnight. I tilted my head and saw a brightly painted sign above me: Wintergreen Gardens. Turning my head this way and that, scanning the landscape before me with my one good eye, I saw a cluster of unfinished abodes: foundations without houses, houses without rooftops, pale wooden skeletal structures, snow swirling through the big rectangular holes that might someday be windows. I knew where I was. Wintergreen Gardens was meant to be a new development of bland, uniform middle-class manses, constructed just on the outskirts of suburban Arden. But once the recession kicked in a year earlier, the developer had had to stop developing. As I sat on the damp, spiky grass, feeling cold snow collecting in my hair, I realized I was not far from home.

Trudging homeward through the snow, bruised, bloodied, blind in one eye, but still alive, gloriously, gratefully alive, I felt like Marlon Brando stumbling toward his fellow longshoremen at the end of *On the Waterfront.* All I wanted was to get home. To hug my kids, my wife. I was alone, snaking through the streets of suburbia. I was enveloped by the powdery hush of the snowfall, staggering, beaten, one-eyed and urine-stained but silently ecstatic just to be alive. Pirate Jenny and T-Bird were dead—and it cut me to the core. But what the fuck. I was alive. Alive! And I hadn't even been kneed in the balls. I had escaped death, testicles intact.

Maplewood. My street. What a good and blessed thing it was to live on a street named Maplewood in a town called Arden in a place known as Ohio. What a good and blessed thing life was, even with a dent in your kidneys and blood in your mouth. And there was my house! I saw it, swimming in and out of view as I blundered down the street. I wondered if maybe I had suffered a concussion. Then, almost magically, my wife appeared. She was hauling a suitcase, kicking out her path through a blanket of snow. There at the curb—what a sublimely familiar sight it was—sat the dark blue Volvo, the solid, reliable, family car, manufactured by scrupulous Scandinavians. My wife opened the trunk of the car, dropped the suitcase inside. I wobbled closer and closer to her, feeling the accumulated snowflakes on the tops of my sturdy Timberland boots. Penelope closed and locked the trunk.

"Honey," I said, my voice echoing in the snow-cushioned streets.

Pen twirled around to confront me. I had known her since we were both twelve years old and I had never seen her face like this, almost disfigured, contorted in anguish. She moved a step toward me. All I heard was the powdery snowfall hush. My wife made a jerky motion, a convulsion in her lower body. Then came the pain, the harrowing excruciation. My eyeballs rolled back into my head, my innards retracted, seemingly consuming themselves as I crumpled to the sidewalk, air being sucked out of my lungs, my throat, my mouth. I writhed in the cold, wet snow, my mind a fuzzing test pattern. All was pure, hollowed-out pain. Penelope had kneed me in the balls.

My wife stood over me. With an angry flick of the wrist, she threw something to the ground. I heard it land softly in the powder. Penelope got into the car. I looked up and saw the twins sticking their heads out of the backseat window.

"We're going to stay with Grandpa and Grandma Law in Philadelphia," Ashley said. "Are you sure you're gonna be all right, Daddy?"

I heard myself wheeze as I writhed on the ground.

"You really fucked up this time, Dad," Amber said, shaking her head and staring pitilessly down at me.

The engine started, the Volvo pulled away. I saw my little girls, through the rear window, waving to me, their unsmiling faces illuminated in the cone of light from the nearby streetlamp, then disappearing into the darkness as they drove down Maplewood. Only after the Volvo faded from view did I notice the object Pen had dropped beside me. The black, unlabeled computer disk lay sideways in the fluffy snow.

Once the agony had subsided, I rose to my feet. Picked up the disk. Entering the house, I saw my old moth-eaten suede jacket twisted on the floor of the foyer. The meaning was immediately clear. I remembered it only now: that day in December, when I had my reluctant last meeting with Jenny at Cafe Bellafiglia, had been unusually balmy. I had not worn my parka, but the dirty old brown suede jacket I had bought back in my undergraduate days at Cornell, a jacket Pen hated, but which I loved to dig out and sport for a few fall days each year, a jacket I must have been wearing and must have stuffed the diary disk into a pocket of the last time I saw Jennifer Wolfshiem alive. Penelope thought to look for the disk in a place that had not even occurred to me. And, obviously, she had read the contents of the disk. Hence my aching balls.

First, I went to the bathroom. I showered, nursed my bruises, treated my cuts. I put an icepack on my sealed, pulsating eye. I changed clothes and made a pot of coffee. At approximately one a.m. Thursday, February 20, 1992, I walked into my study, sat in front of my desktop computer and turned it on. I inserted the black, unlabeled disk as the machine clicked and hummed. I took a sip from my mug of steaming black coffee and watched neon green letters flicker on the black screen.

I said aloud: "Speak, Jenny."

CHAPTER 13

MAYBE THIS IS A COMMON nightmare for some people, but it was most definitely not one that I had ever had before. Sealed in a coffin, suffocating, scratching on the wood above me, tearing at it with my raw and bloody fingertips, hearing my own desperate clawing in the pitch dark, hearing the sound of dirt being shoveled on top of the lid, sensing the hungry, crawling presence of subterranean dwellers as I am buried alive. I bolted upright just as, in the dream, I was opening my mouth to scream.

Shaking the nightmare from my head, struggling to orient myself to waking life, I saw the ice-blue digits of the VCR clock (6:09 a.m.) glowing in the shadows and realized I was sitting on my living room couch. I clicked on the side table lamp. I saw my briefcase propped open on the coffee table, my parka strewn across an armchair, and realized I had not been asleep very long. Gradually, it dawned on me that my scheduled interrogation with Patsy DeFestina in the Arden police headquarters was a bare fifty minutes away. I could still faintly hear a scratching in my brain as the terror of the nightmare slowly dissipated. I felt a twinge of self-pity. After the night I'd had, capped by the two hours spent reading Pirate Jenny's diary, was it any wonder I was dreaming of horrific death?

Still I heard the faint scratching, even though I was now fully awake. "Dexter?" I asked aloud, wondering if our cat was trapped, abandoned in the pantry. I had simply assumed that Dexter was in the Volvo with Penelope, Amber, and Ashley as they drove away. Even if Pen had packed their bags in a furious rush and hustled them out of the house, there was no way the twins would have left their silver-eyed black cat behind. Maybe Pen had simply refused to take him on the long drive.

The scratching, barely audible, continued. I rose creakily from the couch. My body was sore all over. My left eye, still half-closed, quivered and throbbed. I crept into the kitchen. Through the frilly yellow curtains hanging in front of the window, I could see that the sky was still night-time dark, the snow was still falling steadily. I turned on the small lamp on the kitchen table. I no longer heard the scratching. The pantry door was shut tight. "Dexter?" I said.

Hearing a sudden click, I turned my head and saw a silhouette outside the door in the corner of the kitchen, the door whose top portion was a clear pane of glass decorated with curtains in that frilly yellow motif, the door that led to our back lawn. The door that Penelope and the girls were always forgetting to lock. Was it unlocked right now? The shadowy outline of a man shifted behind the curtain. I moved toward the back door, realizing that in the six hours since I had watched my wife and daughters drive away from me I had not checked to see if they had forgotten once again to lock the kitchen entrance. I was reaching for the knob when the back door swung open. Into my kitchen stepped the murderer of Jennifer Wolfshiem.

* * *

What I had mainly felt was embarrassment. I was embarrassed to be reading someone's innermost thoughts and feelings, embarrassed by my role in the author's life, embarrassed by the fact that my wife had read it all before I had—so agonizingly embarrassed that, as I sat alone in my study in the wee hours of Thursday morning, rapidly scrolling through Pirate Jenny's diary on my computer screen, I constantly had the creepy sensation that someone was standing behind me, reading over my shoulder. I could have done a "keyword" search, plugging in CLAY or ROBINETTE or T-BIRD or BROGUS. I could have gone hopping here and there around the text. Instead I read every word, as quickly as I could with my one good eye, racing chronologically through the sixty single-spaced pages, the chronicle of the life and misadventures, the memories and dreams and nightmares of Jennifer Esther Wolfshiem from Sunday, September 1, 1991, the day after she arrived in Arden,

Ohio, to Friday, December 13, 1991, the day before she handed me her diary disk in Cafe Bellafiglia.

She is happiest in September. New school. New beginning. Far enough away from Papa. No explanation of what the trouble with Papa is but she is happy to have escaped his current base of Washington, D.C. Jennifer writes of classes she plans to take, books she must read, wonders if she should focus more on fiction or nonfiction in her creative endeavors. She fondly describes her new "flat" but makes no mention at all of her flatmate and chirpy future eulogist Brittney Applefield. She is listening constantly to a CD of Lotte Lenya singing Brecht/Weill songs and decides to make "Pirate Jenny" her moniker. Despite the general good cheer of these early diary entries, there is always an undertow of loneliness, of sorrow. The vulnerability I had glimpsed in our first meeting lies behind every other line of Jenny's journal. She laments that she cannot help but feel a natural distance, a disengagement from other people. Everywhere she has ever lived, she has been a foreigner. She wonders if there will ever be anyplace she can truly call home.

I leaned close to the computer, my one good eye rapidly scanning the green letters glowing on the black screen. Sometimes, the diary was disappointingly banal. Jenny seemed much younger in her journal than she had in person. Other times, Jenny seemed more the way I remembered her, her observations clear and sharp, her prose sparkling, crystalline. This was a strange, gruesome way of getting to know a person, I thought, reading her journal posthumously. Then again, Jenny had hoped I'd read it while she was still alive. But why? Was it a cheap ploy to reestablish intimacy? Or the proverbial cry for help? I charged headlong through the text, looking for clues.

In mid-September, Pirate Jenny writes of her affinity for African Americans. In her eyes, we seem to know some secret that the rest of the United States is not in on. White female students try to befriend Jenny. She gives them the cold shoulder. White guys ask her out on dates. She turns them all down. Jenny tries to hang with Euphrasia, Tamika, Yolanda, and Shereena. They tolerate her company but seem to wish she would go away. Through them she meets T-Bird Williams. She likes him a lot but says she isn't sexually attracted to him. T-Bird courts her stealthily. He brings candy and flowers to her flat late at night. They sit on the futon and talk. He is always reluctant to leave, but never gets aggressive about it. He accepts his little goodnight peck on the lips and goes back to his dorm. T-Bird gets no play.

Professor Robinette, or "Prof Rob," makes his first appearance. Here Jennifer gets all schoolgirl crushy. How poignantly she looks up to the older man who takes her seriously! My good eye fondled her glowing green words of admiration. Even though I had helped chase an innocent young man to his death, been beaten to within an inch of my life, and been abandoned by my wife and children in the previous thirteen hours, I felt my spirit puff up with pride, my peacock soul blooming vibrantly. For the most part, Pirate Jenny simply recounts our talks about books and movies and music and politics. Yet she captures the seductive magic of good talk, the thing that, beyond physical attraction, truly drew us to each other.

I remembered the old Billy Joel love song in which he crooned, "I don't want clever conversation." Well, I *did* want clever conversation. And lots of it. Penelope and I had had a beautiful conversational communion, from the age of twelve right up until our second year of parenthood, at twenty-eight. From that point on, almost all of our talk centered on practical matters, basic survival issues about aspects of food and shelter, the health and education of our children, the attainment of money to maintain our standard of living. Logistical hassles, scheduling conflicts, priority juggling. For five years, this was what we talked about. At least ninety percent of the time. Whenever we did manage to squeeze in a philosophical debate, an aesthetic dialogue or an uninterrupted session of playful bullshitting, I was reminded of what we had lost, the verbal-erotic energy we had to suppress, the pleasure we had unthinkingly denied ourselves, all we had sacrificed in the name of quotidian family maintenance.

After a couple of entries, "Prof Rob" becomes "Clay." Pirate Jenny feels a certain sexual tension during her Wednesday evening office hours with him. Jenny writes that she has been having erotic dreams about her adviser. Ever since she wrote her imagined postcoital reverie, "Perceptions of a Languid and Bittersweet Tuesday Afternoon." By the last September entry, she is certain that, under the right circumstances, she could have "a romance" with Clay.

Reading Jenny's coquettish calculations—and remembering my self-deluding Gandhi test—my spiritual peacock plumes withered in shame. I thought of Penelope and how she must have felt scrolling through this diary. I could barely imagine the disgust, the revulsion, the killing sense of betrayal she must have experienced. I remembered the look of unspeakable anguish on her face just before she kneed me in the balls. Yet . . . and yet . . . as I stared into the glowing green-and-black computer screen, I was already thinking of how I could rationalize this illicit relationship to my wife—if she would even talk to me—when I called her at her parents' home in Philadelphia later in the day. I would ask Pen to remember how respectfully Jenny had written of me. I would explain that I was a protective and comforting authority figure to a sad and lonesome girl. I was her benevolent polestar, a role model. As I plotted my self-defense, I continued to tap the downward-pointing arrow on the computer keyboard and the first October entry appeared on the screen.

"Clay is a shit. Just like every other man I've ever known. I was so wrong about him. He's a coward. He wasn't even that good in bed."

Pirate Jenny is writing in mid-October, ten days after Clay delivered his lame breakup speech during Wednesday evening office hours. It seems to be Clay's "fear" that disgusts her most. She thinks he would like to sleep with her again, that he has no moral qualms about it. He's just afraid of getting caught.

"But Clay must know I would never report him. I would never reveal our romance to anyone at all! He *must* know that."

Despite a sudden attack of nausea, I continued to scroll the text up the computer screen. In Jenny's next diary entry, her father is pestering her to come visit him in Johannesburg. He expects to be there "on business" for several months. "You were happy here before. We can be happy here together again," he tells his daughter. I remembered the pained, halting voice of the old man on the answering machine message that was played at Jenny's candlelight vigil. In the journal, Jenny writes that she was never happy in Johannesburg. She does not want to go back there. But, as always, she says, she cannot resist her father.

By the next entry she has bought her round-trip ticket to South Africa. She is no longer quite so pissed off at Clay. She misses their conversations. She considers phoning him but thinks the better of it. One night T-Bird shows up again with candy and flowers. They sit and chat on her futon. He pounces on her. She pushes him away. He wants to know why she won't sleep with him. She tells him she doesn't know him well enough but knows she is lying. She is too timid to tell him the truth: that the spark of sexual chemistry is just not there for her. She feels guilty because she likes T-Bird "as a person." And he has been helpful to her research, driving her to Impediment twice and showing her around the deteriorating city. Jenny tells T-Bird they should get to know each other better. She suggests they meet for coffee at Cafe Bellafiglia the following afternoon. T-Bird tells her that if he were to be seen on campus with a white girl his "rep" would be ruined. Jenny sees him to the door. Once again, T-Bird gets no play.

Jenny returns from South Africa on October 28. The tone of the diary changes, becoming bleaker, more fraught with the lingering pain of trauma. She hated her trip to "Johburg." Her father kept kissing her, touching her, in inappropriate ways. He twice entered the bathroom while she was bathing, sat on the stool, talking, watching her, refusing to leave. At night, he came into her bed while she slept. She would wake up with her father's arms wrapped around her. She would tell him to leave but he would beg her to let him stay in the bed with her. "Like in the old days," he said.

Jenny has also been having dreams about her mother. About her mother sitting beside the bed while her father fondles her in the dark. Jenny's mother tells her that soon the two of them will be together, "in the silent place."

I sat alone in my study, staring into the computer screen, feeling like a fool. How could I not have seen the agony Pirate Jenny was in? I had sensed it, back when I was her academic adviser, but I hadn't wanted to deal with it. I made sure to keep our conversations buoyant and fun, fucked her for my own pleasure (not even hers!), and promptly tried to push her out of my life. It was obvious when I had last seen Jenny, in Cafe Bellafiglia, that she was in torment. But did I try to comfort her? Fuck no. Instead, I ran from the restaurant while she was in the bathroom. My nausea increased. Reading Jenny's diary, I was making myself sick.

The next entry is in early November, soon after Reggie Brogus barged in on Pirate Jenny—costumed as a black militant of the sixties—going down on Clay in his office. Jenny says she was totally stoned that night (though she doesn't specify on what). This is her first mention of Brogus at all. Even from under Clay's desk, she recognizes his voice. She had come to Clay's office to tease and cajole him into renewing their romance. After Brogus has left and she sees the abject fear in Clay's eyes she knows the chance of any further romance is nil. There is no bitterness. She actually seems to feel sorry for her professor.

Jenny writes of her longing to be someone different, someone else, anyone but herself. She is having nightmares now. When, as she sleeps, Papa comes into her bed, now he tries to strangle her. She feels his bony fingers around her neck, choking the life out of her. Jenny's mother hovers above. There is a huge, red, smile-shaped gash in her mother's white throat. It flaps up and down and oozes blood as her mother struggles to speak. Jenny always wakes up crying.

Mid-November. A Saturday afternoon. T-Bird knocks on her door. He invites her out for coffee. The whole time they sit together in Cafe Bellafiglia, T-Bird is glancing nervously about, clearly afraid of being seen with a white girl and subsequently having his precious rep devalued. He gallantly walks Jenny home. At her doorstep she tells him she has a lot of work to catch up on. He offers to take her to Impediment the next day. She agrees. He kisses her. She pushes him away. She explains that she wants to remain "just friends." He tells her he loves her. It doesn't matter. T-Bird *still* gets no play.

Nevertheless, the next day, he shows up in his Nissan Z at the scheduled time. As they approach Impediment, T-Bird asks Pirate Jenny, "Are you fuckin' that faggot Robinette?" She says he's not a faggot and she's not fucking him. They drive in silence through streets Jenny does not recognize. T-Bird suddenly stops and tells her to get out of the car. She says no. He says "Get out or I'll *make* you get out." She gets out. "Now, *find* your way home, bitch!" T-Bird cries. He drives away, his laughter trailing behind him.

The thing that makes her most angry as she watches the car fade away into the distance is that T-Bird seems to have assumed she would be lost and helpless, a hysterical wreck in this scary inner city. Because T-Bird thought of her as a white girl, in the same way that her ridiculous flat-mate Brittney Applefield (this is the only mention of her name in the journal) is just a white girl. But T-Bird can only think in terms of a suburban American archetype. Pirate Jenny is a European-American hybrid who has been acculturated to places and peoples all over the world. She walks through the gray tenement-lined streets of Impediment, Ohio, unafraid. Had T-Bird expected her to scream, to scamper about frantically? Jennifer Esther Wolfshiem walks the mean streets of Impediment with the same purposeful, casually intrepid stride with which she had negotiated the mean streets of cities from Amsterdam to Calcutta, from Naples to Hanoi. She walks past black women her age pushing babies in strollers, past clusters of black men her age who look at her threateningly, then, almost bashfully, turn away when they realize she is not threatened. She walks briskly along, as she would in any other strange city in any other foreign country, looking for a sign indicating the town center, or the nearest railway or bus station.

A car horn honks behind her. She turns and sees the gray BMW pull up to the curb. Through the windshield, she recognizes him immediately. But out of context, in a peculiar setting, away from the Arden U. campus, she sees something in the man's face she has never noticed before. She sees her father.

*   *   *

"Sorry to just barge in like this, old bean, but the door *was* open." Roger Pym-Smithers, wearing his battered black fedora and overcoat, stamped his feet, knocking slush off his galoshes and onto my kitchen floor. He flashed a friendly leer and waggled his devilish eyebrows. "We need to *talk*," he said, sounding at once grave and sardonic.

Staring at Pirate Jenny's murderer as we stood in my kitchen, I felt that strange new rage, the bloodlust, returning, warming my insides. But the fury now had a calming effect. I felt almost tranquil. I knew I was capable of killing this man, right here, without hesitation; without doubt, pity, or remorse. I actually thought I might even enjoy it. "Have a seat, Roger," I said, my voice sounding serene.

As he moved toward the kitchen table, Roger suddenly took note of my swollen eye. "Bloody hell! What happened to *you?*"

"Oh, I just met some old friends of Reggie Brogus's last night," I said evenly. "Sit down. I was just about to make some coffee. Would you like some?"

"Tea for me, please," Roger said politely. He took off his hat and over-coat, sat down in the same spindly chair Brogus had strained seventy-odd hours earlier. "I know I should have rung you first instead of popping up so impulsively—and at such an ungodly hour. But when I saw the light on in here, I took the liberty of tapping at your back door. I suppose you didn't hear it. Or did you? What about your lovely wife and children? Are they still asleep?"

"They're not here," I said. I moved dreamily about the kitchen, spooning ground beans into the coffee machine filter, pouring water into a kettle for my guest's tea, setting the kettle atop a burner.

"Oh really?" Roger said, an edge of skepticism in his voice, as if he didn't believe me. "Early risers all, eh? I was up quite early myself. Kwanzi's in New York, you know. She's going to be appearing on live television in about ten minutes. She rang me from the studio about a half hour ago. She was with the *makeup* girl! She really is quite excited about it all. Perhaps we could tune in."

I sat across from Roger at the kitchen table. "There's a TV right there," I said, nodding toward the tiny model on the table.

"That wee thing! Oh, well, fortunately I set the video recorder at home. And, of course, I had fully intended to be there, in my home, watching Kwanzi live. But just as I rang off with Kwanzi, I received an unexpected call from dear Detective DeFestina." Roger stared intently, rheumy-eyed, at me. "She requested that I come round to the station at seven this morning. She said you would be there, too. Patsy would not divulge what this was all about. But I thought I'd stop by here first to chat with you about it—whatever *it* is. Perhaps we can then go visit little Patsy together. What do you say to that, Clay?"

I said nothing. I leaned back in my chair, stuffed my hands into the pockets of the ratty old cardigan sweater I liked to wear around the house. I could feel, in the right-hand pocket, the unlabeled computer disk.

"Perhaps you could enlighten me as to why Patsy wants to see the two of us?" Roger asked, somehow snidely.

I pulled the disk from my pocket, dropped it on the table between Roger and me. It landed with a metallic little clack. "Jennifer kept a diary," I said tonelessly.

Roger focused his filmy gray eyes on the disk. I saw the raspberry color draining from his jowls. "Am I in it?" he whispered.

I didn't bother answering Roger. Nor did I tell him that, after reading the diary quickly, twice, with my one good eye, I copied it onto my hard drive and onto another floppy disk, that I printed it out, called Bernie's All-Nite Taxi Service, and had a cab take me to the English Department where I retrieved my briefcase, checked my email (no messages), got into my Honda, drove to the Arden police headquarters, and dropped off the duplicate disk and the paper version of Jenny's journal for Patsy DeFestina. I didn't tell Roger that I then drove back home and dozed off on my living room couch at around five o'clock this morning, hoping to get a call from Patsy after she read the diary and before our scheduled interrogation.

No, I said nothing to Roger Pym-Smithers as he gazed at the disk on the table, then gazed at me, then gazed back at the disk. The bloodlust raged inside me.

*   *   *

Jenny calls it the sickness. It runs in her family. Usually infects the victim around the early twenties, then tortures her for a decade or two before doing her in. The sickness got Jenny's mother. And, by December 1991, a few months shy of her twentieth birthday, Jenny is convinced it will get her, too. She already experiences it, in her nightmares. During the day, she feels more and more abstracted from herself. She is doing a lot of drugs—again, not specifying which kind—by herself, alone in her bedroom. Every day, she thinks about dying. Americans, she writes, would tell her to get help. They would never understand that she doesn't want it. The sickness, she believes, is her destiny.

Scrolling through the diary, I could hardly believe that this suicidal fatalist inhabited the same mind and body as the bold and vivacious aspiring writer I had known. Surely, that was why Pirate Jenny had given me the diary, to make me see that afflicted other side. Despite her protests, she *did* want help—desperately. And I didn't give it to her. I wondered what I would have done had I read this journal back in December. Would I have tried to stop her from having an affair with her British history professor?

* * *

"Come, come now, old bean," Roger Pym-Smithers said, sitting across my kitchen table from me, six-twentyish this snowy February morning. "Friends mustn't keep secrets from one another. Mustn't have any unnecessary rows." He chuckled uncertainly. "How did you come into possession of this digital document anyway?"

"Jennifer gave it to me," I said. "Of course."

"Of course," Roger repeated dryly. "And does Patsy DeFestina know of the existence of this journal?"

I looked Roger in the eye. "No," I lied.

All the tension in Roger's body was instantly released. The color returned to his jowls. "Well, that's a relief! I suppose you must be mentioned in Jenny's memoirs as well."

"How do you know?"

"I don't. I simply present a hypothesis. Perhaps it's best, old bean, if we speak only hypothetically at this point."

"You met Jenny in Impediment. That's not a hypothesis. It's a fact. You were there visiting a West Indian prostitute."

"Independent businesswoman, Clay. I prefer to call Lucille an independent businesswoman. Though Jennifer was keeping even worse company. She had just been abandoned by the egregious T-Bird."

"And you rescued her?"

"A valiant knight in shining armor am I. Now let's hear your side of the story, old bean. Presumably we are now both suspects in this crime. No doubt we are both innocent as the day is long. We might as well share our information so that we can both, as they say in the Jimmy Cagney movies, beat this bum rap."

"She wrote that she was repulsed by you. Yet she couldn't resist you. Somehow you reminded her of her father. She was repulsed by him, too. But she couldn't resist him either."

"My, my, the girl did kiss and tell, didn't she?"

"Not that much kissing. You didn't have sex with her until December 13th. After a month of begging."

"Good Lord, Clay, you're well informed!"

"I thought you hadn't fucked a white woman since 1969, Roger? That's what you told me on December 26th."

"Well, obviously, that was a lie, old bean."

"And you liked tying Jenny up, didn't you?"

Roger leered sheepishly. "The English Disease, some call it. One hates to generalize, of course, but, in my experience, Clay, black women don't particularly go for bondage and submission. Unless they're getting paid for it. Kwanzi used to fancy it. Back in the old days. But I guess you could say she was getting paid for it, too. No, Clay, I find it takes a ripe Anglo-Saxon wench to really appreciate the pleasures of the lash. The gag and the ropes. Our Jenny was such a wench. Did this surprise you, old bean, when you read it in her diary?"

I said nothing. But, no, it had not surprised me. It did make me feel naive, somehow out of my depth. Reading Jenny's diary I realized again what a normal guy I was. People like Jenny and Roger plunged into depths of weirdness I could hardly even contemplate. I would never want to cause pain to someone I was having sex with. And I wouldn't want to be subjected to pain. I understood, reading Jenny's diary, how she wound up becoming a masochistic victim. Now I could only wonder what manner of childhood catastrophe might have produced a twisted fuck like Roger.

The tea kettle whistled on the stove. I rose and turned down the heat. I dropped a teabag into a mug, poured in the boiling water. My raging bloodlust was balanced by a calm, sharp-edged lucidity, a cool alertness. "Milk or sugar?" I asked politely.

"I'll take it black, thanks," Roger said.

I returned to my seat across the table from Roger, handed him his tea. "You killed her," I said.

"If you would like to present a hypothesis for how I might have committed this murder," Roger said magnanimously, "I'd be happy to hear it." He fiddled with his teabag. "Tell you what? If you give me your hypothesis for my guilt, I'll give you my hypothesis for yours. And I think you will come to see, old bean, that we're both better off playing on the same side. We are, if you will, partners in crime. Whether one likes it or not."

*   *   *

"We're the same," Professor Pym-Smithers tells Pirate Jenny. "Two European outsiders." Surely, it was fate that they met the way they did, that Sunday afternoon in Impediment, after T-Bird had deserted Jenny, after Roger had finished his business with Lucille. "As my wife likes to say," Roger tells Jenny, "there *are* no coincidences." A diligent student, Jenny had dutifully attended Roger's lectures on the Victorian age twice a week. And he had noticed her in the lecture hall. In late November and early December, she attends his weekly office hours. She feels as if she is putting on an act as they talk. She pretends to enjoy these sessions as she enjoyed her sessions with Clay. But she is faking it. Roger does not really talk to her. He talks *at* her. He listens to what she says but doesn't seem to absorb it. He baldly tells her he would like to have sex with her. She laughs it off. Laughs and laughs. But inside, she feels the sickness. The sickness is devouring her. And she knows that Roger Pym-Smithers is somehow part of her infection. He is younger, plumper, of a different nationality, but he is her father. Jenny sees the same helplessness, the same cruelty in him. Like her father, Roger cannot help but be cruel.

"Blackness," Roger says. "Don't you find it rather intriguing that we're both so drawn to blackness? That we both feel the lure of the forbidden?"

Jenny says the same thing to Roger that she had said to me in my office on Halloween Eve, about the forbidden and the permitted in Germany and the permitted and the forbidden in America. It is a line I will repeat to Roger a few weeks later, on Boxing Day.

She would like to see Clay, but is reluctant to call him. One day, Roger asks her out of the blue if she has had sex with Clay. They have talked about him before. Jenny had told Roger that Clay was her academic adviser for a few weeks. That was all. Now, when she hesitates at the question, Roger demands an answer: "Have you or have you not fucked him?" Jenny denies having ever had any physical relationship with Clay. "I would never betray our intimacy to anyone," she writes. "Never."

Roger calls Jenny at night, phoning from his study while his wife sleeps upstairs. He reads Jenny passages from the Marquis de Sade. She always wants to hang up but cannot make herself do it. She feels as if she must listen to Roger, like it is some sort of duty, or punishment, a penance that must be endured. The nightmares continue. They grow so terrifying that Jenny no longer wants to write them down.

By the final entry of the diary, Jenny feels she must "befriend" the sickness. She believes her history professor can help her do this. Roger Pym-Smithers had phoned her at two o'clock that morning. He asked if it was safe for him to come over. As Jenny's flatmate was sleeping at her boyfriend's place, it was. Roger showed up with a black doctor's bag, filled with what he called "goodies."

Jenny is writing in her diary at dawn, after Roger has left. She feels degraded, defiled. And this, she writes, is exactly what she deserves. She looks at the scars Roger left on her body, the bruises, the rope burn. Maybe this is her destiny.

Jenny suddenly decides to call Clay. She will phone him at his office, later in the day. She will try to meet with him for coffee. She needs to talk to him, needs for him to know what is happening to her. Maybe, Pirate Jenny wonders, she should give him a copy of this diary.

Alone in my study, at three in the morning, I scrolled through the last line of neon green text, then stared into the blank, black screen. I contemplated the depth of my stupidity. Faced with the most serious crisis of my life I had not behaved like the shrewd and fearless Hollywood hero.

In fact, from the moment I let Reggie Brogus into my home in the middle of Sunday night, I had made one boneheaded decision after another. Actually, I was being too kind in my self-assessment. My addiction to idiocy had begun even earlier, when I was stupid enough to get involved with Jenny, stupid enough not to read her diary but so abysmally stupid as to leave it someplace where my wife would find it. I could faintly see my reflection in the lamplight bouncing off the computer screen, my half-closed eye glimmering like a badge of my feeblemindedness. I decided it was time to do something smart.

*   *   *

"Hypothesis," I said. "You were supposed to be at an academic conference in New York last weekend. But you didn't go. Or you *did* go. You flew to New York on Saturday, rented a car, and drove back to Ohio on Sunday, then drove back to New York all night Sunday and caught the return flight to Ohio Monday afternoon."

Roger Pym-Smithers, eyebrows awaggle, sipped his tea. He actually seemed to revel in this situation, as if it were all an amusing parlor game. "Credible so far, old bean. Carry on."

"You saw Jennifer Sunday night. Either you killed her during sex, by accident. Or you killed her after sex, by design."

"As Kwanzi likes to say, there *are* no accidents."

For a long moment, neither of us spoke. The kitchen was so deadly quiet, I imagined I could hear the snowfall outside. I smelled the coffee brewing on the counter behind me. Roger, insouciant, practically gleeful, continued sipping his tea. As in the barn with Special Agent Guffin, I had the sense that I was in the presence of some almost cosmic force of malevolence. Or was it more a monstrosity, the same distorted humanity, that Penelope had detected in Reggie Brogus?

"You killed her," I said. "Intentionally."

"*Hypothetically* intentionally, old bean. Remember, we are speaking only hypothetically here."

"And brought her body to the Afrikamerica Studies suite, dumped her on Reggie's couch. Maybe you had strangled her with a pair of suspenders identical to Reggie's. Or, having strangled Jenny in your own bed, you brought her to Reggie's office and, knowing that he always kept a change of clothes in his closet, you wrapped a pair of his suspenders around her neck."

"Or," Roger said, "this hypothetical killer of yours had managed to secure a pair of braces—or, as you people call them—suspenders, from Brogus's office beforehand."

"I hadn't thought of that," I said. I could no longer look at Roger. I stared past his head, at the frilly yellow curtains. Through the gauzy fabric I could see the sky lightening, the snow cascading relentlessly. "But you must have thought Brogus was already out of town for the holiday weekend. Otherwise you would never have taken the chance of planting a body in his office on Sunday night."

"Hypothetically, I would not have expected anyone to discover the body until Tuesday morning. As Pops Mulwray did."

"All for a chair," I said, struggling to comprehend. "You took a young woman's life. And tried to frame Reggie Brogus. Because you thought he was going to take a department chairmanship from Kwanzi."

"According to *your* hypothesis, old bean."

"Would Kwanzi, hypothetically, have been in on this?"

"Absolutely not," Roger pronounced, completely without irony. "Her husband would have protected her from any knowledge of this affair."

"So Reggie was right. He told me this wasn't about sex. It was about politics. But even he couldn't have imagined that it was about *office* politics."

"The only type of politics that matters these days, my dear Clay. The only politics that really counts. But I wouldn't remove sex from the equation. Hadn't Brogus shagged Jenny?"

"Actually, Roger, I don't think the two of them ever even met."

"Hmmm. I was afraid of that. But you can hardly blame me for assuming otherwise. You should have seen the way Jenny blushed whenever I mentioned Brogus's name. I felt as if I'd caught them right in the midst of some intimate encounter."

"So you thought you had an easy frame-up. But then Brogus's guilt became a little shaky. You knew Jenny was friends with T-Bird so you told Patsy D. that he was a likely suspect. And if not T-Bird, then it must have been Clay Robinette."

"All's fair, Clay."

"You confronted Jenny about me back in December. I read it in her diary. Didn't she tell you we weren't involved?"

"So she said, old bean, so she said. And for a time I believed her. But she was constantly quoting you, parroting your opinions. I'd hear you pontificating about some topic at a faculty cocktail party, then hear Jenny utter the exact same words during our office hours the next day. I felt like I was talking to a bloody ventriloquist's dummy. You got into her head, Clay. And into her heart. I envy you."

"Is that why you tried to frame me?"

Roger cocked his head and squinted at me. "Yes, there was that," he said, a taint of melodrama in his voice. "And also the fact that you, too, were pursuing Kwanzi's job."

"What?" After three straight days of improbable outrages, this may have been the most improbable and outrageous thing I had heard yet. "Roger, I don't even teach in the fucking department!"

Roger nodded, smirking knowingly at me. "Oh, yes, old bean. Don't think I couldn't spot your ruthless ambition. Kwanzi never saw through you, but I did!"

At long last, I saw the madness, the complete irrationality, in Roger's rheumy eyes. "What did you say to Kwanzi about our talk in your study," I asked, "after the dinner on Boxing Day?"

Roger twinkled mischievously. "Well, at that point, once I'd heard you quote Jenny as she had quoted you, I was certain you had shagged her. So I told Kwanzi that you had confessed to having an affair with a student. One of those forbidden white girls. Yesterday, I told her that the girl was Jenny."

"You lied."

"Yes and no. Because, though she had denied it in December, Jenny confessed in February, just last Sunday night, in fact. Oh, how she protected you, Clay! I asked her again and again and again if you'd fucked her. I was determined to torture the truth out of her. And still she denied it. Finally, old bean, with her last choking words, she confessed. What loyalty, Clay! I should hardly think you deserve it."

The fever, the dizziness, returned, then quickly passed. "Well, Roger, I have a confession for you, too," I said carefully. "I lied earlier when I said Patsy didn't know about Jenny's diary. She's probably read it all by now. I gave her a copy. And you know what? My guess is that Jenny kept other journals. This one only covers September to December. I'll betcha anything Patsy has read other diaries of Jenny. Later ones. And my hunch is that you are now hypothetically, circumstantially, and probably even forensically, the most obvious person to have killed Jenny."

Roger's face had lost its color once more. He stared glumly at the black computer disk on the table. "Oh, hell," he sighed. With what seemed to be tremendous effort, Roger rose from the table. He put on his overcoat, picked up his floppy hat and his half-empty mug. He walked around the table. Watching him, I coiled tight inside, ready to spring into violence. His back to me, Roger leaned on the edge of the kitchen sink, hunching over the small monument of plates and bowls and glasses and silverware waiting to be placed in the dishwasher. Roger, ever the gentleman, appeared to be placing his used mug in the sink. When he turned to face me, he was holding "the machete." That's what Penelope and I called it: the huge, glass-handled carving knife with an inordinately large blade that had been given to us by a cousin of hers as a wedding present. The machete. Roger Pym-Smithers clutched it in his hand. "Now, old bean," he said, "I must kill *you.*"

Oh really? I thought. But I remained silent. I stared at Roger, feeling irradiated by this animal alertness, my bloodlust. I was prepared to leap from my chair, to take the machete from Roger and plunge it into his throat. Still, I had to wonder why Roger had said he "must" kill me. Was he driven by some implacable rage for vengeance? Or did he see killing me as some sort of practical necessity? Maybe Roger thought that by killing me, he might still get away with Jenny's murder. Would he try to claim that he and Jenny and I were caught in a lust triangle, that I had killed Jenny in a seizure of jealousy and then attacked him when he dropped by my kitchen for a chat? Would he try to say that he murdered me in self-defense? I don't know how long I sat there in the chair, staring at Roger as he stood a few feet away from me, clutching the machete. Probably no more than two eternal seconds. But in that moment, I saw doubt in Roger's rheumy eyes. I knew that if this was indeed a kill-or-be-killed situation, I would prevail. I was ready. I was actually eager. And then—

Enter Brogus. I would like to say it was with a clap of thunder but I heard nothing. I saw the pantry door fly open. And then I saw Reggie Brogus, standing in my kitchen, backlit by the naked bulb dangling from a rubbery cord in the pantry. Brogus seemed to glow with surreality. But he was cool. He simply stood there, almost posing, his gray down jacket over his blue warm-up suit with the white trim, dirty white Nikes on his feet, furry hat with earflaps atop his head, laptop computer in its black canvas carrying case strung across his shoulder.

"If anybody gonna be doin' any killin' 'round here," Brogus said deliberately, "it gon' be *me!*"

Only then did I see the gun in Reggie's hand. As he pointed the weapon at Roger, I saw the little tubular appendage at the end of the barrel. The word *silencer* was just flashing across my mind as I heard the hissy sound—*pssssst!*—like a dainty little fart. Roger dropped the machete, its glass handle shattering on the linoleum tiles of the kitchen floor. Roger clutched his belly. The awkward, almost comical look of surprise on his face reminded me of T-Bird's slapstick grimace as he tumbled off the rooftop. The face, at the brink of death, was a mask of the ridiculous.

"You shot me!" Roger wailed. He crumpled to his knees, clutching his belly. "Fucking hell! I can't believe you shot me!"

I, meanwhile, could hardly believe that Reginald T. Brogus—if that was indeed his name—was standing in my kitchen, a thin cloud of smoke spiraling upward from the barrel of his gun. He stared down at Roger Pym-Smithers, without the faintest hint of mercy in his bullfrog eyes. "Actually, muthafucka, I *gut*-shot you. Enjoy!" Reggie watched Roger sprawl on the kitchen floor, wheezing, struggling to speak, still clutching his belly, a puddle of his blood spreading over the linoleum tiles. Calmly, Reggie turned to me and said, in an easygoing, greeting-upon-a-chance-encounter tone: "What's up, Clay?"

"Hey, Reg," I managed to say.

Denial! Where were my prodigious powers of denial when I needed them most? I tried to imagine this wasn't really happening just as I had tried on Monday to imagine that I hadn't seen Pirate Jenny's body in Brogus's office, that I hadn't even seen Brogus in my kitchen in the middle of the night. Now Reggie Brogus was back in my kitchen. I realized that he must have walked in through the carelessly unlocked back door and hid in the pantry while I was out delivering Jenny's diary to the Arden police station—or maybe even while I snoozed on the couch. He was an armed, three-hundred-pound fact of life. Undeniable.

I would also have liked to deny the existence of Roger Pym-Smithers, writhing in agony at my feet, trying to keep his intestines from spilling out of his body. At the same time, however, the fact sank in that this white man had not only murdered Jenny, but had then tried to frame three black men, including me, for the crime. Roger looked up at me, choking, gurgling, pure horror in his eyes. I cannot say I enjoyed his suffering. But I certainly didn't *mind* seeing Roger die. I only wished he weren't doing it on my kitchen floor.

Reggie, matter-of-fact as could be, walked up to the counter, stepping over wriggling Roger, and poured himself a mugful of coffee. "You don't seem surprised to see me, Clay."

"I'm way past the realm of surprise by now, Reggie." In fact, I was struggling to stay cool, to be as blasé as Reggie was being. My new primary goal in life was to avoid getting shot. "Most people think you're in Mississippi," I said.

Brogus snorted. "I ain't never been to Mississippi in my *en*-tire fucking life." His mug of coffee in one hand, his gun in the other, computer strapped over his shoulder, Reggie moved toward the kitchen table, intentionally brushing Roger's forehead with the toe of his running shoe. "How ya doin', Rog?" he said, barely looking down.

"Aaaaauuuuuuccccccccgggggggghhhhhhhhhhhh!" Roger replied. The stench of his blood filled the kitchen. It was the harsh and vinegary smell of red wine turned bad, a bottle of Côtes du Rhône uncorked and left open for weeks to spoil.

Reggie sat across from me at the table, set down his gun, took a sip of his coffee. "You get my email?" he asked.

"Yeah. Where have you been, man?"

Brogus glared at me from behind his black-framed eyeglasses. "What the fuck do you care? You left me out on the road alone. Don't think I forgot that."

"I'm sorry, Reggie," I said as sincerely as I could. "I just panicked."

"Uh-huh." Reggie slurped his coffee, glanced at his wristwatch. "Hey!" he suddenly cried. "It's after six-thirty! We're gonna miss Kwanzi!"

Brogus reached across the table and switched on the tiny black-and-white TV. A plasticine white woman stood in front of a map of the United States. The volume on the TV was turned very low. The meteorologist pointed to Ohio and said something about a "major blizzard."

"Guess she'll be on after the weather," Brogus muttered. "Hey, Rog!" he called out. "Can you see all right?"

I could hear Roger on the floor behind me, sluicing about in his blood-wine. "Ggggrrrrrccccccccchhhhhhhhhhh," he said. It occurred to me that, if and when Penelope returned to our home, she was going to be furious about this mess.

"So you wanna know where I was?" Reggie said. "After you abandoned me out on the road in my hour of need?" I nodded solemnly, apologetically. "Pops Mulwray hooked me up. Good ole Pops, man. He lives out by the airfield. After you dumped me, I found my way to his house."

"You've been in Pops Mulwray's house all this time?"

"Fuck no! But Pops hooked me up, man. He knew the perfect hideout. Right under everybody's fuckin' nose. I told you I was gonna go underground, right? Well, at the time I wasn't speaking literally. But Pops knew that underneath the Math building is a big ole bomb shelter. Most people never even knew about it. Those who did forgot about it a long time ago. I betcha even Shamberg doesn't know about the cold war bunker. Hardly anybody but Pops has been down there since the Cuban missile crisis back in '62. But shit, man, they got everything down there. Canned food, TV, radio, liquor, guns and ammo! It took some work but I was eventually able to hook my computer up to an old phone line. That's how I emailed you."

"I saw Pops," I said, "entering the Math building last night."

"Yeah, I know. He was bringin' me fresh sandwiches and a six-pack."

"So Pops protected you. Obviously, he didn't tell the cops about the bomb shelter."

"Fuck no! *Some* black folks understand the meaning of loyalty, Clay."

The rage bubbled up inside me again. Where the hell did this militant fraud get off talking to me about loyalty? "So why did you come above ground?" I said.

"Had to. Pops's wife knows and she's gettin' scared. Pops told me she was gonna go to the pigs today. So I need to get outta town."

"Okay, Reg," I said eagerly. "Don't tell me: You need a car. Great! Take my Honda. Please."

"Well, that's right generous of you, Clay," Brogus said with unctuous mock gratitude. "But I didn't trudge over here in the snow just to ask for a favor. You see, I'm a marked man. I might not have long to live. But I figure if I'm gonna go down, I'm damn sure gonna take anybody who betrayed me with me. So I got a question for you, Clay: Why did you try to sell me out?"

"Yo, Reggie, didn't you just hear my little conversation with Roger? I have exonerated you, man!" I spoke quickly, adamantly. "Now the cops are gonna know Roger killed the girl. There'll be no more price on your head, Reggie. You'll be a free man!"

"T-t-t-tellllll," Roger gurgled behind me. I turned and saw him twisting and convulsing on the floor. "Kwachhh. Neeee. Zeeee . . ." Roger spat up grape-colored blood. "I luh-luh-lucccccchhhhh . . ."

"Shut up, bitch!" Reggie barked.

At that moment, Roger Pym-Smithers stopped squirming. His body went abruptly rigid. He was looking up at the instant of his death, his gaze riveted to the tiny TV on top of the table. Kwanzi's face was on the four-inch screen. "Let there be no rush to judgment," I heard her say.

Reggie paid no attention to the television. "What about that shit you wrote in the paper yesterday?" he said

"Hey, Reggie, *you* told me to report this story, to find out what the real deal was. Remember?"

"Yeah, but you didn't do that," Reggie snarled. "Instead you sold me out! You betrayed me!"

I closed my eyes and took a deep breath. I wished that all this was as unreal as it seemed. But even if I were dreaming, I had a feeling I was about to die in my sleep. "Reggie," I said slowly, "I saw Guffin last night. He told me everything."

There was a sudden shock in Brogus's huge eyes. "Say *what?*"

"Guffin told me you were Cointelpro all along."

"Fuck," Reggie whispered. He continued to stare at me, the fear and wrath and bewilderment of exposure all over his face. "Now they'll never let me live."

"I'm sorry if you think I tried to sell you out, Reggie. But it seems you've sold out a whole lotta people. Betrayed a lot of people. Even betrayed Dr. King."

"You better shut the fuck up right now, Clay."

"I'm just trying to understand, Reggie. What it's like to be you."

Brogus shook his head. "You'll never fucking know, Clay. 'Cause I have a faith you can never comprehend. I *believe* in this country. I sacrificed my youth for this country. And I deserve to be properly compensated for that. Because I lived by my belief! But you. Don't matter how much education you've got, or how clever you think you are. You're just like all the other ignorant niggas in America who don't know how to believe! Who *refuse* to believe!"

"I'm not the enemy, Reggie."

This seemed to infuriate Brogus. "The fuck you ain't!" He picked up his gun from the table and pointed it directly in my face.

At that moment I was eleven years old again and it was not a fat man of fifty in a furry hat I saw before me but a young fervent black-bereted urban guerrilla sprung to life from a book jacket, the black radical who would pull the trigger because he just could not stop himself from pulling the trigger. I realized I was experiencing some sort of psycho time warp, that it was not 1969 but 1992 and I even thought how strange it was that the last vision I would have of this life would be a hallucination. The red dot snapped me out of it. I saw it swirling in space, then found myself back in real time, in my kitchen, the fat man of fifty preparing to shoot me between the eyes. The red dot swirled, then came to rest on Brogus's left cheek, a scarlet speck in the scraggly black-and-white nest of his beard. And I wondered: Is that a laser?

All I hear is shattering glass, a crashing waterfall of shards, ringing in my ears. All I see is colors, colors in violent motion. A red geyser exploding from Brogus's face. Splotches of red on twirling yellow. Reggie's blood splattered on the frilly yellow curtains, flapping and splashing in a crazed wind. Suddenly everything goes white. I feel the wind whipping all around me, snow swirling into the kitchen, seemingly from every direction. Now I see black figures moving jerkily in the turbulent whiteness. Then comes the screaming. Many men's voices, all saying the same thing: "FREEZE! FREEZE! FREEZE! GET DOWN ON THE GROUND! HANDS ON YOUR HEAD! FREEZE!"

I am kneeling in snow and blood and broken glass, hands folded on top of my head. Two men dressed completely in black, with black ski masks stretched over their heads, are aiming black rifles at me. I sense the presence of other gunmen behind me. The back door is swinging loosely on its hinges. The window that was once its top portion is completely gone. I see Brogus sprawled in the opposite corner of the kitchen. He lies on his back, his head turned away from me. I see the back of his furry hat but not his face. He still clutches the gun in his beefy right hand. The body of Roger Pym-Smithers is splayed beside me, eyes still open. The kitchen table has been overturned. The television lies on the floor, upside down. I hear Kwanzi's voice, small and staticky. "We need to learn the truth about this crime," she states. "For only the truth shall set us free."

Maybe I am hallucinating again. Or maybe I am dead and already in Hell. This is what I think when I see the tall man in the black trenchcoat and the aviator sunglasses, with his bald, walnut head, walk into my kitchen, through the hanging back door. If I am not hallucinating and not already dead, then surely Special Agent Guffin will kill me now. Or order the men in ski masks pointing their rifles at me to fire away. But

Guffin does not even look at me as I kneel, trembling, hands atop my head. Guffin walks over to Reggie Brogus's body. He pauses for only a second before reaching down and scooping up Brogus's computer. The black canvas case is thickly dripping blood. Computer in hand, still not even acknowledging me, Guffin walks out the same way he came in.

Snow is swirling all around the kitchen now. Flakes cling to my eyelashes. I can barely see Patsy DeFestina as she walks in through the hanging back door, wearing her plaid coat and earmuffs. "Hiya, Clay," she says brightly. Patsy walks right up to me. On my knees, I am almost at eye level with her. "This is gonna hurt you more than it does me," she says. She lunges forward. Her tiny fist lands just above my wounded eye. I am unconscious before my head hits the floor.

CHAPTER 14

"THIS IS THE OFFICIAL VERSION," Patsy DeFestina said. "Take it or leave it."

Friday, February 21, 1992, noon. I was propped up in my hospital bed, a bandage over my left eye, my neck in a brace, an intravenous tube stuck in my arm. Having spent most of the past thirty hours unconscious, I had awakened, Rip Van Winkle–like, to an altered reality. Today's *Arden Oracle* lay on a tray on top of a small table in front of me. The front page read: BROGUS MANHUNT ENDS IN FACULTY BLOODBATH. Under the banner headline was a picture of my house on Maplewood Road and four black-and-white head shots: of Reggie Brogus, Roger Pym-Smithers, Jennifer Wolfshiem, and me. The lead article was written by Andrew V. Chadwick. Andy, marveling at his own good fortune, explained in a sidebar that he had just returned to Arden, Ohio, from Mississsppi—where the Brogus trail had gone cold—minutes before the Maplewood shootout occurred. Groggily—the doctors told me I'd suffered a severe concussion—I listened to Detective DeFestina, who was perched atop a high stool at my bedside. In her flat, raceless accent, she recited the "facts" to me, pedantically, like a nun drilling a pupil on cathecism that must be memorized.

"Last Sunday, Reggie Brogus, out for a late night jog, stopped by his office and found the dead body of a woman he'd never met before. He flipped out, figured he'd best get out of town. But his car was in the repair shop. He had a flight scheduled for Monday morning but suddenly he was too scared to call the taxi service to take him out to the airfield. He called you, Clay, at two-thirty in the morning. He didn't tell you what it was about. He was just panicked. You told him that whatever the problem was, it could wait till morning. You then hung up the phone and went back to sleep."

Patsy paused and gave me her black button stare.

I swallowed hard. "Okay," I said.

"Somehow Reggie made his way out to Pops Mulwray's in the predawn hours Monday. Maybe he walked, maybe he hitched. Who knows? But Reggie convinced Pops to hide him. Of course, Pops would never willingly help a fugitive. Reggie must have threatened the poor old man and Pops must have acted out of duress."

"What does Pops say about that?" I asked, my voice dry and creaky.

"Pops doesn't say a whole lot at the moment. He had another mild stroke yesterday. He's a patient in this very hospital. Two floors down. He's okay. He'll live. But he can't speak. His wife is telling us what she knows. When she found out yesterday morning where Brogus was hiding, she told Pops she would go to the police. Pops told Brogus and Brogus came out from underground. One of your early bird neighbors saw him walking toward your house at about six a.m. Presumably, Brogus wanted your car. But he might also have wanted to shoot you for not helping him out Sunday night. By six-thirty, the SWAT team had your house surrounded. A marksman saw Brogus draw on you. So he fired. That is the reason why you, Clay, are still alive."

"What about Roger?" I croaked.

"How do ya like that for bizarre coincidences?" Patsy fairly trilled. "I mean, is this life an intricate tapestry of serendipity, or what? Ten minutes after Brogus is seen stalking down your driveway, headed for your back door, the same watchful neighbor who spotted him sees Roger Pym-Smithers follow the same path! The first police probably showed up a minute or two later. Reggie comes to your house to kill you and in walks the man who framed him! As it turned out, nobody had a view into your kitchen when Reggie shot Roger." Patsy adjusted her oversized, rectangular glasses on her little leprechaun nose. She just barely suppressed a smile. "Shame about the old chap, huh?"

"Where does Roger fit into the official version?"

"Oh, he murdered the Wolfshiem girl, no doubt about it. Thank you, by the way, for dropping off that diary. I had, in fact, just read a later one, that Jennifer had written in longhand. She made it plain that if anybody was going to kill her, it would be that creep. And the forensic evidence is overwhelming. I figure he met up with her somewhere Sunday evening and somehow lured her up to the Afrikamerica Studies suite. Maybe he told her he had to pick something up in Kwanzi's office."

Now I was confused. "What do you mean?"

"Roger killed her in Kwanzi's office. It was pretty obvious. And the girl must have put up a hell of a struggle. Then Roger dragged her down the hall into Reggie's office, undressed her, dumped her body on the couch. But here's where jolly Roger got sloppy. He left a semen stain on Brogus's couch."

"Patsy!" I gasped.

I shook my head no. Patsy nodded her head yes.

"He raped her *after* he killed her. Guess he couldn't control himself. Or on some level he wanted to get caught. Or he figured his scheme was so solid he would never get caught. Anyway, he missed a drop."

"Oh my God, that's so sick."

"Sick?" Patsy cried. "This was nothing! You want sick? Oh, Clay, the stories I could tell you! Stories that would make Jeffrey Dahmer lose his appetite!"

"Does Kwanzi know?"

"I met with her last night. Showed her the diaries, the results of the DNA tests, all the evidence. Explained the history, the likely motive. Told her that, in his twisted way, Roger thought he was helping her. Kwanzi wasn't having it. She's in total denial mode." Patsy suddenly clicked into an uncanny impersonation of Kwanzi, tilting her head, speaking in a husky voice and staring, spacey-eyed and beatific, into the distance: "'Roger would never do that to me. Oh, no, you're wrong. Roger would never do that to me. He loves me too much. I don't believe it. Roger would never do that to me.'" Patsy switched back into her normal voice. "I didn't bother telling her that Roger probably did this before. That's why he thought he could get away with it. He passed himself off as an amateur sleuth but a lot of people in Scotland Yard thought that Roger had gotten away with murder back in '64 when he was in graduate school. There was a professor who Roger thought was going to flunk his thesis or something, somehow stand in the way of his career. The professor was found strangled in his study. No necrophilia in this case. A janitor at the university, a Jamaican man, went to prison for the murder. Died in prison, some time ago. Like I say, this Roger was a real sicko. But some people found him charming. Go figure. Hitler was a vegetarian who loved animals."

"But you, Patsy," I said accusingly, angry at myself for having believed her, "you thought either Brogus or T-Bird did it."

Patsy shrugged. "Even God makes her mistakes."

"And where do I fit into the official version?"

"You're an exploiter," Patsy said, a cursory condemnation in her voice. "You exploited a student for your carnal pleasure, she trusted you, and you abandoned her. But you didn't murder her. You have that in your favor. Otherwise, you don't come out of this looking too good, Clay. Your business is all out in the street now. Dean Shamberg has suspended you indefinitely. Good luck getting another teaching job in the English-speaking world. I also saw your wife last night. She came back to town. Whooooaaaaa, Daddy! I don't envy you, Clay. You may escape this whole episode of your life without needing criminal counsel, but I hope to God you have a good divorce lawyer 'cause Penelope is loaded for bear!"

"I throw myself on the mercy of the court."

"But getting back to the official version: You provided what evidence you had, when you found it, to the proper authorities. That's a good thing. Roger came by your house because I had phoned him. He knew you'd had a fling with Jenny, assumed you were both now suspects and wanted to, how do they say it in England, suss you out?"

"As well as being official," I said, "that's actually true."

"Anyway," Patsy continued, "it was just Roger's luck that Reggie Brogus should have decided to pay you a visit as well. The three of you got into a scuffle. That's how you got so beat up. That's how Roger wound up dead. And your ass was saved just before Reggie could finish you off."

"Is that all?"

"That pretty much concludes the official version."

I leaned forward, gripped the metal railing on the side of my hospital bed. "And what if I decide to tell the truth, Patsy? About how I really got beat up. About Guffin."

"Who?"

"Special Agent Guffin. Mack Guffin. Of Cointelpro."

"What on earth are you talking about?"

"Yes, Roger killed Jenny, Roger set up Reggie. But there really *were* people—government agents!—out to get Brogus. Because he was blackmailing them. With secret files on the King assassination. Brogus was Cointelpro all along!"

Patsy DeFestina just stared at me, her eyes expressionless behind her windshield glasses.

"Come on, Patsy! You must have talked with Guffin in the last few days. He walked into my fucking kitchen—yesterday morning! Right before you! I know damn well you know exactly what I'm talking about!"

Patsy was quiet for a long moment. "You can say whatever you want, Clay," she said in her bland, pancake voice. "You can publish, or try to publish, any theories you like. But you are a known fabricator of quotes and sources. Who would ever believe you? You've already compromised your credibility in this case by writing about the Wolfshiem girl in the *Oracle.* Do you think anyone in their right mind would take seriously, credulously, anything you have to say now?"

I slouched back in the bed. I knew when I was beat. "Guess not."

"Lemme give you a little advice, Clay. Focus on your wife. Focus on your kids. Salvage what you can. And just be thankful you're not facing prosecution on any felony charges. I don't know, Clay, for some reason I still like you. But you're a sinner and you've got some serious repenting to do."

Detective DeFestina hopped off the stool, walked toward the door.

"Hey, Patsy," I said. She turned to face me, her hand on the doorknob. "I'm sorry if you find this question off-putting, but I just gotta know. I've been trying to figure it out since I first laid eyes on you and I'm just . . . well, I just don't know. Maybe I'm not the first person to ask you this but . . . What race are you?"

Patsy, smiling faintly, said, "Human."

*   *   *

Ashley raced toward me as soon as she saw my face and leapt into my arms. Amber hung back, lingering in the doorway of the hospital's fourth-floor visitors' lounge, fidgeting, maybe even a little bit afraid of me. Though I was standing up and dressed in street clothes, I still sported a scary neck brace and a gruesome bandage over my left eye. Perhaps, to Amber, her father had inexplicably transmogrified into a hideous Frankenstein-Cyclops monster. Or maybe Penelope had told her what an ogre I was. Or maybe someone else had: Pen and the girls were staying with Mrs. Henderson before returning to Philadelphia. But once I squatted and set Ashley back on her feet, Amber walked shyly over to me, then suddenly threw her arms around my shoulders and squeezed us together tight, with a pure and ferocious love. Then the three of us—we were, fortunately, the only people in the lounge this Monday afternoon—curled up on the couch together.

"Were you really in a shootout, Daddy?" Ashley asked excitedly.

"Do you think somebody will make a movie about this?" Amber wanted to know.

For three days, from the time I woke up in Arden General and saw the headline in the *Oracle,* I had agonized over the trauma that this awful notoriety might inflict on my daughters. What I had never imagined was that they would have found the whole thing kinda neat. The cops and camera crews in front of our house. The rumors of my heroism as I fought with two murderers. The girls' strange new celebrity status in Arden, Ohio. Amber and Ashley seemed to be enjoying it all.

"Aren't you sad about Uncle Reggie?" I asked.

"Mommy says not to call him that," Ashley said.

"Mommy says he was a bad man," Amber added.

"Well, there are a lot of bad people in the world," I said. "Reggie was no worse than many of them." I hesitated before continuing. I didn't want the girls to know that since their mother kneed me in the balls I had only communicated with her through her attorney and Mrs. Henderson ("No, Clay," the formidable old churchgoing black lady would bellow over the phone, "you most definitely may *not* speak to your wife"). I cleared my throat and asked, "Does Mommy say I'm a bad man, too?"

"No," Amber said. "She says you're stupid, cowardly, and totally lost, but she doesn't say you're a bad man."

"She says you need to work on yourself," Ashley informed me.

"I let you all down," I said. "I let your mother down. I let you girls down. I want you to know I'm sorry." I struggled not to cry. "I'll do anything to make it up to you."

"We forgive you, Daddy," Ashley said.

"But we can't speak for Mom," Amber said.

"Did she say when we could be together again as a family?" I asked.

Ashley stared down at the floor and shook her head. Amber, meanwhile, looked me straight in the eye. "Daddy," my eldest daughter said sagely, "I think you're in for a long, hard struggle."

*   *   *

If I had known how true Amber's words were on Febraury 24, 1992, I certainly would have broken down and wept right there in the hospital lounge. The next three years were the worst of my life. I confessed all in a letter to Pen. She did not want a divorce, but she wanted no part of me. I wound up moving to Portland, Oregon, where my brother and his wife lived. They were the only family members who were not completely disgusted with me. I worked different jobs: bookstore clerk, telephone pollster, freelance copy editor. My only contact with Pen was listening to her long tortured telephone diatribes. She called me every name in the book. I had no defense. All I could do was beg forgiveness. For three years, I didn't get it. Most excruciating of all, I was allowed to see the girls only twice a year.

No, my penance did not make up for the lives of Pirate Jenny or T-Bird Williams. But three years of virtual exile was the price of repentance to my family. Even once we were reunited, I remained aware of how I had scarred my relationship with my wife. It took a long time, but Penelope eventually trusted me again. A year after she left Arden, Ohio, Pen finished writing her book, *Making Diversity Pay Off for YOU!* The manual on workplace multiculturalism became a runaway bestseller, a standard text. Pen and the girls moved to San Francisco in 1995. For a year, I visited them regularly from Portland. Finally, Pen let me move back in. She was much in demand on the lecture circuit and I turned out to be quite an efficient handler of her appointments and engagements. Very, very slowly, my wife and I grew closer than we had ever been.

But on February 24, 1992, as I sat in the visitors' lounge, curled up on the couch with Amber and Ashley, I couldn't know how anything would turn out. I wouldn't have been able to stand the idea that I would barely see my daughters over the next three years, that it would be more than forty months before I would make love to my wife again, before I could again fall asleep in Penelope's arms, soothed by her gentle, lullaby snore.

*   *   *

There was so much I didn't know, couldn't know, would not even have wanted to know about the near future, back in late February '92.

I could not have dreamed then that a jury—even a white jury—in California would, in April '92, acquit the white cops who had been captured brutalizing the black motorist on videotape. In the wake of the verdict, South Central Los Angeles went up in flames. Cities all over America exploded. Lootings, shootings, sixty dead. Burn, baby, burn! It was the worst civil uprising since April 4, 1968, when black people erupted after the murder of our greatest leader. In twenty-four years, America had moved from the age of Martin Luther King to the age of Rodney King. Everyone in the Godforsaken nation was staring into the racial abyss. There was nothing to do but step gingerly away from the chasm. And, in the words of the first baby boomer president: "Deny, deny, deny!"

I did not know then that I would rarely hear Reggie Brogus's name uttered again. Yet there would be more and more black men of his generation popping up here and there throughout the decade, spokesmen for the right ideas, products of the sixties cashing in in the nineties, seeking not to challenge the establishment, but to be it. Maybe they talked the radical talk back in the day. But near century's end, the bogus brothers had got with the program. Reggie Brogus was dead; but the ghastly march of the Brogi was just beginning.

How could I have guessed on that slushy Monday, February 24, 1992, that Arden University's Afrikamerika Studies Department would not only survive but thrive, with Brogus's boy Trevor Bledsoe III at the helm? Maybe I should have known that somehow Dean Jerry Shamberg could turn even an on-campus murder into a publicity bonanza for a university. Arden U. was in excellent shape when Dean Jer quit in '95 to become a deputy secretary of education in the Clinton administration.

I didn't know that, in another year's time, Pops Mulwray would die quietly in his sleep. I had no idea that former ambassador Heinrich Wolfshiem would slit his throat in a Berlin hotel room. I would never have guessed that, in just a few months' time, Andy Chadwick would become a reporter for the *New York Times*. Or that a biopic on Patsy DeFestina would soon be in development in Hollywood. Or that Kwanzi Authentica Parker would take her $5 million inheritance from Roger Pym-Smithers and move to Johannesburg, South Africa, where, rumor had it, she was going to try to finish writing her dissertation.

Most unpredictable was how easy it was to forget Jenny, T-Bird, and Roger. I would still see Jenny sometimes, in dreams. And she usually seemed happy.

On February 24, 1992, as I tried to begin to recover from the madness of the previous week, as I tried to commit myself to Patsy DeFestina's "official version" of events, I did not know that, two years later, as I walked alone, drunk and miserable, down a deserted Portland street at four in the morning, a black Lincoln Town Car with darkened windows would glide slowly, menacingly, past me. There would be no other possible signs of Special Agent Guffin. But I would always know that he was out there somewhere.

And I could not predict in February '92 how beautifully my daughters would grow between the ages of six and nine or how their absence from my life during my three-year penance would rip me apart inside.

*   *   *

Maybe it's a blessing, the unknowability of the future. The present is an incomprehensible improvisation and the past a riot of official and unofficial versions. On February 24, 1992, my only ideology, my supreme belief, consisted of the two little girls I held under my arms.

Once the visiting hour was over, I walked with the twins through the wide glass entrance of the hospital. We stood in front of the massive white complex. I saw the Volvo, parked at the end of the walkway, Mrs. Henderson behind the wheel.

"We love you, Daddy," Amber said.

I knelt down and embraced my daughters in a three-way hug. "I love you, too, Amber. And I love you, Ashley."

I watched them as they trundled down the walkway. Ashley suddenly turned around and called out, "Keep the faith, Daddy!"

"I'll try."

As the Volvo pulled away from the curb, the twins rolled down the backseat window. Each of them stuck out an arm and flashed the two-fingered salute. I smiled as the car disappeared down the street, the little arms still hanging out the window, the two little hands waving the peace sign.

ABOUT THE AUTHOR

Jake Lamar was born in 1961 in the Bronx, New York. After graduating from Harvard in 1983 he spent six years writing for *Time* magazine. He is the author of the memoir *Bourgeois Blues* (1991) and the novels *The Last Integrationist* (1996) and *Close to the Bone* (1999). He lives in Paris.